## *"FIRE AS YOU BEAR!"*

Bolitho drew his hanger and walked amongst his men as they came alive again. A ball whined past his face and a seaman fell kicking and screaming.

Rowhurst cursed as one of his men reeled away, a massive hole punched through his forehead. He yelled, "Ready, sir!" He waited for the *Faithful* to complete another swing on her cable and then thrust his slow-match to the breech . . .

# ALEXANDER KENT

# IN GALLANT COMPANY

A JOVE BOOK
PUBLISHED BY G.P. PUTNAM'S SONS
DISTRIBUTED BY JOVE PUBLICATIONS, INC.

For Winifred with love

This Jove book contains the complete
text of the original hardcover edition.
It has been completely reset in a typeface
designed for easy reading, and was printed
from new film.

IN GALLANT COMPANY

A Jove Book / published by arrangement with
G. P. Putnam's Sons

PRINTING HISTORY
G. P. Putnam's edition published 1977
Berkley Medallion edition / December 1978
Jove edition / June 1983

ISBN: 0-515-07064-5

Jove books are published by Jove Publications,
Inc., 200 Madison Avenue, New York, N.Y. 10016.
The words "A JOVE BOOK" and the "J" with sunburst
are trademarks belonging to Jove Publications, Inc.
PRINTED IN THE UNITED STATES OF AMERICA

Our foe was no skulk in his ship I tell you, . . . His
        was the surly English pluck, and there is no
        tougher or truer,
     and never was, and never will be.

# Contents

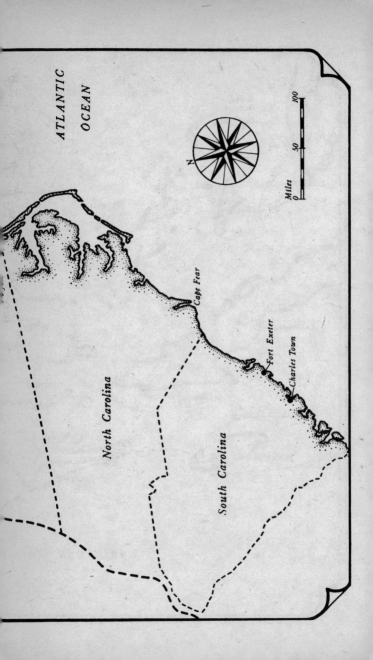

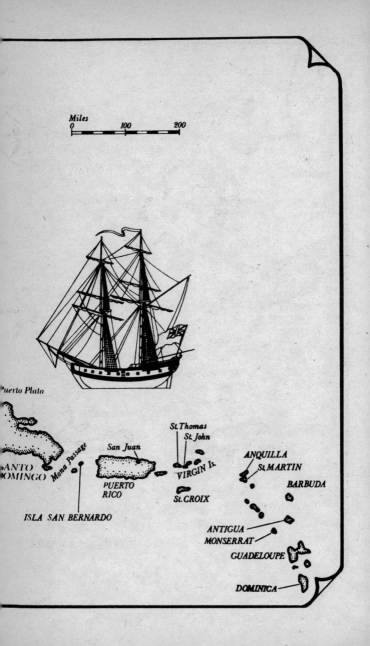

Miles
0      100      200

Puerto Plata

St. Thomas
St. John

San Juan

ANTO
DOMINGO   Mona Passage

ANQUILLA
St. MARTIN

VIRGIN Is.

BARBUDA

PUERTO
RICO

St. CROIX

ISLA SAN BERNARDO

ANTIGUA
MONSERRAT

GUADELOUPE

DOMINICA

# 1

# Show of Strength

The stiff offshore wind, which had backed slightly to the north-west during the day, swept across New York's naval anchorage, bringing no release from the chilling cold and the threat of more snow.

Tugging heavily at her anchor cables, His Britannic Majesty's Ship *Trojan* of eighty guns might appear to a landsman's unpractised eye as indifferent to both wind and water. But to the men who continued with their work about her decks, or high above them on the slippery yards and rigging, her swaying motion made her anything but that.

It was March 1777, but to Lieutenant Richard Bolitho, officer of the afternoon watch, it felt like midwinter. It will be dark early, he thought, and the ship's boats would have to be checked, their moorings doubly secured before night closed in completely.

He shivered, not so much because of the cold, but because he knew there would be little relief from it once he was allowed to go below. For despite her massive size and armament, the *Trojan*, a two-decked ship of the line, whose complement of six hundred and fifty officers, seamen and marines lived out their

1

lives within her fat hull, had no more than the galley fires and
body-warmth to sustain them, no matter what the elements
might do.

Bolitho raised his telescope and trained it towards the fading
waterfront. As the lens passed over other anchored ships of the
line, frigates and the general clutter of small supporting craft he
found time to wonder at the change. It had been just last summer
when *Trojan*, in company with a great fleet of one hundred and
thirty ships, had anchored here, off Staten Island. After the
shock of the actual revolution within the American colonies, the
occupation of New York and Philadelphia with such a show of
force had seemed to those involved as a start on the way back, a
compromise.

It had been such a simple and leisurely affair at the time.
After placing his troops under canvas along the green shoreline
of Staten Island, General Howe, with a token force of infantry,
had gone ashore to take possession. All the preparations by the
Continentals and local militia had come to nothing, and even the
Staten Island force of four hundred men, who had been commanded by General Washington to defend the redoubts at all
costs, had grounded their muskets and obligingly sworn alle-
giance to the Crown.

Bolitho lowered the glass as it blurred in drifting snow. It was
hard to recall the green island and crowds of onlookers, the
Loyalists cheering, the rest watching in grim silence. Now all the
colours were in shades of grey. The land, the tossing water, even
the ships seemed to have lost their brightness in the persistent
and lingering winter.

He took a few paces this way and that across *Trojan*'s spacious quarterdeck, his shoes slipping on the planking, his damp
clothes tugging at him in the wind. He had been in the ship for
two years. It was beginning to feel a lifetime. Like many others
throughout the fleet, he had felt mixed feelings at the news of the
revolution. Surprise and shock. Sympathy and then anger. And
above all the sense of helplessness.

The revolution, which had begun as a mixture of individual
ideals, had soon developed into something real and challenging.
The war was like nothing they had known before. Big ships of
the line like *Trojan* moved ponderously from one inflamed
incident to another, and were well able to cope with anything
which was careless enough to stray under their massive broad-

sides. But the real war was one of communications and supply, of small, fast vessels, sloops, brigs and schooners. And throughout the long winter months, while the overworked ships of the inshore squadrons had patrolled and probed some fifteen hundred miles of coastline, the growing strength of the Continentals had been further aided by Britain's old enemy, France. Not openly as yet, but it would not be long before the many French privateers which hunted from the Canadian border to the Caribbean showed their true colours. After that, Spain too would be a quick if unwilling ally. Her trade routes from the Spanish Main were perhaps the longest of all, and with little love for England anyway, she would likely take the easiest course.

All this and more Bolitho had heard and discussed over and over again until he was sick of it. Whatever the news, good or bad, the *Trojan*'s role seemed to be getting smaller. Like a rock she remained here in harbour for weeks on end, her company resentful, the officers hoping for a chance to leave her and find their fortunes in swifter, more independent ships.

Bolitho thought of his last ship, the twenty-eight gun frigate *Destiny*. Even as her junior lieutenant, and barely used to the sea-change from midshipman's berth to wardroom, he had found excitement and satisfaction beyond belief.

He stamped his feet on the wet planks, seeing the watchkeepers at the opposite side jerk round with alarm. Now he was fourth lieutenant of this great, anchored mammoth, and looked like remaining so.

*Trojan* would be better off in the Channel Fleet, he thought. Manoeuvres and showing the flag to the watchful French, and whenever possible slipping ashore to Plymouth or Portsmouth to meet old friends.

Bolitho turned as familiar footsteps crossed the deck from the poop. It was Cairns, the first lieutenant, who like most of the others had been aboard since the ship had recommissioned in 1775 after being laid up in Bristol where she had originally been built.

Cairns was tall, lean and very self-contained. If he too was pining over the next step in his career, a command of his own perhaps, he never showed it. He rarely smiled, but nevertheless was a man of great charm. Bolitho both liked and respected him and often wondered what he thought of the captain.

Cairns paused, biting his lower lip, as he peered up at the

towering criss-cross of shrouds and running rigging. Thinly coated with clinging snow, the yards looked like the branches of gaunt pines.

He said, 'The captain will be coming off soon. I'll be on call, so keep a weather-eye open.'

Bolitho nodded, gauging the moment. Cairns was twenty-eight, while he was not yet twenty-one. But the span between first and fourth lieutenant was still the greater.

He asked casually, 'Any news of our captain's mission ashore, sir?'

Cairns seemed absorbed. 'Get those topmen down, Dick. They'll be too frozen to turn-to if the weather breaks. Pass the word for the cook to break out some hot soup.' He grimaced. 'That should please the miserly bugger.' He looked at Bolitho. 'Mission?'

'Well, I thought we might be getting orders.' He shrugged. 'Or something.'

'He has been with the commander-in-chief certainly. But I doubt we'll hear anything stronger than the need for vigilance and an eye to duty!'

'I see.' Bolitho looked away. He was never sure when Cairns was being completely serious.

Cairns tugged his coat around his throat. 'Carry on, Mr Bolitho.'

They touched their hats to each other, the informality laid aside for the moment.

Bolitho called, 'Midshipman of the watch!' He saw one of the drooping figures break away from the shelter of the hammock nettings and bound towards him.

'Sir!'

It was Couzens, thirteen years old, and one of the new members of the ship's company, having been sent out from England aboard a transport. He was round-faced, constantly shivering, but made up for his ignorance with a willingness which neither his superiors nor the ship could break.

Bolitho told him about the cook, and the captain's expected return, then instructed him to arrange for piping the relief for the first dog-watch. He passed his instructions without conscious thought, but watched Couzens instead, seeing not him but himself at that tender age. He had been in a ship of the line, too. Chased, harried, bullied by everyone, or so it had seemed. But he had had one hero, a lieutenant who had probably never even noticed him as a human being. And Bolitho had always remembered him. He had never lost his temper without cause. Never found escape in humiliating others when he had received a telling-off from his captain. Bolitho had hoped he would be like that lieutenant one day. He still hoped.

Couzens nodded firmly. 'Aye, aye, sir.'

*Trojan* carried nine midshipmen, and Bolitho sometimes wondered how their lives would take shape. Some would rise to flag rank, others drop by the wayside. There would be the usual sprinkling of tyrants and of leaders, of heroes and cowards.

Later, as the new watch was being mustered below the quarterdeck, one of the look-outs called, 'Boat approaching, sir!' The merest pause. ''Tis the captain!'

Bolitho darted a quick glance at the milling confusion below the quarterdeck. The captain could not have chosen a better time to catch them all out.

He yelled, 'Pass the word for the first lieutenant! Man the side, and call the boatswain directly!'

Men dashed hither and thither through the gloom, and while the marines tramped stolidly to the entry port, their cross-belts very white in the poor light, the petty officers tried to muster the relieving watchkeepers into some semblance of order.

A boat appeared, pulling strongly toward the main chains, the bowman already standing erect with his hook at the ready.

'*Boat ahoy?*'

The coxswain's cry came back instantly. '*Trojan!*'

Their lord and master was back. The man who, next to God, controlled each hour of their lives, who could reward, flog, promote or hang as the situation dictated, was amongst their crowded world once more.

When Bolitho glanced round again he saw that where there had been chaos there was order, with the marines lined up, muskets to their shoulders, their commanding officer, the debonair Captain D'Esterre, standing with his lieutenant, apparently oblivious to wind and cold.

The boatswain's mates were here, moistening their silver calls on their lips, and Cairns, his eyes everywhere, waited to receive his captain.

The boat hooked on to the chains, the muskets slapped and cracked to the present while the calls shrilled in piercing salute.

The captain's head and shoulders rose over the side, and while he doffed his cocked hat to the quarterdeck he too examined the ship, his command, with one sweeping scrutiny.

He said curtly, 'Come aft, Mr Cairns.' He nodded to the marine officers. 'Smart turn-out, D'Esterre.' He turned abruptly and snapped. 'Why are *you* here, Mr Bolitho?' As he spoke, eight bells chimed out from the forecastle. 'You should have been relieved, surely?'

Bolitho looked at him. 'I think Mr Probyn is detained, sir.'

'Do you indeed.' The captain had a harsh voice which cut above the din of wind and creaking spars like a cutlass. 'The responsibility of watchkeeping is as much that of the relief as the one awaiting it.' He glanced at Cairns' impassive face. ''Pon my soul, Mr Cairns, not a difficult thing to learn, I'd have thought?'

They walked aft, and Bolitho breathed out very slowly.

Lieutenant George Probyn, his immediate superior, was often late taking over his watch, and other duties too for that matter. He was the odd man in the wardroom, morose, argumentative, bitter, although for what reason Bolitho had not yet discovered. He saw him coming up the starboard ladder, broad, untidy, peering around suspiciously.

Bolitho faced him. 'The watch is aft, Mr Probyn.'

Probyn wiped his face and then blew his nose in a red handkerchief.

'I suppose the captain was asking about me?'

Even his question sounded hostile.

'He noted you were absent.' Bolitho could smell brandy, and added, 'But he seemed satisfied enough.'

Probyn beckoned to a master's mate and scanned quickly through the deck log which the man held below a lantern.

Bolitho said wearily, 'Nothing unusual to report. One seaman injured and taken to the sickbay. He fell from the boat tier.'

Probyn sniffed. 'Shame.' He closed the book. 'You are relieved.' He watched him broodingly. 'If I thought anyone was making *trouble* for me behind my back . . .'

Bolitho turned away, hiding his anger. Do not fret, my drunken friend. You are doing that for yourself.

Probyn's rumbling voice followed him to the companion as he put his men to their stations and allotted their tasks.

As he ran lightly down the companion ladder and made his

way aft towards the wardroom, Bolitho wondered what the captain was discussing with Cairns.

Once below, the ship seemed to enfold him, contain him with her familiarity. The combined smells of tar and hemp, of bilge and packed humanity, they were as much a part of Bolitho as his own skin.

Mackenzie, the senior wardroom servant, who had ended his service as a topman when a fall from aloft had broken his leg in three places and made him a permanent cripple, met him with a cheery smile. If everyone else was sorry for him, Mackenzie at least was well satisfied. His injuries had given him as much comfort and security as any man could hope to find in a King's ship.

'I've some coffee, sir. Piping hot, too.' He had a soft Scottish accent which was very like Cairns'.

Bolitho peeled off his coat and handed it with his hat to Logan, a ship's boy who helped in the wardroom.

'I'd relish that, thank you.'

The wardroom, which ran the whole breadth of the ship's stern, was wreathed in tobacco smoke and touched with its own familiar aromas of wine and cheese. Right aft the great stern windows were already in darkness, and as the counter swung slightly to the pull of the massive anchor it was possible to see an occasional light glittering from the shore like a lost star.

Hutchlike cabins, little more than screens which would be torn down when the ship cleared for action, lined either side. Tiny havens which contained the owner's cot, chest and a small hanging space. But each was at least private. Apart from the cells, about the only place in the ship a man could be alone.

Directly above, and in a cabin which matched in size and space that which contained most of his officers, was the captain's domain. Also on that deck was the master and the first lieutenant, to be in easy reach of the quarterdeck and the helm.

But here, in the wardroom, was where they all shared their moments off-duty. Where they discussed their hopes and fears, ate their meals and took their wine. The six lieutenants, two marine officers, the sailing master, the purser and the surgeon. It was crowded certainly, but when compared with the below-the-waterline quarters of the midshipmen and other warrant officers and specialists, let alone the great majority of seamen and marines, it was luxury indeed.

Dalyell, the fifth lieutenant, sat beneath the stern windows, his legs crossed and resting on a small keg, a long clay pipe balanced in one hand.

'George Probyn adrift again, eh, Dick?'

Bolitho grinned. 'It is becoming a habit.'

Sparke, the second lieutenant, a severe-faced man with a coin-shaped scar on one cheek, said, 'I'd drag him to the captain if *I* were the senior here.' He returned to a tattered news-sheet and added vehemently, 'These damned rebels seem to do what they like! Two more transports seized from under our frigates' noses, and a brig cut out of harbour by one of their bloody privateers! We're too soft on 'em!'

Bolitho sat down and stretched, grateful to be out of the wind, even though he knew the illusion of warmth would soon pass.

His head lolled, and when Mackenzie brought the mug of coffee he had to shake his shoulder to awaken him.

In companionable silence the *Trojan*'s officers drew comfort from their own resources. Some read, others wrote home letters which might never reach those for whom they were intended.

Bolitho drank his coffee and tried to ignore the pain in his forehead. Without thinking, his hand moved up and touched the rebellious lock of black hair above his right eye. Beneath it was a livid scar, the source of the pain. He had received it when he had been in *Destiny*. It often came back to him at moments like this. The illusion of safety, the sudden rush of feet and slashing, hacking weapons. The agony and the blood. Oblivion.

There was a tap at the outer screen door, and then Mackenzie said to Sparke, who was the senior officer present, 'Your pardon, sir, but the midshipman of the watch is here.'

The boy stepped carefully into the wardroom, as if he was walking on precious silk.

Sparke snapped curtly, 'What is it, Mr Forbes?'

'The first lieutenant's compliments, sir, and will all officers muster in the cabin at two bells.'

'Very well.' Sparke waited for the door to close. 'Now we will see, gentlemen. Maybe we have something of importance to do.'

Unlike Cairns, the second lieutenant could not conceal the sudden gleam in his eyes. Promotion. Prize money. Or just a chance for action instead of hearing about it.

He looked at Bolitho. 'I suggest *you* change into a clean shirt. The captain seems to have his eye on you.'

Bolitho stood up, his head brushing the deckhead beams. Two years in this ship, and apart from a dinner in the cabin when they had recommissioned the ship at Bristol, he had barely crossed one social barrier to meet the captain. He was a stern, remote man, and yet always seemed to possess uncanny knowledge of what was happening on every deck in his command.

Dalyell carefully tapped out his pipe and remarked, 'Maybe he really likes you, Dick.'

Raye, the lieutenant of marines, yawned. 'I don't think he's human.'

Sparke hurried to his cabin, shying away from involvement with any criticism of authority. 'He is the captain. He does not require to be human.'


Captain Gilbert Brice Pears finished reading the daily log of events aboard his ship and then scrawled his signature, which was hastily dried by Teakle, his clerk.

Outside the stern windows the harbour and the distant town seemed far-away and unconnected with this spacious, well-lit cabin. There was some good furniture here, and in the neighbouring dining cabin the table was already laid for supper, with Foley, the captain's servant, neat as a pin in his blue coat and white trousers, hovering to tend his master's needs.

Captain Pears leaned back in his chair and glanced round the cabin without seeing it. In two years he had got to know it well.

He was forty-two years old, but looked older. Thickset, even square, he was as powerful and impressive as the *Trojan* herself.

He had heard gossip amongst his officers which amounted almost to discontent. The war, for it must now be accepted as such, seemed to be passing them by. But Pears was a realistic man, and knew that the time would eventually come when he and his command would be able to act as intended when *Trojan*'s great keel had first tasted salt water just nine years ago. Privateers and raiding parties were one thing, but when the French joined the fray in open strength, and their ships of the line appeared in these waters, *Trojan* and her heavy consorts would display their true worth.

He looked up as the marine sentry stamped his boots together outside the screen door, and moments later the first lieutenant rejoined him.

'I have passed the word to the wardroom, sir. All officers to be here at two bells.'

'Good.'

Pears merely had to look at his servant and Foley was beside him, pouring two tall glasses of claret.

'The fact is, Mr Cairns'—Pears examined the wine against the nearest lantern—'you cannot go on forever fighting a defensive war. Here we are in New York, a claw-hold on a land which is daily becoming more rebellious. In Philadelphia things are a little better. Raids and skirmishes, we burn a fort or an outpost, and they catch one of our transports, or ambush a patrol. What is New York? A besieged city. A town under reprieve, but for how long?'

Cairns said nothing, but sipped the claret, half his mind attending to the noises beyond the cabin, the sigh of wind, the groan of timbers.

Pears saw his expression and smiled to himself. Cairns was a good first lieutenant, probably the best he had ever had. He should have a command of his own. A chance, one which only came in war.

But Pears loved his ship more than hopes or dreams. The thought of Sparke taking over as senior lieutenant was like a threat. He was an efficient officer and attended to his guns and his duties perfectly. But imagination he had not. He thought of Probyn, and dismissed him just as quickly. Then there was Bolitho, the fourth. Much like his father, although he sometimes seemed to take his duties too lightly. But his men appeared to like him. That meant a lot in these hard times.

Pears sighed. Bolitho was still a few months short of twenty-one. You needed experienced officers to work a ship of the line. He rubbed his chin to hide his expression. Maybe it was Bolitho's youth and his own mounting years which made him reason in this fashion.

He asked abruptly, 'Are we in all respects ready for sea?'

Cairns nodded. 'Aye, sir. I could well use another dozen hands because of injury and ill-health, but that is a small margin these days.'

'It is indeed. I have known first lieutenants to go grey-haired because they could not woo, press or bribe enough hands even to work their ships out of port.'

At the prescribed time the doors were opened and *Trojan*'s officers, excluding the midshipmen and junior warrant officers, filed into the great cabin.

It was a rare event, and took a good deal of time to get them into proper order, and for Foley and Hogg, the captain's coxswain, to find the right number of chairs.

It gave Pears time to watch their varying reactions, to see if their presence in strength would make any sort of difference.

Probyn, relieved from his duties by a master's mate, was flushed and very bright-eyed. Just too steady to be true.

Sparke, prim in his severity, and young Dalyell, were seated beside the sixth and junior lieutenant, Quinn, who just five months ago had been a midshipman.

Then there was Erasmus Bunce, the master. He was called the Sage behind his back, and was certainly impressive. In his special trade, which produced more characters and outstanding seamen than any other, Bunce was one to turn any man's head. He was well over six feet tall, deep-chested, and had long, straggly grey hair. But his eyes, deep-set and clear, were almost as black as the thick brows above them. A sage indeed.

Pears watched the master ducking between the overhead beams and was reassured.

Bunce liked his rum, but he loved the ship like a woman. With him to guide her she had little to fear.

Molesworth, the purser, a pale man with a nervous blink, which Pears suspected was due to some undiscovered guilt. Thorndike, the surgeon, who always seemed to be smiling. More like an actor than a man of blood and bones. Two bright patches of scarlet by the larboard side, the marine officers, D'Esterre and Lieutenant Raye, and of course, Cairns, completed the gathering. It did not include all the other warrant officers and specialists. The boatswain, and gunner, the master's mates, and the carpenters, Pears knew them all by sight, sound and quality.

Probyn said in a loud whisper, 'Mr Bolitho doesn't seem to be here yet?'

Pears frowned, despising Probyn's hypocrisy. He was about as subtle as a hammer.

Cairns suggested, 'I'll send someone, sir.'

The door opened and closed swiftly and Pears saw Bolitho sliding into an empty chair beside the two marines.

'Stand up, that officer.' Pears' harsh voice was almost caressing. 'Ah, it is you, sir, at last.'

Bolitho stood quite still, only his shoulders swaying slightly to the ship's slow roll.

'I—I am sorry, sir.' Bolitho saw the grin on Dalyell's face as drops of water trickled from under his coat and on to the black and white checkered canvas which covered the deck.

Pears said mildly, 'Your shirt seems to be rather *wet,* sir.' He turned slightly. 'Foley, some canvas for that chair. It is hard to replace such things out here.'

Bolitho sat down with a thump, not knowing whether to be angry or humiliated.

He forgot Pears' abrasive tone, and the shirt which he had snatched off the wardroom line still wringing wet, as Pears said more evenly, 'We will sail at first light, gentlemen. The Governor of New York has received information that the expected convoy from Halifax is likely to be attacked. It is a large assembly of vessels with an escort of two frigates and a sloop-of-war. But in this weather the ships could become scattered, some might endeavour to close with the land to ascertain their bearings.' His fingers changed to a fist. '*That* is when our enemy will strike.'

Bolitho leaned forward, ignoring the sodden discomfort around his waist.

Pears continued, 'I was saying as much to Mr Cairns. You cannot *win* a defensive war. We have the ships, but the enemy has the local knowledge to make use of smaller, faster vessels. To have a chance of success we must command and keep open every trade route, search and detain any suspected craft, make our presence felt. Wars are not finally won with ideals, they are won with powder and shot, and *that* the enemy does not have in quantity. *Yet.*' He looked around their faces, his eyes bleak. 'The Halifax convoy is carrying a great deal of powder and shot, cannon too, which are intended for the military in Philadelphia and here in New York. If just one of those valuable cargoes fell into the wrong hands we would feel the effects for months to come.' He looked round sharply. 'Questions?'

It was Sparke who rose to his feet first.

'Why us, sir? Of course, I am most gratified to be putting to sea in my country's service, to try and rectify some—'

Pears said heavily, '*Please* get on with the bones of the matter.'

Sparke swallowed hard, his scar suddenly very bright on his cheek.

'Why not send frigates, sir?'

'Because there are not enough, there never *are* enough. Also, the admiral feels that a show of strength might be of more value.'

Bolitho stiffened, as if he had missed something. It was in the captain's tone. Just the merest suggestion of doubt. He glanced at his companions but they seemed much as usual. Perhaps he was imagining it, or seeking flaws to cover up his earlier discomfort under Pears' tongue.

Pears added, 'Whatever may happen this time, we must never drop our vigilance. This ship is our first responsibility, our main concern at all times. The war is changing from day to day. Yesterday's traitor is tomorrow's patriot. A man who responded to his country's call,' he shot a wry smile at Sparke, 'is now called a Loyalist, as if he and not the others was some sort of freak and outcast.'

The master, Erasmus Bunce, stood up very slowly, his eyes peering beneath a deckhead beam like twin coals.

'A man must do as he be guided, sir. It is for God to decide who be right in this conflict.'

Pears smiled gravely. Old Bunce was known to be very religious, and had once hurled a sailor into Portsmouth harbour merely for taking the Lord's name into a drunken song.

Bunce was a Devonian, and had gone to sea at the age of nine or ten. He was now said to be over sixty, but Pears could never picture him ever being young at all.

He said, 'Quite so, Mr Bunce. That was well said.'

Cairns cleared his throat and eyed the master patiently. 'Was that all, Mr Bunce?'

The master sat down and folded his arms. 'It be enough.'

The captain gestured to Foley. No words seemed to be required here, Bolitho thought.

Glasses and wine jugs followed, and then Pears said, 'A toast, gentlemen. To the ship, and damnation to the King's enemies!"

Bolitho watched Probyn looking round for the jugs, his glass already emptied.

He thought of Pears' voice when he had spoken of the ship.

God help George Probyn if he put her on a lee shore after taking too many glasses.

Soon after that the meeting broke up, and Bolitho realized that he had still got no closer to the captain than by way of a reprimand.

He sighed. When you were a midshipman you thought a lieutenant's life was in some sort of heaven. Maybe even captains were in dread of somebody, although at this moment it was hard to believe.

The next dawn was slightly clearer, but not much. The wind held firm enough from the north-west, and the snow flurries soon gave way to drizzle, which mixed with the blown spray made the decks and rigging shine like dull glass.

Bolitho had watched one ship or another get under way more times than he could remember. But it never failed to move and excite him. The way every man joined into the chain of command to make the ship work as a living, perfect instrument.

Each mast had its own divisions of seamen, from the swift-footed topmen to the older, less agile hands who worked the braces and halliards from the deck. As the calls shrilled, and the men poured up on deck through every hatch and companion, it seemed incredible that *Trojan*'s hull, which from figurehead to taffrail measured two hundred and fifteen feet, could contain so many. Yet within seconds the dashing figures of men and boys, marines and landmen were formed into compact groups, each being checked by leather-lunged petty officers against their various lists and watch-bills.

The great capstan was already turning, as was its twin on the deck below, and under his shoes Bolitho could almost sense the ship stirring, waiting to head towards the open sea.

Like the mass of seamen and marines, the officers too were at their stations. Probyn and Dalyell to assist him on the forecastle, the foremast their responsibility. Sparke commanded the upper gundeck and the ship's mainmast, which was her real strength, with all the spars, cordage, canvas and miles of rigging which gave life to the hull beneath. Lastly, the mizzen mast, handled mostly by the afterguard, where young Quinn waited with the marine lieutenant and his men to obey Cairns' first requirements.

Bolitho looked across at Sparke. Not an easy man to know, but a pleasure to watch at work. He controlled his seamen and every halliard and brace with the practised ease of a dedicated concert conductor.

A hush seemed to fall over the ship, and Bolitho looked aft to see the captain walking to the quarterdeck rail, nodding to old Bunce, the Sage, then speaking quietly with his first lieutenant.

Far above the deck from the mainmast truck the long, scarlet pendant licked and hardened to the wind like bending metal. A good sailing wind, but Bolitho was thankful it was the captain and old Bunce who were taking her through the anchored shipping and not himself.

He glanced over the side and wondered who was watching. Friends, or spies who might already be passing news to Washington's agents. Another man-of-war weighing. Where bound? For what purpose?

He returned his attention inboard. If half what he had heard was true, the enemy probably knew better than they did. There were said to be plenty of loose tongues in New York's civil and military government circles.

Cairns raised his speaking trumpet. 'Get a move on, Mr Tolcher!'

Tolcher, the squat boatswain, raised his cane and bellowed, 'More 'ands to th' capstan! *'Eave*, lads!'

He glared at the shantyman with his fiddle. 'Play up, you bugger, or I'll 'ave you on th' pumps!'

From forward came the cry, 'Anchor's hove short, sir.'

'Hands aloft! Loose tops'ls!' Cairns' voice, magnified by the trumpet, pursued and drove them like a clarion. 'Loose the heads'ls!'

Released to the wind the canvas erupted and flapped in wild confusion, while spread along the swaying yards like monkeys the topmen fought to bring it under control until the right moment.

Sparke called, 'Man your braces! Mr Bolitho, take that man's name!'

'Aye, sir!'

Bolitho smiled into the drizzle. It was always the same with Sparke. *Take that man's name*. There was nobody in particular, but it gave the seamen the idea that Sparke had eyes everywhere.

Again the hoarse voice from the bows, 'Anchor's aweigh, sir.'

Released from the ground, her first anchor already hoisted and catted, *Trojan* side-stepped heavily across the wind, her sails spreading and thundering like a bombardment as the men hauled at the braces, their bodies straining back, angled down almost to the deck.

Round and further still, the yards swinging to hold the wind, the sails freed one by one to harden like steel breastplates until the ship was thrusting her shoulder in foam, her lower gunports awash along the lee side.

Bolitho ran from one section to the next, his hat knocked awry, his ears ringing with the squeal of blocks and the boom of canvas, and above all the groaning and vibrating chorus from every stay and shroud.

When he paused for breath he saw the outline of Sandy Hook sliding abeam, some men waiting in a small yawl to wave as the great ship stood over them.

He heard Cairns' voice again. 'Get the t'gan's'ls on her!'

Bolitho peered up the length of the mainmast with its great bending yards. He saw midshipmen in the tops, and seamen racing each other to set more canvas. When he looked aft again he saw Bunce with his hands thrust behind him, his face like carved rock as he watched over his ship. Then he nodded very slowly. That was as near to satisfaction as Bolitho had ever seen him display.

He pictured the ship as she would look from the land, her fierce, glaring figurehead, the Trojan warrior with the red-crested helmet. Spray bursting up and over the beakhead and bowsprit, the massive black and buff hull glistening and reflecting the cruising whitecaps alongside, as if to wash herself clean from the land.

Probyn's voice sounded raw as he shouted at his men to secure the second anchor. He would need plenty to drink after this, Bolitho thought.

He looked aft, past his own seamen as they slid down stays and vaulted from the gangways to muster again below the mast. Then he saw the captain watching him. Along the ship, over all the bustle and haste their eyes seemed to meet.

Self-consciously, Bolitho reached up and straightened his hat, and he imagined he saw the captain give a small but definite nod.

But the mood was soon broken, for *Trojan* rarely gave much time for personal fancies.

'Man the braces there. Stand by to come about!'

Sparke was shouting, *'Mr Bolitho!'*

Bolitho touched his hat. 'Aye, I know, sir. Take that man's name!'

By the time they had laid the ship on her chosen tack to both the captain's and Bunce's satisfaction the land was swallowed in mist and rain astern.

# 2

# A Wild Plan

Lieutenant Richard Bolitho crossed to the weather side of the quarterdeck and gripped the hammock nettings to hold his balance. Towering above and ahead of him, *Trojan*'s great pyramids of sails were impressive, even to one accustomed to the sight. Especially after all the frustration and pain in the last four and a half days, he thought.

The wind which had followed them with such promise from Sandy Hook had changed within hours, as if driven or inspired by the devil himself. Backing and veering without warning, with all hands required to reef or reset the sails throughout each watch. It had taken one complete, miserable day just to work round and clear of the dreaded Nantucket shoals, with sea boiling beneath the long bowsprit as if heated by some force from hell.

Then after raising their progress to four and even five knots the wind would alter yet again, bellowing with savage triumph while the breathless seamen fought to reef the hard canvas, fisting and grappling while their pitching world high above the decks went mad about them.

But this was different. *Trojan* was standing almost due north, her yards braced round as far as they would to take and hold the wind, and along her lee side the water was creaming past as evidence of real progress.

Bolitho ran his eyes over the upper gundeck. Below the quarterdeck rail he could see the hands resting and chatting, as was the custom while awaiting to see what the cook had produced for the midday meal. By the greasy plume which fell downwind from the galley funnel, Bolitho guessed that it was another concoction of boiled beef hacked from salted casks, mixed with a soggy assortment of ship's biscuit, oatmeal and scraps saved from yesterday. George Triphook, the senior cook, was hated by almost everyone but his toadies, but unlike some he enjoyed the hatred, and seemed to relish the groans and curses at his efforts.

Bolitho felt suddenly ravenous, but knew the wardroom fare would be little better when he was relieved to snatch his share of it.

He thought of his mother and the great grey house in Falmouth. He walked away from Couzens, his watchful midshipman, who rarely took his eyes off him. How terrible the blow had been. In the Navy you could risk death a dozen ways in any day. Disease, shipwreck or the cannon's roar, the walls of Falmouth church were covered with memorial plaques. The names and deeds of sea-officers, sons of Falmouth who had left port never to return.

But his mother. Surely not her. Always youthful and vivacious. Ready to stand-in and shoulder the responsibility of house and land when her husband, Captain James Bolitho, was away, which was often.

Bolitho and his brother, Hugh, his two sisters, Felicity and Nancy, had all loved her in their own different and special ways. When he had returned home from the *Destiny*, still shocked and suffering from his wound, he had needed her more than ever. The house had been like a tomb. She was dead. It was impossible to accept even now that she was not back in Falmouth, watching the sea beyond Pendennis Castle, laughing in the manner which was infectious enough to drive all despair aside.

A chill, they had said. Then a sudden fever. It had been over in a matter of weeks.

He could picture his father at this very moment. Captain James, as he was locally known, was well respected as a magistrate since losing his arm and being removed from active duty. The house in winter, the lanes clogged with mud, the news always late, the countryside too worried by pressures of cold and wet, of lost animals and marauding foxes to heed much for this far-off war. But his father would care. Brooding as a ship-of-war anchored or weighed in Carrick Roads. Needing, pining for the life which had rejected him, and now completely alone.

It must be a million times worse for him, Bolitho thought sadly.

Cairns appeared on deck, and after scrutinizing the compass and glancing at the slate on which a master's mate made his half-hourly calculations he crossed to join Bolitho.

Bolitho touched his hat. 'She holds steady, sir. Nor' by east, full and bye.'

Cairns nodded. He had very pale eyes which could look right through a man.

'We may have to reef if the wind gets up any more. We're taking all we can manage, I think.'

He shaded his eyes before he looked to larboard, for although there was no sun the glare was intent and harsh. It was difficult to see an edge between sea and sky, the water was a desert of restless steel fragments. But the rollers were further apart now, cruising down in serried ranks to lift under *Trojan*'s fat quarter to tilt her further and burst occasionally over the weather gangway before rolling on again towards the opposite horizon.

They had the sea to themselves, for after beating clear of Nantucket and pushing on towards the entrance of Massachusetts Bay they were well clear of both land and local shipping. Somewhere, some sixty miles across the weather side, lay Boston. There were quite a few aboard *Trojan* who could remember Boston as it had once been before the bitterness and resentment had flared into anger and blood.

The Bay itself was avoided by all but the foolhardy. It was the home of some of the most able privateers, and Bolitho wondered, not for the first time, if there were any stalking the powerful two-decker at this moment.

Cairns had a muffler around his throat, and asked, 'What make you of the weather, Dick?'

Bolitho watched the men streaming to the hatches on their way to the galley and their cramped messes.

He had taken over the watch as Bunce had been keeping a stern eye on the ritual taking of noon sights, although it was more a routine than to serve any real purpose in this poor visibility. The midshipmen lined up with their sextants, the master's mates watching their progress, or their lack of it.

Bolitho replied calmly, 'Fog.'

Cairns stared at him. 'Is this one of your Celtic fantasies, man?'

Bolitho smiled. 'The master said fog.'

The first lieutenant sighed. 'Then fog it will be. Though in this half gale I see no chance of it!'

'*Deck there!*'

They looked up, caught off guard after so much isolation.

Bolitho saw the shortened figure of the mainmast look-out, a tiny shape against the low clouds. It made him dizzy just to watch.

'Sail on th' weather beam, sir!'

The two lieutenants snatched telescopes and climbed into the shrouds. But there was nothing. Just the wavecrests, angrier and steeper in the searching lens, and the hard, relentless glare.

'Shall I inform the captain, sir?'

Bolitho watched Cairns' face as he returned to the deck. He could almost see his mind working. A sail. What did it mean? Unlikely to be friendly. Even a lost and confused ship's master would not fail to understand the dangers hereabouts.

'Not yet.' Cairns glanced meaningly towards the poop. 'He'll have heard the masthead anyway. He'll not fuss until we're ready.'

Bolitho thought about it. Another view of Captain Pears which he had not considered. But it was true. He never did rush on deck like some captains, afraid for their ships, or impatient for answers to unanswerable questions.

He looked at Cairns' quiet face again. It was also true that Cairns inspired such trust.

Bolitho asked, 'Shall I go aloft and see for myself?'

Cairns shook his head. 'No. I will. The captain will doubtless want a full report.'

Bolitho watched the first lieutenant hurrying up the shrouds, the telescope slung over his shoulders like a musket. Up and up, around the futtock shrouds and past the hooded swivel gun there to the topmast and further still towards the look-out who sat so calmly on the crosstrees, as if he was on a comfortable village bench.

He dragged his eyes away from Cairns' progress. It was something he could never get used to or conquer. His hatred of heights. Each time he had to go aloft, which was mercifully rare, he felt the same nausea, the same dread of falling.

He saw a familiar figure on the gundeck below the quarter-deck rail and felt something like affection for the big, ungainly man in checkered shirt and flapping white trousers. One more link with the little *Destiny*. Stockdale, the muscular prize-fighter he had rescued from a barker outside an inn when he and a dispirited recruiting party had been trying to drum up volunteers for the ship.

Stockdale had taken to the sea in a manner born. As strong as five men, he never abused his power, and was more gentle than many. The angry barker had been hitting Stockdale with a length of chain for losing in a fight with one of Bolitho's men. The man in question must have cheated in some way, for Bolitho had never seen Stockdale beaten since.

He spoke very little, and when he did it was with effort, as his vocal chords had been cruelly damaged in countless barefist fights up and down every fair and pitch in the land.

Seeing him then, stripped to the waist, cut about the back by the barker's chain, had been too much for Bolitho. When he had asked Stockdale to enlist he had said it almost without thinking of the consequences. Stockdale had merely nodded, picked up his things and had followed him to the ship.

And whenever Bolitho needed aid, or was in trouble, Stockdale was always there. Like that last time, when Bolitho had seen the screaming savage rushing at him with a cutlass snatched from a dying seaman. Later he had heard all about it. How Stockdale had rallied the retreating seamen, had picked him up like a child and had carried him to safety.

When Bolitho's appointment to *Trojan* had arrived, he had imagined that would be an end to their strange relationship. But somehow, then as now, Stockdale had managed it.

He had wheezed, 'One day, you'll be a cap'n, sir. Reckon you'll need a coxswain.'

Bolitho smiled down at him. Stockdale could do almost anything. Splice, reef and steer if need be. But he was a gun captain now, on one of *Trojan*'s upper battery of thirty eighteen-pounders. And naturally he just *happened* to be in Bolitho's own division.

'What d'*you* think, Stockdale?'

The man's battered face split into a wide grin. 'They be watching us, Mr Bolitho.'

Bolitho saw the painful movements of his throat. The sea's bite was making it hard for Stockdale.

'You think so, eh?'

'Aye.' He sounded very confident. 'They'll know what we're about, an' where we're heading. I wager there'll be other craft hull down where we can't see 'em.'

Cairns' feet hit the deck as he slid down a stay with the agility of a midshipman.

He said, 'Schooner by the cut of her. Can barely make her out, it's so damn hazy.' He shivered in a sudden gust. 'Same tack as ourselves.' He saw Bolitho smile at Stockdale, and asked, 'May I share the joke?'

'Stockdale said that the other sail is watching us, sir. Keeping well up to wind'rd.'

Cairns opened his mouth as if to contradict and then said, 'I fear he may be right. Instead of a show of strength, *Trojan* may be leading the pack down on to the very booty we are trying to protect.' He rubbed his chin. 'By God, that is a sour thought. I had expected an attack to be on the convoy's rear, the usual straggler cut out before the escort has had time to intervene.'

"All the same.' He rubbed his chin harder. 'They'll not try to attack with *Trojan*'s broadsides so near.'

Bolitho recalled Pears' voice at the conference. The hint of doubt. His suspicion then had now become more real.

Cairns glanced aft, past the two helmsmen who stood straddle-legged by the great double wheel, their eyes moving from sail to compass.

'It's not much to tell the captain, Dick. He has his orders. *Trojan* is no frigate. If we lost time in some fruitless manoeuvres we might never reach the convoy in time. You have seen the wind's perverse manners hereabouts. It could happen tomorrow. Or now.'

Bolitho said quietly, 'Remember what the Sage said. *Fog.*' He watched the word hitting Cairns like a pistol ball. 'If we have to lie to, we'll be no use to anyone.'

Cairns studied him searchingly. 'I should have seen that.

These privateersmen know more about local conditions than any of us.' He gave a wry smile. 'Except the Sage.'

Lieutenant Quinn came on deck and touched his hat.

'I'm to relieve you, sir.'

He looked from Bolitho to the straining masses of canvas. Bolitho would only go for a quick meal, especially as he wanted to know about Pears' reactions. But to the sixth lieutenant, eighteen years old, it would seem a lifetime of awesome responsibility, for to all intents and purposes he would control *Trojan*'s destiny for as long as he trod the quarterdeck.

Bolitho made to reassure him but checked himself. Quinn must learn to stand on his own. Any officer who depended on help whenever things got awkward would be useless in a real crisis.

He followed Cairns to the companionway, while Quinn made a big display of checking the compass and the notes in the log.

Cairns said softly, 'He'll be fine. Given time.'

Bolitho sat at the wardroom table while Mackenzie and Logan endeavoured to present the meal as best they could. Boiled meat and gruel. Ship's biscuit with black treacle, and as much cheese as anyone could face. But there was a generous supply of red wine which had arrived in New York with the last convoy. From the look on Probyn's face he had made very good use of it.

He peered across at Bolitho and asked thickly, 'What was all that din about a sail? Somebody getting a bit nervous, eh?' He leaned forward to peer at the others. 'God, the Navy's changing!'

Bunce sat at the head of the table and intoned deeply without looking up, 'It is not His doing, Mr Probyn. He has no time for the Godless.'

Sparke said unfeelingly, 'This bloody food is swill. I shall get a new cook at the first chance I can. That rogue should be dancing on a halter instead of poisoning us.'

The deck tilted steeply, and hands reached out to seize plates and glasses until the ship rolled upright again.

Bunce took out a watch and looked at it.

Bolitho asked quietly, 'The fog, Mr Bunce. *Will* it come?'

Thorndike, the surgeon, heard him and laughed. He made a braying sound.

'Really, Erasmus! Fog, when she pitches about in this wind!'

Bunce ignored him and replied, 'Tomorrow. We will have to

lie to. There is too great a depth to anchor.' He shook his massive head. 'Time lost. More knots to recover.'

He had spoken enough and stood up from the table. As he passed Probyn's chair he said in his deep voice, 'We will have time to see who is nervous then, I'm thinking.'

Probyn snapped his fingers for some wine and exclaimed angrily, 'He is becoming mad in his old age.' He tried to laugh, but nothing happened.

Captain D'Esterre eyed him calmly. 'At least he seems to have our Lord on his side. What do *you* have, exactly?'

In the cabin above, Captain Pears sat at his large table, a napkin tucked into his neckcloth. He caught the gust of laughter from the wardroom and said to Cairns, 'They seem happier at sea, eh?'

Cairns nodded. 'So it would appear, sir.' He watched Pears' bowed head and waited for his conclusions or ideas.

Pears said, 'Alone or in company the schooner is a menace to us. If only we had been given a brig or a sloop to chase off these wolves. As it is . . .' He shrugged.

'May I suggest something, sir?'

Pears cut a small piece of cheese for himself and examined it doubtfully.

'It is what you came for, surely.' He smiled. 'Speak out.'

Cairns thrust his hands behind him, his eyes very bright.

'You have heard the master's views on the chance of fog, sir?'

Pears nodded. 'I know these waters well. Fog is common enough, though I would not dare to make such a bold prediction this time.' He pushed the cheese aside. 'But if the master says a thing it is usually right.'

'Well, sir, we will have to lie to until it clears.'

'I have already taken that into account, damn it.'

'But so too will our watchdog. Both for his own safety and for fear of losing us. The fog might be an ally to us.' He hesitated, sensing the captain's mood. 'If we could *find* her and take her by boarding—' He got no further.

'In God's name, Mr Cairns, what are you saying? That I should put boats down, fill them with trained hands and send them off into a damned fog? Hell's teeth, sir, they would be going to certain death!'

'There is a chance there may be another vessel in company.'

Cairns spoke with sudden stubbornness. 'They will display lights. With good care and the use of a boat's compass, I think an attack has a good chance.' He waited, seeing the doubts and arguments in Pears' eyes. 'It would give us an extra vessel, and maybe more. Information, news of what the privateers are doing.'

Pears sat back and stared at him grimly. 'You are a man of ideas, I'll give you that.'

Cairns said, 'The fourth lieutenant put the thought in my mind, sir.'

'Might have guessed it.' Pears stood up and walked towards the windows, his thickset frame angled to the deck. 'Damned Cornishmen. Pirates and wreckers for the most part. Did you know that?'

Cairns kept his face stiff. 'I understood that Falmouth, Mr Bolitho's home, was the last place to hold out for King Charles against Cromwell and Parliament, sir?'

Pears gave a tight grin. 'Well said. But this idea is a dangerous thing. We might never find the boats again, and they may not discover the enemy, let alone seize her.'

Cairns insisted, 'The fog will reach the other vessel long before us, sir. I would suggest that as soon as that happens we change tack and close with her with every stitch which will draw.'

'But if the wind goes *against* us.' Pears held up his hand. '*Easy*, Mr Cairns, I can see your disappointment, but it is my responsibility. I must think of everything.'

Overhead, and beyond the cabin doors, life was going on as usual. The clank of a pump, the padding of feet across the poop as the watch hurried to trim a yard or splice a fraying halliard.

Pears said slowly, 'But it does have the stuff of surprise about it.' He made up his mind. 'My compliments to the master and ask him to join us in the chart room.' He chuckled. 'Although, knowing him as I do, I suspect he is already there.'

Out on the windswept quarterdeck, his eyes smarting to salt spray, Bolitho watched the men working overhead, the shivering power of each great sail. Time to reef soon, for the captain to be informed. He had seen the activity beneath the poop, Pears with Cairns entering the small chart room which adjoined Bunce's cabin.

A little later Cairns walked out into the drizzle, and Bolitho noticed that he was without his hat. That was very unusual, for Cairns was always smartly turned out, no matter how bad the circumstances.

'Have you had further reports from the masthead?'

'Aye, sir.'

Bolitho ducked as a sheet of spray burst over the nettings and soaked them both. Cairns barely flinched.

Bolitho said quickly, 'As before, the stranger is holding to wind'rd of us, on the same bearing.'

'I will inform the captain.' Cairns added, 'No matter, he is here.'

Bolitho made to cross to the lee side as was customary when the captain came on deck, but the harsh voice caught him.

'Stay, Mr Bolitho.' Pears strode heavily to the quarterdeck rail, his hat tugged down to his eyes. 'I believe you have been hatching some wild plan with the first lieutenant?'

'Well, sir, I—'

'Madness.' Pears watched the straining main-course as it billowed out from its yard. 'But with a grain, a very *small* grain of value.'

Bolitho stared at him. 'Thank you very much, sir.'

Pears ignored him and said to Cairns, 'The two cutters will have to suffice. I want you to hand-pick each man yourself. You know what we need for this bloody work.' He watched Cairns' face and then said almost gently, 'But you will not be going.' As Cairns made to protest he added, 'I cannot spare you. I could die tomorrow, and with you gone too, what would become of *Trojan*, eh?'

Bolitho watched both of them. It was like being an intruder to see the disappointment showing for the first time on Cairns' face.

Then Cairns replied, 'Aye, sir. I'll attend to it.'

As he strode away, Pears said bluntly, 'But you can send *this* one, he'll not be missed.'

Pears returned to the poop where Bunce was waiting for him, his straggly hair blowing in the wind like spunyarn.

He barked, 'Pass the word to the second lieutenant to lay aft.'

Bolitho considered his feelings. *He was going.* So was Sparke. *Take that man's name.*

He thought of Cairns as his one chance of showing his mettle had been taken from him. It was another measure of the man,

Bolitho thought. Some first lieutenants would have kept all the credit for the idea of boarding the other craft, hoarding it for the final reward.

It was getting dark early again, the low cloud and steady drizzle adding to the discomfort both below and on deck.

Cairns met Bolitho as he came off watch, and said simply, 'I have selected some good hands for you, Dick. The second lieutenant will be in command, assisted by Mr Frowd, who is the ablest master's mate we have, and Mr Midshipman Libby. You will be assisted by Mr Quinn and Mr Couzens.'

Bolitho met his even gaze. Apart from Sparke and Frowd, the master's mate, and to a lesser extent himself, the others were children at this sort of thing. He doubted if either the nervous Quinn or the willing Couzens had ever heard a shot fired other than at wildfowl.

But he said, 'Thank you, sir.' He would show the same attitude that Cairns had displayed to the captain.

Cairns touched his arm. 'Go and find some dry clothing, if you can.' As he turned towards his cabin he added, 'You will have the redoubtable Stockdale in your cutter. I would not be so brave as to try and stop him!'

Bolitho walked through the wardroom and entered his little cabin. There he stripped naked and towelled his damp and chilled limbs until he recovered a sensation of warmth.

Then he sat on his swaying cot and listened to the great ship creaking and shuddering beneath him, the occasional splash of spray as high as the nearest gunport.

This time tomorrow he might be on his way to disaster, if not already dead. He shivered, and rubbed his stomach muscles vigorously to quell his sudden uncertainty.

But at least he would be doing something. He pulled a clean shirt over his head and groped for his breeches.

No sooner had he done so than he heard the distant cry getting louder and closer.

'*All hands! All hands! Hands aloft and reef tops'ls!*'

He stood up and banged his head on a ring-bolt.

'*Damnation!*'

Then he was up and hurrying again to that other world of wind and noise, to the *Trojan*'s demands which must always be met.

As he passed Probyn's untidy shape, the lieutenant peered at him and grinned. 'Fog, is it?'

Bolitho grinned back at him. 'Go to hell!"

It took a full two hours to reef to the captain's satisfaction
and to prepare the ship for the night. The news of the proposed
attack had gone through the ship like fire, and Bolitho heard the
many wagers which were being made. The sailor's margin between life and death in this case.

And it would all probably come to nothing. Such things had
happened often enough on this commission. Preparation, and
then some last-minute hitch.

Bolitho imagined it was going to be an almost impossible
thing to find and take the other ship. Equally, he knew he would
feel cheated if it was called off.

He returned to the wardroom to discover that most of the
officers had turned into their bunks after such a day of wind and
bustle.

The surgeon and Captain D'Esterre sat beneath a solitary
lantern playing cards, and alone by the streaming stern windows, staring at the vibrating tiller-head, was Lieutenant Quinn.

In the glow of the swaying lantern he looked younger than
ever, if that were possible.

Bolitho sat beside him and shook his head as the boy, Logan,
appeared with an earthenware wine jug.

'Are you feeling all right, James?'

Quinn looked at him, startled. 'Yes, thank you, sir.'

Bolitho smiled. 'Richard. Dick, if you like.' He watched the
other's despair. 'This is not the midshipman's berth, you know.'

Quinn darted a quick glance at the card players, the mounting pile of coins beside the marine's scarlet sleeve, the dwindling
one opposite him.

Then he said quietly, 'You've done this sort of thing before,
sir—I mean, Dick.'

Bolitho nodded. 'A few times.'

He did not want to break Quinn's trust now that he had
begun.

'I—I thought it would be in the ship when it happened.'
Quinn gestured helplessly around the wardroom and the cabin
flat beyond. 'You know, all your friends near you, *with* you. I
think I could do that. Put up with the first time. The fighting.'

Bolitho said, 'I know. The ship is home. It can help.'

Quinn clasped his hands and said, 'My family are in the

leather trade in the City of London. My father did not wish me to enter the Navy.' His chin lifted very slightly. 'But I was determined. I'd often seen a man-o'-war working down river to the sea. I knew what I wanted.'

Bolitho could well understand the shock Quinn must have endured when he was faced with the reality of a King's ship with all the harsh discipline and the feeling that you, as a new midshipman, are the only one aboard who is in total useless ignorance.

Bolitho had grown up with it and to it. The dark portraits which adorned the walls and staircase of the old Bolitho home in Cornwall were a constant reminder of all who had gone before him. Now he and his brother Hugh were carrying on the tradition. Hugh was in a frigate, now probably in the Mediterranean, while he was here, about to embark in the sort of action they often yarned about in the taverns of Falmouth.

He said, 'It will be all right, James. Mr. Sparke is leading us.'

For the first time he saw Quinn smile as he said, 'I must admit he frightens me more than the enemy.'

Bolitho laughed, wondering why it was that Quinn's fear had somehow given him strength.

'Turn into your cot while you can. Try to sleep. Tell Mackenzie you'd like a tot of brandy. George Probyn's cure for everything!'

Quinn stood up and almost fell as the ship quivered and lunged across the hidden sea.

'No. I must write a letter.'

As he walked away, D'Esterre left the table, pocketing his winnings, and joined Bolitho by the tiller-head.

The surgeon made to follow, but D'Esterre said, 'No more, Robert. Your poor play might blunt my skill!' He smiled. 'Be off with you to your bottles and pills.'

The surgeon did not give his usual laugh, but walked away, feeling for handholds as he went.

D'Esterre gestured towards the silent cabins. 'Is he worried?'
'A little.'

The marine tugged at his tight neckcloth. 'Wish to God I was coming with you. If I can't put my lads to a fight, they will be as rusty as old pikes!'

Bolitho gave a great yawn. 'I'm for bed.' He shook his head as D'Esterre flicked the cards between his fingers. 'I'd not play with you anyway. You have the uncomfortable knack of winning.'

As he lay in his cot, hands thrust behind his head, Bolitho listened to the ship, identifying each sound as it fitted into the pattern and fabric of the hull.

The watch below, slung in their close-packed hammocks like pods, the air foul around them because of the bilges, and because the gunports had to be tightly sealed against sea and rain. Everything bloomed with damp, the deckheads dripping, the pumps clanking mournfully as *Trojan* worked her massive bulk over a stiff quarter-sea.

On the orlop deck beneath the waterline the surgeon would soon be asleep in his sickbay. He had only a handful of ill or injured men to deal with. It was to be hoped it remained like that.

Further forward in the midshipman's berth all would be quiet, although probably a flickering glim would betray somebody trying to read a complicated navigational problem, with a solution expected in the forenoon by Bunce.

Their own world. Seamen and marines. Painters and caulkers, ropemakers and gun captains, coopers and topmen, as mixed a crowd as you could meet in a whole city.

And right aft, doubtless still at his big table, the one who ruled all of them, the captain.

Bolitho looked up at the darkness. Pears was almost directly above him. With the watchful Foley nearby, and a glass at his elbow as he pondered over the day's events and tomorrow's uncertainties.

That was the difference, he decided. We obey and execute his orders as best we can. But he has to give them. And the reward or the blame must be on his shoulders.

Bolitho rolled over and buried his face in the musty pillow.

There were certain advantages in remaining a mere lieutenant.

# 3

## The Faithful

The following day was little different from the preceding ones. Overnight the wind had backed slightly but had lost much of its strength, so that the great, dripping sails filled and sagged in noisy confusion and added in some way to the general air of tension.

Towards noon, with the drizzle as heavy as ever and the sea an expanse of dirty grey, the pipe echoed around the ship, 'Hands lay aft to witness punishment!' It was common enough and under normal conditions might have excited little comment. In a King's ship discipline was hard and quickly executed, and the punishment given by members of the company to one of their own caught stealing from a shipmate's meagre possessions was far worse.

But today should have been different. After all the weeks and months of frustration and waiting, of being cooped up in harbour with little more comfort than a prison hulk, or beating up and down the coastline on some fruitless mission or other, it had been hoped that this would bring a change.

The weather did nothing to help. As Bolitho stood with the other lieutenants, while the marines clattered up and across the poop in two scarlet lines, the ship's company hurried aft. They had to squint against the blown spray and rain, and the biting wind which stirred the dripping canvas with long, uneven gusts. A sullen, unhappy start, Bolitho thought.

The man to be punished came to the larboard gangway, flanked by Paget, the swarthy master-at-arms, and Mr Tolcher, the boatswain. Paget was a tight-lipped, bitter man, and set against him and the squat boatswain the prisoner looked by far the most innocent.

Bolitho watched him, a young Swede named Carlsson. He had a clean-cut face with long flaxen hair, and was staring around as if he had never laid eyes on the ship before. He was typical of the *Trojan*'s mixture, Bolitho thought. You never knew what sort of man you would confront from day to day. Many tongues and races had been gathered up into *Trojan*'s hull in two years, and yet somehow they all seemed to settle in a very short while of coming aboard.

Bolitho hated floggings, even though they were a part of a sailor's life. There still seemed to be no alternative for a captain to maintain discipline when far away from higher authority and the company of other ships.

The grating was rigged by the gangway, and Balleine, a muscular boatswain's mate, stood waiting beside it, the red baize bag dangling at his side.

Cairns crossed the quarterdeck as Pears appeared beneath the poop.

'Company assembled, sir.' His eyes were expressionless.

'Very well.'

Pears glanced at the compass and then walked heavily forward to the quarterdeck rail. There was a hush over the crowded seamen who filled the gundeck and overflowed on to the gangways and into the shrouds themselves.

Bolitho glanced at the midshipmen grouped alongside the older warrant officers. He had been sick at a flogging when he had been a midshipman.

He thought about Carlsson. Found asleep on watch after a whole day of fighting wind and rebellious canvas.

With some officers it might have made a difference. But Lieutenant Sparke had no such weakness as sentiment. Bolitho wondered if he was thinking about it now. How it had cast a blight over the very day he was going to lead a boat attack. He glanced sideways at him but saw nothing but Sparke's usual tight severity.

Pears nodded. 'Uncover.' He removed his hat and tucked it beneath his arm, while the others followed his example.

Bolitho looked to larboard, half expecting to see the sails of their faithful shadow. During the night the schooner had edged closer, and was now visible from the tops of the lower shrouds, but not from the quarterdeck as yet. That made it harder to accept in a sailor's simple reasoning. A Yankee rebel cruising along as safe as you please, and one of their own about to be flogged.

Pears opened the Articles of War and read the relevant numbers with little change from his normal tone. He finished with the words, '. . . he shall be punished according to the Laws and Customs of such cases used at sea.' He replaced his hat, adding, 'Two dozen lashes.'

The rest of the proceedings moved swiftly. Carlsson was stripped to the waist and seized up to the grating, his arms spread up and out as if he was crucified.

Balleine had taken his cat-o'-nine-tails from the red baize bag and was running it through his fingers, his face set in a grim frown. He was to be in Bolitho's boat for the attack. Was he thinking of that?

Pears said in his harsh voice, 'Do your duty.'

Balleine's thick arm came back, over and down, the lash swishing across the man's naked shoulders with a dull crack. Bolitho heard the man gasp as the air was knocked from his lungs.

'One,' counted the master-at-arms.

Nearby, the surgeon and his mates waited to attend the man should he faint.

Bolitho made himself watch the ritual of punishment, his heart like lead. It was unreal. The grey light, the stark clarity of the sailmaker's patches on the heavily flapping main-course. The lash rose and fell, and the scars across the Swede's skin soon changed to overflowing red droplets, which altered into a bloody mess of torn flesh as the flogging continued. Some of the blood had spattered across the man's flaxen hair, the rest eddied and faded in the drizzle across the deck planking.

'*Twenty-one!*'

Bolitho heard a midshipman sobbing quietly, and saw

Forbes, the youngest one aboard, gripping his companion's arm to control himself.

Carlsson had not cried out once, but as the final stroke cracked over his mutilated back he broke, and started to weep.

'Cut him down.'

Bolitho looked from the captain's profile to the watching company. Two dozen lashes was nothing to what some captains awarded. But in this case it might destroy the man. Bolitho doubted if Carlsson had understood more than a few words of what had been said to him.

The surgeon's assistants moved in to carry the sobbing man below. Two seamen started to swab up the blood, and others hurried to obey Tolcher's order to unrig the grating and replace it.

The marines trooped down either poop ladder, and Captain D'Esterre sheathed his bright sword as the company broke up and continued about its affairs.

Sparke said to Bolitho, 'We had best go over the raid again, so that we know each other's thinking.'

Bolitho shrugged. 'Aye, sir.'

Maybe Sparke's attitude was the right one. Bolitho liked Carlsson, what he knew of him. Obedient, cheerful and hard-working. But suppose it had been one of the ship's real trouble-makers who had been caught sleeping on watch. Would he still have felt the same dismay?

Sparke leaned his hands on the quarterdeck rail and peered down at the two cutters which had already been manhandled away from the other boats on the tier in readiness for swaying out.

He said, 'I am not too hopeful.' He gestured at the vibrating shrouds and halliards. 'Mr Bunce is usually right, but this time—'

A seaman yelled from the maintop, 'Deck there! T'other vessel's fallin' off, sir!'

Dalyell, who was officer of the watch, snatched a glass and climbed into the weather shrouds.

He exclaimed, 'Right, by God! The schooner's falling down-wind. Not much, but she'll be visible to all hands by the time they've had their spirit ration!' He laughed at Bolitho's face. 'Damme, Dick, that bugger is a saucy one!'

Bolitho shaded his eyes against the strange light and saw a brief blur across the tumbling water. Perhaps the schooner's master believed the same as Bunce and was drawing nearer so as not to lose his large quarry. Or maybe he was merely trying to provoke the captain into doing something foolish. Bolitho pictured Pears' face as he had read from the Articles of War. There was no chance of the latter.

Sparke was saying, 'It will have to be very fast. They might have boarding nets, but I doubt it. It would hamper her people more than ours.'

He was thinking aloud, seeing his name and citation in the *Gazette*, Bolitho guessed. It was clear in his eyes, like fever, or lust.

'I will go and see the master.' Sparke hurried away, his chin thrusting forward like a galley prow.

Stockdale emerged from somewhere and knuckled his forehead.

'I've seen to the weapons, sir. I've put all the cutlasses and boarding axes to the grindstone.' He wheezed painfully. 'We still going, sir?'

Bolitho crossed to the side and took a telescope from the midshipman of the watch.

'I hope so.'

Then he saw that the midshipman was Forbes, the one who had been holding on to his friend during the flogging.

'Are you well, Mr Forbes?'

The boy nodded wretchedly and sniffed. 'Aye, sir.'

'Good.' He trained the glass across the nettings. 'It comes hard to see a man punished. So we must always be on the lookout to remove the cause in the first place.'

He held his breath as the other vessel's topmasts flitted above the heaving water, as if the rest of her were totally submerged. She had a red square stitched against the throat of her mainsail. A makeshift patch, he wondered, or some special form of recognition? He shivered, feeling the rain trickling over his collar, plastering his hair to his forehead. It was uncanny to see the disembodied masts, to know nothing of the vessel and crew.

He turned to speak with Stockdale, but he had vanished as silently as he had appeared.

Dalyell lurched up the sloping deck and said hoarsely, 'It

looks as if you'll be staying with us, Dick.' He grinned unfeelingly. 'I'm not sorry. I've no wish to do George Probyn's work when he's in his cups!'

Bolitho grimaced. 'I'm coming round to everyone else's view, Simon. I'll go below now.' He looked up at the flapping masthead pendant. 'It seems I shall have the afternoon watch after all.'

But it appeared that the captain had other ideas and still retained some powerful faith in his sailing master. Bolitho was relieved from his watchkeeping duties, and spent most of the time compiling a letter to his father. He merely added to the same long letter whenever he found the opportunity, and ended it just as abruptly whenever they spoke with a homebound packet. It would be a link with his father. The reverse would also be true as Bolitho described daily events, the sighting of ships and islands, the life which was no more for Captain James.

He sat on his sea chest, squinting his eyes as he tried to think of something new to put in his letter.

A chill seemed to run up his spine. As if a ghost had suddenly entered his tiny cabin. He looked up, startled, and saw the deckhead lantern flickering as before. But was it? He stared, and then peered round at the small hanging space where his other clothing had been swaying and creaking just moments earlier.

Bolitho stood up, but remembered to duck his head as he rushed out and aft into the wardroom. The stern windows were dull grey, streaked with spindrift and caked salt.

He pressed his face against them and exclaimed. 'My God, The Sage was right!'

He hurried up to the quarterdeck, instantly aware of the motionless figures all around him, their eyes peering across the quarter or up at the sails which were lifting and then drooping, shaking against the pressures of rigging and spars.

Cairns had the watch, and looked at him gravely. 'The fog, Dick.' He pointed across the nettings. 'It is coming now.'

Bolitho watched the slow progress, the way it seemed to smooth the turbulence from the waves and flatten the crests as it approached.

'Deck there! Oi've lost sight o' th' schooner, zur!'

Pears' voice cut across the speculation and gossip. 'Bring her up two points, Mr Cairns!' He watched the sudden bustle, the shrill calls between decks.

'Man the braces there!'

Pears said to the deck at large, 'We'll gain a cable or so.'

He looked up as the wheel squeaked and the yards began to swing in response to the braces. With her great spread of canvas still holding the dying wind, *Trojan* heeled obediently and pointed her jib boom further to windward. Flapping canvas, chattering blocks and the yells of petty officers did not cover his voice as he said to the tall sailing master, 'That was *well done*, Mr Bunce.'

Bunce dragged his gaze from the helmsmen and the swaying compass card. In the dull light his eyes and brows stood out from all else.

He replied humbly, 'It is His will, sir.'

Pears turned away as if to hide a smile. He barked, 'Mr Sparke, lay aft. Mr Bolitho, attend the cutters and have them swayed out presently.'

Steel clashed between decks, and more men swarmed up to the boat tier, their arms filled with cutlasses, pikes and muskets.

Bolitho was on the gundeck, watching the second cutter's black painted hull rising on its tackles. Then he turned to look aft and saw that the upper poop and the taffrail were already misty and without substance.

He said, 'Lively, lads, or we'll not find our way over the bulwark!' It brought a few laughs.

Pears heard them and said soberly to Sparke, 'Tend well what the master tells you about the set of the current hereabouts. It will save us a mile of unnecessary boat pulling, and not see you arriving on your prize with no breath to lift a blade.' He watched Sparke's eyes as they took it all in. 'And take care. If you cannot board, then stand off and wait for the fog to clear. We'll not drift that much apart.'

He cupped his hands. 'Shorten sail, Mr Cairns! Bring her about and lie to!'

More shouted commands, and moments later as the courses and topsails were brailed up to the yards the two boats detached themselves from the shadowy gundeck and swung up and over the gangway.

Bolitho came aft and touched his hat. 'The people are mustered and armed, sir.'

Sparke handed him a scribbled note. 'Estimated course to steer. Mr Bunce has allowed for the schooner's drift and the strength of the current.' He looked at the captain. 'I'll be away, sir.'

Pears said, 'Carry on, Mr Sparke.' He was going to add good luck, but set against Sparke's severe features it seemed superfluous.

He did say to Bolitho, however, 'Do not get lost, sir. I'll not hunt around Massachusetts Bay for a year!'

Bolitho smiled. 'I will do my best, sir.'

As he ran down to the entry port, Pears said to Cairns, 'Young rascal.'

But Cairns was watching the pitching boats alongside, already filled with men and waiting for Sparke and Bolitho to take them clear of their ship. His heart was with them. It did him no good to realize that the captain's decision had probably been the right one.

Pears watched the black hulls turning end on, the confused splash and thud of oars suddenly picking up the stroke and taking them deeper into the wet, enveloping mist.

'Double the watch on deck , Mr Cairns. Have swivels loaded and set to withstand any boarding attempt on ourselves.'

'What will you do now, sir?'

Pears looked up at his ship's strength. Each sail was either furled or motionless, and *Trojan* herself was paying off to the current, rolling deeply on a steady swell.

'Do?' He yawned. 'I am going to eat.'


Bolitho stood up in the sternsheets and gripped Stockdale's shoulder while he found his balance. Through the man's checkered shirt his muscles felt like warm timber.

The mist swirled into the boat, clinging to their arms and face, making their hair glisten as if with frost.

Bolitho listened to the steady, unhurried pull of the oars. *No sense in urgency. Save the strength for later.*

He said, 'Hold her nor'-west, Stockdale, I am assured that is the best course to take.'

He thought of Bunce's wild eyes. Could there be any other course indeed!

Then, leaving Stockdale at the tiller, crouching over the boat's compass, Bolitho groped his way slowly towards the bows, climbing over thwarts and grunting seamen, treading on weapons and the feet of the extra passengers.

The twenty-eight foot cutter had a crew of eight and a coxswain in normal times. Now she held them and an additonal party which in total amounted to eighteen officers and men.

He found Balleine, the boatswain's mate, crouching above the stem like a figurehead, peering into the wet mist, a hand cupped around his ear to pick up the slightest sound which might be a ship, or another boat.

Bolitho said quietly, 'I cannot see the second lieutenant's cutter, so we must assume we are dependent on our own resources.'

'Aye, sir.' The reply was blunt.

Bolitho thought Balleine might be brooding over the flogging, or merely resentful in being given a look-out's job while Stockdale took the tiller.

Bolitho said, 'I am depending on your experience today.' He saw the man nod and knew he had found the right spot. 'I fear we are somewhat short of it otherwise.'

The boatswain's mate grinned. 'Mr Quinn and Mr Couzens, sir. I'll see 'em fair.'

'I knew it.'

He touched the man's arm and began to make his way aft again. He picked out individual faces and shapes. Dunwoody, a miller's son from Kent. A dark-skinned Arab named Kutbi who had enlisted in Bristol, although nobody knew much about him even now. Rabbett, a tough little man from the Liverpool waterfront, and Varlo, who had been crossed in love, and had been picked up by the press-gang while he he'd been drowning his sorrows at his local inn. These and many more he had grown to know. Some he knew very well. Others stayed away, keeping the rigid barrier between forecastle and quarterdeck.

He reached the sternsheets and sat down between Quinn and Couzens. Their three ages added together only came to fifty-two. The ridiculous thought made him chuckle, and he felt the others turning towards him.

*They think me already unhinged. I have lost sight of Sparke, and am probably steering in quite the wrong direction.*

He explained, 'I am sorry. It was just a thought.' He took a deep breath of the wet salt air. 'But getting away from the ship is reward enough.' He spread his arms and saw Stockdale give his lopsided grin. 'Freedom to do what we want. Right or wrong.'

Quinn nodded. 'I think I understand.'

Bolitho said, 'Your father will be proud of you after this.' *If we live that long.*

Cairns had explained to Bolitho what Quinn had meant about his family being in the leather trade. Bolitho had imagined it to be a tanyard of the kind they had in Falmouth. Bridles and saddles, shoes and straps. Cairns had almost laughed. 'Man, his father belongs to an all-powerful city company. He has contracts with the Army, and influence everywhere else! When I look at young Quinn I sometimes marvel at his audacity to refuse all that power and all that money! He must be either brave or mad to exchange it for *this*!'

A large fish broke surface nearby and flopped back into the water again, making Couzens and some of the others gasp with alarm.

'Easy all.' Bolitho held up his arm to still the oars.

Again he was very conscious of the sea, of their isolation, as the oars rose dripping and motionless along the gunwales. He heard the gurgle of water around the rudder as the boat idled forward into the swell. The splash of another fish, the heavy breathing of the oarsmen.

Then Quinn said in a whisper, 'I hear the other cutter, sir!'

Bolitho nodded, turning his face to starboard, picking up the muffled creak of oars. Sparke was keeping about the same pace and distance. He said, 'Give way all!'

Beside him Couzens gave a nervous cough and asked, 'H-how many of the enemy will there be, sir?'

'Depends. If they've already taken a prize or two, they'll be short of hands. If not, we may be facing twice our number or more.'

'I see, sir.'

Bolitho turned away. Couzens did not see, but he was able to discuss it in a manner which would do justice to a veteran.

He felt the fog against his cheek like a cold breath. Was it moving faster than before? He had a picture of the wind rising and driving the fog away, laying them bare beneath the schooner's guns. Even a swivel could rip his party to shreds before he could get to grips.

He looked slowly along the straining oarsmen and the others

waiting to take their turn. How many would change sides if that happened? It had occured often enough already, when British seamen had been taken by privateers. It was common practice in the Navy, too. *Trojan* had several hands in her company caught or seized in the past two years from both sea and land. It was thought better to fight alongside their old enemy rather than risk disease and possible death in a prison hulk. While there was life there was always hope.

Bolitho reached up and touched his scar, it was throbbing again, and seemed to probe right through his skull.

Stockdale opened the shutter of his lantern very slightly and examined his compass.

He said, 'Steady as she goes, sir.' It seemed to amuse him.

On and on, changing the men at the oars, listening for Sparke's cutter, watching for even a hint of danger.

Bolitho thought that the schooner's master, being a local man, may have made more sail and outpaced the fog, might already be miles away, laughing while they pulled slowly and painfully towards some part of New England.

He allowed his mind to explore what was fast becoming a real possibility.

They might get ashore undetected and try to steal a small vessel and escape under sail. Then what?

Balleine called hoarsely. 'There's a *glow* of sorts, sir!'

Bolitho stumbled forward again, everything else forgotten. 'There, sir.'

Bolitho strained his eyes through the darkness. A glow, that described it exactly, like the window of an alehouse through a waterfront fog. No shape, no centre.

'A lantern.' Balleine licked his lips. 'Hung very high. So there'll be another bugger nearby.'

Bunce had been very accurate. But for his careful calculations they might have passed the other vessel without seeing her or the light. She was standing about a mile away, maybe less.

Bolitho said, 'Easy all!' When he returned to the sternsheets he said, 'She's up ahead, lads. From our drift I'd say she'll be bows on or stern on. We'll take what comes.'

Quinn said in a husky voice, 'Mr Sparke is coming, sir.'

They heard Sparke call, 'Are you ready, Mr Bolitho?' He sounded impatient, even querulous, his earlier doubts forgotten.

'Aye, sir.'

'We will take her from either end.' Sparke's boat loomed through the fog, the lieutenant's white shirt and breeches adding to the ghostlike appearance. 'That way we can divide their people.'

Bolitho said nothing, but his heart sank. Either end, so the boat which pulled the furthest would have a good chance of being seen before she could grapple.

Sparke's oars began to move again and he called, '*I* will take the stern.'

Bolitho waited until the other was clear and then signalled his own men to pull.

'You all know what to do?'

Couzens nodded, his face compressed with concentration. 'I will stay with the boat, sir.'

Quinn added jerkily, 'I'll support you, sir, er, Dick, and take the foredeck.'

Bolitho nodded. 'Balleine will hold *his* men until they are ready to use their muskets.'

Cairns had been insistent about that, and rightly so. Any fool might set off a musket too šoon if it was loaded and primed from the start.

Bolitho drew his curved hanger and unclipped the leather scabbard, dropping it to the bottom boards. There it would wait until he needed it. But worn during an attack it might trip and throw him under a cutlass.

He touched the back of the blade, but kept his eyes fixed on the wavering glow beyond the bows. The nearer they got, the smaller it became, as the fog's distortion had less control over it.

From one corner of his eye he thought he saw a series of splashes as Sparke increased his stroke and went in for the attack.

Bolitho watched as with startling suddenness the masts and booms of the drifting schooner broke across the cloudy sky like black bars and the lantern sharpened into one unwinking eye.

Stockdale touched Couzens' arm, making the boy jump as if he had cut him.

'Here, your fist on the tiller-bar, sir.' He guided him as if Couzens had been struck blind. 'Take over from me when I give the word.' With his other hand Stockdale picked up his outdated boarding cutlass which weighed as much as two of the modern ones.

Bolitho held up his arm and the oars rose and remained poised over either beam like featherless wings.

He watched, holding his breath, feeling the drag of current and holding power of the rudder. They would collide with the schooner's raked stem, right beneath her bowsprit with any sort of luck.

'Boat your oars!' He was speaking in a fierce whisper although surely his heart-beats against his ribs would be heard all the way to Boston. His lips were frozen in a wild grin which he could not control. Madness, desperation, fear. It was all here.

'Ready with the grapnel!'

He watched the slender bowsprit sweeping across them as if the schooner was riding at full power to smash them under her forefoot. Bolitho saw Balleine rising with his grapnel, gauging the moment, ducking to avoid losing his head on the schooner's bobstay.

There was a sudden bang, followed by a long drawn-out scream. Bolitho saw and heard it all in a mere second. The flash which seemed to come from the sea itself, the response from the vessel above him, yells and startled movements before more explosions ripped across the water towards the scream.

He jumped to his feet. 'Ready, lads!'

He shut Sparke from his mind. The fool had allowed somebody to load a musket, and it had gone off, hitting one of his men. It was too late now. For any of them.

Bolitho threw up his arm and seized the trailing line as the grapnel thudded into the schooner's bowsprit and slewed the cutter drunkenly around the bows.

*'At 'em, lads!'*

Then he was struggling with feet and hands, the hanger dangling from his wrist as he fought his way up and around the flared hull.

The other end of the vessel was lit by exploding muskets, and as Bolitho's men clambered over the forecastle and cannoned into unfamiliar pieces of gear, more shots hammered into the deck around them or whined above the rocking cutter like maddened spirits.

He heard Quinn gasping and stumbling beside him, Stockdale's heavy frame striding just a bit ahead, the cutlass moving before him as if to sniff out the enemy.

Something flew out of the darkness and a man fell shrieking, a pike driven through his chest. More cracks, and two more of Bolitho's men dropped.

But they were nearer now. Bolitho gripped his hanger and yelled, 'Surrender in the King's name!'

It brought a chorus of curses and derisive shouts, as he knew it would. But it gave him just the few more seconds he needed to get to grips. He hacked out and knocked a sword from somebody's hand. As the man ran to retrieve it, Bolitho heard Stockdale's cutlass smash into his skull, heard the big man grunt as he wrenched it free.

Then they were chest to chest, blade to blade. Behind him Bolitho heard Balleine yelling and blaspheming, the sporadic bang of muskets as he managed to get off a few shots at the shrouds where sharpshooters were trying to find their targets.

A bearded face loomed through the others, and Bolitho felt his blade grate against the man's sword with a clang of steel as they parried, pushed each other clear to find the space to fight. Around them figures staggered and reeled like crazed drunkards, their cutlasses striking sparks, the voices distorted and wild with hate and fear.

Bolitho ducked, slashed the man across the ribs, and as he lurched clear he brought the hanger down on his neck with such force he numbed his wrist.

But they were being pushed back towards the forecastle all the same. Somewhere, a hundred miles away, Bolitho heard a cannon shot, and through his dazed mind he guessed that it was another vessel nearby, trying to show that help was on its way.

His shoes slipped on blood, and a dying sailor, trodden and kicked by the fighting, hacking mass of men above him, tried to seize Bolitho's ankle.

Another man screamed and fell from aloft, dead from a musket ball before he hit the deck. But carried by the desperately fighting seamen he still seemed to cling to life, like a tipsy dancer.

Bolitho saw a pair of white legs against the bulwark and knew it was Quinn. He was being attacked by two men at once, and even as Bolitho slashed one of them across the shoulder and dragged him screaming to one side, Quinn gasped and dropped to his knees, his sword gone, and both hands pressed to his chest.

His attacker was so wild with the lust of battle he did not seem to see Bolitho. He stood above the lieutenant and drew back his arm for the kill. Bolitho caught him by the sleeve,

swung him round, using the impetus of the man's sword-thrust
to take him off balance. Then he drove the knuckle guard of his
hanger into his face, the pain jarring his wrist again like a
wound.

The man lurched upright, and seemed to be spitting out teeth
as he bore down for another attack.

Then he stopped stock-still, his eyes white in the gloom like
pebbles, as he slowly pirouetted around and then fell. Balleine
pounced forward and tore his boarding axe from the man's back
as he would from a chopping block.

There was a commotion alongside, and moments later the
retreating boarders heard Sparke's penetrating voice as he
shouted, 'To me, Trojans, to me.'

Attacked from both ends of the schooner, and with the
obvious possibility of other boats nearby, the fight ended as
swiftly as it had begun.

There were not even any curses thrown at the British seamen
this time. *Trojan*'s men were too wild and shocked with the
hand-to-hand fighting, which had left several of their own dead
and badly wounded to accept insults as well. The schooner's
crew seemed to sense this, and allowed themselves to be dis-
armed, searched and then herded into two manageable groups.

Sparke, a pistol in either hand, strode amongst the corpses
and whimpering wounded, and when he saw Bolitho snapped,
'Might have been worse.' He could not control his elation. 'Nice
little craft. Very nice.' He saw Quinn and leaned over him. 'Is it
bad?'

Balleine, who had torn open the lieutenant's shirt and was
trying to stem the blood, said, 'Slit his chest like a peach, sir. But
if we can get him to . . .'

But Sparke had already gone elsewhere, bellowing for
Frowd, his master's mate, to attend to the business of getting
under way at the first breath of a breeze.

Bolitho was on his knees, holding Quinn's hands away from
the wound, as Balleine did his best with a makeshift bandage.

'Easy, James.' He saw Quinn's head lolling, his efforts to
control his agony. His hands were like ice, and there was blood
everywhere. 'You will be all right. I promise.'

Sparke was back again. 'Come, come, Mr Bolitho, there's a
lot to do. And I'll wager we'll have company before too long.'

He dropped his voice suddenly, and Bolitho was confronted

by a Sparke he had not seen before in the two years he had known him.

'I *know* how you feel about Quinn. *Responsible*. But you must not show it. Not now. In front of the people, d'you see? They're feeling the shock, the fight's going out of them. They'll be looking to us. So we'll save our regrets for later, eh?'

He changed back again. 'Now then. Cutters to be warped aft and secured. Check the armament, or lack of it, and see that it is loaded to repel attack. Canister, grape, anything you can lay hands on.' He looked for somebody in the foggy darkness. 'You! Archer! Train a swivel on the prisoners. One sign that they might try to retake the ship and you know what to do!'

Stockdale was wiping his cutlass on a piece of some luckless man's shirt.

He said, 'I'll watch over Mr Quinn, sir.' He rubbed the cutlass again and then thrust it through his belt. 'A good tot would suit him fine, I'm thinking.'

Bolitho nodded. 'Aye, see to it.'

He walked away, the sobs and groans from the darkened deck painting a better picture than any sight could do.

He saw Dunwoody, the miller's son, groping around an inert shape by the bulwark.

The seaman said brokenly, 'It's me mate, sir, Bill Tyler.'

Bolitho said, 'I know. I saw him fall.' He recalled Sparke's advice and added, 'Get that lantern down from aloft directly. We don't want to invite the moths, do we?'

Dunwoody stood up and wiped his face. 'No, sir. I suppose not.' He hurried away, but glanced back at his dead friend as if to tell himself it was not true.

Sparke was everywhere, and when he rejoined Bolitho by the wheel he said briskly, 'She's the *Faithful*. Owned by the Tracy brothers of Boston. Known privateers, and very efficient at their trade.'

Bolitho waited, feeling his wrists and hands trembling with strain.

Sparke added, 'I Have searched the cabin. Quite a haul of information.' He was bubbling with pleasure. 'Captain Tracy was killed just now.' He gestured to the upturned white eyes of the man killed by Balleine's boarding axe. 'That's him. The other one, his brother, commands a fine brig apparently, the *Revenge*, taken from us last year. She was named *Mischief* then.'

'Aye, sir, I remember. She was taken off Cape May.' It was amazing that he could speak so calmly. As if they were both out for a stroll instead of standing amidst carnage and pain.

Sparke eyed him curiously. 'Are you steadier now?' He did not wait for an answer. 'Good. The only way.'

Bolitho asked, 'Does she have any sort of cargo, sir?'

'None. She was obviously expecting to get *that* from our convoy.' He looked up at the bare masts. 'Put some hands to work on this deck. It's like a slaughter-house. Drop the corpses over the side and have the wounded carried below. There's precious little comfort for them, but it's a sight warmer than on deck.'

As Bolitho made to hurry away, Sparke added calmly, 'Besides which, I want them to be as quiet as possible. There may be boats nearby, and I intend to hold this vessel as our prize.'

Bolitho looked round for his hat which had gone flying in the fight. That was more like it, he thought grimly. For a brief moment he had imagined that Sparke's reason for moving the injured was solely for humanity's sake. He should have known better.

The work to clear up the deck and to search out the vessel's defences and stores went on without a break. The fit and un-wounded men did the heavy work, the ones with lesser injuries sat with muskets and at the loaded swivels to watch over the prisoners. The badly wounded, one of whom was the man who had foolishly fired his musket and had lost half his face in doing so, managed as best they could.

Sparke had not mentioned the musket incident. But for it the casualties would have been much reduced, even minimal. The schooner's crew were brave enough, but without that warning, and lacking as they did the hardened discipline of *Trojan*'s seamen, it would likely have ended with little more than a bloody nose or two. Bolitho knew Sparke must have thought about this. He would doubtless be hoping that Pears would see only the prize and forget the oversight.

Several times Bolitho climbed down to the master's cabin where the late Captain Tracy had lived and made his plans. There, Quinn was lying white-faced on a rough bunk, his bandages soaked in blood, his lip cut where he had bitten it to stem the anguish.

Bolitho asked Stockdale what he thought and the man

answered readily, 'He has a will to live, sir. But he's precious little hope, I'm thinking.'

The first hint of dawn came with the lightening of the surrounding mist.

The schooner's lazaret had been broken open and a generous ration of neat rum issued to all hands, including the two young midshipmen.

Of the attacking force of thirty-six officers and seamen, twelve were already dead, or as near to as made no difference, and several of the survivors had cuts and bruises which had left them too weak and dazed to be of much use for the moment.

Bolitho watched the paling mist, seeing the schooner taking shape around them. He saw Couzens and Midshipman Libby from Sparke's boat staring at the great bloodstains on the planking, perhaps realizing only now what they had seen and done.

Mr Frowd, the master's mate, waited by the wheel, watching the limp sails which Bolitho's men had shaken out in readiness for the first breeze. The only sounds were the clatter of loose gear, the creak of timbers as the vessel rolled uncomfortably on the swell.

With the dawn came the awareness of danger, that which a fox might feel when it crosses open land.

Bolitho looked along the deck. The *Faithful* carried eight six-pounders and four swivel guns, all of which had been made in France. This fact, added to the discovery of some very fine and freshly packed brandy in the captain's lazaret, hinted at a close relationship with the French privateers.

She was a very handy little vessel, of about seventy-five feet. One which would sail to windward better than most and outpace any heavier, square-rigged ship.

Whoever Captain Tracy had once been, he would not have planned to be dead on this new dawn.

The boom of the large gaff-headed mainsail creaked noisily, and the deck gave a resounding tremble.

Sparke shouted, 'Lively there! Here comes the wind!'

Bolitho saw his expression and called, 'Stand by the fores'l!' He waved to Balleine. 'Ready with stays'l and jib!' The schooner's returning life seemed to affect him also. 'A good hand at the wheel, Mr. Frowd!'

Frowd showed his teeth. He had picked a helmsman already, but understood Bolitho's mood. He had been in the Navy as long as the fourth lieutenant had been on this earth.

Every man had at least two jobs to do at once, but watched by the silent prisoners, they bustled about the confined deck as if they had been doing it for months.

'Sir! Mastheads to starboard!'

Sparke spun round as Bolitho pointed towards the rolling bank of fog. Two masts were standing through above it, one with a drooping pendant, but enough to show it was a larger vessel than the *Faithful*.

The blocks clattered and squealed as the seamen hauled and panted while the foresail and then the big mainsail with its strange scarlet patch at its throat were set to the wind. The deck tilted, and the helmsman reported gruffly. 'We 'ave steerage way, sir!'

Sparke peered at the misty compass bowl. 'Wind seems as before, Mr Frowd. Let her fall off. We'll try and hold the wind-gage from this other beauty, but we'll run if needs be.'

The two big sails swung out on their booms, shaking away the clinging moisture and yesterday's rain like dogs emerging from a stream.

Bolitho said, 'Mr Couzens! Take three hands and help Balleine with the stays'l!'

As he turned again he saw what Sparke had seen. With the fog rolling and unfolding downwind like smoke, the other vessel seemed to leap bodily from it. She was a brig, with the now-familiar striped Grand Union flag with its circle of stars set against the hoist already lifting and flapping from her peak.

Something like a sigh came from the watching prisoners, and one called, 'Now you'll see some iron, before they bury you!'

Sparke snapped, 'Keep that man silent, or put a ball in his head, I don't care which.' He glanced at Frowd. 'Fall off two points.'

'Steer nor'-east!'

'Will I have the six-pounders run out, sir?'

Sparke had found a telescope and was training it on the brig. 'She's the old *Mischief*.' He steadied the glass. 'Ah. I see her captain. Must be the other Tracy.' He looked at Bolitho. 'No. If we get close enough to use these little guns, the brig will reduce us to toothpicks within half an hour. Agility and speed is all we have.'

He tugged out his watch and studied it. He did not even blink as a gun crashed out and a ball slapped through the foresail like an invisible fist.

Spray lifted over the bows and pattered across the busy seamen there. The wind got stronger as the fog hurried ahead of the little schooner, as if afraid of being impaled on the jib boom.

The brig had set her topsails and forecourse now and was in hot pursuit, trying to beat to windward and outsail the schooner in one unbroken tack. Her two bow-chasers were shooting gun by gun, the air cringing to the wild scream which could only mean chain-shot or langridge. Just one of those around a mast and it would be the start of the end.

Another gun must have been trained round to bear on the elusive *Faithful*, and a moment later a ball ripped low over the poop, cutting rigging, and almost hitting one of the prisoners who had risen to watch.

A seaman snarled at him, 'Y'see, matey? Yankee iron is just as bloody for *you* this time!'

Balleine hurried aft and asked, 'Shall I cut the boats adrift, sir? We might gain half a knot without them.'

Another ball slammed down almost alongside, hurling spray clean over the poop like tropical rain.

A seaman yelled in disbelief, 'The Yankee's goin' about, sir!'

Sparke permitted himself a small smile of satisfaction. With the fog retreating rapidly through her towering masts and rigging like ghostly gunsmoke, the *Trojan* loomed to meet them, her exposed broadside already run out in twin lines of black muzzles.

Sparke said, 'Bless me, Mr Bolitho! They'll have *us* if we're not careful!'

Midshipman Libby ran aft like a rabbit, and seconds later the British ensign broke from the gaff, bright scarlet to match the one above *Trojan*'s gilded poop.

Below, in the tiny cabin, Stockdale wiped Quinn's forehead with a wet rag and looked at the skylight.

Quinn moved his lips very slowly. 'What was that sound?'

Stockdale watched him sadly. 'Cheering, sir. Must've sighted the old *Trojan*.'

He saw Quinn swoon away again on a tide of pain and the brandy which he had been forcing into him. If he lived he might never be the same again. Then he thought of the splashes alongside as the corpses, friends and enemies alike, had been buried at sea. Even so, he'd be better off than them.

# 4

## *Rendezvous*

Bolitho strode aft and paused beneath the *Trojan*'s poop, conscious of the many watching eyes which followed him along the deck, just as they had greeted his return on board. He was aware too of his dirty and bedraggled appearance, the tear in his coat sleeve, and smears of dried blood across his breeches.

He looked over his shoulder and saw the prize, more graceful than ever at a distance, riding comfortably beneath *Trojan*'s lee. It was hard to picture what had happened aboard her during the night, let alone accept he had managed to survive it.

Sparke had come across to the *Trojan* immediately they had made signal contact, and had left Bolitho to attend to the transfer of wounded and the burial of the man whose musket had exploded in his face.

Before reporting to the captain, Bolitho had hurried down to the orlop, almost dreading what he would find. *Responsible*, that was what Sparke had said. It was how it had felt as he had looked at the spread-eagled body on the surgeon's table, shining like a corpse in the swaying deckhead lanterns. Quinn had been stripped naked, and as Thorndike had slit away the last of the matted bandage, Bolitho had seen the gash for the first time.

From the point of Quinn's left shoulder, diagonally across his breast, it opened like an obscene mouth.

Quinn was unconscious, and Thorndike had said curtly, 'Not too bad. But another day,' he shrugged, 'different story.'

Bolitho had asked, 'Can you save him?'

Thorndike had faced him, displaying his bloody apron, as he had snapped, 'I'll do what I can. I have already taken off a man's leg, and another has a splinter in his eye.'

Bolitho had said awkwardly, 'I am sorry. I'll not delay you further.'

Now, as he made his way towards the stern cabin where a scarlet-coated marine stood stiffly on guard, he felt the same dull ache of failure and despair. They had taken a prize, but the cost had been too great.

The marine stamped his boots together, and then Foley, as neat as ever, opened the outer door, his eyes widening as he took in Bolitho's crumpled appearance with obvious disapproval.

In the stern cabin Captain Pears was at his desk, some papers strewn across it, a tall goblet of wine in one hand.

Bolitho stared at Sparke. He was smartly dressed, shaved, and looked as if he had never left the ship.

Pears ordered, 'Wine for the fourth lieutenant.'

He watched Bolitho as he took the goblet from his servant, saw the strain, the dragging weariness of the night's work.

'Mr Sparke has been telling me of your impressive deeds, Mr Bolitho.' Pears' face was devoid of expression. 'The schooner is a good catch.'

Bolitho let the wine warm his stomach, soothe the ache in his mind. Sparke had come straight to the ship, had changed and cleaned himself before presenting his report to the captain. How much had he told him about the first part? The startling crash of the musket which had added so much to the bill.

Pears asked, 'How is Mr Quinn, by the way?'

'The surgeon is hopeful, sir.'

Pears eyed him strangely. 'Good. And I understand both midshipmen behaved well, too.'

He turned his attention to the littered papers, the rest apparently put aside. Finished.

Pears said, 'These papers were found by Mr Sparke in the *Faithful*'s cabin. They are of even greater value than the prize herself.' He looked at them grimly. 'They give details of the schooner's mission after she had taken on any captured powder and weapons from the convoy. The escorts would have been hard put to protect the whole convoy and keep it intact after the sort of weather we have been experiencing. And I have no doubt it was even worse coming out of Halifax. As it is, the brig will have to manage without her, although I would expect there to be other wolves tailing such rich cargoes even now.'

Bolitho asked, 'When will you expect to sight the ships, sir?'

'Mr Bunce and I believe tomorrow.' He spoke as if it no longer mattered. 'But there is something else which must be done without delay. The *Faithful* was to rendezvous with the enemy near the mouth of Delaware Bay. Our Army in Philadelphia is hard put to force supplies upriver to the garrison. There are patrols and skirmishers every mile of the way to fire on our boats and barges. Just think how much worse it will get if the enemy can lay hands on more arms and powder.'

Bolitho nodded and took another goblet from Foley, his mind seeing it exactly.

Delaware Bay was some four hundred miles south of where he was standing. A fast, lively craft could reach the rendevous in three days if the weather favoured her.

They had been that confident, he thought. The red patch on the mainsail. The signal to the watchers on the shore. It was just the right place for it, too. Very shallow and treacherous at low tide, where no prowling frigate would dare give chase for fear of tearing out her keel.

He said, 'You will send the *Faithful*, sir?'

'Yes. There will be some risk of course. The passage might take longer than we plan for. The enemy know that *Faithful* has been seized, and will use every ruse to pass the word south without losing a moment. Signals, fast horsemen, it can be done.' He permitted himself a wintry smile. 'Mr Revere has established that point beyond question.'

Sparke drew himself up very stiffly and looked at Bolitho. 'I have been given the honour of commanding this mission.'

Pears said calmly, 'If you wish, Mr Bolitho, you may go with the second lieutenant as before. The choice is yours, this time.'

Bolitho nodded, marvelling that he did not even hesitate. 'Aye, sir. I'd like to go.'

'That is settled then.' Pears dragged out his gold watch. 'I will have your orders written at once, but Mr Sparke already knows the bones of the matter.'

Cairns entered the cabin, his hat tucked under his arm.

'I have sent some hands across to the schooner, sir. The gunner is attending to the armament.' He paused, his eyes on Bolitho. 'Mr Quinn is still unconscious, but the surgeon says his heart and breathing are fair.'

Pears nodded. 'Tell my clerk to come aft at once.'

Cairns hesitated by the door. 'I have brought the prisoners aboard, sir. Shall I swear them in?'

Pears shook his head. 'No. Volunteers I will accept, but this war has taken too firm a hold to expect a change of loyalties as a matter of course. They would be like bad apples in a barrel, and I'll not risk discontent in my ship. We'll hand them to the authorities in New York when we return there.'

Cairns left, and Pears said, 'The written orders will not protect you from the cannon of our patrols in the area. So show them a clean pair of heels. If there are spies about, it will make your guise even more acceptable.'

Teakle, the captain's clerk, scurried into the cabin, and Pears dismissed them. 'Go and prepare yourselves, gentlemen. I want you to keep that rendezvous, and destroy what you discover there. It will be worth a great deal, and may put heart into our troops at Philadelphia.'

The two lieutenants left the cabin, and Sparke said, 'We will be taking some marines this time.' He sounded as if he disliked the idea of sharing his new role. 'But speed is the thing. So go and hurry our people to ferry the rest of the stores and weapons across to the schooner.'

Bolitho touched his hat and replied, 'Aye, sir.'

'And replace Midshipman Couzens with Mr Weston. This is no work for children.'

Bolitho walked out into the chilling air and watched the boats plying back and forth between the unmatched vessels like water-beetles.

Weston was the signals midshipman and, like Libby, who had been in Sparke's boat, would be the next on the list for examination for lieutenant. If Quinn died, the promotion of one of them would be immediate.

He saw Couzens watching from the lee gangway as *Trojan*

rolled and complained while she lay hove to for the transfer of men and equipment.

Couzens had obviously already been told of the change, and said breathlessly, 'I'd like to come with you, sir.'

Bolitho eyed him gravely. Couzens at thirteen would be worth two of Weston. He was an overweight, ginger-haired youth of seventeen, and something of a bully when he could get away with it.

He replied, 'Next time, maybe.' He looked away. 'We shall see.'

It was odd that he rarely thought of being replaced himself, of being just another name marked D.D. *Discharged Dead*.

To be killed was one thing. To be *replaced* by someone he actually knew at this moment brought it home like a dash of ice water.

He saw Stockdale, arms folded, on the schooner's little poop as she rolled sickeningly on a procession of troughs. *Waiting*. Knowing with his inner sense that Bolitho would be going across at any moment to join him.

The marines were climbing down into the boats now, pursued by all the usual insults from the watching seamen.

Captain D'Esterre, accompanied by his sergeant, joined Bolitho on the gangway.

'Thanks to you, Dick, my lads will get some exercise, I trust.' He waved to his lieutenant who was remaining aboard with the rest of the marines. 'Take care! I'll outlive you yet!'

The marine lieutenant grinned and touched his hat. 'At least I may have a chance of winning a hand of cards while you're away, sir!'

Then the captain and his sergeant followed the others into the nearest boat.

Bolitho saw Sparke speaking with Cairns and the master, and said impetuously, 'Visit Mr Quinn whenever you can. Will you do that for me?'

Couzens nodded with sudden gravity. It was a special task. Something just for him alone.

'Aye, sir.' He stood back as Sparke came hurrying from the quarterdeck and added quickly, 'I will pray for you, sir.'

Bolitho stared at him with surprise. But he was moved, too. 'Thank you. That was well said.'

Then, touching his hat to the quarterdeck and nodding to the faces along the gangway, he hurried into the boat.

Sparke thumped down beside him, his written orders bulging from an inner pocket. As the boat shoved off Bolitho saw the seamen hurrying along the *Trojan*'s decks and yards getting ready to make sail again once she had retrieved her boats.

Sparke said, 'At last. Something to make them all sit up and take notice.'

D'Esterre was looking at the dizzily swaying schooner with sudden apprehension.

'How the deuce will we all get settled into her, in heaven's name?'

Sparke bared his teeth. 'It will not be for long. Sailors are used to such small hardships.'

Bolitho let his mind drift away, seeing his own hand as he continued with the last letter to his father, as if he were actually writing it at this moment.

*Today I had the chance to stay with the ship, but I chose to return to the prize.* He watched the masts and booms rising above the labouring oarsmen. *Perhaps I am wrong, but I believe that Sparke is so full of hope for the future he can see nothing else.*

The boat hooked on and the last of the marines clambered and clattered over the bulwark, swaying on the deck like toy soldiers in an unsteady box.

Shears, their sergeant, soon took charge, and within minutes there was not a red coat to be seen as one by one they climbed down into the vessel's main hold.

One of *Trojan*'s nine-pounders had been ferried across, and was now firmly lashed on the deck, with tackles skilfully fitted to the schooner's available ring-bolts and cleats. How William Chimmo, *Trojan*'s gunner, had managed to get it ferried over, remounted and set in its present position was evidence of a real expert, a professional warrant officer. He had sent one of his mates, a taciturn man called Rowhurst, to tend the nine-pounder's needs, and he was looking at the gun, rubbing it with a rag, and probably wondering what would happen to the schooner's deck planking when he had to lay and fire it.

By the time they had sorted out the hands, the new ones and those of the original party who were still aboard, and put them to work, *Trojan* was already standing downwind, with more and more canvas ballooning from her yards. One boat was still being lowered inboard on to the tier, Pears was so eager to make up for lost time.

Bolitho watched her for some minutes, seeing her from a distance, as Quinn had once seen the great ships heading down the Thames. Things of power and beauty, while within their hulls they carried as much hope and pain as any landlocked town. Now Quinn was lying on the orlop. Or perhaps already dead.

Mr Frowd touched his hat. 'Ready to get under way, sir.' He glanced meaningly at Sparke who was peering at his written orders, entirely absorbed.

Bolitho called, 'We are ready, sir.'

Sparke scowled, irritated at the interruption. 'Then please be so good as to turn the hands to.'

Frowd rubbed his hands as he looked at the big boomed sails and the waiting seamen.

'She'll fly, this one.' He became formal again. 'I suggest we take account of the present wind, sir, and steer sou'-east. That'll take us well clear of the bay and prepare us for old Nantucket again.'

Bolitho nodded. 'Very well, Bring her about and lay her on the starboard tack.'

Sparke came out of his trance and crossed the deck as the man ran to bring the schooner under command.

'It is a good plan.' He stuck out his narrow chin. 'The late and unlamented Captain Tracy wrote almost everything about the rendezvous except the colour of his countrymen's eyes!'

He gripped a stay as the wheel went over and the two great booms swung above the gurgling water alongside and each sail filled until it looked iron-hard.

Bolitho noticed that even the hole in the foresail made by the brig's cannon had been deftly patched during the last few hours. The dexterity of the British sailor when he put his mind to something was beyond measure, he thought.

The *Faithful* was responding well, in spite of her changed ownership. With spray leaping over her stem and sluicing into small rivers along her lee scuppers, she came about like a thoroughbred, the sails filling again and thundering to the wind.

Eventually, leaning over stiffly to take full advantage of the new tack, Frowd was satisfied. After serving under Bunce, he had learned to take nothing for granted.

Sparke watched, unblinking, from right aft by the taffrail. He said, 'Dismiss the watch below, Mr Bolitho.'

He turned and shaded his eyes to seek out the *Trojan*, but she was hidden in a rain squall, little more than a shadow, or a smudge on an imperfect painting.

Sparke lurched unsteadily to the cabin hatch.

'I will be below if you need me.'

Bolitho breathed out slowly. Sparke was no longer a lieutenant. He had become a captain.


'Mr Bolitho, sir!'

Bolitho rolled over in the unfamiliar bunk and blinked at a shaded lantern. It was Midshipman Weston, leaning over him, his shadow looming across the cabin like a spectre.

'What is it?'

Bolitho dragged his mind reluctantly from the precious sleep. He sat up, massaging his eyes, his throat sore from the stench of the sealed cabin, the damp, and foul air.

Weston watched him. 'The second lieutenant's compliments, sir, and would you join him on deck.'

Bolitho threw his legs over the bunk and tested the schooner's motion. It must be nearly dawn, he thought, and Sparke was already about. That was strange, to say the least, as he usually left the matters of watchkeeping and routine alterations of tack and course to Bolitho or Frowd.

Weston said nothing, and Bolitho was disinclined to ask what was happening. It would show doubt and uncertainty to the midshipman, who had enough of his own already.

He scrambled through the companion hatch and winced to the greeting of needle-sharp spray and wind. The sky was much as he had last seen it. Low scudding clouds, and with no sign of a star.

He listened to the boom of canvas, the creak of spars as the schooner plunged drunkenly across a deep trough with such violence it almost flung him to the deck.

It had been like this for three days. The wind had become their enemy more often than not, and they had been made to change tack again and again, beating back and forth for miles to make an advance of just a few cables, or indeed for a complete loss of progress.

Sparke had been almost desperate as day by day they had driven south and then south-west towards the land and the mouth of the Delaware.

Even the most disciplined seaman aboard had become sullen and resentful at Sparke's attitude. He was intolerant of everyone, and seemed totally obsessed by the task entrusted to him, and now the possibility of failure.

Bolitho crossed the slippery planking and shouted above the wind, 'You sent for me, sir?'

Sparke swung round, retaining his grip on the weather shrouds, his usually immaculate hair streaming in the wind as he replied angrily, 'Of course, damn it! You have taken long enough!'

Bolitho controlled his sudden anger, knowing that Sparke's shouted rebuke must have been heard by most of the men on deck. He waited, sensing the lieutenant's mood, his all-consuming need to drive the ship with every stitch she would carry.

Sparke said abruptly, 'The master's mate has suggested we stay on this tack until noon.'

Bolitho forced his mind to grapple with it, to picture their wavering progress on the chart.

He answered without hesitation, 'Mr Frowd means we are less likely to run foul of local shipping, or worse, one of our own patrols.'

'Mr Frowd is an *idiot*!' He was yelling again. 'And if you agree with him, you are equally so, damn your eyes!'

Bolitho swallowed hard, counting seconds as he would for a fall of shot.

'I have to agree with him, sir. He is a man of much experience.'

'And I am not, I suppose!' He held up his free hand. 'Do not bother to argue with me. My mind is settled on it. We will change tack in one hour and head directly for the rendezvous. It will cut the time considerably. On *this* tack we could be another full day!'

Bolitho tried again. 'The enemy will not know our exact time of arrival, sir, or indeed if we are coming at all. War leaves no room for such planning.'

Sparke had not heard him. 'By the living God, I'll not let them get away now. I've waited long enough, watching others being handed gilt-edged commands because they *know* some-body at the Admiralty or in Court. Well, Mr Bolitho, not me. I've worked all the way. Earned each step up the ladder!'

He seemed to realize what he had said, that he had laid himself wide open before his subordinate, and added, 'Now, call the hands! Tell Mr Frowd to prepare his chart.' He eyed him fixedly, his face very pale in the gloom. 'I'll have no arguments. Tell him that also!'

'Have you discussed it with Captain D'Esterre, sir?'

Sparke laughed. 'Certainly not. He is a marine. A *soldier* as far as I am concerned.'

In the cupboard-like space adjoining the master's cabin which was the *Faithful*'s chart room, Bolitho joined Frowd and peered at the calculations and compass directions which had become their daily fare since leaving *Trojan*'s company.

Frowd said quietly, 'It will get us there more quickly, sir. But...'

Bolitho was bent low to avoid the deckhead, conscious of the vessel's violent motion, the nearness of the sea through the side.

'Aye, Mr Frowd, there are always the *buts*. We will just have to hope for some luck.'

Frowd grinned bitterly. 'I've no wish to be killed by my own countrymen, by mistake or otherwise, sir.'

An hour later, with all hands employed on deck, *Faithful* clawed around to starboard, pointing her bowsprit towards the invisible land, a single reef in main and foresail, all that Sparke would tolerate. She was leaning right over to leeward, the sea creaming up and over the bulwark, or sluicing across the teth-ered nine-pounder like surf around a rock.

It was still extremely cold, and what food the cook managed to produce was soon without warmth, and soggy with spray after its perilous passage along the upper deck.

As the light strengthened, Sparke sent an extra look-out aloft with orders to report anything he saw. '*Even if it is a floating log.*'

Bolitho watched Sparke's anxiety mount all through the forenoon as the schooner pushed steadily westward. Only once did the look-out sight another sail, but it was lost in spray and distance before he could give either a description or the course she was steering.

Stockdale was rarely out of Bolitho's sight, and was using his strength to great advantage as the seamen were ordered from one mast to the other, or made to climb aloft to repair and splice fraying rigging.

The cry from the masthead when it came was like an unexpected shot.

'*Land ho!*'

Men temporarily forgot their discomfort as they squinted through the curtain of rain and spray, searching for the landfall.

Sparke hung on to the shrouds with his telescope, all dignity forgotten as he waited for the schooner to leap on a steep crest and he found the mark he had been hoping for.

He jumped down to the deck and glared triumphantly at Frowd.

'Let her fall off a point. That is Cape Henlopen yonder to the nor'-west of us!' He could not contain himself. 'Now, Mr Frowd, how about your caution, eh?'

The helmsman called, 'West by north, sir! Full an' bye!'

Frowd replied grimly, 'The wind's shifted, sir. Not much as yet, but we're heading for shallows to the south'rd of Delaware Bay.'

Sparke grimaced. '*More* caution!'

'It is my duty to warn you on these matters, sir.' He stood his ground.

Bolitho said, 'Mr Frowd is largely responsible for this final landfall, sir.'

'That I will acknowledge at the right time, provided—'

He stared up the mast as a look-out yelled, 'Deck there! Sail on th' larboard quarter!'

'*God damn!*' Sparke stared up until his eyes brimmed over with water. 'Ask the fool what she is!'

Midshipman Libby was already swarming up the weather shrouds, his feet moving like paddles in his efforts to reach the look-out.

Then he shouted, 'Too small for a frigate, sir! But I think she's sighted us!'

Bolitho watched the tossing grey water. They would all be able to see the newcomer soon. Too small for a frigate, Libby had said. But *like* one in appearance. Three masts, square-rigged. A sloop-of-war. *Faithful*'s slender hull would be no match for a sloop's sixteen or eighteen cannon.

'We had better come about, sir, and hoist our recognition

signal.' He saw the uncertainty on Sparke's narrow features, the scar very bright on his cheek, like a red penny.

The other look-out called excitedly, 'Two small craft to loo'rd, sir! Standin' inshore.'

Bolitho bit his lip. Probably local coasting craft, in company for mutual protection, and steering for the bay.

Their presence ruled out the possibility of parleying with the patrolling sloop. If they were nearby, so too might other, less friendly eyes.

Frowd suggested helpfully, 'If we come about now, sir, we can outsail her, even to wind'rd. I've been in schooners afore, and I know what they can do.'

Sparke's voice rose almost to a scream. 'How dare you question my judgement! I'll have you disrated if you speak like that to me again! Come about, wait and see, run away. God damn it, you're more like an old woman than a master's mate!'

Frowd looked away, angry and hurt.

Bolitho broke in, 'I know what he was trying to say, sir.' He watched Sparke's eyes swivel towards him but did not drop his gaze. 'We can stand off and wait a better chance. If we continue, even with the darkness soon upon us, that sloop-of-war has only to bide her time, to hold us in the shallows until we go aground, or admit defeat. The people we are supposed to meet and capture will not wait to share the same fate, I think.'

When Sparke spoke again he was very composed, even calm. 'I will overlook your anxiety on Mr Frowd's behalf, for I have observed your tendency to become involved in petty matters.' He nodded to Frowd. 'Carry on. Hold this tack as long as the wind favours it. In half an hour send a good leadsman to the chains.' He smiled wryly. 'Will that satisfy you?'

Frowd knuckled his forehead. 'Aye, aye, sir.'

When the half-hour glass was turned beside the compass the other vessel's topgallant sails were in sight from the deck.

D'Esterre, very pale from the hold's discomfort, came up to Bolitho and said hoarsely, 'God, I am so sick, I would wish to die.' He peered at the sloop's straining sails and added, 'Will she catch us?'

'I think not. She's bound to go about soon.' He pointed to the creaming wash alongside. 'There's barely eight fathom under our keel, and it'll soon be half as much.'

The marine stared at the water with amazement. 'You have done nothing to reassure me, Dick!'

Bolitho could imagine the activity aboard the pursuing sloop. She would be almost as big as the *Destiny*, he thought wistfully. Fast, agile, free of the fleet's ponderous authority. Every glass would now be trained on the scurrying *Faithful* and her strange red device. The bow-chasers were probably run out with the hope of a crippling shot. Her captain would be waiting to see what the schooner might do and act accordingly. After months of dreary patrol work, with precious little help from the coastal villages, he would see the schooner as some small reward. When the truth was discovered, and Sparke had to explain what he had been doing, there would be a double-hell to pay.

He could understand Sparke's eagerness to get to grips with the enemy and do what Pears expected of him. But Frowd's advice had been sound, and he should have taken it. Now, they would have the sloop to contend with while they hunted for the Colonists and the craft they would be using to ferry powder and shot to a safe hiding place.

There was a muffled bang, the sound blown away by the wind almost as quickly.

A ball slashed along the nearest wave crest, and Stockdale said admiringly, 'Not bad shooting.'

A second ball ripped right above the schooner's poop, and then Sparke, who had been standing rigidly like a statue, shouted harshly, '*There!* What did I tell you? She's wearing! Going about, just as I said she would!'

Bolitho watched the angle of the sloop's yards changing, the momentary confusion of her sails before she leaned over on the opposite tack.

Midshipman Weston exclaimed, 'That was most clever of you, sir. I would never have believed . . .'

Bolitho felt his lips crease into a smile, in spite of his anxiety. Sparke, no matter what mood he was in, had little time for crawlers.

'Hold your tongue! When I want praise from you I will ask for it! Now be about your duties, or I'll have Balleine lay his rattan across your fat rump!'

Weston scurried away, his face screwed up with humiliation

as he pushed through some grinning seamen.

Sparke said, 'We will shorten sail, Mr Bolitho. Tell Balleine to close up his anchor party in case we have to let go in haste. See that our people are all armed, and that the gunner's mate knows what to do when required.' His eyes fell on Stockdale. 'Get below and put on one of the coats in the cabin. Captain Tracy was about your build, I believe. You'll not be near enough for them to spy the difference.'

Bolitho gave his orders, and felt some relief at Sparke's sudden return to his old self. Right or wrong, successful or not, it was better to be with the devil one knew.

He came out of his thoughts as Sparke snapped, *'Really, must I do everything?'*

As the evening gloom followed them towards the land, *Faithful's* approach became more stealthy and cautious. The hands waited to take in the sails, or to put the schooner into the wind should they run across some uncharted sandbar or reef, and every few minutes the leadsman's mournful chant from the forecastle reminded anyone who might still be in doubt of their precarious position.

Later, a little before midnight, *Faithful's* anchor splashed down, and she came to rest once again.

# 5

# The Quality of Courage

'It's getting lighter, sir.' Bolitho stood beside the motionless wheel and watched the water around the anchored schooner until his eyes throbbed with strain.

Sparke grunted but said nothing, his jaw working up and down on a nugget of cheese.

Bolitho could feel the tension, made more extreme by the noises of sea and creaking timbers. They were anchored in a strange, powerful current, so that the *Faithful* repeatedly rode forward until her anchor was almost apeak. If the tide fell sharply, and you could not always trust the navigational instructions, she might become impaled on one of the flukes.

Another difference was the lack of order and discipline about the decks. Uniforms and the familiar blue jackets of the boatswain's and master's mates had been put below, and the men lounged around the bulwarks in varying attitudes of relaxed indifference to their officers.

Only the marines, crammed like fish in a barrel, were still sealed in the hold, awaiting the signal which might never come.

Sparke remarked quietly, 'Even this schooner would make a fine command, a good start for any ambitious officer.'

Bolitho watched him cut another piece of cheese, his hands quite steady as he added, 'She'll go to the prize court, but after that...'

Bolitho looked away, but it was another jumping fish which had caught his eye. He must not think about *afterwards*. For Sparke it would mean almost certain promotion, maybe a command of his own, this schooner even. It was obviously uppermost in his mind just now.

And why not? Bolitho pushed his envy aside as best he could. He himself, if he avoided death or serious injury, would soon be back in *Trojan*'s crowded belly. He thought of Quinn as he had last seen him and shivered. Perhaps it was because of the wound he had taken on his skull. He reached up and touched it cautiously, as if expecting the agony to come again. But injury was more on his mind than it had been before he had been slashed down. Seeing Quinn's gaping wound had made it nearer, as if the odds were going against him with each new risk and action.

When you were very young, like Couzens or Midshipman Forbes, the sights were just as terrible. But pain and death only seemed to happen to others, never to you. Now, Bolitho knew differently.

Stockdale trod heavily across the deck, his head lowered as if in deep thought, his hands locked behind him. In a long blue coat, he looked every inch a captain, especially one of a privateer.

Metal rasped in the gloom, and Sparke snapped, 'Take that man's name! I want absolute silence on deck!'

Bolitho peered up at the mainmast, searching for the masthead pendant. The wind had shifted further in the night and had backed almost due south. If that sloop had sailed past their position in the hope of beating back again at first light, she would find it doubly hard, and it would take far longer to achieve.

Another figure was beside the wheel, a seaman named Moffitt. Originally from Devon, he had come to America with his father as a young boy to settle in New Hampshire. But when the revolution had been recognized as something more than some ill-organized uprisings, Moffitt's father had found himself on the wrong side. Labelled a Loyalist, he had fled with his family to Halifax, and his hard-worked farm had been taken by his new enemy. Moffitt had been away from home at the time and had been seized, then forced into a ship of the Revolutionary Navy, one of the first American privateers which had sailed from Newburyport.

Their activities had not lasted for long, and the privateer had been chased and taken by a British frigate. For her company it had meant prison, but for Moffitt it had been a chance to change sides once more, to gain his revenge in his own way against those who had ruined his father.

Now he was beside the wheel, waiting to play his part.

Bolitho heard the approaching hiss of rain as it advanced from the darkness and then fell across the deck and furled sails in a relentless downpour. He tried to keep his hands from getting numb, his body from shivering. It was more than just the discomfort, the anxious misery of waiting. It would make the daylight slow to drive away the night, to give them the vision to know what was happening. Without help they had no chance of finding those they had come to capture. This coastline was riddled with creeks and inlets, bays and the mouths of many rivers, large and small. You could hide a ship of the line here provided you did not mind her going high and dry at low water.

But the land was there, lying across the choppy water like a great black slab. Eventually it would reveal itself. Into coves and trees, hills and undergrowth, where only Indians and animals had ever trod. Around it, and sometimes across it, the two armies manoeuvred, scouted and occasionally clashed in fierce battles of musket and bayonet, hunting-knife and sword.

Whatever the miseries endured by seamen, their life was far the best, Bolitho decided. You carried your home with you. It was up to you what you made of it.

'Boat approaching, sir!'

It was Balleine, a hand cupped round his ear, reminding Bolitho of the last moments before they had boarded this same schooner.

For a moment Sparke did not move or speak, and Bolitho imagined he had not heard.

Then he said softly, 'Pass the word. Be ready for treachery.'

As Balleine loped away along the deck Sparke said, 'I hear it.'

It was a regular splash of oars, the efforts noisy against a powerful current.

Bolitho said, 'Small boat, sir.'

'Yes.'

The boat appeared with startling suddenness, being swirled towards the schooner's bows like a piece of driftwood. A stout fishing dory with about five men aboard.

Then just as quickly it was gone, steered or carried on the current, it was as if they had all imagined it.

Frowd said, 'Not likely to be fishing, sir. Not this time o' day.'

Surprisingly, Sparke was almost jovial as he said, 'They are just testing us. Seeing what we are about. A King's ship would have given them a dose of canister or grape to send them on their way, as would a smuggler. I've no doubt they've been passing here every night and day for a week or more. Just to be on the safe side.' His teeth showed in his shadowy face. 'I'll give them something to remember all their lives!'

The word went along the deck once more and the seamen relaxed slightly, their bodies numbed by the rain and the raw cold.

Overhead the clouds moved swiftly, parting occasionally to allow the colours of dawn to intrude. Grey and blue water, the lush dark green of the land, white crests and the snakelike swirls of an inshore current. They could have been anchored anywhere, but Bolitho knew from his past two years' service that beyond the nearest cape, sheltered by the bay and the entrance to the Delaware River, were towns and settlements, farms and isolated families who had enough to worry about without a war in their midst.

Bolitho's excitement at being at sea again in the calling which had been followed by all his ancestors had soon become soured by his experiences. Many of those he had had to fight had been men like himself, from the West Country, or from Kent, from Newcastle and the Border towns, or from Scotland and Wales. They had chosen this new country, risked much to forge a new life. Because of others in high places, of deep loyalties and deeper mistrusts, the break had come as swiftly as the fall of an axe.

The new Revolutionary government had challenged the King, that should have been enough. But when he thought about it honestly, Bolitho often wished that the men he fought, and those he had seen die, had not called out in the same tongue, and often the same dialect, as himself.

Some gulls circled warily around the schooner's spiralling masts, then allowed themselves to be carried by the wind to more profitable pickings inland.

Sparke said, 'Change the look-outs, and keep one looking to seaward.'

In the strengthening light he looked thinner, his shirt and breeches pressed against his lean body by the rain, shining like snakeskin.

A shaft of watery sunlight probed through the clouds, the first Bolitho had seen for many days.

The telescopes would be watching soon.

He asked, 'Shall I have the mains'l hoisted, sir?'

'Yes.' Sparke fidgeted with his sword-hilt.

The seamen hauled and panted at the rain-swollen halliards until, loosely set, the sail shook and flapped from its boom, the red patch bright in the weak sunlight.

The schooner swung with it, tugging at the cable, coming alive like a horse testing bit and bridle.

'Boat to starboard, sir!'

Bolitho waited, seeing what looked like the same dory pulling strongly from the shore. It was unlikely that anyone would know or recognize any of the *Faithful*'s company, otherwise the recognition patch would be superfluous. Just the sight of the schooner would be enough. Bolitho knew from his childhood how the Cornish smugglers came and went on the tide, within yards of the waiting excisemen, with no more signal than a whistle.

But someone knew. Somewhere between Washington's army and growing fleet of privateers were the link-men, the ones who fixed a rendezvous here, hanged an informer there.

He looked at Stockdale as he strode to the bulwark, and was impressed. Stockdale gestured forward, and two seamen swung a loaded swivel towards the boat, while he shouted in his hoarse voice, 'Stand off there!'

Moffitt stepped up beside him and cupped his hands. 'What d'you want of us?'

The boat rocked on the choppy water, the oarsmen crouched over with the rain bouncing on their shoulders.

The man at the tiller shouted back, 'That Cap'n Tracy?'

Stockdale shrugged. 'Mebbe.'

Sparke said, 'They're not sure, look at the bloody fools!'

Bolitho turned his back on the shore. He could almost feel the hidden telescopes searching along the deck, examining them all one at a time.

'Where you from?' The boat idled slowly nearer.

Moffitt glanced at Sparke, who gave a curt nod. He shouted, 'There's a British man-o'-war to seaward! I'll not wait much longer! Have you no guts, man?'

Frowd said, 'That's done it. Here they come.'

The open mention of the British sloop, and Moffitt's colonial accent, seemed to have carried more weight than the scarlet patch.

The dory grated alongside and a seaman caught the line thrown up by one of the oarsmen.

Stockdale stood looking down at the boat, and then said in an offhand manner which Bolitho had not heard before, 'Tell the one in charge to step aboard. I'm not satisfied.'

He turned towards his officers and Bolitho gave a quick nod. Sparke hissed, 'Keep him away from the nine-pounder, whatever happens.' He gestured to Balleine. 'Start opening the hold.'

Bolitho watched the man climb up from the boat, trying to picture the *Faithful*'s deck through his eyes. If anything went wrong now, all they would have to show for their plans would be five corpses and a dory.

The man who stood on the swaying deck was solidly built but agile for his age. He had thick grey hair and a matching beard, and his clothing was roughly stitched, like that of a woodsman.

He faced Stockdale calmly. 'I am Elias Haskett.' He took another half pace. 'You are not the Tracy I remember.' It was not a challenge but a statement.

Moffitt said, 'This is Cap'n Stockdale. We took over the *Faithful* under Cap'n Tracy's orders.' He smiled, letting it sink in. 'He went in command of a fine brig. Like his brother.'

The man named Elias Haskett seemed convinced. 'We've been expecting you. It ain't easy. The redcoats have been pushing their pickets across the territory, and that ship you told of has been up and down the coast for weeks, like a nervous rabbit.' He glanced at the others nearby, his eyes resting momentarily on Sparke.

Moffitt said, 'Mostly new hands. British deserters. You know how it goes, man.'

'I do.' Haskett became businesslike. 'Good cargo for us?'

Balleine and a few hands had removed the covers from the hold, and Haskett strode to the coaming to peer below.

Bolitho watched the pattern of men changing again, just as they had practised and rehearsed. The first part was done, or so it appeared. Now he saw Rowhurst, the gunner's mate, stroll casually to join Haskett, his hand resting on his dirk. One note of alarm and Haskett would die before he hit the deck.

Bolitho peered over a seaman's shoulder and tried not to think of the marines who were packed in a hastily constructed and almost airless chamber below a false platform. From the deck it looked as if the hold was full of powder kegs. In fact, there was just one layer, and only two were filled. But it only needed a marine to sneeze and that would be the end of it.

Moffitt clambered down and remarked coolly, 'Good catch. We cut out two from the convoy. We've muskets and bayonets too, and a thousand rounds of nine-pound shot.'

Bolitho wanted to swallow or to clear his parched throat. Moffitt was perfect. He was not acting, he *was* the intelligent mate of a privateer who knew what he was about.

Haskett said to Stockdale, 'I'll hoist the signal. The boats are hid yonder.' He waved vaguely towards some overlapping trees which ran almost to the water's edge. It could be a tiny cove or the entrance of a hitherto unexplored bay.

'What about the British sloop?' Moffitt glanced briefly at Sparke.

'She'll take half a day to claw back here, an' I've put some good look-outs where they can get a first sight of her.'

Bolitho watched Haskett as he bent on a small red pendant and ran it smartly to the foremast truck. He was no stranger to ships and the sea, no matter how he was dressed.

He heard one of the seamen gasp, and saw what looked like part of a tree edging clear of the shore. Then he realized it was a fat, round-bowed cutter, her single mast and yard covered with branches and gorse, while her broad hull was propelled slowly but firmly by long sweeps from either beam. She was followed by her twin. They looked Dutch built, and he guessed they had probably been brought here from the Caribbean, or had made their own way to earn a living from fishing and local trading.

He knew that Sparke had been counting on a single vessel, or several small lighters, even pulling boats. Each of these broad-beamed cutters was almost as large as the *Faithful* and built like a battering-ram.

Moffitt saw his quick nod and said, 'One will be enough. They look as if they could carry a King's arsenal.'

Haskett nodded. 'True. But we have other work after this, south towards the Chesapeake. Our boys captured a British ordnance brigantine a week back. She's aground, but filled to the gills with muskets and powder. We will off-load her cargo into one of the cutters. Enough to supply a whole army!'

Bolitho turned away. He could not bear to look at Sparke's face. He could read his mind, could picture his very plan of attack. With the sloop too far away to be of help, Sparke would seize the whole credit for himself.

The next few moments were the worst Bolitho could recall. The slow business of manoeuvring the two heavy cutters, with their strange disguise and long, galley-like sweeps. They must hold thirty or forty men, he decided. Some seamen, and the rest probably from the local militia, or an independent troop of Washington's scouts.

The *Faithful*'s masthead pendant flapped wetly in the wind, and Bolitho saw the nearest cutter start to swing across the current. Minutes to go. Mere minutes, and it would be too late for her to work clear, or set her sails.

Moffitt murmured, 'Stand by there.' If he was nervous, he was not showing it.

A seaman called, 'Aye, aye, sir!'

Bolitho chilled. It might have been expected. That somebody, even himself who had helped to plan the deception, should overplay his part. The smart acknowledgement to Moffitt's order was not that of a defecting sailor or half-trained privateersman.

Haskett swung round with an oath. 'You dirty scum!'

The crash of a pistol made every man freeze. Voices from the dory alongside mingled with the shrill cries of startled seabirds, but Bolitho could only stare at the grey-haired stranger as he staggered towards his bulwark, blood gushing from his mouth, while his hands clutched at his stomach like scarlet claws.

Sparke lowered his pistol and snapped, 'Swivels! *Open Fire!*'

As the four swivels cracked from their mountings, sweeping the side and deck of the nearest cutter with whining canister,

Rowhurst's men tore the tarpaulin from the nine-pounder and threw their weight on tackles and handspikes.

A few shots came from the nearest cutter, but the unexpected attack had done what Sparke had intended. The packed canister had swept amongst the men at the long sweeps, cutting them down, and knocking the stroke into chaos. The cutter was broaching to, drifting abeam, while Rowhurst's other crews waited by the stubby six-pounders which would bear, their slow-matches ready, the guns carefully loaded in advance with grapeshot.

'Fire as you bear!' Bolitho drew his hanger and walked amongst his men as they came alive again. *'Steady!'* A ball whined past his face and a seaman fell kicking and screaming beside the dead Elias Haskett.

Sparke took his reloaded pistol from a seaman and remarked absently, 'I hope Rowhurst's aim is as good as his obscenities.'

Even the taciturn Rowhurst seemed shocked out of his usual calm. He was capering from side to side of the nine-pounder's breech, watching as the second cutter managed to set her mainsail and jib, the sweeps discarded and drifting away like bones, the disguise dropping amongst them as the wind ballooned into the canvas.

Rowhurst cursed as one of his men reeled away, a massive hole punched through his forehead. He yelled, 'Ready, sir!' He waited for the *Faithful* to complete another swing on her cable and then thrust his slow-match to the breech.

Double-shotted, and with grape added for good measure, the gun hurled itself back on its makeshift tackles like an enraged beast. The crash of the explosion rolled around the sea like thunder, and the billowing smoke added to the sense of horror as the cutter's mast disintegrated and fell heavily in a tangle of rigging and thrashing canvas.

'Reload! Run out when you're ready and fire at will!'

The shock of Sparke's pistol shot had given way to a wave of wild excitement. This was something they understood. What they had been trained for, day by backbreaking day.

While the swivels and six-pounders kept up their murderous bombardment on the first cutter, Rowhurst's crew maintained a regular attack on the other. With mast and sails gone, she was soon hard aground on a sandbar and even as someone gave a cheer a savage plume of fire exploded from her stern and spread rapidly with the wind, the rain-soaked timbers spurting steam until the fire took hold and she was ablaze from stem to stern.

Through and above the din of cannon-fire and yelling men Bolitho heard D'Esterre call, 'Lively, Sar'nt Shears, or there'll be little left for us to do!' D'Esterre blinked in the billowing smoke from the cutter and Rowhurst's nine-pounder and said, 'By God, this one will be up to us shortly!'

Bolitho watched the first cutter swinging drunkenly toward the *Faithful*'s bows. There were more men in evidence on her deck now, but there were many who would never move again. Blood ran in bright threads from her scuppers to mark the havoc left by the canister and packed grape.

'Marines, forward!'

Like puppets they stepped up to the bulwark, their long muskets rising as one.

'Present!' The sergeant waited, ignoring the balls which buzzed overhead or thudded into the timbers. '*Fire!*'

Bolitho saw those who had gathered at the point where both vessels would come together stagger and sway like corn in a field as the carefully aimed volley ripped amongst them.

The sergeant showed no emotion as he beat out the time with his handspike while the ramrods rose and fell together as if on a range.

'Take aim! *Fire!*'

The volley was upset by the sudden collision of both hulls, but not enough to save another handful of the yelling, defiant men who started to clamber aboard, cutlasses swinging, or firing at the nine-pounder's crew on the forecastle.

Sparke shouted, 'Strike, damn you!'

'I'll see you in hell!'

Bolitho ran to the bulwark, briefly aware that someone had defied Sparke even in the face of death.

Sergeant Shears shouted, 'Fix bayonets!' He looked at D'Esterre's raised sword. 'Marines, advance!'

Bolitho shouted, 'Tell them again to strike, sir!'

Sparke looked wild as he retorted, 'They had their chance, damn them!'

The marines moved with precision, shoulder to shoulder, a living red wall which cut the boarders off from the gun crews, separated them from their own craft, and from all hope.

Bolitho saw a figure duck past a bayonet and run aft, a cutlass held across his body like a talisman.

Bolitho raised his hanger, seeing the clumsy way he was holding the cutlass. Worse, he was no more than a youth.

'Surrender!'

But the youth came on, whimpering with pain as Bolitho turned his blade aside and with a twist of the wrist sent his cutlass clashing into the scuppers. Even then he tried to get to grips with Bolitho, sobbing and almost blinded with fury and tears.

Stockdale brought the flat of his cutlass down on the youth's head and knocked him senseless.

Sparke exclaimed, 'It's done.'

He walked past D'Esterre and regarded the remaining attackers coldly. There not many of them. The rest, dead or wounded by the lunging line of bayonets, sprawled like tired onlookers.

Bolitho sheathed his hanger, feeling sick, and the returning ache in his head.

The dead were always without dignity, he thought. No matter the cause, or the value of a victory.

Sparke shouted, 'Secure the cutter! Mr Libby, take charge there! Balleine, put those rebels under guard!'

Frowd came aft and said quietly, 'We lost three men, sir. An' two wounded, but they'll live, with any fortune.'

Sparke handed his pistol to a seaman. 'Damn it, Mr Bolitho, look what we have achieved!'

Bolitho looked. First at the blackened carcass of the second cutter, almost burnt out and smoking furiously above a litter of wreckage and scattered remains. Most of her crew had either died under Rowhurst's solitary bombardment or had been carried away to drown on the swift current. Few sailors could even swim, he thought grimly.

Alongside, and closer to the eye, the other cutter was an even more horrific sight. Corpses and great patterns of blood were everywhere, and he saw Midshipman Libby with his handful of seamen picking his way over the deck, his face screwed up, fearful of what he would see next.

Sparke said, 'But the hull and spars are intact, d'you see, eh? Two prizes within a week! There'll be some envious glances when we reach Sandy Hook again, make no mistake!' He gestured angrily at the wretched Libby. 'For God's sake, sir! Stir yourself and get that mess over the side. I want to make sail within the hour, damn me if I don't!'

Captain D'Esterre said, 'I'll send some marines to help him.'

Sparke glared. 'You will not, sir. That young gentleman wishes to become a lieutenant. And he probably will, shortages in the fleet being what they are. So he must learn that it rates more than the uniform, damn me so it does!' He beckoned to the master's mate. 'Come below, Mr Frowd. I want a course for the Chesapeake. I'll get the exact position of the brigantine at leisure.'

They both vanished below, and D'Esterre said quietly, 'What a nauseating relish he displays!'

Bolitho saw the first of the corpses going over the side, drifting lazily past, as if glad to be free of it all.

He said bitterly, 'I thought you craved action.'

D'Esterre gripped his shoulder. 'Aye, Dick. I do my duty with the best of 'em. But the day you see me gloat like our energetic second lieutenant, you may shoot me down.'

The youth who had been knocked unconscious by Stockdale was being helped to his feet. He was rubbing his head and sobbing quietly. When he saw Stockdale he tried to hit out at him, but Moffitt caught him easily and pinioned him against the bulwark.

Bolitho said, 'He could have killed you, you know.'

Through his sobs the youth exclaimed, 'I wish he had! The British killed my father when they burned Norfolk! I swore to avenge him!'

Moffitt said harshly, 'Your people tarred and feathered my young brother! It blinded him!' He pushed the youth towards a waiting marine. 'So we're equal, eh?'

Bolitho said quietly, 'No, opposite, is how I see it.' He nodded to Moffitt. 'I did not know about your brother.'

Moffitt, shaking violently now that it was over, said, 'Oh, there's more, sir, a whole lot more.'

Frowd reappeared on deck and walked past the sobbing prisoner without a glance.

He said grimly, 'I thought this day's work would be an end to it, sir. For the moment at least.'

He looked up at the pendant and then at the cutter alongside, the hands working with buckets and swabs to clear the blood-stains from the scarred and riddled planking.

'She's named the *Thrush*, I see.' His professional eye confirmed Bolitho's opinion. 'Dutch built. Handy craft, and well able to beat to wind'rd, better even than this one.'

Midshipman Weston hovered nearby, his face as red as his hair. He had shouted a lot during the brief engagement, but had hung back when the Colonials had made their impossible gesture.

Frowd was saying, 'I'd hoped that sloop might have joined us.' He sounded anxious. 'Mr Sparke's got the name of the cove where they beached the brigantine. I know it, but not well.'

'How did he discover that?'

Frowd walked to the rail and spat into the water. 'Money, sir. There's always a traitor in every group. If the price is right.'

Bolitho made himself relax. He could forget Frowd's bitterness. He had been afraid that Sparke, in his desperate eagerness to complete his victory, would use harsher methods of obtaining his information. His face as he had killed Elias Haskett had been almost inhuman.

How many more Sparkes were there still to discover? he pondered.

In a steady wind, both vessels eventually got under way and started to work clear of the sandbars and shoals, the smoke from the burned-out cutter following them like an evil memory.

Charred remains and gaping corpses parted to allow them through, when with all sails set both vessels started the first leg of their long tack to seaward.

Sparke came on deck during the proceedings. He peered through a telescope to see how Midsipmhan Libby, ably assisted by the boatswain's mate, Balleine, and a handful of seamen, were managing aboard the *Thrush*. Then he sniffed at the air and snapped, 'Run up our proper colours, Mr Bolitho, and see that Mr Libby follows our example.'

Later, with both vessels in close company, heeling steeply on the starboard tack, Bolitho felt the stronger upthrust of deeper water, and not for the first time was glad to be rid of the land.

From the rendezvous point where they had won such a bloody victory, to the next objective, a cove just north of Cape Charles which marked the entrance to Chesapeake Bay, it was approximately one hundred miles.

Sparke had hoped for a change of wind, but on the contrary, it soon became worse and more set against them. Both vessels were able to keep company, but each tack took longer, each mile gained could be quadrupled by the distance sailed to achieve it.

Every time that Sparke went on deck he showed no sign of apprehension or dismay. He usually examined the *Thrush* through his glass and then looked up at his own flag. Bolitho had heard one of the marines whispering to his friend that Sparke had made himself an admiral of his own squadron.

The weather and the constant demands of working the schooner to windward had cleared most of the tension and bitterness from Bolitho's thoughts. On the face of it, it had been a success. A vessel seized, another destroyed, and many of the enemy killed or routed. If the plan had misfired, and the trap laid in reverse, he doubted if the enemy would have showed them any mercy either. Once aboard the schooner, the combined numbers of both cutters would have swamped Sparke's resistance before the nine-pounder could have levelled the balance.

It took three days to reach the place where the brig was supposedly hidden. The rugged coastline which pointed south towards the entrance of Chesapeake Bay was treacherous, even more than that which they had left astern. Many a coasting vessel, and larger ships as well, had come to grief as they had battered through foul weather to find the narrow entrance to the bay. Once within it there was room for a fleet, and then some. But to get there was something else entirely, as Bunce had remarked often enough.

Once again, the sad-faced Moffitt was the one to step forward and offer to go ashore alone and spy out the land.

The *Faithful*'s boat had taken him in, while close to the nearest land both vessels had anchored and mounted guard to ward off any attack.

Bolitho had half expected Moffitt not to return. He had done enough, and might be pining to rejoin his family.

But five hours after being dropped on a tiny beach, while the long-boat laid off to wait for his return, Moffitt appeared, wading through the surf in his eagerness to bring his news.

It was no rumour. The ordnance vessel, a brigantine, was beached inside the cove, exactly as Sparke's informer had described. Moffitt had even discovered her name, the *Minstrel*, and thought her too badly damaged even to be moved by expert salvage parties.

He had seen some lanterns nearby, and had almost trodden on a sleeping sentry.

Sparke said, 'I will see that you are rewarded for this work, Moffitt.' He was almost emotional as he added, 'This is the quality of courage which will always sustain us.'

Ordering that Moffitt be given a large tot of brandy or rum, both if he wished, Sparke gathered his officers and senior rates together. There was barely room to draw breath in the schooner's cabin, but they soon forgot their discomfort when Sparke said bluntly, 'Dawn attack. We will use our own and *Thrush*'s boat. Surprise attack at first light, right?' He eyed them searchingly. 'Captain D'Esterre, you will land with your contingent under cover of darkness, and find some cover above the cove. Stay there to mark our flank, and our withdrawal if things go wrong.'

Sparke looked at the rough map which Moffitt had helped to make.

'I will of course take the leading boat. Mr Libby will follow in the other.' He looked at Bolitho. 'You will assume command of *Thrush* and bring her into the cove for the transfer of cargo once I have smashed whatever opposition which may still be near the brigantine. The marines will then move down and support us from the beach.' He clapped his hands together. 'Well?'

D'Esterre said, 'I'd like to leave now, if I may, sir.'

'Yes. I shall need the boats very soon.' He looked at Bolitho. 'You were about to say something?'

'A hundred miles in three days, sir. Another half day by dawn. I doubt very much if we will surprise them.'

'You're not getting like Mr Frowd, surely? A real Jeremiah indeed.'

Bolitho shut his mouth tightly. It was pointless to argue, and anyway, with the marines in position to cover them they could fall back if it was a trap.

Sparke said, 'It is settled then. Good. Mr Frowd will take charge here in our absence, and the nine-pounder will be more than a match for any foolhardy attacker, eh?'

Midshipman Weston licked his lips. His face was glistening with sweat. 'What shall *I* do, sir?'

Sparke smiled thinly. 'You will be with the fourth lieutenant. Do what he says and you might learn something. Do *not* do what he says and you may well be dead before you fill yourself with more disgusting food!'

They trooped up on deck, where a few pale stars had appeared to greet them.

Moffitt reported to Captain D'Esterre, 'I'm ready, sir. I'll show you the way.'

The marine nodded. 'You are a glutton for punishment, but lead on, with my blessing.'

The two boats were already filling with marines and would now be in continuous use. That left only the captured dory. It was as well somebody had kept it secured during the fighting.

Stockdale was by the taffrail, his white trousers flapping like miniature sails.

He wheezed, 'Glad you're not going this time, sir.'

Bolitho stiffened. 'Why did you say that?'

'Feeling, sir. Just a feeling. I'll be happier when we're out of here. Back with the Navy again.'

Bolitho watched the boats pulling clear, the marines' crossbelts stark against the black water.

The trouble with Stockdale was that his 'feelings', as he called them, were too often transformed into actual deeds.

Bolitho moved restlessly around the *Thrush*'s tiller, very conscious of the stillness, the air of expectancy which hung over the two vessels.

The wind was from the same direction but was dropping with each passing minute, allowing the warmth to replace the night's chill, the sun to penetrate the full-bellied clouds.

He trained his telescope towards the nearest hillside and saw two tiny scarlet figures just showing above the strange, tangled gorse. D'Esterre's marines were in position, pickets out. They would have a good view of the little cove, although from the *Thrush*'s deck there was nothing to see but fallen, rotting trees by the entrance and the swirl of a cross-current by some scattered rocks.

He heard Midshipman Weston with some seamen sorting out the good sweeps from those broken by the swivels' canister. He could also hear him retching as he found some gruesome fragment which Libby's men had overlooked.

Stockdale joined him by the rail, his face black with stubble and grime.

'Should be there by now, sir. Not heard a shot nor nothin'.'

Bolitho nodded. It was uppermost in his mind. The wind was dropping, and that made movement difficult if urgently required. He would need to move the *Thrush* under sweeps, and the longer it took the more chance of an ambush there was.

He cursed Sparke's eagerness, his blind determination to take all the rewards for himself. At any time of day a frigate might pass nearby and they could depend on support by the boatload, even at the expense of sharing the victory.

He said, 'Get in the dory. I'm going to that little beach yonder.' He pointed to the two scarlet shapes on the hillside. 'I'll be safe enough.'

Midshipman Weston panted along the deck, his ungainly feet catching and jarring on splinters from the raked planking.

Bolitho said, 'You take charge here.' He could almost smell his fear. 'I'll be in view the whole time.'

He saw Stockdale and two seamen climbing down to the dory, eager to be doing something to break the strain of waiting. Or maybe to get away from the scene of such carnage.

When Bolitho stepped on to the firm beach, which was not much bigger than the boat itself, it felt good. To smell the different scents, to hear birds and the vague rustling of small creatures nearby was like a balm.

Then one of the seamen exclaimed, 'There, sir! 'Tis Mr Libby's boat!'

Bolitho saw the midshipman's head and shoulders even before he heard the swish of oars.

'Over here!'

Libby waved his hat and grinned. Relief, and more, was plain on his tanned face.

He shouted, 'The second lieutenant says to bring the cutter, sir! There's no sign of anyone ashore, and Mr Sparke thinks they must have run when they saw the boats!'

Bolitho asked, 'What is he doing now?'

'He is about to board the brigantine, sir. She is a fine little vessel, but is badly holed.'

Sparke probably wanted to make quite sure there was no chance of adding her, as well as her cargo, to his little squadron.

Feet slithered on the hillside, and Bolitho swung round to see Moffitt, followed by a marine, stumbling and falling towards him.

'What is it, Moffitt?' He saw the anguish on his face.

'*Sir!*' He could barely get the words out. 'We tried to signal, but Mr Sparke did not see us!' He gestured wildly. 'Them devils have laid a fuse, I can see the smoke! They're going to blow up the brigantine! They must've been waiting!'

Libby looked appalled. 'Man your oars! We'll go back!'

Bolitho ran into the water to stop him, but even as he spoke the earth and sky seemed to burst apart in one tremendous explosion.

The men in the boat ducked and gasped, while around and across them pieces of splintered wood and rigging rained down, covering the water with leaping feathers of spray.

Then they saw the smoke, lifting and spreading above the cove's shoulder until the sunlight was completely hidden.

Bolitho groped his way to the dory, his ears and mind cringing from the deafening explosion.

Marines blundered down the slope and waited until Libby's oarsmen had recovered sufficiently to bring their boat towards the tiny beach.

But all Bolitho could see was Sparke's face as he had outlined his last plan. *The quality of courage.* It had not sustained *him.*

Bolitho pulled himself together as D'Esterre with his sergeant and two skirmishers walked toward him.

Again he seemed to hear Sparke's crisp voice. Speaking as he had aboard the schooner when the shocked aftermath of battle had begun to take charge.

'*They'll be looking to us. So we'll save our regrets for later.*'

It could have been his epitaph.

Bolitho said huskily, 'Get the marines ferried over as quickly as you can.' He turned away from the stench of burning wood and tar. 'We'll get under way directly.'

D'Esterre eyed him strangely. 'Another few minutes and it could have been Libby's boat. Or yours.'

Bolitho met his gaze and replied, 'There may not be much time. So let's be about it, shall we?'

D'Esterre watched the last squad of marines lining up to

await the boat's return. He saw Bolitho and Stockdale climb from the dory to the *Faithful*'s deck, Frowd hurrying across to meet them.

D'Esterre had been in too many fights of one sort or another to be affected for long. But this time it had been different. He thought of Bolitho's face, suddenly so pale beneath the black hair with its unruly lock above one eye. Determined, using every ounce of strength to contain his feelings.

Junior he might be in rank, but D'Esterre had felt in those few moments that he was in the presence of his superior.

# 6

## A Lieutenant's Lot

Lieutenant Neil Cairns looked up from the small bulkhead desk
in response to a knock on his cabin door.

'Come.'

Bolitho stepped inside, his hat beneath his arm, his features
tired.

Cairns gestured to the only other chair. 'Take those books off
there and sit yourself down, man.' He groped amongst piles of
papers, lists and scribbled messages and added, 'There should be
some glasses here, too. You look as if you need a drink. I am
certain I do. If anyone advises you to take on the role of first
lieutenant, I suggest you tell him to go to hell!'

Bolitho sat and loosened his neckcloth. There was the hint of
a cool breeze in the cabin, and after hours of walking around
New York, and the long pull across the harbour in *Trojan's*
launch he was feeling sweaty and weary. He had been sent
ashore to try to get some new hands to replace those killed or
injured aboard the *Faithful* and later when Sparke's cutter and
his men had been blasted to fragments. It all seemed like a vague,
distorted dream now. *Three months ago*, and already it was hard
to put the order of things together properly. Even the weather
made it more obscure. Then it had been miserably cold and

bleak, with fierce running seas and the fog which had then seemed like a miracle. Now it was bright sunshine and long periods without any wind at all. The *Trojan*'s hull creaked with dryness and her deck seams shone moistly in the glare, clinging to the shoes and to the seamen's bare feet.

Cairns watched him thoughtfully. Bolitho had changed a great deal, he decided. He had returned to New York with the two prizes a different man. More mature, and lacking the youthful optimism which had marked him out from the others.

The events which had changed him, Sparke's terrible death in particular, had even been noticed by the captain.

Cairns said, 'Red wine, Dick. Warm, but better than anything else to hand. I bought it from a trader ashore.'

He saw Bolitho tilt back his head, the lock of hair clinging to his forehead and hiding the cruel scar. Despite his service in these waters, Bolitho looked pale, and his grey eyes were like the winter they had long since left behind.

Bolitho knew he was being watched, but he had become used to it. If he had changed, so too had his world. With Sparke dead, the officers had taken another step on promotion's ladder. Bolitho was now the third lieutenant, and the most junior post, then left vacant, had been taken by Midshipman Libby. He was now *Trojan*'s acting sixth lieutenant, whether he was able to take his proper examination or not. The age difference between the captain and his lieutenants was startling. Bolitho would not be twenty-one until October, and his juniors were aged from twenty to Libby's mere seventeen years.

It was a well-used system in the larger ships, but Bolitho could find little comfort in his promotion, even though his new duties had kept him busy enough to hold most of the worst memories to the back of his mind.

Cairns said suddenly, 'The captain wants you to accompany him to the flagship this evening. The admiral is "holding court", and captains will be expected to produce a likely aide or two.' He refilled the glasses, his features impassive. 'I have work to do with the damned victualling yard, so I'll not be able to go. Not that I care much for empty comversation when the whole world is falling apart.'

He said it with such bitterness that Bolitho was moved to ask, 'Is something troubling you?'

Cairns gave a rare smile. 'Just everything. I am heartily sick of inactivity. Of writing down lists of stores, begging for new cordage and spars, when all those rogues ashore want is for you to pass them a few pieces of gold, damn their eyes!'

Bolitho thought of the two prizes he had brought back to New York. They had been whisked away to the prize court, sold and recommissioned into the King's service almost before the new ensigns had been hoisted.

Not one man of the *Trojan's* company had been appointed to them, and the lieutenant given command of the *Faithful* had barely been out from England more than a few weeks. It was unfair, to say the least, and it was obviously a sore point with Cairns. In about eighteen months he would be thirty. The war could be over, and he might be thrown on the beach as a half-pay lieutenant. It was not a very enjoyable prospect for a man without means beyond his naval pay.

'Anyway,' Cairns leaned back and looked at him, 'the captain has made it plain he'd rather have you with him in his admiral's presence than our tippling second lieutenant!'

Bolitho smiled. It was amazing how Probyn survived. He was fortunate perhaps that after *Trojan's* return from escorting the convoy from Halifax the ship had barely been to sea at all. Two short patrols in support of the Army and a gunnery exercise with the flagship well within sight of New York was the extent of her efforts. A few more storms and Probyn's weakness might have put an end to him.

Bolitho stood up. 'I'd better get changed then.'

Cairns nodded. 'You're to meet the captain at the end of the first dog-watch. He'll be taking the barge, so make sure the crew are smart and ready. He's in no mood to suffer slackness, I can tell you.'

Sharp at four bells Captain Pears strode on to the quarter-deck, resplendent in his full-dress uniform and carrying his sword at his side like a pointer. If anything, the glittering gold lace set off against the dark blue coat and white breeches made him appear younger and taller.

Bolitho, also dressed in his best clothes, waited by the entry port, a sword, instead of his usual hanger, slung across his waistcoat on a cross-belt.

He had already examined the barge to ensure it was ready and suitable for *Trojan's* captain. It was a fine-looking boat, with a dark red hull and white painted gunwales. In the stern-sheets there were matching red cushions, while across the transom was the ship's name in gilt. Swaying against *Trojan's* side, with the oars tossed in two vertical lines, her crew dressed in red and white checkered shirts and black tarred hats, the barge looked good enough for an emperor, Bolitho thought.

Cairns hurried to the side and murmured something to the captain. Molesworth, the nervous-looking purser, was waiting by the mizzen, and Bolitho guessed that Cairns was going ashore with him to bolster his dealings with the victuallers, who, like ships' chandlers, thought more of personal profit than patriotism.

Captain D'Esterre snapped, 'Marines, present *arms*!'

The bayoneted muskets jerked up almost to the canvas awning overhead, and Bolitho momentarily forgot Pears as he recalled the marines on the *Faithful*'s deck as they had cut down the boarders with the same crisp precision.

Pears seemed to see Bolitho for the first time. 'Ah, it *is* you.' He raised his eye over Bolitho's best cocked hat, his white lapels and freshly pressed waistcoat. 'I thought I had a new officer for a while.'

Bolitho smiled. 'Thank you, sir.'

Pears nodded. 'Carry on.'

Bolitho ran down the ladder to the boat, where Hogg, the burly coxswain, stood in readiness, his hat in his hand like a grim-faced mourner.

The pipes trilled and then the barge tilted to Pears' weight as he stepped down and into the sternsheets.

'Shove off! Out oars!' Hogg was conscious of his captain and watching telescopes from nearby warships. 'Give way *all*!'

Bolitho sat stiffly with his sword between his knees. He found it impossible to relax when he was with the captain. So he watched *Trojan* instead, seeing her curved tumblehome change shape as the boat swung round and beneath her high stern. He saw the red ensign curling listlessly above the taffrail, the glitter of gilt paint and polished fittings.

Every gunport was open to catch the offshore air, and at each one, withdrawn like a resting beast, *Trojan*'s considerable artillery showed a round black muzzle. They too were as clean as D'Esterre's silver buttons.

Bolitho glanced at Pears' grim profile. What news there was of the war was bad. Stalemate at best, real losses too often for comfort. But whatever Pears thought about the situation and the future he was certainly not going to let down his ship by any sign of slackness.

Beneath her furled sails and crossed yards, shimmering in her own haze of black and buff, *Trojan* was a sight to stir even the most doubting heart.

Pears said suddenly, 'Have you heard from your father?'

Bolitho replied, 'Not of late, sir. He is not much for writing.'

Pears looked directly at him. 'I was sorry to learn of your mother's death. I met her just the once at Weymouth. You were at sea, I believe. A gracious lady. It makes me feel old even to remember her.'

Bolitho looked astern at *Trojan*. So that was part of it, and no wonder. Suppose, just suppose, that *Trojan* had to fight. Really fight with ships of her own size and fire power. He thought of the officers Pears would carry into battle. Probyn, getting more difficult and morose every day. Dalyell, cheerful but barely equipped to take over his new role as fourth lieutenant. And poor Quinn, tight-lipped and in constant pain from his wound, and confined to light duties under the surgeon's attention. Now there was Libby, one more boy in a lieutenant's guise. Pears had good cause to worry about it, he thought. It must be like having a shipload of schoolboys.

'How many men did you get today!'

Bolitho stared. Pears knew everything. Even about his trip ashore.

'Four, sir.' It was even worse when you said it aloud.

'Hmm. We may have better luck when the next convoy arrives.' Pears shifted on the red cushion. 'Damned knaves. Prize seamen, protected by the East India Company or some bloody government warrant! Hell's teeth, you'd think it was a crime to fight for your country! But I'll get my hands on a few of 'em, exemptions or not.' He chuckled. 'By the time their lordships hear about it, we'll have changed 'em into King's men!'

Bolitho turned his head as the flagship loomed around another anchored man-of-war.

She was the *Resolute*, a second-rate of some ninety guns, and a veteran of twenty-five years of service. There were several boats at her booms, and Bolitho guessed it was to be quite a gathering. He looked up at the drooping flag at her mizzen and wondered what their host would be like. Rear-Admiral Graham Coutts, in command of the inshore squadron, had controlled *Trojan*'s destiny since her first arrival in New York. Bolitho had never laid eyes on him and was curious to know what he was like. Probably another Pears, he decided. Rocklike, unbreakable.

He shifted his attention to the professional side of their arrival. The marines at the entry port, the gleam of steel, the bustle of blue and white and the faint shout of commands.

Pears was sitting as before, but Bolitho noticed that his strong fingers were opening and closing around the sharkskin grip of his sword, the first sign of agitation he had ever noticed in him.

It was a fine sword and must have cost a small fortune. It was a presentation sword, given to Pears for some past deed of individual courage, or more likely a victory over one of England's enemies.

'Ready to toss yer oars!' Hogg was leaning on the balls of his feet, his fingers caressing the tiller-bar as he gauged the final approach. 'Oars *up!*'

As one the blades rose and remained motionless in paired lines, the sea water trickling unheeded on to the knees of the bargemen.

Pears nodded to his crew and then climbed sedately up the side, doffing his hat to the shrill calls and the usual ceremony which greeted every captain.

Bolitho counted seconds and then followed. He was met by a thin-nosed lieutenant with a telescope jammed beneath his arm who looked at him as if he had just emerged from some stale cheese.

'You are to go aft, sir.' The lieutenant gestured to the poop where Pears, in company with *Resolute*'s flag captain, was hurrying towards the shade.

Bolitho paused to look around the quarterdeck. Very like *Trojan*'s. The lines of tethered guns, their tackles neatly turned on to cleats or flaked down on the snow-white planking. Seamen going about their work, a midshipman studying an incoming brig through his glass, his lips moving silently as he read her flag hoist of numbers which would reveal her name and that of her captain.

Down on the gundeck a seaman was standing beside a corporal of marines, while another midshipman was speaking rapidly to a lieutenant. A crime committed? A man about to be taken aft for punishment? Or he might be up for promotion or discharge. It was a familiar scene which could mean so many things.

He sighed. Like the *Trojan*. And yet again, she was completely different.

Bolitho walked slowly beneath the poop and was startled by the sound of music and the muted laughter of men and women. Every screen had been removed and the admiral's quarters had been opened up into one huge cabin. By the open stern windows some violinists were playing with great concentration, and amongst the jostling crowd of sea officers, civilians and several ladies, servants in red jackets carried trays laden with glasses, while others stood at a long table refilling them as fast as they could.

Pears had been swallowed up, and Bolitho nodded to several lieutenants who, like himself, were only here under sufferance.

A tall figure emerged from the crush, and Bolitho saw it was Lamb, the flagship's captain. He was a steady-eyed man with features which might at first appear to be severe, even hard. But when he smiled, everything changed.

'You are Mr Bolitho, I understand?' He held out his hand. 'Welcome aboard. I heard about your exploits last March and wanted to meet you. We can use men of mettle who have seen what war is all about. It is a hard time, but also one of opportunity for young men such as yourself. If the moment comes, seize your chance. Believe me, Bolitho, they rarely come twice.'

Bolitho thought of the graceful schooner, even the stubby-hulled *Thrush*. His own chance had already come and gone.

'Come and meet the admiral.' He saw Bolitho's expression and laughed. 'He will not eat you!'

More pushing to get through the crowd. Flushed faces, loud voices. It was difficult to imagine that the war was just miles away.

He saw a hunched set of blue shoulders and a gold-laced collar, and groaned inwardly. Ponderous. Slow-moving. A disappointment after all.

But the flag captain pushed the big man aside and revealed a slight figure who barely came up to his shoulder.

Rear-Admiral Graham Coutts looked more like a lieutenant than a flag officer. He had dark brown hair which was tied to the nape of his neck in a casual fashion. He had an equally youthful face, devoid of lines or the usual mask of authority which Bolitho had seen before.

He thrust out his hand. 'Bolitho, is it? Good.' He nodded and smiled impetuously. 'Proud to meet you.' He beckoned to some hidden servant. 'Wine over here!'

Then he said lightly, 'I know all about you. I suspect that if

you and not your superior officer had been leading that boat
attack you might even have recaptured the brigantine!' He
smiled. 'No matter. It showed what can be done, given the will.'

An elegant figure in blue velvet walked from a noisy group by
the quarter galley and the admiral said quietly, 'See that man,
Bolitho? That is Sir George Helpman, from London.' His lip
curled slightly. 'An "expert" on our malaise here. A very important person. One to be heard and respected at all times.'

The mood changed, and just as swiftly he was the admiral
again. 'Be off with you, Bolitho. Enjoy what you wish. The food
is palatable today.'

He turned away and Bolitho saw him greeting the man from
London. He got the impression that Rear-Admiral Coutts did
not like him very much. It had sounded like a warning, although
what a lowly lieutenant could do to upset matters was hard to
imagine.

He thought about Coutts. Not a bit what he had expected. He
shied away from what he felt. Admiration. A strange sense of
loyalty for the man he had met for just a few minutes. But it was
there. It was useless to deny it.

It was getting dark by the time the guests started to leave.
Some were so drunk they had to be carried to their boats, others
lurched, glassy-eyed and unsupported, fighting each step of the
way for fear of disgracing themselves.

Bolitho waited on the quarterdeck, watching the civilians
and the officials, the ladies and a few of the military being
helped, pushed or lowered by tackles into the bobbing flotilla of
boats alongside.

He had just passed a cabin which he guessed was that of
Coutts' flag lieutenant. The door had been slightly ajar, and
Bolitho had caught just a brief view before it had swung shut. A
woman's body, naked to the waist, her arms wrapped around the
officer's head as he tore at her clothing like a madman. And she
had been giggling, bubbling with sheer enjoyment.

Her husband or escort was probably lying in one of the boats
right now, Bolitho thought. He smiled. Was he shocked or
envious again?

A boatswain's mate harassed by his additional duties, called,
'Yer captain's comin', sir!'

'Aye. Call the barge.' Bolitho adjusted his swordbelt and
straightened his hat.

Pears appeared with Captain Lamb. The two men shook

hands and then Pears followed Bolitho down into the boat.

As the barge edged clear and swung on a swift moving current, Pears made one comment. 'Disgusting, was it not?'

He then lapsed into silence and did not move until *Trojan*'s lighted gunports were close by. Then he said curtly, 'If that was diplomacy, then thank God I'm a simple sailor!'

Bolitho stood in the swaying boat beside the coxswain, and as Pears reached out for the ladder his foot slipped. Bolitho thought he heard him swear but was not certain. But he felt vaguely honoured to share the moment. Pears was in perfect control again, but only just. That made him seem more human than Bolitho could remember.

Pears' harsh voice came down from the entry port, 'Don't stand there like a priest, Mr Bolitho! 'Pon my soul, sir, others have work to do, if you do not!'

Bolitho looked at Hogg and grinned. That was more like it.

Amongst other tasks required of ship's lieutenants was the wearying and thankless duty of officer of the guard. In New York, to ease the work of the shorebound authorities, the various ships at anchor were expected to supply a lieutenant for a full twenty-four-hour duty. It entailed checking the various guardboats which pulled around the jetties and moored ships, to make certain they allowed no enemy agents to get near enough to do damage or discover secret information. Equally, they were required to prevent any of the fleet's seamen from deserting to seek shelter and more doubtful pleasures on the waterfront.

Seamen entrusted with work ashore were often tempted, and drunken, wild-eyed sailors had to be sorted out to await an escort back to their rightful ships, and a few lashes for good measure.

Two nights after his visit to the flagship it fell to *Trojan*'s third lieutenant to place himself at the disposal of the port admiral and provost marshal for such duty. New York made him feel uneasy. A city waiting for something to happen, a pattern to settle once and for all. It was a city of constant movement. Refugees arriving from inland, others thronging offices and government buildings in search of relatives lost in the fighting. Some were already leaving for England and for Canada. Others waited to reap rich rewards from the victors, no matter what colour their coats might be. It could be a dangerous place at night, especially along the crowded waterfront with its taverns and brothels, boarding houses and gaming rooms, where anything was available so long as there was gold for the taking.

Bolitho, followed by a file of armed seamen, walked slowly along a line of sun-dried planked buildings, careful to stay close to the wall and avoid any filth which might be thrown or accidentally dropped on to his patrol.

He heard Stockdale's wheezing breath behind him, the occasional clink of weapons as they made their way towards the main jetty. Few people were in view, although behind most of the shuttered windows he could hear music and voices raised in song or blasphemy.

One house stood silhouetted against the swirling water, and he saw the usual marine sentries outside the entrance, a sergeant pacing up and down by a small lantern.

''Alt! 'Oo goes there!'

'Officer of the guard!'

'Advance an' be recognized.'

It was always the same, even though the marines knew most of the fleet's lieutenants by sight, night or day.

The sergeant stamped to attention. 'Two men for the *Vanquisher*, sir. Fightin' drunk they are.'

Bolitho walked through some doors and into a large hall. It had once been a fine house, the home of a tea merchant. Now it served the Navy.

'They seem quiet enough, Sergeant.'

The man grinned unfeelingly. 'Ah, sir, *now* they is!' He gestured to two inert shapes in leg irons. ''Ad to quieten 'em, like.'

Bolitho sat down at a scarred desk, half listening to the noises beyond the doors, the clatter of wheels across the Dutch cobbles, the occasional shriek of some whore.

He looked at the clock. Past midnight. Another four hours to go. At times like this he longed for the *Trojan*, when hours earlier he had pined to be free from her regulated routine.

When the fleet had first arrived off Staten Island, someone had described it as being like London afloat. It had become too much of a reality to be mentioned nowadays. Bolitho had seen two lieutenants from one of the frigates as they had gone into a gaming house. He knew both by sight but little more. In those few moments he had caught a snatch of their conversation.

*Sailing on the tide. Going to Antigua with despatches.* What it was to be free. Able to get clear away from this floating muddle of ships.

The sergeant reappeared and regarded him doubtfully.

'I got a crimp outside, sir.' He jerked his thumb towards the door. 'I know 'im of old, a rogue but reliable. 'E says there are some 'ands from the brig *Diamond*. Jumped ship afore she weighed three days back.'

Bolitho stood up, reaching for his hanger. 'What was she?'

The sergeant grinned hugely. 'No bother, sir. She weren't under no warrant, she was with general cargo from an English port.'

Bolitho nodded. A brig from England. That implied trained seamen, deserters or not.

He said, 'Bring the, er, crimp inside.'

The man was typical of his trade. Small, greasy, furtive. They were common enough in any seaport. Boarding-house runners who sold information about likely hands to officers of the Press.

'Well?'

The man whined, 'It be my duty, sir. To 'elp the King's Navy.'

Bolitho eyed him coldly. The man still retained the accent of the London slums.

'How many?'

'Six, sir!' His eyes glittered. 'Fine strong lads they be.'

The sergeant said offhandedly, 'They're in Lucy's place.' He grimaced. 'Poxed to the eyebrows, I shouldn't wonder.'

'Tell my men to fall in, Sergeant.' Bolitho tried not to think of the delay this would cause. He would probably miss his sleep altogether.

The crimp said, 'Could we come to an agreement nah, sir?'

'No. You wait here. If I get the men, you'll get paid. If not . . .' He winked at the grinning marines. 'We'll have you seized up and flogged.'

He strode out into the night, hating the crimp, these detestable methods of getting enough men. Despite the hardships of naval life, there were plenty of volunteers. But there were never enough. Death by many means, and injury by many more, saw to that.

Stockdale asked, 'Where, sir?'

'A place called Lucy's.'

One of the seamen chuckled. 'Oi bin there, zur.'

Bolitho groaned. 'Then you lead. Carry on.'

Once in the narrow, sloping street which stank like an open sewer, Bolitho split his men into two groups. Most of the trusted hands had done it before several times. Even pressed men, once settled in their new life, were ready enough to bring the Navy's rough justice to the fore. *'If we have to go, why not you!'* seemed to be their only yardstick.

Stockdale had vanished to the rear of the building, his cutlass in his belt and carrying instead a cudgel as big as a leg of pork.

Bolitho stood for a few more seconds, taking deep breaths while he stared at the sealed door, beyond which he could hear someone crooning quietly like a sick dog. They were probably sleeping it off, he thought grimly. If they were there at all.

He drew his hanger and smashed the pommel against the door several times, shouting. 'Open, in the King's name!'

The response was immediate. Shuffles and startled cries, the muffled tinkle of breaking glass followed by a thud as a would-be escaper fell victim to Stockdale's cudgel.

Then the door was flung open, but instead of a rush of figures Bolitho was confronted by a giant of a woman, whom he guessed to be the notorious Lucy. She was as tall and as broad as any sailorman, and had the language to match as she screamed abuse and waved her fists in his face.

Lanterns were appearing on every hand, and from windows across the street heads were peering down to enjoy the spectacle of Lucy routing the Navy.

'Why, you poxy young bugger!' She placed her hands on her hips and glowered at Bolitho. ''Ow dare you come accusin' me of 'arbouring deserters!'

Other women, some half-naked, were creeping down a rickety stairway at the back of the hallway, their painted faces excited and eager to see what would happen.

'I have my duty.' Bolitho listened to his own voice, disgusted with the jeering woman, humiliated by her contempt.

Stockdale appeared behind her, his face unsmiling as he wheezed, 'Got 'em, sir. Six, like 'e said.'

Bolitho nodded. Stockdale must have found his own way through the rear.

'Well done.' He felt sudden anger running through him. 'While we're here we shall take a look for more *innocent* citizens.'

She reached out and seized his lapels, and pursed her lips to spit into his face.

Bolitho got a brief view of bare, kicking legs and thighs as Stockdale gathered her up in his arms and carried her screaming and cursing down the steps to the street. Without further ado he dropped her face down in a horse trough and held her head under the water for several seconds.

Then he released her, and as she staggered, retching and gasping for breath, he said, 'If you talks to the lieutenant like that again, my beauty, I'll take my snickersnee to yer gizzard, see?'

He nodded to Bolitho. 'All right now, sir.'

Bolitho swallowed hard. He had never seen Stockdale behave like it before.

'Er, thank you.'

He saw his men nudging each other and grinning, and tried to assert himself. 'Get on with the search.' He watched the six deserters lurching past, one holding his head.

From one of the other houses an anonymous voice yelled, 'Leave 'em be, you varmints!'

Bolitho entered the door and looked at the upended chairs, empty bottles and scraps of clothing. It was more like a prison than a place for pleasure, he thought.

Two additional men were brought down the stairs, one a lobster fisherman, the other protesting that he was not a sailor at all. Bolitho looked at the tattoos on his arms and said softly, 'I suggest you hold your tongue. If, as I suspect, you are from a King's ship, it were better to say nothing.' He saw the man pale under his sunburn, as if he had already seen the noose.

A seaman clattered down the stairs and said, 'That's the lot, sir. 'Cept for this youngster.'

Bolitho saw the youth being pushed through the watching girls and decided against it. Probably someone's young son, out on an errand, seeking a first thrill in this foul place.

'Very well, Call the others.'

He looked at the youth, slim-shouldered, eyes downcast and in shadow.

'This is no place for you, boy. Be off, before something worse happens. Where do you live?'

When there was no reply, Bolitho reached out and lifted the other's chin, allowing the lantern light to spill over the frightened face.

He seemed to stand locked in the same position for an age, and yet he was aware of other things happening elsewhere. The feet shuffling on the cobbles as his men sorted their new hands into file, and the distant shout of orders as a military patrol approached from the end of the street.

Then events moved swiftly. The figure twisted away and was out and through the door before anyone could move.

A seaman bellowed, *'Stop that man!'* And along the street Bolitho heard a challenge from the soldiers.

Bolitho ran out shouting, *'Wait!'* But it was too late, and the crash of the musket seemed like a cannon in the narrow street.

He walked past his men and stood over the sprawled figure as a corporal of infantry ran forward and rolled the body on to its back.

'Thought 'e was escapin' from you, sir!'

Bolitho got down and unbuttoned the youth's rough jerkin and shirt. He could feel the skin, still hot and inflamed, and very smooth like the chin had been. There was blood too, glittering in the lantern light as if still alive.

Bolitho ran his hand over the breast. There was no heart-beat, and he could feel the dead eyes staring at him in the darkness. Hostile and accusing.

He stood up, sickened. 'It's a girl.'

Then he turned and added, 'That woman, bring her here.'

The woman called Lucy edged closer, gripping her hands together as she saw the sprawled corpse.

Gone was the bluster and coarse arrogance. Bolitho could almost smell her terror.

He asked, 'Who was she?' He was surprised at the sound of his own voice. Flat and unemotional. A stranger's. 'I'll not ask a second time, woman.'

More noises echoed along the street, and then two mounted figures cantered through the army patrol, and a voice barked, 'What the *hell* is going on here?'

Bolitho touched his hat. 'Officer of the guard, sir.'

It was a major, who wore the same insignia as the man who had shot the unknown girl.

'Oh, I see. Well then.' The major dismounted and stooped over the body. He put his hand under the girl's head, letting it roll stiffly towards the beam.

Bolitho watched, unable to take his eyes from the girl's face.

The major stood up and said quietly, 'Fine kettle of fish, Lieutenant.' He rubbed his chin. 'I'd better rouse the governor. He'll not take kindly to it.'

'What is it, sir?'

The major shook his head. 'What you don't know will do you no harm.' He became businesslike as he snapped to the other mounted soldier, 'Corporal Fisher! Ride to the post and rouse the adjutant, I want him and a full platoon here on the double.' He watched the man gallop away and then added, 'This damned house will be closed and under guard, and *you*,' his white-gloved finger shot out towards the shivering Lucy, 'are under arrest!'

She almost fell as she pleaded, 'Why *me*, sir? What have *I* done?'

The major stood aside as two soldiers ran to seize her arms. 'Treason, *madam*. That's what!'

He turned more calmly to Bolitho. 'I suggest you go about your affairs, sir. I have no doubt you will hear more of this.' Surprisingly, he gave a quick smile. 'But if it's a consolation, you may have stumbled on something of real value. Too many good men have fallen to treachery. Here's one who will betray no more.'

Bolitho walked back towards the waterfront in silence. The major had recognized the dead girl, and from the fineness of her bones, the smoothness of her skin, she came from a good family.

He tried to guess what had been happening before he and his men had burst in, but all he could remember were her eyes as she had looked at his face, when they had both known the truth.

# 7

## Hopes and Fears

Bolitho moved a few paces across the quarterdeck in an attempt
to stay in the shadow of *Trojan*'s great spanker. It was oppres-
sively hot, and despite a steady wind across the quarter it was
impossible to draw comfort from it.

Bolitho turned as a ship's boy reversed the half-hour glass
and six bells chimed out from the forecastle. An hour of the
forenoon still to run.

He winced as the sun smashed down between the sails'
shadows and seared his shoulders like a blacksmith's forge. He
took a telescope from its rack and trained it ahead, seeing the
flagship *Resolute* leap to meet him. How quickly things had
changed, he thought. Just the day after the mystery of the dead
girl orders had been received to weigh and put to sea with the
first favourable wind. No mention was made of the destination
or the purpose, and up to the last some of the wardroom cynics
had expected it to turn into another exercise, a brief display of
strength for the Army's moral support.

That had been four days ago. Four long days of crawling
south with barely a ripple around the rudder to show some
progress. It had taken them four days to make good four hundred miles.

Bolitho swung the glass slowly across the quarter and saw the sun shimmering on the topgallant sails of the frigate *Vanquisher*, well out to windward, ready to dash down to assist her ponderous consorts if she were needed. He returned to study the flagship again. Just occasionally, as she pitched heavily in a deep swell, he caught sight of another, smaller set of sails far ahead of the squadron, the admiral's 'eyes'.

As *Trojan* had weighed anchor and prepared to leave Sandy Hook, Bolitho had watched the sloop-of-war *Spite* spreading her sails and speeding out of harbour with the minimum of fuss. She was up there now, ready to pass back her signals if she sighted anything which might interest the admiral.

She was a lovely little vessel of eighteen guns, and Bolitho had discovered her to be the one which had fired on the *Faithful* before Sparke's attempt to seize the ordnance brigantine. Her commander was only twenty-four years old, and, like the three other captains here today, knew exactly what he was doing and where he was ordered to go.

Secrecy seemed to have crept into their world like the first touch of a disease.

The deck trembled, and he heard the port-lids on the lower battery's starboard side being opened, and after a pause the squeak of gun trucks as thirty of *Trojan*'s thirty-two-pounders were run out as if to give battle. If he looked over the side he would be able to see them easily. Just the thought of it was enough. Even the touch of the tinder-dry bulwark or quarterdeck rail was like a burn. What Dalyell, now appointed in charge of the lower gundeck, was suffering, he could barely imagine.

The sails clapped, and rustled overhead, and he glanced up at the trailing pendant, looking for a shift of wind. It seemed steady enough from the north-west, but without the strength they needed to drive the humidity and discomfort from between decks.

Rumble, rumble, rumble, the thirty-two-pounders were being run in again, and no doubt Dalyell was peering at his watch and consulting with his midshipmen and petty officers. It was taking too long, and Captain Pears had made his requirements plain from the start of the commission. Clear for action in ten minutes or less, and when firing, three rounds every two minutes. This last exercise had sounded twice as long.

He could picture the stripped and sweating gun crews, struggling to run out those massive cannon. With the ship leaning over on the starboard tack, the guns, each weighing over three tons, had to be hauled bodily up the sloping deck to the ports. This was not the weather for it, but then, it never was, as Cairns had often remarked.

Bolitho stared across the nettings, picturing the invisible land as he had studied it on the chart during each watch. Cape Hatteras and its shoals lay some twenty miles abeam, and beyond, Pamlico Sound and the rivers of North Carolina.

But as far as Bolitho and the look-outs were concerned the sea was theirs. Four ships, spread out to obtain best advantage of wind and visibility, moving slowly towards a secret destination. Bolitho thought about their combined companies, which must amount to close on eighteen hundred officers and men.

Just a few moments earlier he had seen the purser with his clerk hurrying down the main companion, Molesworth carrying his ledger, his clerk with a box of tools which he used for opening casks and checking the quality of their contents.

It was Monday, and Bolitho could imagine the scribbled instructions in Molesworth's ledger. Per man this day, one pound of biscuit, one gallon of small beer, one pint of oatmeal, two ounces of butter and four ounces of cheese.

After that, it was up to Triphook and his mates to do what they could with it.

No wonder pursers were always worried or dishonest. Sometimes both. Multiply a man's daily ration by the whole company and by the long days and weeks at sea, and you got some idea of his problems.

Midshipman Couzens, standing discreetly by the lee rail with his telescope ready to train on the flagship, hissed, '*Captain,* sir!'

Bolitho turned swiftly, the effort making the sweat run between his shoulder blades and gather at his waistband like hot rain.

He touched his hat. 'Sou'-sou'-west, sir. Full and bye.'

Pears glanced at him impassively. 'The wind appears to have veered in the last hour. But not enough to make any difference.'

He said nothing further, and Bolitho crossed to the lee side to allow his captain the freedom of the deck.

Pears paced slowly up and down, his face totally absorbed. What was he thinking about, Bolitho wondered? His orders or his wife and family in England?

Pears paused and swivelled his head towards him. 'Pipe some hands forrard, Mr Bolitho. The weather forebrace is as slack as this watch, dammit! 'Pon my soul, sir, you'll have to do better!'

Bolitho nodded. 'Aye, sir. At once.'

He gestured to Couzens, and a moment later some seamen were hauling lustily, each knowing he was under the captain's scrutiny.

Bolitho found himself pondering over Pears' behaviour. The forebrace had seemed no slacker than you might expect in the rising and falling gusts of wind. Was it just to keep him on his toes? He thought suddenly of Sparke and his, *take that man's name*.

The memory saddened him.

He saw Quinn coming up the ladder from the gundeck and nodded to him, adding a quick shake of the head to warn him of Pears' presence.

Quinn was doing far better than Bolitho had dared hope. He had got his colour back, and could walk without twisting his face in readiness for the pain.

Bolitho had seen the great scar on Quinn's breast. If his attacker had not been startled and taken off guard, his blade would have sliced through bone and muscle to the heart itself.

The voice settled on the young fifth lieutenant like a mesh. 'Mr Quinn!'

'Sir!' He hurried across the deck, his face working anxiously as to what he had done wrong.

Pears studied him grimly. 'I am indeed glad to see you are up and about.'

Quinn smiled gratefully. 'Thank you, sir.'

'Quite so.' Pears continued with his daily walk. 'You will exercise your men at repelling boarders this afternoon. *Then*, if we remain on this tack, you will put the new hands aloft for sail drill.' He nodded curtly. 'That should restore your well-being better than any pills, eh?'

Couzens yelled excitedly, 'Signal from Flag, sir!' He was peering through his big telescope, his forehead wrinkled like that of an old man as he read the hoist of coloured bunting at *Resolute*'s yard. '*Make more sail*, sir!'

Pears growled, 'Call the hands. Get the royals on her. Stuns'ls too if she can take them.' He strode aft as the master appeared beneath the poop, and Bolitho heard him say in his harsh tone 'More sail, that is all *he* can think of, damn it!'

Cairns hurried up as the calls trilled between decks and

brought the watch below scampering to their stations.

'Hands aloft! Set the royals!'

Cairns saw Bolitho and shrugged. 'The captain is in a foul mood, Dick. We lay each course a day ahead, but I am as wise as you as to where we are bound.' He looked to see that Pears was not close by. 'It has always been *his* way to explain, to share his views with us. But now, it seems our admiral has other ideas.'

Bolitho thought of the admiral's youthful enthusiasm. Maybe Pears had become staid, out of touch with things.

But there was nothing wrong with his eyes as he yelled, 'Mr Cairns, sir! Get those topmen aloft, flog them if you must! I'll not be goaded again by the flagship!'

It was noon by the time the royals and then the great, batlike studding sails had been set on either beam. The flagship had also made as much sail as she could carry, and appeared to be buried under the towering pyramids of pale canvas.

Lieutenant Probyn relieved Bolitho without his usual sarcasm or complaint, but remarked, 'I see no gain in this at all. Day after day, with ne'er a word of explanation. It makes me uneasy, and that's no lie!'

But two more days were to pass before anyone had settled on the truth of the matter.

Rear-Admiral Coutts' little squadron continued on its southerly course and then swung south-east, skirting Cape Fear, so aptly named, to take advantage of the wind's sudden eagerness to help them.

Bolitho was about to go off watch when he was unexpectedly summoned aft to the great cabin.

But it was not a conference, and he found the captain alone at his desk. His coat was hanging across his chairback, and he had loosened his neckcloth and shirt.

Bolitho waited. The captain looked very calm, so it seemed unlikely there was to be a reprimand for something he had done, or not done.

Pears glanced up at him. 'The master, and now the first lieutenant, know the extent of my orders. You may think it strange for me to confide in you before the rest of my officers, but under the circumstances I think it is fair.' He bobbed his head. *'Do sit down.'*

Bolitho sat, sensing the sudden irritation which was never far from Pears' manner.

'There was some trouble at New York. You played no small part in it.' Pears smiled wryly. 'Which did *not* surprise me, of course.'

Bolitho pricked up his ears. Somehow he had known that the matter of the dead girl would come up again. Even that it might be connected in some small way with the squadron's unexpected departure from Sandy Hook.

'I will not go into full detail, but the girl you discovered in that brothel was the daughter of a New York government official, a very important one to boot. It could not have come at a worse time. Sir George Helpman is out from England under the direct instructions of both Parliament and Admiralty to discover what is being done to pursue the war, to prevent the whole campaign being bogged down in stalemate. If, or rather when, the French come into the open to fight in strength, we will be hard put to hold what we have, let alone make any gains.'

'I thought we were doing all we could, sir.'

Pears looked at him pityingly. 'When you are more experienced, Bolitho . . .' He looked away, frowning angrily. 'Helpman will see it for himself. The corrupt officials, the dandies of the military government who dance and drink while our soldiers in the field pay the price. And now this. An important official's daughter is discovered to be working hand-in-glove with the rebels. She has been leaving her home in a carriage and changing into boy's clothes just so that she can meet one of Washington's agents and pass him any tidbit of secret information she could lay her hands on.'

Bolitho could well imagine the fury and consternation it must have caused. He could find pity for the blowzy whore who had tried to spit in his face. With so much at stake, and with important heads on the block, her interrogators would have few scruples in the manner of gaining information.

Pears said, 'Due to her treachery, the Tracy brothers were able to plot our every move, and but for taking the *Faithful*, and Mr Bunce's liaison with the Almighty on matters concerning the weather, we might never have known anything. Links in a chain. And now we have one more scrap to play with. That damned whore had her ear to the keyhole more often than not. The Colonials have a new stronghold, constructed with the express purpose of receiving and transporting powder and weapons to their ships and soldiers.'

Bolitho licked his lips. 'And we are heading there now, sir?'

'That's the strength of it, yes. Fort Exeter, in South Carolina, about thirty miles north of Charles Town.'

Bolitho nodded, remembering clearly what happened near there about a year ago, at another rebel fort, only that had been to the south of Charles Town. A large squadron, with troops as well as marines embarked, had sailed to seize the fort which commanded the inshore waters, and would thus interdict all trade and privateer traffic to and from Charles Town, the busiest port south of Philadelphia. Instead of victory, it had ended in humiliating defeat. Some of the ships had gone aground because of wrongly marked charts, while elsewhere the water had been too deep for the soldiers to wade ashore as had been intended. And all the time the Colonials, snug behind their fortress walls, had kept up a steady bombardment on the largest British vessels, until Commodore Parker, whose flagship had taken the worst of it, had ordered a complete withdrawal. *Trojan* had been on her way to offer support when she had met the returning ships.

In the Navy, unused to either defeat or failure, it had seemed like an overwhelming disaster.

Pears had been watching his face. 'I see you have not forgotten either, Bolitho. I only hope we all live to remember this new venture.'

With a start Bolitho realized the interview was over. As he made to leave, Pears said quietly, 'I told you all this because of your part in it. But for your actions, we might not have found out about that girl. But for her, Sir George Helpman would not be raising hell in New York.' He leaned back and smiled. 'And but for *him*, our admiral would not now be trying to prove he can do what others cannot. Links in a chain, Bolitho, as I said earlier. Think about it.'

Bolitho walked out and cannoned into Captain D'Esterre. The marine said, 'Why, Dick you look as if you have seen a ghost!'

Bolitho forced a smile. 'I have. Mine.'


When the time came for Lieutenant Cairns to share Pears' orders with the lieutenants and warrant officers, even the most unimaginative one present could not fail to marvel at their admiral's impudence.

While out of sight of land, and with the frigate patrolling to ensure they were left undisturbed, the sloop *Spite* was to embark all of the flagship's and *Trojan*'s marines, and with boats under tow would head inshore under cover of darkness. The two-deckers, in company with *Vanquisher*, would then continue along the coast towards the same fort which had routed Commodore Parker's squadron the previous year.

To any watchers along the coast, and to the officers of the fort and the Charles Town garrison, it would not seem an unlikely thing for the British to attempt. Hurt pride, and the fact that the fort was still performing a useful protection for privateers and the landing of stores and powder, were two very good reasons for a second attempt.

Fort Exeter, on the other hand, was easier to defend to seaward, and would feel quite safe when the small squadron had sailed past in full view of the Colonial pickets.

Bolitho, when he had listened to Cairns' level, unemotional voice as he explained the extent of their orders, had imagined he could detect Rear-Admiral Coutts speaking directly to him.

*Spite* would land the marines, a party of seamen and all the necessary tackle and ladders for scaling walls, and then stand out to sea again before dawn. The rest, an attack from inland towards the rear of the fort, would be left to the discretion of the senior officer. In this case, he was Major Samuel Paget, commanding officer of the flagship's marines.

D'Esterre had said of him in confidence, 'A very hard man. Once he has made up his mind nothing will shift him, and no argument is tolerated.'

Bolitho could well believe it. He had seen Paget a few times. Very erect and conscious of the figure he made in his scarlet coat and matching sash, impeccable white lapels and collar, he was nevertheless having difficulty in concealing his growing corpulence. His face had once been handsome, but now, in his middle thirties, the major had all the signs of a heavy drinker, and one who enjoyed a good table.

D'Esterre had also said, 'This little jaunt might take some of the fat off him.'

But he had not smiled, and Bolitho had guessed that he had wished he and not the major was to command.

Once their mission was out in the open the ship's company got down to work and preparation with the usual mixture of attitudes. Grim resignation for those who would be taking part, cheerful optimism from those who would not.

At the chosen time the work of ferrying the marines and

seamen to the little sloop-of-war was begun without delay. After the blazing heat of a July day the evening brought little respite, and the gruelling, irksome work soon roused tempers and on-the-spot justice from fist and rope's end.

Bolitho was counting the last group of seamen and making sure they were all armed, as well as being equipped with flasks of water and not hoarded rum, when Cairns strode up to him and snapped, 'There has been another change.'

'How so?'

Bolitho waited, expecting to hear that the raid was being delayed.

Cairns said bitterly, 'I am remaining aboard.' He looked away, hiding his hurt. '*Again.*'

Bolitho did not know what to say. Cairns had obviously set his heart on going with the attack as senior lieutenant. Having missed the chance of being a prize-master, or even of taking part in the *Faithful*'s capture, he must have seen the landing as his rightful reward, although by going he stood as much chance of being killed as anyone else.

'Someone from the flagship, sir?'

Cairns faced him. 'No. Probyn is to lead. God help you!'

Bolitho examined his feelings. 'And young James Quinn is to go with us also.'

Quinn had said nothing when he had been told, but he had looked as if someone had struck him.

Cairns seemed to read his thoughts. 'Aye, Dick. So it may fall to you to look after our people.'

'But why not the flagship? Surely they have a lieutenant and more to spare?'

Cairns regarded him curiously. 'You don't understand admirals, Dick. They never let go of their own. They must always show a perfect front, a well ordered world of officers and men. Coutts will be no exception. He'll want perfection, not a rabble of old men and boys like we are fast becoming.'

He could have said more, Bolitho thought. That Quinn was being sent to prove that his wound had not destroyed his resolution and courage, and Probyn because he would not be missed. He thought of his own position and almost smiled. Pears was only doing what the admiral had done. Keeping the best for himself. Anyone below Cairns in rank and quality would be sacrificed first.

Cairns said, 'I am glad you can still discover humour in this affair, Dick. For myself, I find it intolerable.'

Midshipman Couzens, hung about with telescope, dirk, pistols and a bulging sack of food, called breathlessly, '*Spite* has signalled, sir! Last party to go across now.'

Bolitho nodded. 'Very well. Man your boats.'

He watched a second midshipman, a serious-faced sixteen-year-old named Huyghue, climbing down into the cutter to sit beside the coxswain, who was probably twice his age.

'I see you are ready, Mr Bolitho.'

Probyn's thick voice made him turn towards the quarterdeck. The second lieutenant could only just have been told of Pears' change of plans, but he looked remarkably unworried. He was very flushed, but that was quite usual, and as he leaned on the quarterdeck rail to peer at the boats alongside he seemed calm to the point of indifference.

Cairns straightened his back as the captain's heavy tread came across the deck. 'Good luck. Both of you.' He glanced at the dizzily swaying sloop. 'By God, I wish I was coming with you.'

Probyn said nothing but touched his hat to the quarterdeck before following the others down into a crowded boat.

Bolitho saw Stockdale in one of the other boats and nodded to him. If for some reason he had not been taking part, it would have been like an ill-omen, something final. Seeing him there, big and quiet-faced, made up for many of the other, nagging doubts.

Probyn said, 'Shove off, cox'n. I don't want to fry in this damn heat!'

As they drew closer to the sloop, her commanding officer hurried to the side and cupped his hands. 'Move yourselves, damn you! This is a King's ship, not a bloody lobster boat!'

Only then did Probyn show some mettle. 'Hear that? Impudent young chicken! God, how command changes a man!'

Bolitho shot him a quick glance. In just those few angry words Probyn had revealed a lot. Bolitho knew he had been beached on half-pay before the war. Whether it was because of his drinking, or he had simply become a hardened drinker because of his ill-luck, he was not sure. But he had certainly been passed over for promotion, and to be shouted at by the *Spite*'s youthful commander would not make it any easier.

As they clambered up on to the sloop's busy deck, he wondered where all the marines had gone. As in the *Faithful*, they had been swallowed up within minutes of boarding. Aft by the taffrail he saw Major Paget speaking with D'Esterre and the two marine lieutenants.

The sloop's commander walked across to meet the last arrivals.

He nodded curtly and then shouted, '*Mr Walker!* Get the ship under way, if you please!'

To Bolitho he added, 'I suggest you go below. My people have enough to contend with at present, without being faced by unknown officers from every hand!'

Bolitho touched his hat. Unlike Probyn, he could undetstand the young man's sharpness. He was very conscious of his command and the mission suddenly thrust upon him. Close by, two ships of the line, his admiral and some senior post captains would be watching, waiting to find fault, to compare his efficiency with others.

The commander swung on his heel. 'I understand that you were the officer *involved* with my ship two weeks back, eh?'

He had a sharp, incisive tone, and Bolitho guessed he would be a difficult man to get on with. Twenty-four years old. What had Probyn said? *How command changes a man.*

'*Well?*'

'Aye, sir. I was second in command of the raid. My senior was killed.'

'I see.' He nodded. 'My gunner nearly did that to you earlier.' He walked away.

Bolitho made his way aft, pushing through the bustling seamen as they ran to braces and halliards, oblivious to everyone but their own officers.

The pulling boats were already falling obediently astern on their lines, and almost before Bolitho's head had passed into the shadow of the companionway the *Spite* was heeling over to the wind and presenting her counter to the big two-deckers.

The wardroom was crowded with officers, and *Spite*'s purser soon produced bottles and glasses for all the additional guests.

When it came to Probyn he shook his head and said abruptly, 'Not for me, but thankee. Later maybe.'

Bolitho looked away, unable to bear the sight of the man's battle. Probyn had never refused a drink before. And it had cost him a great deal to do it now.

He thought of Probyn's bitterness about the sloop's commander and what lay ahead of them tomorrow.

It was of paramount importance to Probyn that he should succeed, and for that he would give up a lot more than brandy.

During the night and through the following day, *Spite* tacked back and forth, biding her time while she continued a slow approach towards the land.

Fort Exeter stood on a sandy four-mile-long island which was shaped rather like an axe-head. At low water it was connected to the mainland by an unreliable causeway of sand and shingle, and the entrance to a lagoon-like anchorage was easily protected by the fort's carefully sited artillery.

As soon as the landing party was ashore, *Spite* would withdraw and be out of sight of land by the following dawn. If the wind died, the attack would be postponed until it returned. Whatever happened, it would not be abandoned unless the enemy were ready and waiting.

When Bolitho thought of Major Samuel Paget, the man who would be leading the attack, he doubted if it would be cancelled even then.

# 8

# *Fort Exeter*

The landing, which took place at one in the morning, was carried
out with unexpected ease. A favourable wind carried the sloop
close inshore, where she dropped anchor and started to ferry the
marines ashore as if it were part of a peacetime manoeuvre.

Major Samuel Paget went with the first boat, and when
Bolitho eventually stepped on to glistening wet sand and
squelched after a hurrying file of marines, he found time to
admire the man's sense of planning. He had brought two Cana-
dians with him, and had explained they were better at scouting
'than any damn dogs'. They were both fierce-looking men with
beards and rough trapper's clothing, and a smell to match any
pelt.

One, a sad-eyed Scot named Macdonald, had originally lived
for some years in South Carolina, and had been driven from his
land when the main Loyalist force in the area had been beaten in
a pitched battle by the Patriot militia. His hate reminded Bolitho
of the resourceful Moffitt.

Paget greeted Bolitho with his usual abruptness. 'All quiet. I
want our men positioned before first light. We'll issue rations
and water.' He scanned the starry sky and grunted, 'Too bloody
hot for my liking.'

Stockdale said hoarsely, 'Mr Couzens is comin' with the last lot, sir.'

'Very well.' Bolitho watched as Probyn blundered out of some dark scrub, sniffing around him like a fox. 'Everyone's ashore, sir.'

Probyn watched the marines plodding past, their weapons and equipment carefully muffled, like silent ghosts from some forgotten battle.

'God, it makes you think. Here we are, bloody miles from anywhere, marching into heaven knows what, and to what purpose, eh?'

Bolitho smiled. He had been thinking much the same. The marines seemed quite at home on land as they did at sea, but he could sense the wary caution of the seamen, the way they tended to bunch together, no matter what they were threatened with.

D'Esterre appeared from somewhere and showed his teeth. 'Come along, Dick, join the marines and see the world!' He went off to find his lieutenant, swinging his sword like a cane.

Bolitho looked at the beach, shining faintly in the darkness. The boats had already gone, and he imagined he could hear the sounds of sails being shaken out above the murmur of breakers. Then it really hit home. They were to all intents and purposes abandoned on this unknown shore, with just the skill of two Canadian scouts whom Paget had 'borrowed from the Army'.

Suppose that even now they were being trailed, their stumbling progress marked as they approached some terrible ambush. The night was still but for the wind in the trees and the occasional cry of a startled bird. Even the wind sounded different here, which was not surprising, Bolitho thought, as he peered at the strange palms which ran almost to the water's edge. They gave the land a tropical touch, something alien.

Lieutenant Raye of *Trojan*'s marines marched out of the darkness and exclaimed cheerfully, 'Ah, here you are. The major says you are to follow with the rearguard, Mr Bolitho. Make certain the men do not crash into each other with their ladders and suchlike.' He touched his hat to Probyn. 'He sends his compliments, sir, and would you join him with the main party.'

Probyn nodded, muttering, 'Bloody soldiers, that's what we are!'

Bolitho stood aside to allow the seamen to lurch past, some with ladders and heavy tackles, others carrying muskets, powder and shot. The remainder were loaded down with food and water.

Lieutenant Quinn was right at the rear, with only the blurred shapes on either side to reveal some of the marine skirmishers who were covering their advance.

Bolitho fell in step beside him and asked quietly, 'How is the wound, James?'

'I don't feel it much.' Quinn sounded as if he were shivering. 'But I wish we were afloat, instead of here.'

Bolitho recalled him saying much the same before the last fight. D'Esterre and Thorndike, the surgeon, playing cards under a lantern, the ship sleeping around them.

Quinn said, 'I'm afraid of what I might *do*.' He was almost pleading. 'If I have to face another hand-to-hand, I think I shall break.'

'Easy, man. Don't start meeting trouble before you must.'

He knew exactly how Quinn felt. As he had done after being wounded. It was worse for Quinn. He had not been in action before that last time.

Quinn did not seem to hear.

'I think of Sparke a lot. How he used to rant and rave. I never really liked him, but I admired his courage, his, his,' he groped for words, 'his *style*.'

Bolitho reached out to steady a seaman as he almost tripped over a root with his load of muskets.

Style. Yes, it described Sparke better than anything else.

Quinn sighed. 'I could never do what he did. Never in a thousand years.'

There was a thud, and a marine raised his musket and brought down the butt a second time on some coarse grass beside the file of seamen.

'Snake!' He mopped his face. 'Cor, that's the bloody potful as far as I'm concerned!'

Bolitho thought suddenly of Cornwall. In July. At this very moment. Hedgerows of lush fields, sheep and cows dotted on the hillsides like scattered flowers. He could almost smell it, hear the bees, the swish of hooks as the farm workers cleared some new land to grow more food. To feed the country, the Army.

Midshipman Couzens said between gasps for breath, 'Sky's brighter, sir.'

Bolitho replied, 'We must be near the place then.'

What would happen if instead of a suitable hideout for the landing party, as remembered by the Canadian, Macdonald, they found an enemy encampment?

Sure enough, the rearguard was already catching up with the main party, where Paget's sergeants and corporals waited like the keepers of invisible gates to guide and push the men into smaller sections. Bolitho watched the white cross-belts and the checkered shirts fading away obediently to the preselected sites.

In the centre of what felt like a shallow, wooded basin, the officers grouped together and waited to receive their orders.

Bolitho felt unusually tired and wanted to keep yawning. And yet his mind was very clear, and he guessed that the yawning might also betray his fear. He had known it before. Too often.

Major Paget, still erect and showing no trace of weariness, said. 'Stay with your people. Issue the rations. But mind they waste nothing and leave no trace of their rubbish.' He looked at D'Esterre meaningly. 'You know what to do. Take control of the perimeter. Double the pickets, and tell them to keep *down*.' To Probyn he said, 'You are in charge here, of course. I shall need an officer with me in a moment.'

Probyn sighed. 'You go, Bolitho. If I send Quinn, the major will eat him for breakfast.'

Bolitho reported to Paget after the others had vanished into the gloom to seek out their men. He took Couzens with him, and answered Stockdale's plea to go too by saying firmly, 'Save your strength for when it is needed, as needed it will be!'

In a fight, or in a raging storm at sea, Stockdale was unbeatable. Creeping through unfamiliar territory, when at any second they might stumble on an enemy look-out or patrol, was not his place. His big frame and powerful limbs were enough to wake an army. But it was painful to sense his hurt all the same.

Couzens, on the other hand, was bubbling with excitement. Bolitho had never known anything like it. He seemed to put the awful sights and sounds behind him, dropping them with the tough resilience of youth in war.

Major Paget was drinking from a silver flask while his orderly checked a brace of pistols for him.

He held out the flask. 'Here. Have some.' He leaned forward, his polished boots squeaking. 'Oh, it's you, Bolitho. I've heard about *you*.' He did not elaborate.

Bolitho gasped as the hot brandy trickled over his tongue.

Paget nodded to the midshipman. 'Him, too. Man's drink for a man's work eh?' He chuckled, the sound like two dry sticks rubbing together.

Couzens smacked his lips. 'Thank you, sir. That was lovely!'

Paget looked at Bolitho and exclaimed, *'Lovely'* In hell's name, what sort of a navy is this?'

With the orderly following respectfully at their heels, they set off in a south-westerly direction, the sea to their left, out of sight but comfortingly close.

Bolitho sensed some of D'Esterre's scouts nearby, flitting through the scrub and trees like forest animals as they protected their commanding officer from attack.

They walked on in silence, aware of the lightening sky, the stars fading obediently as the land took shape from the shadows.

They seemed to be moving up a gentle slope now, weaving occasionally to avoid sprawling clumps of prickly bushes and fallen trees.

A dark figure rose out of the shadows, and Paget said, 'Ah, the Canadian *gentleman!*'

The scout greeted them with a lazy wave. 'This is far enough, Major. The rest o' th' way you gets down on yer belly!'

Paget snapped his fingers, and like a footman serving his master a picnic, the marine orderly brought out with a flourish something like a short green cape.

Paget removed his hat and his sword, then slipped the cape over his head. It completely hid his uniform down as far as his waist.

Bolitho could feel the scout and Couzens staring open-mouthed, but when he glanced at the orderly he saw only stiff indifference, and guessed that Paget's own men knew better than to show amusement.

Paget muttered, 'Had the thing made last year. No sense in getting your head blown off by some backwoodsman, what?'

Bolitho grinned. 'Good idea, sir. I've seen poachers use them, too.'

'Huh.' The major lowered himself carefully on to his hands and knees. 'Well, let's get on with it. We'll be pestered by flies and a million sorts of beetles before another hour. I want to be back at the camp by then.'

It took all of half an hour to discover a suitable observation point, and by that time the sky was considerably brighter, and when Bolitho propped himself on his elbows he saw the sea, the horizon like a thin gold thread. He craned forward, the sharp-pointed grass pricking his face and hands, the soil alive with minute insects. With the sun still below the horizon, the lagoon-shaped bay was in darkness, but against the shimmering water, with the restless procession of white horses further to seaward, he could see the fort clearly. A black, untidy shape perched on the end of the low island. He saw two lanterns, and what appeared to be a sheltered fire outside the wall, but little else.

Paget was breathing heavily as he trained a telescope through the grass and rough scrub.

He seemed to be thinking aloud as he muttered, 'Got to be careful at this angle. If the sun comes up suddenly, some fellow down there might see it reflected in this damn glass.'

Couzens whispered to Bolitho, 'Can you see the guns, sir?'

Bolitho shook his head, picturing the marines charging across the alleged causeway into a hail of canister or worse. 'Not yet.' He strained his eyes again. 'The fort is not square, or even rectangular. Six, maybe seven sides. Perhaps one gun per wall.'

The scout wriggled nearer and said, 'They're supposed to have a flat pontoon, Major.' He raised an arm, releasing an even sourer smell. 'When they get supplies sent by land they put th' wagons an' horses on th' pontoon an' haul the thing across.'

Paget nodded. 'As I thought. Well, that's how we'll go. This time tomorrow. While the devils are still asleep.'

The scout sucked his teeth. 'Night-time'd be better.'

Paget replied scornfully, 'The dark is damn useless to every-body, man! No, we'll watch today. Tomorrow we attack.'

'As you say, Major.'

Paget rolled over heavily and peered at Bolitho. 'You take the first watch, eh? Send the boy to me if you sight anything useful.' Then, with remarkable stealth, he was gone.

Couzens smiled tightly, 'Are we alone, sir?' For the first time he sounded nervous.

Bolitho smiled tightly. 'It would seem so. But you saw where the last picket was. If you go back with a message, put yourself in his hands. I don't want you wandering off.'

He drew a pistol from his belt and felt it carefully. Then he unsheathed his hanger and laid it beside him, thrusting the blade into the sand to hide any reflection.

It was going to be very hot before long. Bolitho tried not to think of fresh drinking water.

Couzens said, 'I feel I'm doing something, sir. Something *useful* at last.'

Bolitho sighed. 'I hope you're right.'

By the time the sun's rim had broken above the horizon and

come spilling down towards the fort and its protected anchorage, Bolitho had learned a lot more about his companion. Couzens was the fifth son of a Norfolk clergyman, had a sister called Beth who intended to marry the squire's son if she got half a chance, and whose mother made the best applie pie in the county.

They both fell silent as they peered at the newly revealed fort and its immediate surroundings. Bolitho had been right about its shape. It was hexagonal, and the walls, which were of double thickness and constructed of stout palmetto wood, had their inner sections filled with rocks and packed earth. Both inner and outer wall was covered by a parapet, and Bolitho guessed that even the heaviest ball would find it hard to penetrate such a barrier.

He saw a squat tower on the seaward side, with a flagpole, and a drifting smear of smoke which suggested a galley somewhere below in the central courtyard.

There were the usual loopholes, and as the light strengthened Bolitho saw two gun embrasures pointing towards the mainland and the causeway, and he could also see the shadow of a gateway between them.

Two small boats were pulled up on to the nearest beach, and the skeleton of another, probably the only remains of some skirmish a year or more ago.

Couzens whispered excitedly, 'There, sir! The pontoon!'

Bolitho lowered his eye to the telescope and scanned first the fort and then the moored pontoon. It was a crude affair, with trailing ropes, and slatted ramps for horses and wagons. The sand on both mainland and beach was churned up to mark the many comings and goings.

He moved the glass carefully towards the anchorage. Small, but good enough for two vessels. Brigs and schooners most likely, he thought.

A trumpet echoed over the swirling water, and moments later a flag jerked up to the top of the pole and broke dejectedly towards them. A few heads moved on the parapet, and then Bolitho saw a solitary figure appear from the pontoon's inner ramp, a musket over his shoulder, gripped casually by the muzzle. Bolitho held his breath. That was worth knowing. He had had no idea there was a space there for a sentry.

With daylight spreading inland, and his companions on the move again, the sentry's night vigil was done. If Paget's scheme was going to work, that sentry would have to be despatched first.

As the first hour dragged by, Bolitho studied the fort carefully and methodically, as much to take his mind off the mounting glare and heat than with any purpose in mind.

There did not appear to be many men in the garrison, and the amount of horse tracks by the pontoon suggested that quite a number had left very recently. Probably in response to the news of the British squadron which had been sighted heading further south.

Bolitho thought of Rear-Admiral Coutts' plan, the simplicity of it. He would like to be here now, he thought. Seeing his ideas taking shape.

The Canadian, Macdonald, slid up beside him without a sound and showed his stained teeth.

'It'd bin no use you reachin' fer yer blade, mister!' His grin widened. 'I could'a slit yer throat easy-like!'

Bolitho swallowed hard. 'Most probably.' He saw Quinn and Midshipman Huyghue crawling through the scrub towards him and said, 'We are relieved, it seems.'

Later, when they reached Paget's command post, Bolitho described what he had seen.

Paget said, 'We must get that pontoon.' He looked meaningly at Probyn. 'Job for seamen, eh?'

Probyn shrugged. 'Of course, sir.'

Bolitho sat with his back to a palm and drank some water from a flask.

Stockdale squatted nearby and asked, 'Is it a bad one, sir?'

'I'm not sure yet.'

He saw the pontoon, the sentry stretching as he had emerged from his hiding place. He'd quite likely been asleep. It would not be difficult for such an easily defended fort to become over-confident.

Stockdale watched him worriedly. 'I've made a place for you to lie, sir.' He pointed to a rough cover of brush and fronds. 'Can't fight without sleep.'

Bolitho crawled under the tiny piece of cover, the freshness of the water already gone from his mouth.

It was going to be the longest day of all, he thought grimly, and the waiting unbearable.

He turned his head as he heard someone snoring. It was Couzens, lying on his back, his freckled features burned painfully by the sun.

The sight of such apparent confidence and trust helped to steady Bolitho. Couzens was probably dreaming of his mother's pies, or the sleepy Norfolk village where something or somebody had put the idea in his mind to be a sea officer and leave the land.

Stockdale leaned back against a tree and watched Bolitho fall asleep.

He was still watching when one of D'Esterre's marines crawled through the scrub and hissed, 'Where is the lieutenant?'

Bolitho awoke reluctantly, his mind trying to grapple with where he was and what he was doing.

The marine explained wearily, 'The major's compliments, sir, and would you join 'im where you was this mornin'.'

Bolitho stood up, each muscle protesting violently.

'Why?'

'Mr Quinn sighted a strange sail, sir.'

Bolitho looked at Stockdale and grimaced. 'What timing! It couldn't be at a worse moment!'

It took longer to reach the look-out the second time. The sun was much higher in the sky and the air so humid it was hard to draw breath.

Paget, complete with green cape, was lying with his telescope carefully shaded by some leaves. Probyn sprawled beside him, and further down the slope, trying to find some shade, Quinn and his midshipman looked like survivors from a desert trek.

Paget snapped, 'So here you are.' He relented slightly and added, 'Look for yourself.'

Bolitho took the glass and trained it on the approaching craft. She was broad in the beam, and from her low freeboard he guessed her to be fully laden. She was moving at a snail's pace, her tan-coloured sails flapping uncomfortably as she tacked towards the fort. Three masts on a small, sturdy hull, she was obviously a coasting lugger. There were plenty of such craft along the east coast, as they were good sea-boats, but equally at home in shallow water.

Bolitho wiped the sweat from his eyes and moved the lens on to the fort's square tower. There were quite a lot of heads there now, watching the approaching lugger, and Bolitho saw that the gates were wide open, and some more men were walking unhurriedly below the walls and making for the beach on the far side of the island.

None of the fort's cannon was run out or even manned.

He said, 'Must be expecting her.'

Paget grunted. 'Obviously.'

Probyn complained, 'It'll make our task damn near impossible. We'll have the enemy on two sides of us.' He swore crudely and added, 'Just our luck!'

'I intend to attack *as planned*.' Paget watched the lugger bleakly. 'I can't waste another full day. A patrol might stumble on our people at any moment. Or the *Spite* may return ahead of time to see what we are about.' He thrust out his heavy jaw. 'No. We attack.'

He crawled awkwardly across some sharp stones and snapped, 'I'm going back. Keep watch and tell me what you think later.'

Probyn glared after him. 'He makes me sick!'

Bolitho lay on his back and covered his face with his arms. He was being stung and bitten by tiny, unseen attackers, but he barely noticed. He thought of the lugger and how the unexpected could rearrange a puzzle in seconds.

Probyn said grudgingly, 'Still, he may be right about another delay. And I can't see him calling off the attack altogether.'

Bolitho knew he was watching him and smiled. 'What about you?'

'Me?' Probyn grabbed the telescope again. 'Who cares what I think?'

It was well into the afternoon before the lugger had worked around the end of the island and into the anchorage. As her sails were carelessly brailed up and her anchor dropped, Bolitho saw a boat pulling from the beach towards her.

Probyn looked and sounded tired out. He asked irritably, 'Well, what d'you see?'

Bolitho levelled the glass on the man who was climbing down into the boat. Bravado, conceit, or was it just to display his confidence? But his uniform, so bright against the lugger's untidiness, was clearer than any message.

Bolitho said quietly, 'That's a French officer down there.' He looked sideways at Probyn's features. 'So now we know.'

# 9

# Probyn's Choice

Midshipman Couzens crawled on his hands and knees until he had reached Bolitho at the top of the rise.

'All accounted for, sir.' He peered down the slope towards the sea and the fort's uncompromising outline.

Bolitho nodded. There were a dozen questions at the back of his mind. Had the seamen's weapons been checked to make sure that some nervous soul had not loaded his pistol despite the threats of what would happen to him? Had Couzens impressed on them the vital importance of silence from now on? But it was too late now. He had to trust every man jack of them. Bolitho could sense them at his back, crouching in their unfamiliar surroundings, gripping their weapons, worrying.

At least there was no moon, but against that, the wind had dropped away, and the slow, regular hiss of surf made the only sound. To get the men down to the beach and across to the island without raising an alarm would be doubly difficult without some noise to cover their approach.

He thought of D'Esterre's cool appraisal of the island and its defences. He had studied it through his telescope from three different angles. The fort had at least eight heavy cannon, and several smaller pieces. The garrison, although depleted, appeared to number about forty. Just a dozen men could hold the fort and sweep away a frontal attack without effort. It was a miracle that some hunter or scout had not stumbled on the hidden marines. But this place was like an abandoned coast. They had seen nothing but a few men around the island and the occasional comings and goings from the anchored lugger.

The French officer was thought to be in the fort, although his purpose for being there was still a mystery.

Stockdale hissed, 'Mr Quinn's party is 'ere, sir.'

'Good.' Poor Quinn, he looked like death, and they had not even begun yet. 'Tell him to get ready.'

Bolitho peered through his glass towards the lugger, but saw nothing but her shadow. No riding light to betray her presence, and even some drunken singing had stopped hours ago.

A hand touched his shoulder, and he heard the Canadian scout say, *'Now!'*

Bolitho stood up and followed him down the steep side of the hill towards the water. His shoes loosened stones and sand, and he could feel the sweat running down his chest. It was like being naked, walking towards levelled muskets which at any moment would cut him down.

*Too late now. Too late now.*

He walked steadily behind the other man's shadow, knowing the rest of his party were close on his heels. He could even picture their faces. Men like Rowhurst, the gunner's mate, Kutbi, the staring-eyed Arab, Rabbett, the little thief from Liverpool who had escaped the rope by volunteering for the Navy.

The sea's noises came to meet them, giving them confidence like an old friend.

They paused by some sun-dried bushes while Bolitho took stock of his position. The bushes had looked much larger from the hilltop. Now the seamen crowded behind and amongst them, peering across the rippling water towards the fort, and probably thinking that they were the last cover until they reached those walls.

The Canadian whispered, 'Them there are th' guide ropes fer th' pontoon.'

He was chewing methodically, his body hunched forward as he studied the shelving strip of beach.

Bolitho saw the great timbers which had been raised to carry

the ropes, and found himself praying that their calculations on
tide and distance were right. If the pontoon was hard aground it
would take an army to move it. He thought of the two big
muzzles he had seen pointing towards the mainland and the
hidden causeway. He doubted if the garrison would give them
time for regrets.

He wondered if Paget was watching their progress from some
vantage point, seething with impatience.

Bolitho took a grip on his racing thoughts. This was no
moment to get flustered.

The scout was stripping off his jerkin as he said, 'I'll be goin'
over then.' He could have been remarking on the weather. 'If you
hear nothin', you'd better follow.'

Bolitho reached out and touched the man's shoulder. It was
covered in grease.

He forced himself to say, 'Good luck.'

The scout left the bushes and walked unhurriedly to the
water's edge. Bolitho counted the paces, four, five, six, but
already the Canadian was merging with the water, then he was
gone altogether.

The sentries around the fort stood three-hour watches. Probably because they were short-handed. It would, with luck, make
them extra weary.

The minutes dragged past, and several times Bolitho thought
he heard something, and waited for the alarm to be raised.

Rowhurst muttered, 'Should be long enough, sir.' He had a
bared cutlass in his fist. "*Must* be all right.'

Bolitho looked at the gunner's mate in the darkness. Was he
that confident? Or did he think his lieutenant had lost his nerve
and was merely trying to jolt him into action?

'One more minute.' He beckoned to Couzens. 'Go and tell Mr
Quinn to prepare his men.'

Again he had to check himself. Make sure the ladders were
muffled. Quinn would have seen to that. He must have.

He nodded to Rowhurst. 'You take the left rope.' He beckoned to Stockdale. 'We'll take the right one.'

The seamen had split into two groups, and he saw them
crossing the open beach towards the massive timbers, then up
and out on the sagging ropes. Dangling at first, and then lower
until their legs and then their bodies were pushed and buffeted
by the swirling current.

After the heat of the day and the discomfort of waiting, the water was like cool silk.

Bolitho dragged himself along the rope. It felt greasy, like the scout's shoulder.

Every man in the party was hand-picked. Even so, he could hear a few grunts and gasps, and felt his own arms throbbing with strain.

Then, all of a sudden, they were there, dropping silently on the pontoon's crude deck, peering round with white eyes, waiting for a challenge.

Instead, the scout moved out of the shadows and drawled, 'All done.' 'E never even woke up.'

Bolitho swallowed. He did not need to be told anything more. The luckless sentry must have fallen asleep, to awake with the scout's double-edged hunting knife already sawing into his throat.

He said, 'Rowhurst, you know what to do. Carry on and collect the others. Let the current move the thing.'

Rowhurst nodded patiently. 'Aye, sir. I'll do that.'

Bolitho stepped carefully off the ramp, his foot brushing against an outflung arm where the dead sentry lay at the water's edge. He shut him from his mind as he tried to remember all he had seen here. The fort was on the other side of the narrow island. About half a mile. Less. The sentries would be watching to seaward, if they were watching at all. They had plenty of reason for confidence, he thought. The lugger had taken an age to work around the point, so even firing blindly the fort could cripple a large man-of-war in no time at all.

Nobody in his right mind would anticipate an attack from inland, without even boats provided for the crossing.

Stockdale whispered huskily, 'She's movin', sir.'

The pontoon was slipping away, merging with the shadows and the black mainland beyond.

Bolitho walked towards the fort, his little group of men spreading out on either side. Now he felt really alone, and completely cut off from aid if things went wrong.

After groping their way towards the fort for some while, they discovered a shallow gully and gratefully clambered into it.

Bolitho lay with his telescope propped over the lip of coarse sand and tried to discover some sign of life. But, like the island itself, the fort seemed dead. The original building, long since destroyed by fire and battle, had been constructed to defend the early settlers from attack by Indians. Those hardy adventurers would be laughing now if they could see us, Bolitho thought grimly.

After what seemed like a lifetime a seaman whispered, 'Mr Couzens is comin', sir.'

Led by the Canadian scout, out of breath and grateful to have discovered his companions, Couzens fell into the gully.

He said, 'Mr Quinn is over here now, sir. And Captain D'Esterre with his first section of marines.'

Bolitho let his breath exhale very slowly. Whatever happened now, he was not alone and unsupported. The pontoon would be on its way back, and with any sort of luck more marines would soon be landing.

He whispered, 'Take two men and feel your way along the beach to those boats.' I want them guarded, in case we have to leave with sudden haste.' He could sense the youth's concentration. 'So be off with you.'

He watched him crawl over the lip of the gully with two armed seamen. One less to worry about. There was no sense in Couzens getting killed for such a hazy plan.

It was easy to picture the marines spreading out in two sections, making their way towards the fort's gates while the next to land took station to cover the eventual attack, or retreat.

Bolitho guessed that Probyn would be with the major, if only to make certain he was not forgotten after the excitement was over.

Another figure slithered amongst the tense seamen. It was Quinn's midshipman, out of breath, and quivering with exertion.

'Well, Mr Huyghue?' Bolitho thought suddenly of Sparke in the heat of a fight. Cool, detached. It was easier said than done. 'Is your party ready?'

Huyghue bobbed his head. 'Aye, sir. Ladders and grapnels.' He licked his lips noisily. 'Mr Quinn says it will be light very soon now.'

Bolitho looked at the sky. Quinn must be ill at ease to mention the obvious to his midshipman.

He said, 'We'd best begin, in that case.'

He stood up and loosened his shirt. How many more times like this? When would it be his turn to fall and never get up again?

Bolitho said harshly, 'Follow me.' The unnatural sound of his own voice made him feel slightly unsteady, light-headed. 'Mr Huyghue, remain here and keep a good watch. If we are repulsed, you will join Mr Couzens at the boats.'

Huyghue was shifting from foot to foot, as if he were standing on hot coals.

'And then, sir?'

Bolitho looked at him. 'You will have to decide on that. For I fear there will be none left to advise you!'

He heard Rabbett's little titter, and wondered how anyone could laugh at such a feeble, gruesome joke.

He felt the breeze on his face, soft and coolly caressing, as he strode towards the corner of the fort. It was still a cable away, and yet he felt starkly visible as he made his way towards Quinn's hiding place.

Someone rose to his knees with an aimed musket, but fell prone again as he recognized Bolitho's party.

Quinn was with his men by the ladders, edgy and nervous as he waited for Bolitho to use his telescope.

Bolitho said, 'Nothing. It looks quiet. Very quiet. I think they must place a lot of trust in the seaward entry and the one we left by the beach.' He saw Quinn flinch and added softly, 'Get a *grip*, James. Our people have nothing but us to judge their chances by.' He forced a grin, feeling his lips tighten as if freezing. 'So let us earn our pay, eh?'

Rowhurst strode from the shadows. 'Ready, sir.' He glanced quickly at Quinn. 'No sign of the buggers on this parapet.'

Bolitho turned his back towards the fort and raised his arm. He saw the crouching figures breaking from cover and knew he had committed all of them. There was no turning back.

The ladders were carried swiftly towards the chosen wall, and on either side of them the first party of seamen loped forward, their cutlasses and boarding axes making them look like figures from an old Norman tapestry Bolitho had once seen at Bodmin.

Bolitho gripped Quinn's wrist, squeezing it until he winced with pain.

'We don't know what we'll find, James. But the gates *must* be opened, do you hear me?' He spoke slowly, despite his tumbling thoughts. It was essential for Quinn to hold out now.

Quinn nodded. 'Yes. I—I'll be all right, sir.'

Bolitho released him. 'Dick.'

Quinn stared at him dazedly. 'Dick!'

The first ladder was already rising against the pale stars, up and up, and the second following even as the waiting seamen hurried to steady them.

Bolitho made sure that his hanger was looped around his wrist and then ran lightly to the nearest ladder, knowing that Stockdale was following.

Rowhurst watched Quinn and then tapped his arm, seeing him jump as he hissed, 'Come along, sir!'

With a gasp Quinn ran to the other ladder, scrambling and panting as he pulled himself towards the hard black edge below the stars.

Bolitho hoisted himself over the rough planking and dropped on to the wooden rampart. It was little different from a ship, he thought vaguely, except for the terrible stillness.

He felt his way along a handrail, past a mounted swivel gun and towards where he thought the gates would be. He sucked breath to his aching lungs, seeing the rounded hump on the wall which he knew was directly above the entrance. He could smell the embers of a wood fire, cooking, horses and men. The smell of a tightly packed garrison almost anywhere in the world.

He twisted round as the seaman Rabbett slid forward and brought down the side of his boarding axe on what Bolitho had thought to be a pile of sacks. It was another sentry, or perhaps just a man who had come up to the parapet to find some cool air. It was such a swift and savage blow that Bolitho thought it doubtful if he would draw breath again.

The shock of it helped to tighten his reactions, to compress every ounce of concentration in what he was doing. He found the top of a ladder and knew the gates were just yards away.

Stockdale moved beside him. 'I'll do it, sir.'

Bolitho tried to see his face but there was only shadow. 'We'll do it together.'

With the remainder of the men kneeling or lying on the parapet, Bolitho and Stockdale stepped very slowly down the uneven wooden stairs.

At the other end of that same wall Quinn and his party would be making towards the watch-tower to protect Bolitho from the rear if the guard turned out.

It had all begun in Rear-Admiral Coutts' mind, many miles from this sinister place. Now they were here, when previously Bolitho had thought they would be attacked and beaten back before they had even found a refuge to hide. It had been so ridiculously easy that it was unnerving at the same time.

He felt the ground under his shoes and knew he had reached the courtyard. He could sense rather than discern the low buildings and stables which lined the inner walls, but when he looked at the tower he discovered he could see the flagpole and the paling sky above.

Stockdale touched his arm and pointed towards a small outthrust hut beyond the gates. There was a soft glow of light through some shutters, and Bolitho guessed it was where the guard took its rest between watches.

He whispered, 'Come.'

It took only seven paces to reach the centre of the gates. Bolitho found he was counting each one as if his life depended on it. There was a long beam resting on iron slots to secure the gates, and nothing more. Stockdale laid down his cutlass and took the weight of the bar at one end while Bolitho watched the hut.

It was just as Stockdale put his great strength under the beam that it happened. A terrified shout, rising to a shrill scream, before being cut off instantly as if slammed behind a massive door.

For an instant longer nobody moved or spoke, and then as startled voices and padding feet echoed around the courtyard Bolitho yelled, 'Open it! Fast as you can!'

Shots cracked and banged haphazardly, and he heard them slamming into timber or whistling harmlessly towards the water. He could imagine the confusion and pandemonium it was causing, and plenty of the garrison must still be thinking the attack was coming from outside the defences.

Light spilled from the guard hut, and Bolitho saw figures running towards him, one firing his musket and then being knocked down by more men who were charging out, palely naked against the shadows.

He heard someone yell, 'Load and fire at will, lads!'

Then steel grated on steel, and more shouts changed to screams and desperate cries before anyone from Bolitho's party could fire.

A man lunged at him with a bayoneted musket, but he parried it away, letting the charge carry his attacker past, gasping with terror, until the hanger slashed him down at Stockdale's feet.

Bolitho yelled, 'To me, Trojans!'

There were more cries and then cheers as the first gate began to move and Stockdale heaved the great beam aside, hurling it amongst the confused figures by the hut like a giant's lance.

But others were appearing from across the courtyard, and some semblance of order came with shouted commands, a responding rattle of musket-fire which hurled two seamen from the parapet like rag dolls.

Stockdale snatched up his cutlass and slashed a man across the chest, turning just enough to take a second in the stomach as he tried to stab under Bolitho's guard.

Kutbi, the Arab, screamed shrilly and ran forward, whirling his axe like a madman, oblivious to everything but the urge to kill.

Another seaman fell coughing blood by Bolitho's feet, and he heard Quinn's men clashing blades with the guards from the tower, getting nearer and louder as they were driven back towards the gates.

Clang, clang, clang. Bolitho thought his arm would break as he hacked and parried at a uniformed figure which had seemingly risen from the ground beneath him. He could feel the man's strength, his determination, as step by step he drove him back, and further still.

Bolitho felt strangely clear-headed, devoid of fear or any recognizable sensation. This must be the moment. What it was like. The end of luck. Of everything.

Clang, clang, clang.

He locked his hilt with the other man's, sensing his power against his own fading strength. Vaguely he heard Stockdale bellowing, trying to cut his way through to help him.

Instinct told him there was no help this time, and as the other man swung him round, using the locked hilts like a hinge, he saw a pistol protruding from his belt. With one last agonizing effort he flung himself forward, letting his sword-arm drop while he snatched for the trigger, cocking the weapon and firing even as he tore it free.

The explosion threw it from his hand, and he saw the man double over, his agony too terrible even for screams as the heavy ball ripped through his groin like molten lead.

Bolitho raised his hanger, swayed over the writhing man and then lowered it again. It would be kinder to free him from his agony forever, but he could not do it.

The next moment the other gate was being thrust aside, and through the drifting smoke of musket and pistol fire Bolitho saw the white cross-belts and the faintly glittering bayonets as the marines surged through.

There were a few last pockets of resistance. Handfuls of men, fighting and dying in a cellar and on the parapet. Some tried to surrender, but were shot down in a wave of madness by the victorious marines. Others burst through the gates and ran for the sea, only to be trapped by Paget's next cordon of muskets.

Probyn limped through the chaos of dying men and prisoners with their hands in the air. He saw Bolitho and grunted, 'That was close.'

Bolitho nodded, leaning against a horse-rail, sucking air into his aching body. He looked at Probyn's limp and managed to gasp, 'Are you wounded?'

Probyn replied hotly, 'Got tripped by some fools with a ladder! Might have broken my damn leg!'

It was so absurd in the midst of all the pain and death that Bolitho wanted to laugh. But he knew if he did he would not be able to stop or control it.

D'Esterre came from beneath the stable roof and said, 'The fort is taken. It's done.' He turned to receive his hat from a marine and brushed it against his leg before adding, 'The devils had a gun already loaded and trained on the causeway. If they had been warned we would have been cut down completely, attacking *or* running away!'

Rowhurst waited until Bolitho had seen him and then said heavily, 'We lost three men, sir.' He gestured with his thumb towards the tower. 'An' two badly wounded.'

Bolitho asked quietly, 'And Mr Quinn?'

Rowhurst replied gruffly, "E's all right, sir.'

What did that mean? Bolitho saw Paget and more marines coming through the open gates and decided not to press further. Not yet.

Paget looked at the hurrying marines and seamen and snapped. 'Where is the fort's commanding officer?'

D'Esterre said, 'He was absent, sir. But we have taken his second-in-command.'

Paget snorted. 'He'll do. Show me to his quarters.' He looked at Probyn. 'Have your people lay a couple of heavy cannon on that lugger. If she tries to make sail, dissuade her, what?'

Probyn touched his hat and muttered sourly, 'He's having a fine time, and no mistake!'

Rowhurst was already looking up at the gun embrasures with a professional eye. 'I'll attend to the lugger, sir.' He strode off, yelling names, glad to be doing something he understood.

The man whose pistol Bolitho had used just minutes earlier gave a single cry and then died. Bolitho stood looking at him, trying to discover his feelings towards someone who had tried to kill him.

A marine from the *Trojan* marched across the courtyard and could barely stop himself from grinning as he reported, 'Beg pardon, sir, but one of your young gennelmen 'as caught a prisoner!'

At that moment Couzens and two seamen came through the gates. Leading them, for that was how it looked, was the French officer, his coat over one arm and carrying his cocked hat as if going for a stroll.

Couzens exclaimed, 'He was making for the boats, sir. Ran right into us!' He was glowing with pride at his capture.

The Frenchman glanced from Bolitho to Probyn and said calmly, 'Not *running*, I assure you! Merely taking advantage of circumstances.' He bowed his head. 'I am Lieutenant Yves Contenay. At your service.'

Probyn glared at him. 'You are under arrest, damn you!'

The Frenchman gave a gentle smile. 'I think not. I command yonder vessel. I put in for...' He shrugged. 'The reason is unimportant.'

He looked up as some seamen used handspikes to train one of the cannon further round towards the anchorage. For the first time he showed alarm, even fear.

Probyn said, 'I see. Unimportant. Well, I shall expect you to tell your people not to attempt to leave, or to damage the vessel in any way. If they do, I will have them fired upon without quarter.'

'I believe that.' Contenay turned to Bolitho and spread his hands. 'I have my orders also, you know.'

Bolitho watched him, the strain dragging at his body like claws. 'Your lugger is carrying gunpowder, is she not?'

The Frenchman frowned. 'Lug-ger?' Then he nodded. 'Ah, yes, *lougre*, I understand.' He shrugged again. 'Yes. If you put one shot into her, *pouf*!'

Probyn snapped, 'Stay with him. I must go and tell the major.'

Bolitho looked at Couzens. 'Well done.'

The French officer smiled. 'Indeed, yes.'

Bolitho watched the bodies being dragged from the gates and the guard hut. Two of the prisoners in their blue and white uniforms were already being put to work with brooms and buckets to clear away the blood.

He said quietly, 'You will be *asked* about your cargo, *m'sieu*. But you know that.'

'Yes. I am under official orders. There is no law to stop me. My country respects the revolution. It does not respect your oppression.'

Bolitho asked dryly, 'And France hopes to gain nothing, of course?'

They both grinned at each other like conspirators, while Couzens, robbed of some of his glory, watched in confusion.

Two lieutenants, Bolitho thought. Caught up in a tidal wave of rebellion and war. It would be hard to dislike this French officer.

But he said, 'I suggest you do nothing to rouse Major Paget.'

'Just so.' Contenay tapped the side of his nose. 'You have officers like that too, do you?'

As Probyn returned with a marine escort, Bolitho asked, 'Where did you learn such good English, *m'sieu*?'

'I lived in England for a long time.' His smile widened. 'It will be useful one day, *oui*?'

Probyn snapped, 'Take him to Major Paget.' He watched the man go with his escort and added angrily, 'You should have shot him, Mr Couzens, dammit! He'll be exchanged for one of our officers, don't doubt it. Bloody privateers, I'd hang the lot of 'em, theirs and ours!'

Stockdale called, 'See the flag, sir!'

Bolitho looked up at the garrison flag which Paget had sensibly ordered to be hoisted in the usual way. There was no sense in drawing suspicion from sea or land until they had finished what they had begun.

But he knew what Stockdale meant. Instead of flapping lazily towards the land, it was lifting and falling towards the brightening horizon. The wind had completely changed direction overnight. Up to now, everyone had been too busy and apprehensive to notice.

He said quietly, '*Spite* will not be able to stand inshore.'

Probyn's palm rasped across his bristles as he replied anxiously, 'But it'll shift back again. You see if it don't.'

Bolitho turned his back on the sea and studied the hillside where he and Couzens had baked in the sun. From the fort it looked different again. Dark and brooding.

'But until it does, *we* are the defenders here!'

Major Paget squatted on the corner of a sturdy table and eyed his weary officers grimly.

Sunlight streamed through the windows of the garrison commander's room, and through a weapon slit Bolitho could see the trees along the shore and a small sliver of beach.

It was halfway into the morning, and still without a sight of friend or enemy.

That did not mean they had not kept busy. On the contrary, with the captured French lieutenant as hostage, Probyn and an escort of armed marines had been pulled across to the lugger.

When he had eventually returned he had described the vessel's cargo for Paget's benefit. She was full to the deck seams with West Indian gunpowder, several stands of French muskets, pistols and numerous pieces of military equipment.

Paget said, 'She is a very valuable capture. Denying the enemy her cargo will do Washington's campaign some damage, I can assure you, gentlemen. If we are attacked here before help comes for us, it seems very likely that the enemy will destroy the lugger if they cannot recapture her. I intend that she should not fall into their hands again.'

Bolitho heard the tramp of marching feet and the hoarse cries of the marine sergeants. Paget's assessment made very good sense. Fort Exeter had to be destroyed, and with it all the defences, weapons and equipment which had been gathered over the months.

But it would take time, and it seemed unlikely that it could be long before the enemy counter-attacked.

'I am in command of this operation.' Paget ran his eyes over them as if expecting an argument. 'It falls to me to appoint a prize crew for the lugger, to sail her without delay to New York, or to report to any King's ship whilst on passage there.'

Bolitho tried to contain his sudden excitement. The lugger had a crew of natives which had been recruited by the French authorities in Martinique. No wonder a man like Lieutenant Contenay had been picked for such a small and lonely command. He was a cut above many officers Bolitho had met, and well suited for such arduous work. It was no mean task to sail the lugger from Martinique in the Caribbean all the way to this poorly charted anchorage.

Even with such a devastating and lethal cargo she would make a pleasant change from this, he thought. And once in New York, anything might happen before *Trojan*'s authority caught up with him again. A frigate perhaps? Going back to the most junior aboard a frigate would be reward enough.

He thought he had misheard as Paget continued, 'Mr Probyn is to command. He will take some of the lesser wounded men to watch over the native crew.'

Bolitho turned, expecting Probyn to explode in protest. Then it came to him. After all, why should not Probyn feel as he did? Go with the prize and present himself to the commander-in-chief in the hopes of getting a better appointment, and promotion to boot.

Probyn was so obsessed with the idea he had not touched a drop of wine or brandy, even after taking the fort. He was not shrewd enough to see beyond the new prize and his eventual entrance to Sandy Hook, not the sort of man to consider that others might think it strange for so senior a lieutenant to take so small a command.

Probyn stood up, his features showing satisfaction better than any speech.

Paget added, 'I will write the necessary orders, unless...' he glanced at Bolitho, 'you intend to change your mind?'

Probyn's jaw lifted firmly. 'No, sir. It is my right.'

The major glared at him. 'Only if I say so.' He shrugged. 'But so be it.'

D'Esterre murmured, 'I am sorry for your missed chance, Dick, but I cannot say the same of your remaining with us.'

Bolitho tried to smile. 'Thank you. But I think poor George Probyn may soon be back in *Trojan*. He is likely to run into a senior ship on his journey whose captain may have other ideas about the lugger's cargo.'

Paget's eyebrows knitted together. 'When you have quite *finished*, gentlemen!'

D'Esterre asked politely, 'What of the French lieutenant, sir?'

'He will remain with us. Rear-Admiral Coutts will be interested to meet him before the authorities in New York get the chance.' He gave a stiff smile. 'If you can see my point?'

The major stood up and flicked some sand from his sleeve. 'Be about your affairs, and see that your men are on the alert.'

Probyn waited by the door for Bolitho and said curtly, 'You are the senior here now.' His eyes glittered through his tiredness. 'And I wish you luck with this rabble!'

Bolitho watched him impassively. Probyn was not that much senior in years, but looked almost as old as Pears.

He asked, 'Why all this bitterness?'

Probyn sniffed. 'I have never had any real luck, or the background of your family to support me.' He raised his fist to Bolitho's sudden anger. 'I came from nothing, had to drag myself up every rung by my fingernails! You think I should have asked for you to be sent with the lugger, eh? What's a damned Frenchie blockade-runner to a senior lieutenant like me, that's what you're thinking!'

Bolitho sighed. Probyn was deeper than he had imagined. 'It did cross my thoughts.'

'When Sparke was killed, the next chance fell to me. I took it, and I intend to exploit it to the fullest range, d'you see?'

'I think so.' Bolitho looked away, unable to watch Probyn's torment.

'You can wait for the relief to arrive, then you can tell Mr bloody Cairns, and anyone else who might be interested, that I'm not coming back to *Trojan*. But if I ever do have to visit the ship, I will be piped aboard as a captain in my own right!'

He swung on his heel and walked off. Whatever pity or understanding Bolitho might have felt melted when he realized that Probyn had no intention of speaking with the men he was leaving behind, or visiting those who would die from their wounds before the lugger had tacked clear of the anchorage.

D'Esterre joined him on the parapet and watched Probyn as he marched purposefully along the beach towards one of the long-boats.

'I hope to God he stays out of his cups, Dick. With a hull full of powder, and a crew of frightened natives, it could be a rare voyage if George returns to his favourite pastime!' He saw his sergeant waiting for him and hurried away.

Bolitho went down one of the stairways and found Quinn

leaning against a wall. He was supposed to be supervising the collection of side-arms and powder flasks, but was letting his men do as they pleased.

Bolitho said, 'Well, you heard what the major had to say, and what Probyn said to me just now. I have a few ideas of my own, but first I want to know what happened at dawn when we attacked.' He waited, remembering the awful cry, the bark of musket fire.

Quinn said huskily, 'A man came out of the watch-tower. We were all so busy, looking at the gates and trying to mark down the sentries. He just seemed to come from nowhere.' He added wretchedly, 'I was the nearest. I could have cut him down easily.' He shuddered. 'He was just a youngster, stripped to the waist and carrying a bucket. I think he was going down to get some water for the galley. He was unarmed.'

'What then?'

'We stood looking at each other. I am not sure who was the more surprised. I had my blade to his neck. One blow, but I couldn't do it.' He looked desperately at Bolitho. 'He knew it, too, We just stood there until . . .'

'Rowhurst, was it?'

'Yes. With his dirk. But he was too late.'

Bolitho nodded. 'I thought we were done for.' He recalled his own feelings as he had stood over the man he had shot to save himself.

Quinn said, 'I saw the look in the gunner's mate's eyes. He despises me. It will go through the ship like fire. I'll never be able to hold their respect after this.'

Bolitho ran his fingers through his hair. 'You'll have to try and earn it, James.' He felt the sand and grit in his fingers and longed for a bath or a swim. 'But we've work here now.' He saw Stockdale and some seamen watching him. 'Take those hands to the pontoon directly. It is to be warped into deep water and broken up.' He gripped his arm and added, 'Think of them, James. *Tell* them what you want done.'

Quinn turned and walked dejectedly towards the waiting men. At least with Stockdale in charge he should be all right, Bolitho thought.

A petty officer knuckled his forehead and asked, 'We've broached the main magazine, zur?' He waited patiently, his eyes like those of a sheepdog.

Bolitho collected his thoughts, while his mind and body still tried to detain him. But it had to be faced. He *was* in charge of the seamen, just as Probyn had said.

He said, 'Very well, I'll come and see what you've found.'

Cannon had to be spiked and made useless, stores to be set alight before the fort itself was blasted to fragments with its own magazine. Bolitho glanced at the empty stables as he followed the petty officer into the shade. He was thankful there were no horses left in the fort. The thought of having to slaughter them to deny them to the enemy was bad enough. What it might have done to the battle-wearied seamen was even worse. Death, injury or punishment under the lash, the average sailor seemed to accept as his lot. But Bolitho had seen a boatswain's mate split open a man's head in Plymouth, merely for kicking a stray dog.

Marines bustled everywhere, in their element as they prepared long fuses, stowed casks of powder and trundled the smaller field-pieces towards the gates.

By the time the work was half completed, the pontoon had been warped into deep water, and from a parapet Bolitho saw the seamen hacking away the ropes and destroying the ramp with their axes. Small in the distance, Quinn stood watching them. The next time he was thrown into a fight he would not be so lucky, Bolitho decided sadly.

He saw Midshipman Couzens in the watch-tower, a telescope trained towards the anchorage. When he turned, Bolitho saw the lugger making sail, her anchor swinging and dripping as it was hoisted to the cathead.

The same wind which would delay *Spite* should carry Probyn and his little command well clear of the land by nightfall. Pity was never a good reason for making friends, Bolitho thought. But it had been a bad parting, and if they ever met again, it would be between them, of that he was certain.

'So there you are, Bolitho!' Paget peered down from his crude window. 'Come up here and I will give you your instructions.'

In the room once again, Bolitho felt the weariness, the aftermath of destruction and fear, pulling him down.

Paget said, 'Another piece of intelligence. We now know where the enemy are getting some of their armaments and powder, eh?' He watched Bolitho narrowly. 'It's up to the admiral now.'

There was a rap at the door, and Bolitho heard someone whispering urgently outside.

'*Wait!*' Paget said calmly, 'I had no choice over the lugger. She was yours by right, in my view, because of the manner in which you opened the fort for us.' He shrugged heavily. 'But the Navy's ways are not mine, and so . . .'

'I *understand*, sir.'

'Good. Paget moved across the room with remarkable speed and flung open the door. '*Well*, man?'

It was Lieutenant FitzHerbert of the flagship's marines.

He stammered, 'We have sighted the enemy, sir! Coming up the coast!'

Together they walked into the blinding sunlight, and Paget calmly took a telescope from one of the sentries. Then after a full minute he handed it to Bolitho.

'There's a sight for you. I reckon your Mr Probyn will be sorry to miss it.'

Bolitho soon forgot his disappointment and the major's sarcasm as he trained the glass towards the shore. There must be a track there, following the sea's edge, probably all the way to Charles Town.

Weaving along it was a slow-moving ribbon of blue and white. It was broken here and there by horses, and shining black shapes which could only be artillery.

Paget folded his arms and rocked back on his heels. 'So here they come. No use trying any more deceptions, I think.' He looked up at the pole, his eyes red-rimmed with strain.

'Run up the colours, Sergeant! It'll give 'em something to rant about!'

Bolitho lowered the glass. Quinn was still down by the partly wrecked pontoon, oblivious to the threatening column coming up the road. Probyn was too involved in working his vessel clear of the sand-pit to notice it, or care much if he did.

He swung the glass towards the horizon, his eyes stinging in the fierce glare. Nothing broke the sharp blue line to betray the presence of a friendly sail.

He thought of the captured French officer. With any luck, his captivity would be one of the shortest on record.

Paget barked, 'Stir yourself, sir! Main battery to be manhandled towards the causeway. You have a good runner with you, I believe? Tell him I want a full charge in each weapon. This is going to be hot work, dammit!'

Bolitho made to hurry away, but Paget added firmly, 'I don't care what they promise or offer. We came to destroy this place, and we will, so help me God!'

When Bolitho reached the courtyard he turned and looked again at the tower. Paget was standing bareheaded in the sun, staring at the newly hoisted Jack which the marines had brought with them.

Then he heard a seaman say quietly to his friend. 'Mister Bolitho don't look too troubled, Bill. Can't be anythin' we won't be able to tackle.'

Bolitho glanced at them as he passed, his heart both heavy and proud. They did not question why they were here, or even where they were. Obedience, trust, hope, they were as much part of these men as their cursing and brawling.

He met Rowhurst by the gate. 'You have heard, no doubt?'

Rowhurst grinned. 'Seen 'em too, sir. Like a whole bloody army on the march! Just for us!'

Bolitho smiled gravely. 'We've plenty of time to get ready.'

'Aye, sir.' Rowhurst looked meaningly at the mounting pile of powder casks and fuses. 'One thing, they won't have to bury us. They'll just have to pick up the bits!'

# *10*

# *Night Action*

Bolitho entered the room at the top of the tower, where the former garrison commander had lived out his spartan days, and found Paget discussing a map with D'Esterre.

Bolitho asked, 'You sent for me, sir?'

He barely recognized his own voice. He had got past tiredness, almost to a point of exhaustion. All through the day he had hurried from one task to another, conscious the whole time of that far-off blue and white column as it weaved in and out of sight along the coast. Now it had vanished altogether, and it seemed likely that the road turned sharply inland before dividing opposite the island.

Paget glanced up sharply. He had shaved, and looked as if he had been freshly pressed with his uniform.

'Yes. Won't be long now, what?' He gestured to a chair. 'All done?'

Bolitho sat down stiffly. *All done*. Like an endless muddle of jobs. Dead had been buried, prisoners moved to a place where they could be guarded by the minimum of men. Stores and water checked, powder stacked in the deep magazine to create one devastating explosion once the fuses were set and fired. The heavy field-pieces manhandled to the landward side to be trained on the causeway and the opposite stretch of shoreline.

He replied, 'Aye, sir. And I've brought all the seamen inside the fort as you ordered.'

'Good.' Paget poured some wine and pushed the goblet across the table. 'Have some. Not too bad, considering.'

The major continued, 'You see, it's mostly a matter of bluff. We know quite a lot about these fellows, but they'll not know much about us. Yet. They'll see my marines, but one redcoat looks much like another. Anyway, why *should* the enemy think we are marines, eh? Could just as easily be a strong force of skirmishers who have cut through their lines. That'll give 'em something to worry about.'

Bolitho glanced at D'Esterre, but his normally agile face was expressionless, so Bolitho guessed he and not Paget had thought up the idea of concealing the presence of his sailors.

It made sense, too. After all, there were no boats, and who better than the returning garrison commander would know the impossibility of getting a man-of-war into the anchorage without passing those heavy cannon?

The wind showed no sign of changing direction, and in fact had gained in strength. All afternoon it had driven a pall of dust from the distant marching column out across the sea like gunsmoke.

Paget said, 'Hour or so to sunset. But they'll make themselves felt before dark. That's my wager.'

Bolitho looked across the room and through a narrow window. He could just see part of the hillside where he had lain with young Couzens, a million years ago. The sun-scorched bushes and scrub were moving in the wind like coarse fur, and everything was painted in fiery hues by the evening light.

The marines were down by the uprooted timbers where the pontoon had been moored. Dug into little gullies, they were invisible to eyes across the restless strip of water.

D'Esterre had done a good job of it. Now they all had to sit and wait.

Bolitho said wearily, 'Water is the problem, sir. They always brought it from a stream further down the coast. There's not much left. If they guess we're waiting for a ship to take us off the island, they will know exactly how much time they have. And us, too.'

Paget sniffed. 'I'd thought of that, naturally. They'll try to bombard us out, but there *we* have the advantage. That beach is too soft to support artillery, and it will take another day at least for them to move their heavier pieces up the hill to hit us from there. As for the causeway, I'd not fancy a frontal attack along it, even at low water!'

Bolitho saw D'Esterre give a small smile. He was probably thinking it was exactly what would have been expected of him and his men if Bolitho had failed to open the gates.

The door banged open and the marine lieutenant from the flagship said excitedly, 'Enemy in sight, sir!'

Paget glared. 'Really, Mr FitzHerbert, this is a garrison, not a scene from Drury Lane, dammit!'

Nevertheless, he got up and walked into the hot glare, reaching for a telescope as he strode to the parapet.

Bolitho rested his hands on the sun-dried wood and stared at the land. Two horsemen, five or six foot soldiers and a large black dog. He had not expected to see the whole enemy column crammed on to the narrow beach, but the little group was a complete anticlimax.

Paget said, 'They're looking at the pontoon ramps. I can almost hear their brains rattling!'

Bolitho glanced at him. Paget really was enjoying it.

One of the horsemen dismounted and the dog ran across to him, waiting for something to happen. His master, obviously the senior officer present, reached down to fondle his head, the movement familiar, without conscious thought.

FitzHerbert asked cautiously, 'What will they do, sir?'

Paget did not answer immediately. He said, 'Look at those horses, D'Esterre. See how their hoofs are digging into the sand. The only piece of supported road led to the pontoon loading point.' He lowered the glass and chuckled dryly. 'Never thought *they'd* have to attack, I imagine!'

Sergeant Shears called, 'Saw some more of 'em on the hillside, sir!'

"Can't hit us with a musket from there, thank God.' Paget rubbed his hands. 'Tell your gunner to put a ball down on the end of the causeway.' He looked at Bolitho sharply. '*Now.*'

Rowhurst listened to Paget's order with obvious enthusiasm. 'Good as done, sir.'

With some of his men at their handspikes, and others slackening or tightening the tackles, he soon trained the cannon towards the wet bank of sand nearest the land.

'Stand clear, lads!'

Bolitho yelled, 'Keep out of sight, you men! Stockdale, see that our people stay down!'

The crash of the single shot echoed around the fort and across the water like thunder. Scores of birds rose screaming from the trees, and Bolitho was just in time to see a tall spurt of sand as it received the heavy ball like a fist. The horses shied violently and the dog ran round and round, his bark carrying excitedly across the water.

Bolitho grinned and touched Rowhurst's arm. 'Reload.' He strode back to the tower and saw Quinn watching him from the other parapet.

Paget said, 'Good. Fine shot. Just close enough for them to know we're ready and able.'

A few moments later Sergeant Shears called, 'Flag o' truce, sir!'

One horseman was cantering towards the causeway where a tendril of smoke still drifted to mark the fall of shot.

Paget snapped, 'Ready with another ball, Mr Bolitho.'

'It's a flag of truce, sir.' Bolitho forgot his tiredness and met Paget's glare stubbornly. 'I cannot tell Rowhurst to fire on it.'

Paget's eyebrows rose with astonishment. 'What is this? A spark of honour?' He turned to D'Esterre. 'Explain it to him.'

D'Esterre said quietly, 'They'll want to sound us out, discover our strength. They are not fools. One sight of a marine's coat and they'll know how we came, and what for.'

FitzHerbert said unhelpfully, 'The horseman is an officer, sir.'

Bolitho shaded his eyes to follow the distant horse and rider. How was it possible to argue over honour and scruples at such a moment? Today or tomorrow he would be expected to cut down that same man if need be, without question or thought. And yet . . .

He said bluntly, 'I'll put a ball in the centre of the causeway.'

Paget turned from studying the little group on the beach. 'Oh, very well. But do get *on* with it!'

The second shot was equally well aimed, and threw spray and sand high into the air while the horseman struggled to regain control of his startled mount.

Then he turned and trotted back along the beach.

'Now they know.' Paget seemed satisfied. 'I think I'd like a glass of wine.' He left them and re-entered his room.

D'Esterre smiled grimly. 'I suspect Emperor Nero was something of a Paget, Dick!'

Bolitho nodded and moved to the seaward side of the tower. Of Probyn's new command there was no trace, and he pictured her gaining more and more distance in the favourable off-shore wind. If the enemy column had seen the vessel leave, they would assume she had turned away at the sight of the redcoats. Otherwise, why should not the fort's new occupiers go with her?

Bluff, stalemate, guessing, it all added up to one thing. What would they do if the sloop did not or could not come to take them off the island? If the water ran out, would Paget surrender? It seemed unlikely the enemy commander would be eager to be lenient after they had blown up his fort and every weapon with it.

He leaned over the parapet and looked at the seamen who were sitting in the shadows waiting for something to do. If the water ran out, could these same men be expected to obey, or keep their hands off the plentiful supply of rum they had unearthed by the stables?

Bolitho recalled Paget's words. He knew where the enemy were getting much of their powder and shot. The information would be little help to Rear-Admiral Coutts if their brave escapade ended here.

Just to be back in *Trojan*, he thought suddenly. After this he would never complain again. Even if he remained one of her lieutenants for the rest of his service.

The very thought made him smile in spite of his uncertainty. He knew in his heart that if he survived this time he would be as eager as ever to make his own way.

He heard Lieutenant Raye of *Trojan*'s marines clattering up the ladder and reporting to D'Esterre.

To Bolitho it was another sort of life. Tactics and strategy which moved at the speed of a man's feet or a horseman's gallop. No majesty of sail, no matter how frail when the guns roared. Just men, and uniforms, dropping into the earth when their time came. Forgotten.

He felt a chill at the nape of his neck as D'Esterre said to the two lieutenants, 'I feel certain they will attack tonight. An

assault to test us out, to be followed up if we are caught un-
awares. I want two platoons on immediate readiness. The guns
will have to fire over their heads, so keep 'em down in their
gullies until I give the word.' He turned and looked meaningly at
Bolitho. 'I'll want two guns by the causeway as soon as it gets
dark. We might lose them if we fall back, but we stand no chance
unless we can give them bloody noses at the first grapple.'

Bolitho nodded. 'I'll see to it.' How calm he sounded. A
stranger.

He remembered his feelings as he had stood facing the fort
with the pontoon moving away in the darkness. If the enemy
broke through the causeway pickets, it was a long way to the
gates for those in retreat.

D'Esterre was watching him gravely. 'It sounds worse than it
is. We must be ready. Keep our men on the alert and together.
We might find ourselves with visitors after dark.' He gestured to
the roughly dressed Canadian scouts. 'Two can play their game.'

As shadows deepened between island and mainland, the
marines and seamen settled down to wait. The beach was empty
once more, and only the churned up sand betrayed where the
horses and men had stood to watch the fort.

Paget said, 'Clear night, but no moon.' He wiped one eye and
swore. 'Bloody wind! Constant reminder of our one weakness!'

Bolitho, with Stockdale close by his side, left the fort and
went to watch the two guns being hauled down to the causeway.
It was hard, back-breaking work, and there were no laughs or
jests now.

It seemed cold after the day's heat, and Bolitho wondered
how he could go through another night without sleep. How any
of them could. He passed little gullies, their occupants revealed
only by their white cross-belts as they crouched and cradled their
muskets and watched the glitter of water.

He found Quinn with Rowhurst, siting the second cannon,
arranging powder and shot so that it would be easily found and
used in total darkness.

Stockdale wheezed, 'Who'd be a soldier, eh, sir?'

Bolitho thought of the soldiers he had known in England.
The local garrison at Falmouth, the dragoons at Bodmin.
Wheeling and stamping to the delight of churchgoers on a
Sunday, and little boys at any time.

This was entirely different. Brute force, and a determination
to match anything which came their way. On desert or muddy

field, the soldier's lot was perhaps the worst of all. He wondered briefly how the marines saw it? The best or the worst of their two worlds?

Quinn hurried across to him, speaking fast and almost incoherent.

'They say it will be tonight. Why can't we fall back to the fort? When we attacked it they said the cannon commanded the causeway and the pontoon. So why not the same for the enemy?'

'Easy, James. Keep your voice low. We must hold them off the island. They know this place. We only think we know it. Just a handful of them around the fort and who knows what could happen.'

Quinn dropped his head. 'I've heard talk. They don't want to die for a miserable little island which none of them had ever heard of before.'

'You know why we came.' He was surprised yet again by the tone of his own voice. It seemed harder. Colder. But Quinn must understand. If he broke now, it would not be a mere setback, it would be a headlong rout.

Quinn replied, 'The magazine. The fort. But what will it matter, really count for, after we're dead? It's a pin-prick, a gesture.'

Bolitho said quietly, 'You wanted to be a sea officer, more than anything. Your father wanted differently, for you to stay with him in the City of London.' He watched Quinn's face, pale in the darkness, hating himself for speaking as he was, as he must. 'Well, I think he was right. More than you knew. He realized you would never make a King's officer. Not now. Not ever.' He swung away, shaking off Quinn's hand and saying, 'Take the first watch here. I will relieve you directly.'

He knew Quinn was staring after him, wretched and hurt.

Stockdale said, 'That took a lot to speak like so, sir. I know 'ow you cares for the young gentleman, but there's others wot depends on 'im.'

Bolitho paused and looked at him. Stockdale understood. Was always there when he needed him.

'Thank you for that.'

Stockdale shrugged his massive shoulders and said, 'It's nothing. But I thinks about it sometimes.'

Bolitho touched his arm, warmed and moved by his ungainly companion. 'I'm sure you do, Stockdale.'

Two hours dragged past. The night got colder, or seemed to,

and the first stiffening tension was giving way to fatigue and aching discomfort.

Bolitho was between the fort and the causeway when he stopped dead and turned his face towards the mainland.

Stockdale stared at him and then nodded heavily. *'Smoke.'*

It was getting thicker by the second, acrid and rasping to eyes and throat as it was urged across the island by the wind. There were flames too, dotted about like malicious orange feathers, changing shape through the smoke, spreading and then linking in serried lines of fires.

Midshipman Couzens, who had been walking behind them, asleep on his feet, gasped, 'What does it mean?'

Bolitho broke into a run. 'They've fired the hillside. They'll attack under the smoke.'

He forced his way through groups of startled, retching marines until he found the cannon.

'Get ready to fire!' He picked out FitzHerbert with one of his corporals, a handkerchief wrapped around his mouth and nose. 'Will you tell the major?'

FitzHerbert shook his head, his eyes streaming. 'No time. He'll know anyway.' He dragged out his sword and yelled, *'Stand to! Face your front!* Pass the word to the other section!'

He was groping about, coughing and peering for his men, as more marines ran through the smoke, D'Esterre's voice controlling them, demanding silence, restoring some sort of order.

Couzens forgot himself enough to seize Bolitho's sleeve and murmur, 'Listen! Swimming!'

Bolitho pulled out his hanger and felt for his pistol. Near his home in Cornwall there was a ford across a small river. But sometimes, especially in the winter, it flooded and became impassable to wagons and coaches. But he had seen and heard horses often enough to know what was happening now.

'They're swimming their mounts across!'

He swung round as above the sounds of water and hissing fires he heard a long-drawn-out cheer.

D'Esterre shouted, 'They're coming from the causeway as well!' He pushed through his men and added, 'Keep 'em down, Sar'nt! Let the cannon have their word first!'

Some armed seamen amongst them blundered out of the darkness and slithered to a halt as Bolitho called, 'Keep with me! Follow the beach!' His mind was reeling, grappling with the swiftness of events, the closeness of disaster.

A cannon roared out, and from somewhere across the water he heard the cheers falter, broken by a chorus of cries and screams.

The second cannon blasted the darkness apart with its long orange tongue, and Bolitho heard the ball smashing into men and sand, and pictured Quinn stricken with fear as the defiant cheers welled back as strong as before.

Stockdale growled, 'There's one of 'em!'

Bolitho balanced himself on the balls of his feet, watching the hurtling shadow charging from the darkness.

Someone fired a pistol, and he saw the horse's eyes, huge and terrified, as it pounded towards the seamen, and then swerved away as another horseman lurched from the water and loomed above them like an avenging beast.

He thought Stockdale was saying to Couzens, 'Easy, son! Keep with me! Stand yer ground!'

*Or he may have been speaking to me*, he thought.

Then he forgot everything as he felt his hanger jerk against steel and he threw himself to the attack.

Lieutenant James Quinn ducked as musket-fire clattered along the causeway and some of the shots clanged and ricocheted from the two cannon. He was almost blinded by smoke, from the burning hillside and now with additional fog of gunfire.

Out in the open it seemed far worse than any gundeck. Metal shrieked overhead, and through the smoke men stumbled and cursed as they rammed home fresh charges and grapeshot to try and hold off the attack.

'*Fire!*'

Quinn winced as the nearest cannon belched flame and smoke. In the swift glare he saw running figures and a gleam of weapons before darkness closed in again and the air was rent by terrible screams as the murderous grape found a target.

A marine was yelling in his ear, 'The devils are on the island, sir!' He was almost screaming. 'Cavalry!'

Lieutenant FitzHerbert ran through the smoke. 'Silence, that man! He fired his pistol along the causeway and added savagely, 'You'll start a panic!'

Quinn gasped, '*Cavalry*, he said!'

Fitz Herbert glared at him, his eyes shining above the handkerchief like stones.

'We'd all be corpses if there was, man! A few riders, no doubt!'

Rowhurst shouted hoarsely, 'Gettin' short of powder!' He blundered towards Quinn. 'Damn yer eyes, sir! Do somethin', fer Christ's sake!'

Quinn nodded, his mind empty of everything but fear. He saw Midshipman Huyghue crouching on one knee as he tried to level a pistol above a hastily prepared earthwork.

'Tell Mr Bolitho what is happening!'

The youth stood up, uncertain which way to go. Quinn gripped his arm. 'Along the beach! Fast as you can!'

A shrill voice shouted, ''Ere the buggers come!'

FitzHerbert threw his handkerchief away and waved his sword. 'Sar'nt Triggs!'

A corporal said, 'He's dead, sir.'

The marine lieutenant looked away. 'God Almighty!' Then as the shouts and whooping cheers echoed across the water he added, '*Forward*, marines!'

Stumbling and choking in the smoke, the marines emerged from their gullies and ditches, their bayonets rising in obedience to the order, their feet searching for firm ground as they peered with stinging eyes for a sign of their enemy.

A hail of musket-fire came from the causeway, and a third of the marines fell dead or wounded.

Quinn stared with disbelief as the marines fired, started to reload and then crumpled to another well-timed volley.

FitzHerbert yelled, 'I suggest you spike those guns! Or get your seamen to reload our muskets!'

He gave a choking cry and pitched through his dwindling line of marines, his jaw completely shot away.

Quinn shouted, 'Rowhurst! Fall back!'

Rowhurst thrust past him, his eyes wild. 'Most of the lads 'ave gone already!' Even in the face of such danger he could not hide his contempt. 'You might as well run, too!'

From over his shoulder Quinn heard the sudden blare of a trumpet. It seemed to grip the remaining marines like a steel hand.

The corporal, earlier on the edge of terror, called, 'Retreat!

Easy, lads! Reload, take aim!' He waited for some of the wounded to hop or crawl through the line. *'Fire!'*

Quinn could not grasp what was happening. He heard the snap of commands, the click of weapons, and somehow knew that D'Esterre was coming to cover the withdrawal. The enemy were barely yards away, he could hear their feet slipping and squelching on the wet sand, sense their combined anger and madness as they surged forward to retake the landing-place. Yet all he could think of was Rowhurst's disgust, the need to win his respect in these last minutes.

He gasped, 'Which gun is loaded?'

He staggered down the slope, his pistol still unloaded, and the hanger which his father had had specially made by the best City sword cutler firmly in its scabbard.

Rowhurst, dazed and bewildered by the change of events, paused and stared at the groping lieutenant. Like a blind man.

It was stupid to go back with him. What safety remained was a long run to the fort's gates. Every moment here cut away a hope of survival.

Rowhurst was a volunteer, and prided himself on being as good a gunner's mate as any in the fleet. In a month or so, if fate was kind, he might gain promotion, proper warrant rank in another ship somewhere.

He watched Quinn's pathetic efforts to find the gun, which because of the marines leaving cover was still unfired. Either way it was over. If he waited, he would die with Quinn. If he escaped, Quinn would charge him with disobeying orders, insolence to an officer. Something like that.

Rowhurst gave a great sigh and made up his mind.

''Ere, this is the one.' He forced a grin. 'Sir!'

A corpse propped against one of the wheels gave a little jerk as more random shots slammed into it. It was as if the dead were returning to life to witness their last madness.

The crash of the explosion as the slow-match found its mark, and the whole double-shotted charge swept through the packed ranks of attackers, seemed to bring some small control to Quinn's cringing mind. He groped for the finely made hanger, his eyes streaming, his ears deafened by that final explosion.

All he could say was, 'Thank you, Rowhurst! Thank you!'

But Rowhurst had been right about one thing. He lay staring angrily at the smoke, a hole placed dead centre through his forehead. No gunner's mate could have laid a better shot.

Quinn walked dazedly away from the guns, his sword-arm at his side. The white breeches of dead marines shone in the darkness, staring eyes and fallen weapons marked each moment of sacrifice.

But Quinn was also aware that the din of shouting had gone from the causeway. They too had taken enough.

He stopped, suddenly tense and ready as figures came down towards him. Two marines, the big gun captain called Stockdale. And a lieutenant with a drawn blade in his hand.

Quinn looked at the ground, wanting to speak, to explain what Rowhurst had done, had made him do.

But Bolitho took his arm and said quietly, 'The corporal told me. But for your example, no one outside the fort would be alive now.'

They waited as the first line of marines came down from the fort, letting the battered and bleeding survivors from the causeway pass through them to safety.

Bolitho ached all over, and his sword-arm felt as heavy as iron. He could still feel the fear and desperation of the past hour. The thundering horses, the swords cutting out of the darkness, and then the sudden rallying of his own mixed collection of seamen.

Couzens had been stunned after being knocked over by a horse, and three seamen were dead. He himself had been struck from behind, and the edge of the sabre had touched his shoulder like a red-hot knife.

Now the horses had gone, swimming or drifting with the current, but gone from here. Several of their riders had stayed behind. For ever.

D'Esterre found them as he came through the thinning smoke and said, 'We held them. It was costly, Dick, but it could save us.' He held up his hat and fanned his streaming face. 'See? The wind is going about at last. If there is a ship for us, then she can come.'

He watched a marine being carried past, his leg smashed out of recognition. In the darkness the blood looked like fresh tar.

'We must get replacements to the causeway. I've sent for a new gun crew.' He saw Couzens walking very slowly towards them, rubbing his head and groaning. 'I'm glad he's all right.' D'Esterre replaced his hat as he saw his sergeant hurrying towards him. 'I'm afraid they took the other midshipman, Huyghue, prisoner.'

Quinn said brokenly, 'I sent him to look for you. It was my fault.'

Bolitho shook his head. 'No. Some of the enemy got amongst us. They'd allowed for failure, I expect, and wanted to seize a few prisoners just in case.'

Bolitho made to thrust his hanger into its scabbard and discovered that the hilt was sticky with blood. He let out a long sigh, trying to fit his thoughts in order. But, as usual, nothing came, as if his mind was trying to protect him, to cushion him from the horror and frantic savagery of hand to hand fighting. Sounds, brief faces and shapes, terror and wild hate. But nothing real. It might come later, when his mind was able to accept it.

Had it all been worthwhile? Was liberty that precious?

And tomorrow, no, *today*, it would all begin again.

He heard Quinn call, 'They will need more powder for those guns! See to it, will you!'

An anonymous figure in checkered shirt and white trousers hurried away to do his bidding. An ordinary sailor. He could be every sailor, Bolitho thought.

Quinn faced him. 'If you want to report to Major Paget, I can take charge here.' He waited, watching Bolitho's strained features as if searching for something. 'I can, really.'

Bolitho nodded. 'I'd be grateful, James. I shall be back directly.'

Stockdale said roughly, 'With Rowhurst gone, you'll need a fair 'and at the guns, sir.' He grinned at Quinn's face. 'Keep up the good work, eh, sir?'

Bolitho made his way into the fort, weaving through groups of wounded, each one a small island of pain in the glow of a lantern. Daylight would reveal the real extent of what they had endured.

Paget was in his room, and although Bolitho knew he had been controlling the defences from the first minutes, he looked as if he had never left the place.

Paget said, 'We will hold the causeway tonight, of course.' He gestured to a bottle of wine. 'But tomorrow we will prepare for evacuation. When the ship comes, we will send the wounded and those who have stood guard tonight, *first*. No time for any bluff. If they've got prisoners, they know what we're up to.'

Bolitho let the wine run over his tongue. God, it tasted good. Better than anything.

'What if the ship does not come, sir?'

'Well, that simplifies things.' Paget watched him coldly. 'We'll blow the magazine, and fight our way out.' He smiled very briefly. 'It won't come to that.'

'I see, sir.' In fact, he did not.

Paget ruffled some papers. 'I want you to sleep. For an hour or so.' He held up his hand. 'That is an order. You've done fine work here, and now I thank God that fool Probyn made the decision he did.'

'I'd like to report on Mr Quinn's part, sir.' The major was getting misty in Bolitho's aching vision. 'And the two midshipmen. They are all very young.'

Paget pressed his fingertips together and regarded him unsmilingly. 'Not like you, of course, an ancient warrior, what?'

Bolitho picked up his hat and made for the door. With Paget you knew exactly where you were. He had selected him for some precious sleep. The very thought made him want to lie down immediately and close his eyes.

Equally, he knew the true reason for Paget's concern. Someone would have to stay behind and light the fuses. You needed a measure of alertness for that!

Bolitho walked past D'Esterre without even seeing him.

The marine captain picked up the wine bottle and said, 'You told him, sir? About tomorrow?'

Paget shrugged. 'No. He is like I was at his age. Didn't need to be *told* everything.' He glared at his subordinate. 'Unlike some.'

D'Esterre smiled and walked to the window. Somewhere across the water a telescope might be trained on the fort, on this lighted window.

Like Bolitho, he knew he should be snatching an hour's rest. But out there, still hidden in darkness, were many of his men, sprawled in the careless attitudes of death. He could not find it in his heart to leave them now. It would be like a betrayal.

A gentle snore made him turn. Paget was fast asleep in the chair, his face completely devoid of anxiety.

Better to be like him, D'Esterre thought bitterly. Then he downed the drink in one swallow and strode out into the darkness.

# II

## Rear-guard

When the sun eventually showed itself above the horizon and felt its way carefully inland, it revealed not only the horror of the night's work, but to those who had survived it also brought new hope.

Hull down with the early sunlight were two ships, and at first it seemed likely that the enemy had somehow found the means to frustrate any attempt of evacuation. But as the vessels tacked this way and that, drawing nearer and nearer to land with each change of course, they were both identified and cheered. Not only had the sloop-of-war, *Spite*, come for them, but also the thirty-two-gun frigate *Vanquisher*, sent, it seemed, by Rear-Admiral Coutts himself.

As soon as it was light enough the work of collecting and burying the dead got under way. Across the causeway, now partially submerged, a few corpses rolled and moved with the current. Most had been carried away to deeper water during the night, or retrieved perhaps by their comrades.

Paget was everywhere. Bullying, suggesting, threatening, and occasionally tossing a word of encouragement as well.

The sight of the two ships put fresh life into his men, and even though neither of them was a match for well-sited shore batteries, they would shorten the work of evacuation. More pulling boats, fresh, rested seamen to work them, officers to take over the strain of command.

Bolitho was in the deep magazine with Stockdale and a marine corporal for much of the morning. The place had a dreadful stillness about it, a quality of death which he could feel like a chill breeze. Keg upon keg of gunpowder, boxes of equipment, and many unpacked cases of new French muskets and side-arms. Fort Exeter had a lot to answer for in past dealings with England's old enemy.

Stockdale hummed to himself as he attached the fuses to the foot of the first mound of explosives, entirely engrossed and glad to be out of the bustle in the fort above.

Boots tramped in the courtyard, and there were sounds of grating metal as the cannons were spiked and then moved to a point above where the explosion would be.

Bolitho sat on an empty keg, his cheeks stinging from the shave which Stockdale had given him when he had awakened from his deep, exhausted sleep. He remembered his father telling him when he had been a small boy, 'If you've not had to shave with salt water, you never know how soft is the life of a landsman by comparison.'

He could have had all the fresh water he wanted. But even now, with the ships so near, you could not be complacent, or certain.

He watched Stockdale's big hands, so deft and gentle as he worked with the fuses.

It was a gamble, always. Light the fuses. Head for safety. Minutes to get clear.

A seaman appeared on the sunlit ladder.

'Beg pardon, sir, but the major would like you with 'im.' He looked at Stockdale and at the fuses and paled. 'Gawd!'

Bolitho ran up the ladder and across the courtyard. The gates were open, and he looked across the trampled ground, the dried blood-stains, the pathetic mounds which marked the hasty graves.

Paget said slowly, 'Another flag of truce, dammit.'

Bolitho shaded his eyes and saw the white flag, some figures standing on the far end of the causeway, their feet touching the water.

D'Esterre came hurrying from the stables where some marines were piling up papers and maps and all the contents of the tower and quartermaster's stores.

He took a telescope from Paget's orderly and then said grimly, 'They've got young Huyghue with them.'

Paget said calmly, 'Go and speak with them. You know what I said this morning.' He nodded to Bolitho. 'You, too. It might help Huyghue.'

Bolitho and the marine walked towards the causeway, Stockdale just behind them with an old shirt tied to a pike. How he had heard what was happening and been here in time to keep Bolitho company was a mystery.

It seemed to take an age to reach the causeway. The whole time the little group at the far end never moved. Just the white flag streaming over a soldier's head to display the wind's impartial presence.

Bolitho felt his shoes sinking into sand and mud the further they walked towards the waiting group. Here and there were signs of battle. A broken sword, a man's hat and a pouch of musket balls. In deep water he saw a pair of legs swaying gently, as if the corpse was merely resting and about to surface again at any moment.

D'Esterre said, 'Can't get any closer.'

The two groups stood facing each other, and although the man who waited by the flag was without his coat, Bolitho knew it was the senior officer from yesterday. As if to prove it, his black dog sat on the wet sand at his side, a red tongue lolling with weariness.

A little to the rear was Midshipman Huyghue. Small, seemingly frail against the tall, sunburned soldiers.

The officer cupped his hands. He had a deep, resonant voice which carried without effort.

'I am Colonel Brown of the Charles Town Militia. Who have I the honour of addressing?'

D'Esterre shouted, 'Captain D'Esterre of His Britannic Majesty's Marines!'

Brown nodded slowly. 'Very well. I have come to parley with you. I will allow your men to leave the fort unharmed, provided you lay down your weapons and make no attempt to destroy the supplies and the arms.' He paused and then added, 'Otherwise my artillery will open fire and prevent evacuation, even at the risk of blowing up the magazine ourselves.'

D'Esterre called, 'I see.' To Bolitho he whispered, 'He is

trying to drag out the time. If he can get cannon on the hilltop he can certainly throw some long shots at the ships when they anchor. It only needs a lucky ball, just one in the right place.' He shouted again, 'And what does the midshipman have to do with all this?'

Brown shrugged. 'I will exchange him here and now for the French officer you are holding prisoner.'

Bolitho said softly, 'I see it. He is going to open fire anyway, but wants the Frenchman in safety first. He fears we might kill him, or that he would be cut down in a bombardment.'

'I agree.' D'Esterre said loudly, 'I cannot agree to the exchange!'

Bolitho saw the midshipman take a pace forward, his hands half raised as if pleading.

Brown called, 'You will regret it.'

Bolitho wanted to turn his head and look for the ships, to see how near they had managed to tack. But any sign of uncertainty now might bring disaster. Another frontal attack perhaps. If the enemy knew about the guns being spiked they would be halfway across the island by now. He felt suddenly vulnerable. But how much worse for Huyghue. Sixteen years old. To be left out here amongst enemies in a strange land where his death or disappearance would excite very little comment.

D'Esterre said, 'I might exchange your second-in-command instead.'

'No.' Colonel Brown's hand was rubbing the dog's head as he spoke, as if to calm his own thoughts.

He obviously had his orders, Bolitho decided. As we all do.

The mention of the second-in-command had changed little, except to prove that Paget still had his prisoners guarded and alive. That knowledge might help Huyghue to survive.

A gun banged out suddenly, the sound hollow and muffled. Bolitho thought the militia had got their guns into position already, and felt the disappointment tug at his heart until he heard distant cheering.

Stockdale wheezed, 'One o' the ships 'as dropped anchor, sir!'

D'Esterre looked at Bolitho and said simply, 'We must go. I'll not prolong the boy's misery.'

Bolitho shouted, 'Take care, Mr Huyghue! All will be well! You will be exchanged soon, I've no doubt!'

Huyghue must have believed up to the last second that he was going to be released. His experiences during the bloody fighting had been enough in his eyes perhaps. Being taken prisoner was beyond his understanding.

He tried to run into the water, and when a soldier seized his arm he fell on his knees, calling and sobbing, '*Help me!* Don't leave me! Please help!'

Even the militia colonel was moved by the boy's despair, and he gestured for him to be taken up the beach again.

Bolitho and his companions turned their backs and started back towards the fort, Huyghue's pathetic cries following them like a curse.

The frigate was anchored well out from the land, but her sails were brailed up and there were boats in the water already, pulling strongly towards the island.

The *Spite*, being smaller, was still working her way inshore, leadsmen busy in the chains to seek out any uncharted reef or bar.

They looked so clean, so efficiently remote, that Bolitho felt suddenly sick of the land. The heavy smell of death which seemed to overpower even that of the night's fires.

Quinn was by the gates, watching his face as he strode into the shade.

'You left him?'

'Yes.' Bolitho looked at him gravely. 'I'd no choice. If all we had to do was exchange our victims, there'd be no point in coming here.' He sighed. 'But I'll not forget his face in a hurry.'

Paget examined his watch. 'First wounded men to the beach.' He glanced at Bolitho. 'Do you think they might try and rush us, eh?'

Bolitho shrugged. 'The smaller swivels could deal with them in daylight, sir. It'd make our work harder though.'

Paget turned to listen as more cheers echoed around the fort. 'Simple fools.' He looked away. 'Bless 'em!'

A marine ran down a ladder from the parapet. 'Mr Raye's respects, and he's sighted soldiers on the hill. Artillery too, he thinks, sir.'

Paget nodded. 'Right. We must make haste. Signal *Spite* to anchor and lower boats as fast as she can.' As Quinn hurried away with the marine, Paget added, 'Warm work for you, Bolitho, I'm afraid. But whatever happens, see that the magazine *goes up*.'

'What about the prisoners, sir?'

'If there's room enough, and time to spare, I'll have them shipped to the frigate.' He smiled wryly. 'If I was left as rearguard, I'd see they went up with the magazine, damned bloody rebels. But as you will be in charge, you may use your discretion. On your head be it.'

The *Vanquisher's* boats were being beached, and seamen were already hoisting wounded marines aboard, their faces shocked at the small number of survivors.

Then the sloop's boats pulled ashore, and more men started on their way to safety and medical care.

Bolitho stood on the parapet above the gates, where he and Stockdale had crouched on that first terrible night when Quinn had lost his nerve.

The fort already felt emptier, and as marines hurried through the gates towards the rear Bolitho watched the little scarlet figures down by the causeway and the two remaining cannon. Once he gave the order for final withdrawal, Sergeant Shears and his handful of pickets would light the fuses which were attached to both guns. Two tightly packed charges would blow off the trunnions and render them as useless as those in the fort.

He wondered if anyone would ever hear about it in England. The small but deadly actions which made up the whole. Few ever wrote of the real heroes, he thought. The lonely men on the prongs of an attack, or those left behind to cover a retreat. Sergeant Shears was probably thinking about it just now. Of the distance to the fort. Of the marines under his charge.

There was a loud bang, followed by a whimpering drone, as a heavy ball passed low overhead and slammed hard into the sand.

Midshipman Couzens pointed at the hillside. 'See, sir? The smoke! They've got one gun at least in position!'

Bolitho watched him. Couzens looked pale and sick. It would take time to recover from the night's fighting, the rearing horses and sabres.

'Go and tell the major. He'll know, but tell him anyway.' As Couzens made for the ladder he added quietly, 'Then report to the senior officer with the boats. Don't come back here.' He saw the emotions flooding across the boy's face. Relief, concern, finally stubbornness. Bolitho added firmly, 'I am not asking. It is an order.'

'But, sir. I want to stay with you.'

Bolitho turned as another bang echoed from the hillside. This time the ball hit the sea and ricocheted over the wavecrests like a maddened dolphin.

'I know. But how will I explain to your father if anything happens to you, eh? Who'd eat your mother's pies?'

He heard what sounded like a sob, and when he turned again the parapet was empty. Time enough for you, Bolitho thought sadly. Three years younger than Huyghue. A child.

He saw the brilliant flash of a cannon, and felt the ball tear above the fort with the sound of ripping canvas. They had the range now. The shot fell directly in line with the anchored frigate, throwing spray over one of her boats as it pulled back to the island for more men.

D'Esterre came up the ladder and looked at him. 'Last section moving out now. They're taking most of the prisioners, too. Major Paget's sent the Frenchman, Contenay, over with the first boat. Taking no chances.' He removed his hat and stared at the causeway. 'Damnable place.'

A voice called from the courtyard, '*Vanquisher*'s shortenin' 'er cable, sir!'

'Getting clear before she gets a piece of Colonel Brown's iron on her quarterdeck.' D'Esterre looked anxious. 'It might spark off an attack, now that they think we're on the run, Dick.'

Bolitho nodded. 'I'll get ready. I hope they've got a fast boat for us.'

It was meant to sound amusing. Relaxed. But it merely added to the strain, the tension which was making it difficult to breathe evenly.

D'Esterre said, '*Spite*'s jolly boat, it's there waiting. Just for you.'

Bolitho said, 'Go now. I'll be all right.'

He watched a small squad of marines scurrying through the courtyard, one pausing to hurl a torch into the pile of papers and stores inside the stables.

D'Esterre watched him walking towards the magazine, and then just as quickly turned and followed his men through the gates.

A ball shrieked above the squat tower, but D'Esterre did not even look up. It seemed to have no menace. All danger and death was here. Like a foul memory.

He saw the frigate's outline shortening as she tacked steeply away from the land, her forecourse filling and flapping even as one of her boats pulled frantically alongside. For the other boats it would be a long hard pull to reach her. But her captain would know the danger of well-hidden artillery. To lose a frigate was bad enough, to allow her to be added to the Revolutionary Navy was even worse.

Bolitho forgot D'Esterre and everything else as he found Stockdale with his slow-match, a solitary marine corporal and a seaman he recognized through the grime and stubble as Rabbett, the thief from Liverpool.

'Light the fuses.'

He winced as a heavy ball crashed through a parapet and came splintering amongst the stables which were now well alight.

He said, 'Get to the gates, Corporal, call back your pickets. Fast as you can.'

The fuses hissed into life, somehow obscene in the gloom, like serpents.

They seemed to be burning at a terrible speed, he thought.

He clapped Stockdale on the shoulder. 'Time for us.'

Another ball smashed into the fort and hurled a swivel gun into the air like a stick.

Two more sharp explosions came from the causeway, and he knew the cannon had been destroyed.

Musket-fire too, remote and without effect at this range. But they would be coming soon.

They ran out into the blinding sunlight, past discarded boxes and blazing stores.

Two loud bangs and then splintering woodwork flying above the parapet told Bolitho that Brown's men must have worked like demons to get their guns up the hill.

The corporal yelled, 'Seargeant Shears is comin' at th' double, sir! The whole bloody rebel army's on their 'eels!'

Bolitho saw the running marines even as one fell headlong and stayed down.

Soldiers were wading and struggling across the causeway too, firing and reloading as they came.

Bolitho measured the distance. It was taking too long.

Round one wall of the fort, along the sloping beach where the jolly boat was waiting. Bolitho noticed that the crew had their oars out, backing water, watching the land, mesmerized.

Sergeant Shears panted down the beach, his men behind him.

'Into the boat!' Bolitho looked up at the tower, their flag still above it.

Then he realized he was alone on the beach, that Stockdale had his arm and was hauling him over the gunwale as a nervous-looking lieutenant ordered, *'Give way all!'*

Minutes later, as the jolly boat bounded over the first lazy roller, some soldiers appeared below the fort, firing at the boat, the shots going everywhere. One hit the side and threw droplets of water across the panting marines.

Shears muttered, 'I'd get the hell out of here, if I was them, sir!'

They were midway between the beach and the sloop when the explosion blasted the day apart. It was not the sound, but the sight of the complete fort being hurled skywards in thousands of shattered fragments which remained fixed in Bolitho's reeling mind, long after the last piece had fallen. As the smoke continued to billow across the island, Bolitho saw there was nothing there but one huge, black wilderness.

All the prisoners had been taken off after all, and he wondered what they must be thinking at this moment. And young Huyghue, too. Would he remember the part he had played, or would he think only of his own plight?

When he turned his head he saw the sloop's masts and yards swaying above him, willing hands waiting to assist them on board.

He looked at Stockdale, and their eyes met. As if to say, once again, we survived. Once more fate stayed her hand.

He heard the sloop's young commander, Cunningham, shouting irritably, 'Lively there! We've not got all damn day!'

Bolitho smiled wearily. He was back.


Captain Gilbert Brice Pears sat at his table, his strong fingers interlaced in front of him, while his clerk arranged five beautifully written copies of the Fort Exeter raid for his signature.

Around him *Trojan*'s great hull creaked and clattered to a stiff quarter sea, but Pears barely noticed. He had read the original report most carefully, missing nothing, and had questioned D'Esterre on the more complex details of the attack and withdrawal.

Nearby, his lean body angled to the deck, and silhouetted against the spray-dappled windows, Cairns waited patiently for some comment.

Pears had fretted at the delay in reaching the rendezvous after their feint attack towards Charles Town. The wind's sudden change, a total absence of news and the general lack of faith he held in Coutts' plan added to his worst fears. Even Coutts must have sensed his uneasiness, and had despatched the frigate to assist *Spite*'s recovery of the landing party. Pears had watched *Trojan*'s seamen and marines climbing back aboard after they had eventually regained contact. The tired, haggard, yet somehow defiant marines, what was left of them, and the filthy seamen. D'Esterre and Bolitho, with young Couzens waving to his fellow midshipmen, half laughing, partly weeping.

Fort Exeter was no more. He hoped it had all been worthwhile, but secretly doubted it.

He nodded grimly to his clerk. 'Very well, Teakle. I'll sign the damn things.' He glanced at Cairns. 'Must have been a bloody business. Our people did well, it seems.'

Pears glared through the dripping windows at the blurred shape of the flagship, close-hauled on the same tack, her courses and topsails filling to the wind.

'Now *this*, blast his eyes!'

Cairns followed his glance, knowing better than most how his captain felt.

It had taken six days for the ponderous ships of the line to rendezvous with *Vanquisher* and *Spite*. Then a further two while their admiral had interviewed the senior officers of his little squadron, watched an interrogation of the disarmingly cheerful French prisoner and had considered the information which Paget had gleaned at the fort.

Now, instead of returning to New York for further orders, and to obtain replacements for the dead and wounded, *Trojan* was to proceed further south. Pears' orders were to seek out and finally destroy an island base which, if half of the intelligence gathered from the prisoners was to be trusted, was the most important link in the supply chain for arms and powder for Washington's armies.

At any other time Pears would have welcomed it as the chance to use his ship as he had always wanted. To make up for the humiliating setbacks and delays, the months of patrol duty or the boredom of being at anchor in harbour.

The flagship *Resolute* would be leaving them shortly and would return to Sandy Hook, taking Coutts' impressive reports to the commander-in-chief, along with the prisoners and most of the badly wounded seamen and marines.

The youthful rear-admiral had taken the unprecedented step, in Pears' view, of appointing his flag captain, Lamb, as acting officer-in-charge of the inshore squadron, while he, Coutts, transferred his flag to *Trojan* to pursue the attack in the south.

Coutts probably guessed that if he returned with his own flagship the commander-in-chief, in connivance with or under direct orders from the government 'expert', Sir George Helpman, would be ordered elsewhere before he could see his strategy brought to a successful end.

There was a tap at the door.

'Enter.'

Pears looked up, watching Bolitho's face from the moment he walked into the great cabin, his cocked hat tucked under one arm.

He looked older, Pears decided. Strained, but more confident in some way. There were lines at the corners of his mouth, but the grey eyes were steady enough. Like those battered marines. Defiant.

Pears noticed how he was holding his shoulder. It was probably stinging badly from that sabre's quick touch, more so from the surgeon's attentions. But in his change of clothing Bolitho appeared restored.

Pears said, 'Good to see you in one piece.' He waved to a chair and waited for his clerk to leave. 'You'll hear soon enough. We're to stand further south, to seek out and destroy an enemy supply headquarters there.' He grimaced. 'French, to all accounts.'

Bolitho sat down carefully. His body clean, his clothes fresh and strangely unfamiliar, he was just beginning to feel the slackening of tension.

They had been good to him. Cairns, the Sage, Dalyell. All of them. And it felt free to be here, in this groaning, over-crowded hull.

He had no idea what was happening, until now. After the swift passage aboard the sloop, the sadness of seeing more survivors die and be buried over the side, he had found little time, other than to scribble his own version of what had happened. Apart from a few quiet words with Pears as he and the others had been helped aboard, he had not spoken with him at all.

Pears said, 'The war makes great demands. We were short of experienced officers, now we are even shorter.' He stared at the empty table where the report had been lying. 'Good men killed, others maimed for life. Half my marines gone in the blink of an eye, and now, with two officers taken prisoner to boot, I am feeling like a clergyman with an empty church.'

Bolitho glanced at Cairns, but his face gave nothing away. He had seen a brig speaking with the flagship that morning, but he knew nothing further.

He asked, '*Two* officers, sir?' He must have missed something.

Pears sighed. 'Young Huyghue, and now the flagship has told me about Probyn. He was apparently run down by a privateer, one day after leaving you at Fort Exeter.' He watched Bolitho's face. 'Shortest command in naval history, I'd imagine.'

Bolitho thought of the last time he had seen Probyn. Angry, triumphant, bitter. Now it had all been taken away. His hopes dashed.

All he could find in his heart was pity.

'*So*,' Pears' voice brought him back with a jerk, 'you are hereby appointed as second lieutenant of this ship, *my* ship.'

Bolitho stared at him dazedly. From fourth to second. He had heard of it happening, but had never expected it like this.

'I—that is, thank you, sir.'

Pears eyed him flatly. 'I am glad you did not crow over Probyn's fate. But I think I could have understood even that.'

Cairns nodded, his lips parted in a rare smile. 'Congratulations.'

Pears waved his large hands. 'Save them for later and spare me, Mr Cairns. Be about your affairs. Appoint another midshipman to Huyghue's duties, and I suggest you consider the master's mate, Frowd, as acting lieutenant. A promising fellow, I think.'

The marine sentry opened the door gingerly. 'Beg pardon, sir, midshipman o' th' watch is 'ere.'

It was little Forbes, somehow grown in stature to his title.

'S-sir. Mr Dalyell's respects, and the flagship has just signalled us to heave to.'

Pears glanced at Cairns. 'See to it. I'll be up presently.'

As the two lieutenants hurried after the midshipman, Bolitho asked, 'Why is this?'

Cairns stared at him. 'You *are* out of touch, Dick!' He pointed to a petty officer with a flag neatly rolled under his arm. 'Today we will hoist the flag to our mizzen. Rear-Admiral Coutts is to be our very present help in trouble!'

*'Flagship?'*

'Acting.' Cairns straightened his hat as they strode forward to the quarterdeck rail. 'Until Coutts reaps his reward, or lays his head on the block.'

Seamen were already running to their stations, and Bolitho had to make himself look at the massive trunk of the mainmast, where he had once taken so many orders and goads from Lieutenant Sparke.

Now he was second lieutenant. With still two months between him and twenty-one years.

He saw Stockdale watching him and nodding. It was thanks to Stockdale, and some missing faces, that he was here at all.

'All hands! Stand by to wear ship!'

Cairns' voice found him with the speaking trumpet. 'Mr Bolitho, sir! Hurry those men at the braces! They are like old cripples today!'

Bolitho touched his hat and kept his face straight.

Across the scrambling seamen he saw Quinn staring at him, still uncertain at his new station. He smiled at him, trying to break the strain that was still there.

'Lively, Mr Quinn!' He hesitated, holding another memory. 'Take that man's name!'

# I2

## Rivals

The day after Rear-Admiral Coutts had shifted his flag to *Trojan* found Bolitho pacing the quarterdeck, keeping an eye on the forenoon watch and enjoying a fresh north-west breeze. During the night the big ninety-gun *Resolute* with the frigate in company had vanished astern, and would now be beating back towards New York, the wind making every mile a battle of its own.

For the *Trojan* things were different, as if Coutts' unexpected arrival had brought a change of circumstances. She must make a fine sight, Bolitho thought as his feet took him up and down the windward side without conscious effort. In her fair-weather canvas, and under courses, topsails and topgallants, she was leaning her shoulder into the blue water, throwing curtains of spray high above her beakhead.

The compass held steady at south, south-east, taking the powerful two-decker well away from the land, down towards the long chain of islands which separated the Atlantic from the Caribbean.

The wind held back the heat, and allowed the less badly wounded and injured men to move about the decks, to find themselves again in their own way. The remainder, some of whom might die before they reached Sandy Hook, had gone with the flagship, as had the prisoners, and Coutts' report of the attack.

Only one captive remained aboard, the Frenchman, Contenay. He took regular walks on deck without an escort, and seemed completely at home in a King's ship.

Bolitho had discovered that he still knew little about his own captain. The brief moments of contact, even warmth, upon his return to the ship had been replaced by Pears' usual stern, remote demeanour. Bolitho thought that the admiral's presence had a lot to do with it.

Coutts had appeared on deck this morning. Youthful, relaxed and apparently interested, he had strolled along the weather gangway, pausing to watch the bare-backed seamen at their work, the carpenter with his crew, the sailmaker and the cooper, the ship's tradesmen who daily changed a man-of-war into a busy street.

He had spoken to the officers and some of the senior hands. The Sage had been impressed by his knowledge of Arctic exploration, and Midshipman Forbes reduced to blushing incoherence by a few well-aimed questions.

If he was troubled at the doubtful prospect of running another enemy supply cache to earth, or at what the commander-in-chief might say at his behaviour, he certainly did not show it. His plans he kept to himself, and only Ackerman, his urbane flag lieutenant, the one Bolitho had seen in a cabin with a half-naked woman, and his personal clerk shared his confidences.

Bolitho decided that would also irritate Pears beyond measure.

A step fell on the deck nearby and Cairns joined him at the rail, his eyes taking in the working parties and the set of each sail with practised authority.

He said, 'The admiral is with our captain. I sense an air of grapeshot close by.' He turned and glanced meaningly at the poop skylight. 'I was glad to leave the great men.'

'No news yet?'

'Not much. Like D'Esterre, the admiral plays a taut hand. He will rise like a comet.' He gestured at the deck. 'Or fall like one.'

With Coutts aboard, Cairns also faced changes. The main result was that he shared more of his thoughts with his second lieutenant.

He added slowly, 'The captain was wanting to know why this ship and not *Resolute* was selected for the mission.' He smiled grimly. 'The admiral explained, as cool as you please, that *Trojan* is the faster vessel, and her company deserving of reward for their work.'

Bolitho nodded. 'I suppose so. *Resolute* has been out here far longer and has had few refits, I believe. She must be foul with weed.'

Cairns eyed him admiringly. 'We'll make a politician of you yet.' He waved Bolitho's confusion aside. 'You see, the back-handed compliment. Coutts lays on treacle with talk of reward and the better ship for the task, then in the next breath he gently reminds Captain Pears that his own flagship is in truth the more deserving.'

Bolitho pursed his lips. 'That is clever.'

'It takes a rogue to recognize one, Dick.'

'In that case, what *is* the real reason?'

Cairns frowned. 'I suspect because he wants the flagship on her proper station. That would make sense. Also, he despatched *Vanquisher* as escort, and because *she* will be sorely needed elsewhere with the growth of privateers everywhere.'

He dropped his voice as Sambell, master's mate of the watch, strolled past with elaborate indifference on his tanned face.

'He will want to follow this plan to the end. Reap the reward, or cover the flaws as best he can. He would not trust our captain to act alone. And if things go disastrously badly, then he will need a scapegoat other than his own flag captain.' Cairns wached Bolitho's eyes. 'I see that *you* see.'

'I'll never understand this kind of reasoning.'

Cairns winked. 'One day, you'll be teaching it!'

More feet thudded on the sun-dried planking, and Bolitho saw Pears and the sailing master leaving the chart room, the latter carrying his leather satchel which he used to stow his navigational notes and instruments.

He looked much as usual, turning briefly to examine the compass and the two helmsmen, his eyes glittering in the sunlight beneath the great black brows.

Pears, by comparison, appeared tired and in ill humour, impatient to get whatever it was over and done with.

'We'll soon know where this blessed spot is to be, Dick.' Cairns loosened his neckcloth and sighed. 'I hope it is not another Fort Exeter.'

Bolitho watched the first lieutenant continue on his daily rounds, wondering if Cairns was still brooding over the chances of leaving *Trojan* and getting a ship of his own.

So far, *Trojan*'s lieutenants had not fared very well away from her protection. Sparke killed, Probyn a prisoner of war, while Bolitho had returned each time like a wayward son.

He saw Quinn without his coat, his shirt sticking to his back like another skin, stepping between the busy sailmaker and his mates, his face still pale and strained. Eighteen years old, he looked far more. Bolitho thought. The savage slash across his chest still troubled him. You could see it in his walk and the tightness of his mouth. A constant reminder of other things, too. That moment at the fort when his nerve had failed, and by the guns when he had almost gone mad because of Rowhurst's scorn.

Midshipman Weston shouted suddenly, '*Spite*'s signalling, sir!'

Bolitho snatched a telescope from its rack and climbed swiftly into the weather shrouds. It took a few moments to find the little sloop-of-war, their only companion on this 'adventure', as Cairns had described it. The glass steadied on *Spite*'s pale topgallant sails and the bright hoist of flags at her yards.

Weston was saying, 'From *Spite*. Sail in sight to the south'rd.'

Bolitho turned and looked at him. Weston was now the senior midshipman, and probably smarting at Pears' advice to promote Mr Frowd to acting lieutenant instead of him. Advice from a captain was as good as a command.

Bolitho felt almost sorry for Weston. Almost. Ungainly, overweight, belligerent. He would be a bad officer if he lived long enough.

'Very well. Keep watching *Spite*. I'll not inform the captain yet.'

Bolitho continued his measured pacing. The air seemed fresh, but when you paused for too long you felt the sun's power right enough. His own shirt was sodden with sweat, and the scar across his shoulder stung like a snakebite.

The sloop's captain would be fretting and eager to be off on his own, he thought. Right now he would be watching the unknown sail, considering, translating details into facts to relay as well as he could with his signal book for his admiral's decision.

Half an hour passed. Smoke gushed from the galley funnel, and Molesworth, the purser, and his clerk appeared en route for the spirit store to check the daily issue of rum or brandy.

Some marines, who had been drilling on the forecastle, holding off imaginary boarders, marched aft and returned their pikes. There was also a small contingent of marines from the flagship to help fill the gaps until proper replacements could be obtained. Bolitho thought of all the little mounds on the island. Who would care?

Weston called, 'From *Spite*, sir. Disregard.'

Another small encounter. Most likely a Dutchman on her lawful occasions. Anyway, Cunningham of the *Spite*, was satisfied. In fact, the strange sail had probably made off at full speed at the first sign of the sloop's topsails. It paid to be careful these days. The margin between friend and foe changed too often for over-confidence.

Stockdale crossed the quarterdeck on his way aft to the starboard battery.

As he passed he whispered, 'Admiral, sir.'

Bolitho stiffened and turned as Coutts walked out of the poop and into the glare.

Bolitho touched his hat, wondering briefly if Weston had deliberately failed to warn him.

Coutts smiled easily. ''Morning, Bolitho. Still on watch, I see.' He had a pleasant, even voice, unaffected.

Bolitho replied, 'A moment more, sir.'

Coutts took a glass and studied the far-off *Spite* for several minutes.

'Good man, Cunningham. Should be posted soon with any luck.'

Bolitho said nothing, but thought of Cunningham's youth. His *luck*. With Coutts' blessing he would be made a full captain, and with the war going as it was he would make post rank within three years. Safe from demotion, on the road to higher things.

'I can hear your mind at work, Bolitho.' Coutts tossed the glass to Weston. Again, the action was casual, yet timed to the second. 'Do not fret. When your time arrives you will discover that a captain's life is not all claret and prize-money.' Just for a moment his eyes hardened. 'But the opportunities are there. For those who will dare, and who do not use their orders as substitutes for initiative.'

Bolitho said, 'Yes, sir.'

He did not know what Coutts was implying. That there was hope for him? Or that he was merely revealing his feelings for Pears?

Coutts shrugged his shoulders and added, 'Dine with me tonight. I will have Ackerman invite a few others.'

Once more, Bolitho discerned the youthful devilment and touch of steel.

'In my quarters of course. I feel certain the captain will not object.'

He strolled away, nodding to Sambell and Weston as if they were yokels on the village green.

The hands were already gathering on the upper gundeck for the afternoon watch, and Bolitho knew that Dalyell would soon be here to relieve him. Unlike George Probyn, he was never late.

Bolitho was confused by what he had heard. He felt excited at Coutts' interest, yet uneasy because of it. It was like disloyalty to Pears. He smiled at his confusion. Pears probably didn't even like him, so what was the matter?

Dalyell appeared, blinking in the sunlight, some crumbs sticking to his coat.

'The watch is aft, sir.'

Bolitho eyed him gravely. 'Very well, Mr Dalyell.'

The both winked, their faces hidden from the men, their good spirits masked by the formality.

Quinn, on the larboard gangway, watched the two lieutenants as they supervised the usual milling confusion of changing watches. He had seen, and had felt, the ache of longing rising to match the pain of his wound. Bolitho had come out of it, or if not, had managed to put his memories behind him. While all he could do was to measure each step, calculate every action as he went along. He kept telling himself that his momentary defiance, his stand at the causeway had not been a fluke. That he had failed once, but had fought to retrieve and hold on to his pride again.

He felt that the ship's company were watching him, rating his confidence. It was why he was lingering on the gangway, waiting for Bolitho before he went below for the noon meal. Bolitho was his strength. His only chance, if chance there was.

Bolitho beckoned to him. 'Not hungry, James? And I am told that we have some fine beef today, barely a year or so in the cask!' He clapped Quinn on the shoulder. 'Make the best of it, eh?'

When Quinn faced him he saw the sudden gravity in Bolitho's eyes and knew his words had nothing to do with food.

With her yards re-trimmed and her great spread of canvas filling and banging in the wind, *Trojan* settled down on her new tack.

Bolitho looked at Cairns and touched his hat. 'Steady as she goes, sir.'

Cairns nodded. 'Dismiss the watch below, if you please.'

As the seamen and the afterguard hurried thankfully below, Bolitho glanced quickly at Pears, who was with the admiral on the weather side of the quarterdeck.

It was another fiery sunset, and against it the two men were in silhouette, their faces hidden. But there was no mistaking Coutts' irritation, Pears' dogged stubbornness.

It all seemed a long, long way from the relaxed supper in the great cabin. Coutts had kept the wit and conversation going with little pause, except to recharge the glasses. He had enthralled the young lieutenants with stories of intrigue and corruption in the New York military government. Of the grand houses in London, the men, and in many cases the ladies who held the reins of power.

Once Pears and the sailing master had concluded their calculations, the ship's destination and purpose had gone through each deck like a bolt of lightning.

There was a small island, one of a group, which lay in the passage between Santo Domingo and Puerto Rico. Avoided by all but the most experienced navigators, it would seem to be the ideal place for transferring arms and powder to Washington's growing fleet of supply vessels.

As Coutts had discussed his hopes for a swift ending of the mission, Bolitho and most of the others had sensed his eagerness, his excitement at the prospect of a quick victory. He had known that nothing could outpace him with a warning, no horseman to carry the word that the British were coming. Not this time. With the vast Atlantic at his back, the keen-eyed *Spite* sweeping well ahead, Coutts had had good reason for confidence.

But that had been fifteen days ago. The delays had been unavoidable, but nevertheless had put a marked strain on Coutts and his officers. Several times *Trojan* had been forced to lie to while *Spite* made off under full sail to investigate a strange vessel and then beat the weary miles round again and make her report. The wind too had backed and veered as Bunce had predicted, but had on the whole favoured their slow advance.

Now, with another sunset closing over the ship, Bolitho could sense a growing impatience, even anger in Coutts' quick movements with head and hands.

Once more *Spite* had been sent ahead to discover if the tiny island was in fact the one described in Paget's documents. If it was, Cunningham was to put a boat ashore and if possible discover the strength of the enemy there. If there was nothing at all, he was to report back instantly. Either way, he should have returned by now. With darkness closing in with its usual swiftness, it was very unlikely they would make contact until tomorrow. Another day. More anxiety.

He stiffened and touched his hat as Pears strode past, his feet thudding loudly on the planking. The slam of the chart room door was further evidence of his mood.

Bolitho waited, knowing Coutts was going to speak with him.

'A long day, Bolitho.'

'Aye sir.' Bolitho faced him, trying to discover the man's feelings. 'But the glass is steady. We should be able to maintain our tack during the night.'

Coutts had not heard. He rested his hands on the quarterdeck rail and stared down intently at the larboard battery of eighteen-pounders. He was without his hat, and his hair was blowing across his forehead to make him appear even younger.

He asked quietly, 'Are you like the others? Do you think me a fool to press on with this mission, a task which has no more substance than a scrap of paper?'

'I am only a lieutenant, sir. I was not aware of any doubt.'

Coutts laughed bitterly. 'Doubt? God, man, there's a mountain of it!'

Bolitho waited, feeling the admiral's urgency, his frustration.

Coutts said, 'When you reach flag rank you believe the world is yours. You are only partly right. I was a frigate captain, and good at my work.'

'I know, sir.'

'Thank you.' Coutts seemed surprised. 'Most people look at an admiral and seem to think he has never been anything else, not an ordinary man at all.' He pointed vaguely through *Trojan*'s black web of shrouds and stays. 'But I believe the information is true. Otherwise I would not have risked my ships and my reputation. I do not care what some soft-spoken official from London thinks of me. I want to get this war over, with more cards on our side than across the enemy's table.' He was speaking quickly, his hands moving eloquently to describe his feelings, his fears. 'Each extra day brings more enemies against us. Ships to seek out and bring to battle. We have no squadrons to spare, but the enemy's agility is such that we must match his every move. No merchantman is safe without escort. We have even been forced to send armed vessels to the Davis Strait to protect our whaling ships! It is no time for the timid, or the one who waits for the enemy to act first.'

His terse, emphatic manner of speaking, of sharing his thoughts, was something new to Bolitho. It was like seeing the world, his world, opening up to reach far beyond the ship's hull, and further still to every sea where Britain's authority was being challenged.

'I was wondering, sir.' Bolitho hesitated and then added, 'Why you did not request ships to be sent from Antigua? We have sailed four times the distance it would have taken the vessels which patrol from there.'

Coutts watched him, his face in shadow, saying nothing, as if he were seeking some criticism in Bolitho's question.

Then he said, 'I could have sent *Spite* to the admiral at Antigua. It would have been faster certainly.' He turned away. 'But would they have acted? I think not. The affairs in New York and the threat of Washington's armies seem a long way off in the Caribbean. Only the commander-in-chief could have made a request, and with Sir George Helpman at his elbow, I doubt he would have done more than enter it in his report for the Admiralty.'

Bolitho understood. It was one thing to hear of a victorious sea fight, but nothing to match the sight of a beaten enemy being brought into port, her flag beneath the British ensign.

Coutts had evidence, but that was insufficient. Too many men had died so far to warrant another haphazard scheme. And with Probyn's prize being re-taken by the enemy, even the destruction of Fort Exeter might appear unimportant in far-off London.

But a sharp, determined attack on a supply base, right under the noses of the French who were flaunting their neutrality like a false flag, might sway the balance. Especially if successfully completed before anyone could say no.

Coutts seemed to read his thoughts. 'Remember this, Bolitho. When you attain high rank, never ask what you shall do. The superior minds of Admiralty tend to say no, rather than encourage risk, which might disturb their rarefied existence. Even if you put your career and your life in jeopardy, do as you believe is right, and in the manner best for your country. Acting merely to placate your superiors is living a lie.'

Pears loomed through the dimming light and said harshly, 'We will shorten sail in one hour, Mr Bolitho. But I'll not lie to. There's too much current for comfort hereabouts.' He looked at the admiral and added curtly, 'We shall need to be on station for *Spite*'s return.'

Coutts took Pears' arm and guided him away, but not far enough for Bolitho to miss the anger in his voice as he snapped, 'By God, you drive me too hard, Captain! I'll brook no insolence from you, or anyone else, d'you hear?'

Pears rumbled something, but they were out of earshot.

Bolitho saw Couzens, his face glowing in the compass light as he wrote his entry on the master's mate's slate. He seemed to symbolize something. Youth, innocence or ignorance, whichever way you looked at it. They were all being carried forward to what might easily turn into a disaster. Coutts' determination to win might soon give way to grasping straws. Pears' mistrust of his superior could do for all of them just as easily.

Bolitho was torn between them. He admired Coutts more than he could say. Yet he could understand Pears' more cautious approach. The old and the new. One man at the peak of his career, whereas the admiral saw himself in a far greater role in the not too distant future.

He heard Cairns on the upper gundeck speaking with Tolcher, the boatswain.

Discussing tomorrow's routine which could never be allowed to falter. Not in war or peace, and no matter what kind of man walked the poop in lordly silence. The ship came first. Tomorrow, and all the other tomorrows. Painting to be done, a man to be flogged, another to be promoted, rigging and spars to be overhauled. It never ceased.

He remembered suddenly what Probyn had said about taking full advantage of any chance which offered itself. It was as if he had heard him speak aloud.

Well, Cairns would be off the ship soon. Even Pears could not refuse the next time. Bolitho sighed, finding no comfort in the fact that in a matter of weeks or days he might be doing Cairns' work until Pears could find himself a more experienced replacement.

Cairns would make a good commander. Fair, firm and intelligent. A few more like him and there would be victories enough to satisfy everyone, he thought bitterly.

Midshipman Couzens crossed the deck and asked, 'Will we see any more action, sir?'

Bolitho considered it.

'You know as much as I.'

Couzens stepped back to hide his expression. He had seen Bolitho discussing important matters with the admiral. Naturally he would not allow himself to share such privileged information with a mere midshipman. But that Bolitho knew that *he* knew was almost as good as sharing it, he thought.

To everyone's relief, and no little surprise, the *Spite*'s topsails were reported by the masthead look-out within minutes of the first dawn light. A tiny, pale pyramid of sails, drawing nearer and nearer with such maddening slowness that Bolitho could sense the mood around him like a threat.

The decks were holystoned, and the hands had their breakfast washed down with beer. Then they mustered for the many tasks throughout the ship, and more than one petty officer had to use threats and brute force to stop his men from peering outboard to see how much nearer the sloop had come.

When she had beaten as close as she could manage, she went about and lay hove to under *Trojan*'s lee, and a boat was dropped smartly in the water to carry Cunningham in person to make his report.

Bolitho stood with the side party to receive the youthful commander, and did not envy him at all. He had seen Coutts pacing the poop and staring at the *Spite*, and had also felt Pears' harsh reprimands more than once during the morning about matters which at any other time he would have thought too trivial for comment.

But Cunningham showed no anxiety as he climbed through the entry port and doffed his hat to the quarterdeck and saluting marines. His eyes passed over Bolitho without even a blink of recognition and then he strode aft to meet the captain.

Later, Bolitho was summoned to the great cabin, where he found Cairns already waiting with the flag lieutenant.

He was not really surprised at being called aft. It was customary for the first lieutenant and his immediate subordinate to be invited, if only to listen, when some important manoeuvre was to be undertaken.

They could hear Pears' voice from the dining cabin, loud and angry, and Cunningham's clipped, almost matter of fact tone as he explained something.

Cairns looked at Lieutenant Ackerman. 'They seem to be in a sour mood today.'

Ackerman kept his face blank. 'The admiral will have his way.'

A screen door was thrust open and the three other men entered the cabin abruptly, like late arrivals in a theatre.

Bolitho looked at Coutts. Gone was the uncertainty.

He said lightly, 'Well, gentlemen, Major Paget's piece of intelligence has proved its worth.' He nodded to Cunningham. 'Tell them.'

Cunningham explained how he had discovered the little island, and under cover of darkness had put a landing party ashore. It had taken longer than expected, but after sighting wood-smoke he had guessed there were people there and every care had to be taken to avoid detection.

Bolitho guessed he had been rehearsing that part on his way over in the boat. To forestall any criticism which, once made, might damage his chances of reward.

He said, 'There is a good anchorage, not large, but well concealed from seaward. There are several huts, and plenty of evidence that ships put in to load and unload cargo, even to refit if need be.'

Pears asked, 'Who did you send?'

Bolitho waited, seeing Coutts' brief smile as the sloop's commander replied just as sharply, 'I went myself, sir. I was not mistaken about what I saw.'

Coutts asked, 'What else?'

Cunningham was still glaring at Pears. 'A sizeable schooner is anchored there. Privateer. No doubt of it.'

They exchanged glances, and Coutts said, 'She'll be waiting for another vessel. I'll lay odds that there are enough weapons to supply two regiments!'

Pears persisted, 'But suppose there's nothing but the schooner.' He looked round the cabin with something like dismay. 'Like taking a cudgel to crack a small egg!'

'The first part of the information is correct, Captain Pears.' Coutts was watching him. Compelling, insisting. 'Why do you still doubt the rest? This island is obviously chosen for its access. From the Leeward or Windward Islands, from as far south as the Spanish Main, it would present an excellent place for exchange, even for rearming a merchant vessel and changing her to a privateer.' He did not conceal his impatience. 'This time we'll cut them off at the roots. For good.'

He started to move around the cabin, as if unable to hold his excitement in check.

'Think of it. All we have to do is trap them in their anchorage and seize whatever vessel tries to enter. The French will think again about allowing their people to be laid so low. A setback like that would also give their Spanish friends something to ponder on before they run like jackals to sample the spoils.'

Bolitho tried to see it like an outsider. To avoid considering Coutts as his superior, someone he had shared a few weeks of his life with.

Was this discovery really that important? Or was Coutts merely blowing it up like a bladder to *make* it appear so?

A few huts and a schooner did not sound very promising, and it was obvious from Pears' resentful expression that he thought much the same.

When he looked again the mood had changed once more. Foley, the cabin servant, was here, and glasses of wine were already being handed round as if to celebrate Cunningham's news.

Coutts raised his glass. 'I'll give you a sentiment.' He was smiling broadly. 'To a victory, gentlemen. And let us make it as painless as we can!'

He had turned to look through the stern windows and did not see Pears place his glass on the tray, untouched.

Bolitho tasted the wine, but like the mood it was suddenly bitter.

# 13

## No More Pretence

'Captain's a'comin', sir!' The boatswain's mate's whisper seemed unnaturally loud in the dawn stillness.

Bolitho turned, seeking out Pears' heavy figure as he moved to the compass, murmured something to Sambell, the master's mate, and then walked forward to the quarterdeck rail.

Bolitho knew better than to say anything at this point. It was early in the morning, and as *Trojan* ploughed a steady southerly course under her topsails and jib, it was as if they were in the middle of a tropical downpour. The rain had burst over the slow-moving ship with the fierceness of a storm, advancing out of the darkness to thunder across canvas and decks and pass just as quickly across the opposite beam. But now, an hour later, the water still trickled and thudded from sails and rigging, from the tops and down through the scuppers in miniature cascades. When the sun rose there would be so much steam it would be like a fire-ship, Bolitho thought.

But Pears knew all this, and required no telling. He had watched too many dawns on so many seas to need some lieutenant to remind him.

It was still quite dark on the upper gundeck, but Bolitho

knew that every cannon was manned and cleared for action within minutes of the galley fires being doused. It was an uncanny, sinister feeling. This great ship, moving like a shadow into deeper darkness, the sails shaking occasionally to a tired wind, the wheel creaking as the helmsmen sought to hold her on course.

Somewhere, up ahead, lay Coutts' objective. The tiny, remote island where he hoped, no, intended to find so much. Isla San Bernardo, little more than a dot on Erasmus Bunce's chart. It was said to have been the last resting place of some exclusive order of friars who had landed there over a hundred years ago. Bunce had remarked scathingly that they had probably arrived there by accident, imagining it to be one of the mainlands. That seemed likely, Bolitho thought. The passage between Santo Domingo and Puerto Rico was some ninety miles wide, a veritable ocean for some tiny, inexperienced boat. The friars had long passed into history, massacred it was said by pirates, by marooned captives, by one of a dozen scourges which still ravaged the length and breadth of the rich Caribbean.

*Spite* was there now, in position and ready to seal the anchorage. Cunningham must be rubbing his hands, seeing the citation in the *Gazette* as if it were already written.

Bolitho heard Pears moving towards him. It was time. He said, 'Wind holding steady, sir, nor' by west.' He waited, sensing the man's responsibility, his doubt.

Pears muttered, 'Very well, Mr Bolitho. We shall get light to see our way before long.' He raised his eyes to the mastheads, to the great rectangles of pale canvas and the fading stars beyond.

Bolitho followed his glance, wondering how it must feel. To command, to carry the final reward, or blame. Cairns seemed exactly ready for it, whereas he felt unsure, too far removed to understand what Pears must be feeling. Cairns would be leaving soon, he thought. Would that bring him closer to Pears? He doubted it.

Cairns came now out of the darkness without causing a stir, as he always did.

He touched his hat to Pears' bulky shape and to Bolitho said, 'I've just been round the lower gundeck. Not enough hands there, but I doubt we'll be fighting a fleet today!'

Bolitho recalled Coutts' excitement over a single schooner and smiled.

'With *Spite*'s aid, I expect we'll give a good account of ourselves!'

Pears turned with sudden anger. 'Get aloft, Mr Bolitho! Use some of your wit on the masthead look-out and report what you see.' He swung away. 'Unless your sickness at heights still prevails!'

His sarcasm was clearly heard by the helmsmen and the quarterdeck gun crews. Bolitho felt both surprised and embarrassed by the outburst, and saw a marine turning away to hide a broad grin.

Cairns said quietly, 'Which gives you some idea of his own anxiety, Dick.'

That simple comment helped to steady Bolitho as he climbed up the mainmast ratlines, purposefully disdaining the lubber's hole at the maintop to climb out and cling with fingers and toes to the futtock shrouds, his body arched above the deck far below. His resentment at Pears' words enabled him to reach the topgallant mast without even a stab of nausea, and when at last, breathless and sweating, he clambered on to the crosstrees beside the look-out, he realized he had climbed that far with more haste than his usual caution.

The seaman said, 'It be lightenin' now, zur. Be a fine old day, I'm thinkin'.'

Bolitho looked at him, drawing deep breaths to recover himself. He recognized the man, an elderly topman named Buller. Elderly by naval standards, but he was probably no more than thirty. Worn out by the endless demands of wind and sea, of fighting maddened canvas in the teeth of a gale, fisting and kicking until every nail was almost torn from his hands, and his muscles strained and ruptured beyond treatment, he would soon be relegated to safer work on the forecastle or with the afterguard.

But the important thing to Bolitho was that the man was untroubled. Not merely by height and discomfort, but by the unexpected appearance of his second lieutenant.

Bolitho thought of the marine's grin. That too was suddenly important. There had been no malice, no pleasure at seeing him trodden on by the captain.

He replied, 'It will be hot anyway,' He pointed past the foremast, strangely bare without its topgallant set at the yard. 'D'you know these waters, Buller?'

The man considered it. 'Can't say I do, zur. But then, can't say I don't. One place is like another to a sailorman.' He chuckled. 'Less 'e's let ashore, o' course.'

Bolitho thought of the brothel in New York, the woman screaming obscenities in his face, the dead girl's breast still warm under his palm.

One place like another. That was true enough, he thought. Even the merchant seamen were the same. Every ship was the last. One more voyage, just enough pay and bounty saved, and it would be used to buy a little alehouse, a chandlery, a small-holding from some country squire. But it never seemed to happen, unless the man was thrown on the beach in peacetime, or rejected as a useless cripple. The sea always won in the end.

The outboard end of the fore-topsail yard paled slightly, and when he twisted round Bolitho saw the first hint of dawn. He peered down and swallowed hard. The deck, darkly ribbed around by the upper batteries of guns, seemed a mile beneath his dangling legs. He would just have to put up with it. If the hatred of heights had plagued him since his first ship when he had been twelve years old, it was not likely to relent now.

Bolitho felt the mast and its spars trembling and swaying beneath him. He had gone to sea as a midshipman in 1768. The year *Trojan* had been launched. He had thought of it before, but this morning, up here and strangely isolated, it seemed like an omen, a warning. He shivered. He was getting as bad as Quinn.

On the quarterdeck, unaware or indifferent to his second lieutenant's fancies, Pears paced back and forth across the damp planking.

Cairns watched him, and aft on the raised poop D'Esterre stood with his arms crossed, thinking of Fort Exeter, of Bolitho, and of his dead marines.

A door opened and slammed, and voices floated around the quarterdeck to announce the admiral's arrival. He was followed by his aide, Ackerman, and even in the poor light looked alert and wide awake.

He paused near the wheel and spoke to Bunce, then with a nod to Cairns said, ''Morning, Captain. Is everything ready?'

Cairns winced. Where Pears was concerned, things were always *ready*.

But Pears sounded unruffled. 'Aye, sir. Cleared for action, but guns not loaded,' the slightest hint of dryness, 'or run out.'

Coutts glanced at him. 'I can see that.' He turned away. '*Spite* must be in position now. I suggest you set more sail, Captain. The time for guessing is done.'

Cairns relayed the order and seconds later, with the topmen rushing out along the upper yards and the wet canvas falling and then billowing sluggishly to the wind, *Trojan* tilted more steeply to the extra pressure.

'I've been looking at the chart again.' Coutts was half watching the activity above the deck. 'There seems to be no other anchorage. Deep water to the south'rd and a shoal or two against the shore. Cunningham put his landing party to the south'rd. A clever move. He thinks things out, that one.'

Pears dragged his eyes from the lithe topmen as they slithered down to the deck again.

He said, 'It was the *only* place, I'd have thought, sir.'

'Really?'

Coutts moved away with his flag lieutenant, the cut well and truly driven home.

A few gulls dipped out of the darkness and circled the ship like pieces of spindrift. They seemed to tell of the land's nearness, and their almost disinterested attitude implied they had other sources of food close by.

From his dizzy perch Bolitho watched the birds as they floated past him. They reminded him of all those other times, different landfalls, but mostly of Falmouth. The little fishing villages which nestled in rocky clefts along the Cornish coast, the boats coming home, the gulls screaming and mewing above them.

He came out of his thoughts as Buller said, ''Ell, zur, *Spite*'s well off station!' He showed some excitement for the first time. 'There'll be the devil to pay now!'

Bolitho found time to marvel that the seaman should care, and be so accurate in his opinions. Coutts would be furious, and it might take *Trojan* a whole day to beat back to her original station and allow Cunningham a second chance.

'I'd better get down and tell the captain.' He was thinking aloud.

Why had he mentioned it? Even thought of it? Had it been to stop another wave of frustration throughout the ship, or merely to protect Coutts' credibility?

Buller grunted. 'She probably lost a man over the side.'

Bolitho did not answer. He hoped Cunningham was the kind
of man who would waste valuable time to look for a man
overboard. But that was as far as it went. He swung the telescope
over his arm and pressed his shoulders against the shivering
mast.

'I'll leave this with you, Buller. When I go down, give us a hail
as soon as you can make out what she's up to.'

He tried not to think of the drop to the deck, how long it
would take if the ship gave a lurch before he could use both
hands to hold on again.

It was like looking through a dark bottle. A few hints of
whitecaps, a glassiness on the sea's face to show that dawn was
nearby. Then he saw the pale squares of canvas, barely clear as
yet, but rising from the darkness like a broken iceberg.

*Spite* must have changed tack considerably, he thought. She
was standing in well towards the hidden anchorage, but she
should have been miles nearer by now. Buller was right, but
there would be more than the devil to pay after this. There would
be . . . he stiffened, momentarily forgetting his precarious position.

'Wot is it, zur?' Buller had sensed something.

Bolitho did not know what to say. He was wrong of course.
Had to be.

He held the swaying blur of sails in his lens and then, straining every nerve until the wound on his forehead began to throb
in time with his heart-beats, he lowered the glass just a fraction.

Still deep in shadow, but it was there right enough. He
wanted it to be a dream, a fault in the telescope. But instead of
*Spite*'s rakish single deck there was something more solid, deep
and hard like a double reflection.

He thrust the glass at the seaman and then cupped his hands
to his mouth.

'Deck there! Sail on the starboard bow!' He hesitated a few
moments longer, imagining the sudden tension and astonishment below him. Then, *'Ship of the line!'*

Buller exclaimed slowly, 'You done it proper now, zur!'

Bolitho was already slithering downwards, groping for a
backstay, his eyes still holding that menacing outline.

Coutts was waiting for him, his head thrust forward as he
asked, 'Are you certain?'

Pears strode past them, his eyes everywhere as he prepared
himself for the next vital hours.

Only once did he glance at Bolitho. Then to Coutts he snapped. 'He's *certain*, sir.'

Cairns said quietly, 'Now here's a fine thing, Dick. She'll not be one of ours.'

The admiral heard him and said curtly, 'I don't care what she is, Mr Cairns. If she stands against us, then damn your eyes, she's an enemy in my book!' He peered after the captain and raised his voice. 'Have the guns loaded, if you please!' He seemed to sense Pears' arguments from the opposite side of the deck. 'And let me see what this ship of yours can do today!'


Along either side of the upper gundeck the crews threw themselves on their tackles and handspikes and manhandled their heavy cannon up to the closed ports.

Bolitho stood by the boat tier, straining his eyes through the gloom as he watched one gun captain after another raise his fist to signify he was loaded and ready.

Midshipman Huss peered over the main hatch and yelled, 'Lower gundeck *ready*, sir!'

Bolitho pictured Dalyell down there with thirty great thirty-two-pounders. Like everyone else in the wardroom, he had risen in rank, but his experience had altered little. Bolitho knew that if and when *Trojan* was required to give battle it would test everyone to the limit.

Quinn crossed from the opposite side and asked, 'What *is* going on, Dick?' He was almost knocked from his feet as some ship's boys hurried aft with carriers of shot for the quarterdeck nine-pounders.

Bolitho looked up at the mainmast, through the shaking rigging and spread canvas, recalling his feelings such a short while back when he had watched the other ship through the telescope. It had been fifteen minutes ago, but the daylight seemed reluctant to reveal the newcomer, and only the look-outs, and perhaps the marines in the tops, could see the ship properly.

He replied, 'Maybe that ship is here on passage for another port in the Caribbean.'

As he said it he knew he was deluding himself, or perhaps trying to ease Quinn's anxiety. The ship was no English man-of-war. Every large vessel was being held within a squadron, just in case France openly joined in the fight. Unlikely to be a Spaniard either. They usually used their larger men-of-war to escort the rich treasure ships from the Main, through the pirate-infested waters and all the way to Santa Cruz and safety. No, it had to be a Frenchman.

Bolitho chilled with excitement. He had seen French ships in plenty. Well designed and built, they were said to be equally well manned.

He looked around the tiered boats and saw Coutts, hands behind his back, speaking with Pears and old Bunce. They all appeared calm enough, although with Pears you could never be sure. It was strange to see the quarterdeck so busy in the first light. Crouching gun crews on either side, and further aft, standing against the hammock nettings, D'Esterre's depleted ranks of marines. Near one battery of nine-pounders he could see Libby, one-time signals midshipman, now acting fifth lieutenant. What must he be thinking, Bolitho wondered? Seventeen years old, and yet if a blast of canister and grape raked the quarterdeck with its bloody furrows he might find himself in temporary command until someone else could reach him. Frowd was there, too. From master's mate to acting sixth lieutenant. It was mad when you considered it, he was even older than Cairns by a year or two. He was standing quite near Sambell, the other master's mate. But that was all. Before Sparke had been killed and Probyn captured it had been Jack and Arthur. Now it was sir and Mr Sambell.

He heard Cairns call, 'Let her fall off a point!'

Then later the helmsman's cry, 'Steady as she goes, sir! Sou'-east by sou'!'

The braces were manned, the yards trimmed for the slight alteration of course. Apart from the rustle and grumble of the sails, the ship's own private sounds, there was silence.

Bolitho pictured the chart, and beyond the bows the island as it must appear to those who could see. A headland sliding out towards the starboard bow, around which lay the entrance to the anchorage. Where *Spite*, presumably, was on station after all. God, she would get a surprise when the newcomer showed herself around the shoulder of land. Cunningham's look-outs would probably mistake her for the *Trojan*.

'Deck there!' Buller's hoarse voice. 'T'other ship's shortenin' sail, zur!'

Someone said, 'She's sighted *Spite*, 'tis my guess.'

The larboard battery dipped over slightly to the pressure of wind in the sails, and Bolitho saw the tethered guns glint suddenly as the daylight lanced through the shrouds and halliards.

Colour was returning to familiar things. Faces emerged as people, features became expressions again. Here and there a man moved, to adjust a gun tackle, or push loose equipment away from a carriage or breech, to brush hair from eyes, to make sure a cutlass or boarding axe was within reach.

The petty officers and midshipmen stood out at intervals, little blue and white markers in the chain of command.

Far above the deck, at the highest point, the long masthead pendant licked out ahead like a scarlet serpent. Wind was holding steady, Bolitho thought. Even so, there was no chance of heading off the other ship.

Quinn whispered, 'What will the admiral do? What can he do? We're not at war with France.'

Midshipman Forbes scurried along the deck, skipping over tackles and flaked halliards like a rabbit.

He touched his hat and said breathlessly, 'Captain's compliments, sir, and would you bring the French lieutenant aft?'

Bolitho nodded. 'Very well.'

Forbes was really enjoying himself. Aft with the mighty, too excited and too young to see the teeth of danger.

Quinn said, 'I'll fetch him.'

Bolitho shook his head, smiling at the absurdity of it. He had to bring the French officer because Cairns was busy on the quarterdeck and everyone else was too junior. Etiquette would be observed even at the gates of hell, he thought.

He found the Frenchman on the orlop deck, sitting with the surgeon outside the sickbay while Thorndike's assistants laid out the makeshift table with his instruments.

Thorndike asked irritably, 'What the hell are we doing now?' He glared at his helpers. 'Wasting time and dirtying my things. They must be short of work to do!'

Bolitho said to Contenay, 'The captain wishes to see you.'

Together they climbed up through the lower gundeck, a place in almost complete darkness with every port shut and only the slow-matches glowing slightly in the tubs by each division of cannon.

Contenay said, 'There is trouble, my friend?'

'A ship. One of yours.'

It was strange, Bolitho thought, it was easier to speak with the Frenchman than the surgeon.

'*Mon Dieu*.' Contenay nodded to a marine sentry at the next hatchway and added, 'I will have to watch my words, I think.'

On deck it was much brighter. It seemed impossible that it had changed so much in the time to go to the orlop and back again.

On the quarterdeck Bolitho announced, '*M'sieu* Contenay, sir.'

Pears glared at him. 'Over here.' He strode across to the nettings where Coutts and the flag lieutenant were training telescopes towards the other ship.

Bolitho stole a quick glance at her. He had not been mistaken. She made a proud sight, leaning over, close-hauled on the starboard tack, her topgallant sails and maincourse already brailed up to the yards, her bilge clearly visible as she tacked towards the entrance.

'The prisoner, sir.' Pears too was looking at the other vessel.

Coutts lowered his glass and regarded the Frenchman calmly. 'Ah yes. The ship yonder, *m'sieu*, do you know her?'

Contenay's mouth turned down, as if he was about to refuse an answer. Then he shrugged and replied, 'She is the *Argonaute*.'

Ackerman nodded. 'Thought as much, sir. I saw her once off Guadeloupe. A seventy-four. Fine looking ship.'

Pears said heavily, 'She too wears a rear-admiral's flag.' He glanced questioningly at Contenay.

He said, 'It is true. *Contre-Amiral* André Lemercier.'

Coutts eyed him searchingly. 'You were one of his officers, am I right?'

'I *am* one of his officers, *m'sieu*.' He looked towards the other two-decker. 'It is all I am prepared or required to say.'

Pears exploded, 'You mind your manners, sir! We don't need to be told more. You were aiding the King's enemies, abetting an unlawful rebellion, and now you expect to be treated as an innocent bystander!'

Coutts seemed surprised at the outburst. 'Well said, Captain. But I think the lieutenant is well aware of what he has done, and where he stands.'

Bolitho watched, fascinated, hoping Pears would not notice him and order him down to the gundeck.

A private drama which excluded everyone else, and yet which could decide their future.

Cairns said quietly, 'Here is a problem for the admiral, Dick. Is it a real stalemate? Or shall we force our views on the Frenchman?'

Bolitho watched Coutts' youthful profile. He was no doubt regretting his shift of flag now. His ninety-gun *Resolute* would be more than a match for the French seventy-four. *Trojan* had no such advantage. About the same size, and with just two more guns than the *Argonaute*, she was undermanned and lacking experienced officers.

If Contenay was typical of *Argonaute*'s wardroom, she would be an adversary to reckon with. What the hell was Cunningham doing? A sloop-of-war was far too frail to match iron with the line of battle, but an extra show of strength, no matter how small, would be doubly welcome.

'Take the prisoner down. I may require him presently.' Coutts beckoned to D'Esterre. 'Attend to it.' To Bolitho he said, 'Warn the masthead to report what *Spite* is doing the instant he sights her.'

Bolitho hurried to the quarterdeck ladder. The masthead look-out, like everyone else above deck, was probably more interested in the French two-decker than in *Spite*.

*Trojan* maintained her set course, every telescope trained on the other ship as she moved at right angles across the bows, nearer and nearer to the headland.

Coutts must be worried. He could not anchor, and if he continued past the entrance he would lose the wind-gage and it might take hours to beat back again. If he stood out to sea, the same must apply. His only course was to follow the Frenchman, who obviously intended to ignore *Trojan*'s intentions, to treat her as if she did not exist.

The headland was sloping more quickly now, to reveal the one on the opposite side of the entrance. Two green arms reaching out to receive them.

Bolitho felt the mounting glare from the sun, the sudden dryness in his throat as the look-out yelled, 'Deck there! *Spite*'s aground, zur!'

Something like a sigh ran along the *Trojan*'s decks.

Of all the bad luck, this was it. Cunningham must have

misjudged his entrance, or had been deceived by the currents. It was humiliating enough for Coutts. For Cunningham it must be the end of the world, Bolitho thought.

Stockdale whispered, 'The Frenchie can do as 'e pleases now, sir.'

The anchorage was opening up with every dragging minute. Bolitho could see the sheltered water beyond the turbulence at the entrance. *Spite*'s three masts, slightly angled and stiffly unmoving. Beyond her the deeper shadows, and a schooner at anchor, close inshore.

The look-out shouted, 'They're tryin' to tow 'er off, zur!'

Bolitho could not see without a telescope, and like the seamen around him, fretted and waited for more news from aloft. Cunningham had boats down and would probably lay out an anchor to kedge his ship free from the ground.

Quinn asked, 'What is the Frenchman doing?' He sounded beside himself with worry.

'He'll no doubt anchor, James. He has beaten us to the island. To attack him there would be a sure way of starting a war.'

He looked away, confused and bitter. Whatever they did, no matter how right the cause, fate seemed to be against them.

The *Argonaute* was quite likely bringing another great cargo of ordnance and powder. Some to be loaded into the schooner, more to be stacked in a safe hiding place to await the next privateer or transport. Contenay must have sailed from here more than a few times. No wonder he found Fort Exeter without any trouble.

As if to bear out his ideas, another look-out shouted wildly, 'Sail on the starboard quarter, sir!'

Figures bustled across the quarterdeck, sunlight glinting on raised telescopes, as the look-out continued, 'Brig, sir! She's goin' about!'

Bolitho looked at Quinn's pale features. 'I'll bet she is, James! Just the sight of us will be enough. She must have been coming here to collect her cargo from the French!'

'Is there nothing we can do?'

Quinn looked up, startled, as Buller yelled again, 'Deck there! *Spite*'s come off, zur! She's shakin' out 'er tops'ls!'

Quinn gripped Bolitho's arm as the news brought a wild burst of cheering from the watching seamen and marines.

They looked aft as Midshipman Weston's signals party burst

into life and sent a hoist of bright flags flying to the yards.

Bolitho nodded. In the nick of time. Coutts had signalled *Spite* to leave the anchorage and give chase. Even the delay at hoisting her boats would not mean much to Cunningham. With a following wind, and his honour very much at stake, he would overhaul and take the brig before noon.

And there was still the schooner. If she was a privateer, the French could not prevent Coutts taking action against her if she attempted to leave.

He shaded his eyes, seeing more sails breaking out from the sloop's yards, imagining the excitement and relief pushing all disappointment aside.

'*Spite*'s acknowledged, sir!'

Midshipman Couzens bounded past on some mission or other, his freckled face alive with anticipation.

'Now it's the Frenchman's turn to be an onlooker, sir!'

Bolitho turned sharply as the anchorage echoed violently to the crash of cannon fire. He saw the gunsmoke hit the calm water and burst skyward, eddying across the pale sunlight like a cloud.

Everyone was yelling and shouting at once, stricken by the unexpected turn of events. *Spite* was turning to one side, still reeling from a savage broadside at extreme range. Like a hurricane the *Argonaute*'s iron had ripped through her masts and rigging, reducing her to an unmanageable wreck in seconds. Her foremast had gone, and while they watched, her maintopmast fell alongside in a welter of spray and tangled cordage. *Spite* stopped moving, and Bolitho guessed she had run aground again on an extension of the same sand-bar. Seeing her go from movement to sudden stillness was like watching something beautiful die.

The *Argonaute* had made certain the brig would not be captured, and even now was coming about, her long jib boom swinging through the smoke of her one, murderous broadside.

Quinn said in a choking voice, 'God, they're coming out!'

Bolitho looked aft as Cairns' voice boomed through his speaking trumpet.

'Hands aloft and shorten sail! Mr Tolcher, rig your nets!'

A bright scarlet ensign rose to the gaff, and Stockdale spat on his hands. Coutts had shown his colours. He was going to fight.

Nets were already being spread above the gundeck, the men

working without thought, as they had so often at their drills.

Bolitho watched the *Argonaute*'s shape shortening as she completed her turn towards the entrance.

She too had run up her colours. The white flag of France. No more pretence or bluff.

Later, higher authorities might argue over excuses and deceptions. But now, today, each captain had his own clear reason to engage an enemy.

'*Open your ports!*'

Tackles squeaked, and along either side a double line of port lids lifted in time with the lesser quarterdeck batteries.

'*Run out!*'

Bolitho drew a deep breath, forcing himself to watch as his own guns trundled noisily to their ports, thrusting out their black muzzles like snouts in the strengthening sunlight.

Two ships of the line, without aid, not even a spectator to watch their ponderous strength as they manoeuvred towards each other, in no haste, and in total silence.

Another glance aft and he saw Coutts lifting his arms to allow the captain's coxswain to buckle on his sword for him.

Bolitho realized that Coutts would never give in. He dare not. It must be victory today. Or nothing.

'Starboard battery, *stand by!*'

Bolitho tugged out his hanger and pulled his hat over his eyes.

'Ready, lads!'

He glanced to left and right, the familiar faces passing his vision, merging, then disappearing as he faced the enemy.

'On the uproll!'

Somewhere, a man started to cough violently, another was pounding a slow, desperate tattoo on the deck beside his gun.

'*Fire!*'

# 14

# A Very High Price

As the upper battery, followed instantly by the thirty-two-pounders on the lower gundeck, roared out in a full broadside, *Trojan* gave a tremendous shudder, as if she would wrench herself apart.

Even though every man had been expecting it, the deafening crash of gun-fire was beyond imagination, the sound going on and on as each cannon hurled itself inboard on its tackles.

Bolitho watched the dense smoke being forced downwind from the starboard bow and stared towards the French ship as the sea around her became a mass of leaping white feathers. The *Argonaute* was steering on a converging tack, her yards braced hard round to carry her away from the nearest spit of land. Without a telescope it was impossible to see if they had hit her, although with such a massive broadside they should have found some targets. But *Trojan* had fired at the first possible moment, and Bolitho estimated the range to be at least eight cables.

On either side of him the gun captains were yelling like demons, the crews ramming home charges and fresh balls, while others stood with handspikes in readiness to control their ponderous weapons.

It sounded blurred, unreal, and Bolitho rubbed his ears rapidly to restore his hearing. The deck tilted very slightly as Pears ordered an alteration of course towards the other ship. How invulnerable she looked. With topsails and forecourse flapping to retain the wind, the French captain was trying to gain sea-room, to escape the blanketing shelter of the land across his quarter.

What was he up to, he wondered? What motive did Coutts' opposite number have in mind? Perhaps he wished to draw *Trojan* away from the island to allow the schooner time to escape. Or maybe, having put the *Spite* out of action, all he wanted to do was slip away himself and avoid further conflict. Perhaps he had other orders, to find a second rendezvous and unload his cargo without delay.

It was incredible that he could think at all. He peered along the deck, seeing the captains raise their fists, their faces masked in concentration.

He looked aft. 'Ready, sir!'

Again, the senior midshipman of the lower gundeck bobbed through the hatch and yelled, '*Ready*, sir!'

Couzens went past at the run, carrying a message from the forecastle to Cairns on the quarterdeck.

As he passed Midshipman Huss he shouted, 'You were slow that time!' They grinned at one another as if it were a huge game.

Bolitho turned towards the enemy again. Nearer now, her deck angled over to the wind, the lines of guns shining in the sunlight like teeth.

He knew in his heart that the French admiral had no intention of telling his captain to haul off. He was going to fight. What the world said later mattered little out here. Justification would be sought and found by both sides, but the winner would have the real say in things.

The side of the French ship vanished in a writhing bank of smoke, broken by darting orange tongues, as she delivered her reply to *Trojan*'s challenge.

Bolitho gritted his teeth, expecting to feel the hull quiver to the crash of the broadside. But only a few balls hit the tumblehome, while above the decks the air became alive with screaming, shrieking chain-shot.

Bolitho saw the boatswain's hastily spread nets jumping with fallen blocks and severed rigging, and then a marine fell headlong from the maintop, struck the gangway and vanished over the side without even a cry.

Bolitho swallowed hard. *First blood.* He looked aft, seeing Pears watching the enemy while his hand rose level with his shoulder.

Bolitho said quickly, 'Ready, lads!'

The captain's arm fell, and once more the air was blasted by the thunder of guns.

'Stop your vents! Sponge out! *Load!*'

The seamen, who had cursed their captain and officers as they had drilled again and again in every kind of condition, went through the motions without even pausing to watch some of their companions hurrying aloft to make repairs.

Bolitho saw the great rent in the main-topsail spreading and ripping as it was pushed by the wind, and knew that the enemy was following a regular French tactic. To cripple the adversary first, render her useless and impossible to handle so that she would fall downwind and present her stern to another murderous broadside. Cleared for action, a ship of the line was open from bow to stern, and a well-timed bombardment through the poop and counter could change the gundecks into a slaughterhouse.

The *Argonaute* was showing some signs of damage, too. Shot-holes in her canvas, and a savage gash in her larboard gangway where two balls had struck home together.

Five cables. Just half a mile between them, and both ships gathering speed as they thrust clear of the land.

Again the writhing bank of smoke, and once more the shriek of chain-shot overhead. It was unbelievable that no spar was hit, but the terrible sound made more than one man gasp with alarm as he worked at his gun.

Stockdale paused at his efforts and shouted. 'We're holdin' the wind, sir!' His battered features were stained with smoke, but he looked unbreakable.

'On the uproll!'

Bolitho heard Midshipman Huss repeating the order to Dalyell below.

'*Fire!*'

The deck rebounded as if the ship was driving ashore, and

then there was a ragged cheer as the enemy's main-topgallant mast swung wildly on its stays before breaking away and plunging down like a lance.

A lucky shot, and nobody would ever know who had aimed it.

Pears' harsh voice carried easily above the squeak of gun trucks and the clatter of rammers.

'Well done, Trojans! Hit 'em again!'

More cheers, quenched by the enemy's return fire, the terrifying crash of iron smashing into the hull and through some of the gunports below.

Bolitho winced, wondering why the Frenchman had changed his tactics. He heard the rumble of a cannon careering across the lower deck, the sudden lurch as it hit something solid. Men were yelling down there, their voices strangely muffled, like souls in torment.

The *Argonaute* seemed to be gaining, drawing slightly ahead, so that her jib boom appeared to be touching *Trojan*'s bowsprit. With the advantage of wind and position, Pears would probably let his ship fall off, then spread more sail and try to cross the enemy's stern.

He heard Cairns' voice through his speaking trumpet. 'Hands aloft! Loose t'gan's'ls!'

Bolitho found himself nodding as if in agreement. The ship was turning again, just a few points, while her topgallant sails flapped and then hardened at their yards.

He watched the other ship, his eyes smarting in the smoke. One giant arrowhead of blue water, and both vessels aiming for some invisible mark which would bring them together.

*'Fire!'*

The seamen leapt aside as their guns crashed inboard, groping in the funnelling smoke to sponge out the muzzles before a packed charge was rammed home.

Bolitho felt the hull quiver and realized the enemy had fired again, and saw part of a gangway splinter apart as if under an invisible axe. A seaman ran screaming and stumbling past his companion, his hands clawing at his face.

A marine seized him and pushed him to a hatchway, and others reached up to drag him below.

Bolitho glanced at Quinn and saw him retching. The seaman had taken a giant wood splinter in his eye as big as a marlinespike.

The sharper crack of the quarterdeck nine-pounders told him that their crews had at last been able to bring them to bear on the enemy.

The noise was growing and spreading as the two ships moved inexorably towards each other. Wood splinters, fragments of cordage and yet another corpse joined the tangle on the nets, and from below Bolitho heard a man screaming like a tortured hare.

A quick glance aft again. Pears still there, unmoving and grim-faced as he studied the enemy. Coutts, apparently untroubled by the din of battle, one foot on a bollard as he pointed to something on the Frenchman's deck for Ackerman's benefit.

'*Fire!*'

The guns were recoiling more unevenly now. The crews were getting tired, stunned by the constant thunder and crash of explosions.

Bolitho made himself walk along the deck, ducking to peer through each port as the men hauled their guns back in readiness to fire. A small world. a square of hazy sunlight in which each crew saw just a portion of the enemy.

He felt unsteady, his gait jerky as he moved behind them. His face was stiff with strain, and he imagined he must look halfway between laughing and squinting from shock.

Stockdale glanced round at him and nodded. Another man, Bolitho recognized him as Moffitt, waved his hand and shouted, 'Hot work, sir!'

More powerful thuds into the lower hull, and then a column of black smoke through an open hatch to bring a chorus of shouts and cries of alarm. But the smoke was quickly brought under control, and Bolitho guessed that Dalyell's men had been ready for such an emergency.

'Cease firing!'

As the men stood back from their smoking guns, Bolitho thought the silence almost as painful as the noise. The enemy had moved further across the bows, so that it was pointless to try to hit her.

Cairns shouted, 'Put some men to larboard!' He gestured with his trumpet. 'We will engage him as we cross his stern!'

Bolitho saw petty officers pushing dazed men across to the opposite side to help the depleted crews there. Pears had timed it well. With the slight change of tack, and extra canvas to give her more speed, *Trojan* would sweep across the enemy's wake and pour a broadside, gun by gun, the length of her hull. Even if she were not dismasted, she would be too crippled to withstand the next encounter.

He shouted, 'Ready, James!' Again he felt his jaw locked in a wild grin. 'Yours is the honour this time!'

A gun captain touched Quinn's arm as he hurried past. 'We'll show 'em, sir!'

'Hands to the braces there!'

Bolitho swung round as Cairns' voice echoed from the quarterdeck.

Stockdale gasped, 'The Frenchie's luffed, by God!'

Bolitho watched, his body like ice, seeing the *Argonaute* swinging steadily up into the wind, her reduced sails almost aback as she turned to face her enemy.

It was all happening in minutes, yet Bolitho could still find time for admiration at the superb seamanship and timing. Round and further still, so that when she had finished her manoeuvre she would be on the reverse tack, while *Trojan* was still struggling to slow her advance.

'Hands aloft! Take in the t'gan's'ls!'

Masts and spars shook and creaked violently as the helm was put over, but it was all taking too long.

As men ran wildly back to the starboard battery, Bolitho saw the enemy's side belch smoke and fire, felt the ship stagger as a carefully timed broadside smashed into the side from bowsprit to quarterdeck. Because of the angle, many of the shots did little damage, but others, which burst through gunports or smashed through the flimsy defences of gangways and nettings, caused terrible havoc. Three guns were upended, their crews either crushed or hurled aside like rubbish, and Bolitho heard the splintering bang of more balls ripping through the boat tier and sending a wave of splinters across the opposite side like tiny arrows. Men were falling and stumbling everywhere, and when Bolitho glanced at his legs he saw they were bloody from the carnage at the nearest gun.

A great chorus of voices made him turn in time to see the fore-topgallant mast fall across the bows and plunge over the side, taking with it a writhing trail of rigging like maddened snakes, spar and canvas, and two screaming seamen.

Momentarily out of control, *Trojan* swung drunkenly away from her enemy, while all the time, as her jubilant crews reloaded, *Argonaute* continued to go about until she had completed one great circle. Then as she settled down on a parallel course, but slightly ahead of the *Trojan*, she opened fire with her sternmost guns.

Blinded by smoke, and fighting to free themselves from the mass of tangled rigging, the forward gun crews aboard the *Trojan* were able to return only half their shots.

Bolitho found himself striding up and down yelling meaningless words until he was hoarse, raw with the stench of battle.

Around him men were fighting back, dying, or sprawled in the bloody attitudes of death.

Others hurried past, following the boatswain and his mates, axes shining in the smoky glare, to hack the wreckage away before it swung the ship stern on towards those merciless guns.

And aft, his face like stone, Pears watched all of it, giving his orders, not even flinching as splinters whipped past him to bring down more of the crouching gun crews.

Midshipman Huss appeared on deck, his eyes white with fear. He saw Bolitho and shouted frantically. 'Mr Dalyell's fallen, sir! I—I can't find...' He spun round, his face gaping with astonishment and freezing there as he pitched forward at Bolitho's feet.

Bolitho shouted, 'Get below, James! Take command of the lower gundeck!'

But Quinn was staring transfixed at the midshipman. Blood was pouring from a great hole in his back, but one hand still moved, as if it and nothing else was holding on to life.

A seaman turned the boy over and rasped, 'Done for, sir.'

'Did you hear?' Bolitho gripped Quinn's arm, Huss and all else forgotten. '*Get below!*'

Quinn half turned, his eyes widening as more cries and screams came up from the other gundeck.

He stammered, 'Can't. Can't...do...it.'

His head fell forward, and Bolitho saw tears running down his face, cutting pale furrows through the grime of gunsmoke.

An unfamiliar voice snapped, 'I'll go.' It was Ackerman the immaculate flag lieutenant. 'I can manage.' He stared at Quinn as if he could not believe what he saw. 'The admiral sent me.'

Bolitho peered aft, shocked by Quinn's collapse, stunned by the horror and bloody shambles all around him.

Through the drifting smoke and dangling creeper of severed rigging their eyes met. Then Coutts gave a slight wave and what could have been a shrug.

The deck shivered, and Bolitho knew that the broken mast had been hacked free.

*Trojan* was turning to windward, laying her enemy in the sights again, seemingly unreachable and beyond hurt.

'*Fire!*'

The men sprang back, groping for their rammers and spikes, cursing and cheering like mad things from bedlam.

Quinn stood as before, oblivious to the hiss of iron overhead, to the crawling wounded, to the danger of his position as the enemy's mizzen and then mainmast towered high above the nettings.

Fifty yards, certainly no more, Bolitho thought wildly. Both ships were firing blindly through the churning smoke which was trapped between them as if to cushion the hammer blows.

A seaman ran from his gun, crazed by the din and slaughter, trying to reach a hatchway. To go deeper and deeper until he found the keel, like a terrified animal going to ground. A marine sentry raised his musket as if to club him down, but let it fall, as if he too was past reason and hope.

Couzens was tugging Bolitho's sleeve, his round face screwed up as if to shut out the awful sights.

'Yes?' Bolitho had no idea how long he had been there. 'What is it?'

The midshipman tore his eyes from Huss's corpse. 'The captain says that the enemy intends to board us!' He stared at Quinn. 'You are to take charge forrard.' He showed his old stubbornness. 'I will assist.'

Bolitho gripped his shoulder. Through the thin blue coat the boy's body was hot, as if burning with fever.

'Go and get some men from below.' As the boy made to run he called, '*Walk*, Mr Couzens. Show the people how calm you are.' He forced a grin. 'No matter how you may feel.'

He turned back to the guns, astounded he could speak like that when at any second he would be dead. Worse, he might be lying pinned on the surgeon's table, waiting for the first touch of his knife.

He watched the set of the enemy's yards, the way the angle was more acute as both ships idled closer together. The guns showed no sign of lessening, even though they were firing at point-blank range, some hurling blazing wads through the smoke which were almost as much danger as the balls.

There were new sounds now. The distant crack of muskets, the thuds of shots hitting deck and gangway, or ripping harmlessly into the packed hammock nettings.

From the maintop he heard the bark of a swivel and saw a cluster of marksmen drop from the enemy's mizzen-top, swept aside like dead fruit by a hail of canister.

Individual faces stood out on the *Argonaute*'s decks, and he saw a petty officer pointing him out to another sharpshooter on the gangway. But he was felled by one of D'Esterre's marines even as he raised his musket to shoot.

He heard men scrambling up from the lower gundeck, the rasp of steel as they seized their cutlasses. Balleine, the boatswain's mate, stood by the mainmast rack, issuing the boarding pikes to anyone who came near him.

'We will touch bow to bow.' Bolitho had spoken aloud without knowing it. 'Not much time.' He drew his curved hanger and waved it over his head. 'Clear the larboard battery! Come with me!'

A single ball crashed through an open port and beheaded a seaman even as he ran to obey. For a few moments the headless corpse stood stock-still, as if undecided what to do. Then it fell, and was forgotten as swearing and cheering the seamen dashed towards the forecastle, nothing in their minds but the towering bank of pockmarked sails alongside, the crimson stab of musket-fire.

Bolitho stared, watching the other ship's great bowsprit and jib boom poking through the smoke, thrusting above the forecastle and beakhead as if nothing could stop it. There were men already there, firing down at *Trojan*'s deck, brandishing their weapons, while beneath them their fierce-eyed figurehead watched the scene with incredible menace.

Then with a violent shudder both hulls ground together. Hacking and stabbing, *Trojan*'s men swarmed to repel boarders, and from aft D'Esterre's men kept up a withering fire on the enemy's quarterdeck and poop.

Bolitho jumped over a fallen seaman and yelled, 'Here they come!'

A French seaman tried to scramble on to the cathead, but a blow with a belaying pin knocked him aside, and a lunge from a pike sent him down between the hulls.

Bolitho found himself face to face with a young lieutenant. His sword-arm came up, the two blades circled warily and with care, despite the surging press of fighting figures all around.

The French officer lunged, his eyes widening with fear as Bolitho side-stepped and knocked his arm aside with his hanger, seeing the sleeve open up, the blood spurting out like paint.

Bolitho hesitated and then hacked him across the collarbone, seeing him die before he hit the water alongside.

More men were hurrying to his aid, but when he twisted his head he saw Quinn standing by his guns as before, as if he would never move again.

Smoke swirled and then enveloped the gasping and struggling men, and Bolitho realized that the wind was strengthening, pushing the ships along in a terrible embrace.

Another figure blocked his path, and again the clang of steel dominated everything else.

He watched the man's face, detached, without feeling, meeting each thrust, testing his strength, expecting an agonizing blade through his stomach if he lost his balance.

There were others beside him. Raye of the marines, Joby Scales, the carpenter, wielding a great hammer, Varlo, the seaman who had been crossed in love, Dunwoody, the miller's son, and of course Stockdale, whose cutlass was taking a terrible toll.

Something struck him on the head and he felt blood running down his neck. But the pain only helped to tighten his guard, to make him examine his enemy's moves like an onlooker.

A dying seaman fell whimpering against the other man, making him dart a quick glance to his right. Just a second, no more than a flash of his eyes in the misty sunlight. It was enough, and Bolitho leapt over the corpse, his hanger still red as he rallied his men around the forecastle. He could not even remember driving the blade into flesh and bone.

Somebody slipped in a pool of blood and crashed into his spine. He fell sprawling, only retaining his hanger because of the lanyard around his wrist.

As he struggled to rise he saw with amazement that there was a glint of water below him, and as he stared down he could see it was widening. The ships were drifting apart.

The French boarders had realized it too, and while some tried to climb back on to the overlapping bowsprit, others made to jump, only to fall headlong into the sea to join the bobbing litter of corpses and frantic swimmers.

A few threw up their hands in surrender, but when a marine was shot dead by an enemy marksman, they too were driven bodily over the side.

Bolitho felt the strength ebbing out of him, and he had to hold on to the bulwark for support. A few guns were still firing haphazardly through the smoke, but it was over. The *Argonaute*'s sails were coming about, and very slowly she began to stand away, her stern turning towards *Trojan*'s poop like the hinges of a gate.

Bolitho realized that he was on his back, looking at the sky, which seemed unnaturally clear and blue. So clean, too. Far away. His thoughts were drifting like the smoke and the two badly mauled ships.

A shadow loomed over him and he realized that Stockdale was kneeling beside him, his battered face lined with anxiety.

He tried to tell him he was all right. That he was resting.

A voice shouted, 'Take Mr Bolitho to the orlop at once!'

Then he did try to protest, but the effort was too much and with it came the darkness.


Bolitho opened his eyes and blinked rapidly to clear his vision. As the pain returned to his head he realized he was down on the orlop deck, a place of semi-darkness at the best of times. Now, with deckhead lanterns swinging to the ship's heavy motion, and others being carried this way and that, it was like looking at hell.

He was propped against *Trojan*'s great timbers, and through his shirt he could feel the hull working through a deep swell. As his eyes grew used to the gloom he saw that the whole area from the sickbay to the hanging magazine was filled with men. Some lay quite still and were probably dead, others rocked back and forth, crouching like terrified animals as they nursed their private pain.

In the centre of the deck, directly below the largest number of lanterns, Throndike and his assistants worked in grim silence on an unconscious seaman, while one of the surgeon's loblolly boys dashed away with a bucket from which protruded an amputated arm.

Bolitho reached up and felt his head. It was crusted in blood, and there was a lump like an egg. He felt the relief welling from his taut stomach muscles like a flood, stinging the back of his eyes so that he could feel tears running down his face. As another figure was carried to the table and stripped of his blackened clothing, Bolitho felt ashamed. He had been terrified of what would happen, but compared with the man who was whimpering and pleading with the surgeon he was unhurt.

'*Please*, sir!' The man was sobbing uncontrollably, so that even some of the other wounded forgot their pain and watched.

Thorndike turned from a locker, wiping his mouth. He looked like a stranger, and his hands, like his long apron, were red with blood.

'I am *sorry*.'

Thorndike nodded to his assistant, and Bolitho saw the injured man's shattered leg for the first time and realized it was one of his own gun crews who had been pinned under a cannon.

He was still pleading, 'Not me leg, sir!'

A bottle was thrust to his lips, and as he let his head fall back, choking and gasping on neat rum, a leather strap was put between his teeth.

Bolitho saw the glitter of the knife and turned his face away. It was wrong for a man to suffer like this, to scream and choke on his own vomit while his stricken messmates watched in silence.

Thorndike snapped, 'Too late. Take him on deck.' He reached out for his bottle again. 'Next!'

A seaman was kneeling beside Bolitho while some wood splinters were plucked from his back.

It was the masthead look-out, Buller.

He winced and then said, 'Reckon I'm a lucky one today, zur.' That was all he said, but it spoke volumes.

'You all right, sir?' It was Midshipman Couzens. 'I was sent by the first lieutenant.' He flinched as someone started to scream. 'Oh God, sir!'

Bolitho reached out. 'Help me up. Must get out of here.' He staggered to his feet and clung to the boy's shoulder like a drunken sailor. 'I'll not forget this, ever.'

Stockdale strode to meet them, ducking beneath the deck-head beams, his face creased with worry.

'Let me take him!'

The journey to the upper deck was in itself another part of the nightmare. The lower gundeck was still wreathed in trapped smoke, the red-painted sides only hiding some of the battle's agony.

He saw Lieutenant Dalyell with his two remaining midshipmen, Lunn and Burslem, discussing with the gun captains what had to be done.

Dalyell saw Bolitho and hurried over, his open face filled with obvious pleasure.

'Thank God, Dick! I had heard you were done for!'

Bolitho tried to smile, but the pain in his skull stopped it.

'I heard much the same about you!'

'Aye. A gun exploded. I was stunned by the blast. But for the men nearby, I would be dead.' He shook his head. 'Poor Huss. He was a brave lad.'

Bolitho nodded slowly. They had begun with nine midshipmen. One promoted, one taken prisoner, and now one killed. The midshipmen's berth would be a sad place after this.

Dalyell looked away. 'So much for the admiral's strategy. A very high price for what we have done.'

Bolitho continued with his two helpers to the upper gundeck, and stood for several moments sucking in the air and looking up at the clear sky above the severed topgallant mast.

Men were being carried below, and Bolitho wondered how Thorndike could go on. Cutting, sawing and stitching. He shuddered violently. Others were being dragged beneath the gangways, limp and without identity, to await the sailmaker and his mates, who would sew them up in their hammocks for the last journey. How far had Bunce said it was? One thousand five hundred fathoms hereabouts. A long, dark passage. Perhaps there was peace there.

He shook himself and winced at the stabbing pain. He was getting hazy again. It had to stop.

Cairns said, 'Good to see you, Dick.' He looked tired and drained. 'I could do with some help,' he hesitated, 'if you feel up to it?'

Bolitho nodded, moved that this man who carried so much had found time to ask about him and how he was faring on the orlop.

'It will be good for me.'

He made himself look along the torn and splintered deck where he had been such a short while ago. Upended guns, great coils of fallen cordage and ripped canvas. Men picking their way amongst it like survivors from a shipwreck. How could any man have lived through it? To see such chaos made it seem impossible.

He asked, 'How is James?'

Cairns' eyes were bleak. 'The *fourth lieutenant* is alive, I believe.' He patted Bolitho's arm. 'I must be off. You remain here and assist the boatswain.'

Bolitho crossed to the first division of eighteen-pounders, where he had been for most of the battle. He could see the *Argonaute*, stern on and a good three miles downwind. Even if they could complete some temporary repairs in time, they would not catch the Frenchman now.

Stockdale spoke for both of them. 'Anyways, we beat 'em off. Short-handed though we was, sir, we gave as good as we got.'

Couzens said huskily, 'But the brig got away.'

The sailing master towered above the quarterdeck rail and boomed, 'Come now, Mr Bolitho, this will not do! I have a ship to steer, a course to lay! To do that I need sails and more halliards than I can see at present!' His black brows descended over his deepset eyes and he added, 'You did well today. I saw.' He nodded firmly, as if he had said far too much.

For the rest of the day the ship's company went about the work of putting *Trojan* to rights as best they could. The dead were buried and the wounded made as comfortable as possible. Samuel Pinhorn, the sailmaker, had kept plenty of spare canvas on deck, knowing that more would die before reaching port.

It was amazing that men could work after what they had been through. Perhaps it was work which saved them, for no ship can sail without care and constant attention.

A jury-mast was hoisted to replace the topgallant, and as the seamen bustled far above the deck the cordage dangled down on either side like weed.

Hammers and saws, tar and paint, needles and twine.

The only thing which happened to make them stop, to stare abeam and remember, was the sudden appearance of the schooner from the anchorage at Isla San Bernardo. *Spite* had been abandoned as a hopeless wreck, then set alight to make sure no pirate or privateer would lay hands on her.

In a short and savage boat action, Cunningham attacked and took the schooner. The one reward of the whole operation.

But Bolitho was certain of one thing. The prize, no matter what secrets she disclosed, would not remove the ache from Cunningham's heart as he had ordered his men to abandon his own command.

At sunset, Cairns ordered a halt. A double ration of spirits was issued to all hands, and after shortening sail for the night *Trojan* was content to reflect and lick her wounds.

Bolitho received a summons to the great cabin without curiosity. Like most of the company, he was drained, and too shocked to care.

But as he made his way aft, ducking his head beneath the poop, he heard Pears' voice, clearly audible through two sets of screen doors.

'I know your father, otherwise I would have you stripped of your appointment *at this very moment!*'

Bolitho hesitated outside the door, feeling the sentry's eyes watching him.

It was Quinn of course. Poor, broken Quinn. He could still see him, standing on the gundeck amongst the litter of dead and dying. Stricken, unable to think or move.

The sentry looked at him. 'Sir?'

Bolitho nodded wearily, and the marine banged his musket on the deck and called, 'Second lieutenant, *sir!*'

The door opened and Teakle, the clerk, ushered Bolitho inside. He had a bandage on his wrist and looked very shaken. Bolitho wondered why he had never thought of a clerk being in as much danger as any of them.

Quinn came from the cabin, his face as white as a sheet. He saw Bolitho and looked as if he were about to speak. Then with a gasp he blundered past him into the shadows.

Pears strode to meet Bolitho. 'Ah, not too knocked about, eh?' He was restless, off balance.

Bolitho replied, 'I was fortunate, sir.'

'Indeed you were.'

Pears looked round as Coutts came from the adjoining cabin.

The admiral said, 'I will be leaving at daylight and transferring to the prize, Bolitho. I intend to head for Antigua and take passage from there in a courier brig, or one of the frigates '

Bolitho looked at him, trying to guess where it was leading. He could feel the tension between the two men, see the bitterness in Pears' eyes. Like physical pain.

Coutts added calmly, '*Trojan* will follow, of course. Full repairs can be carried out there before she returns to the squadron. I will ensure that the people at Antigua give full attention to it, and to obtaining replacements for—'

Pears interrupted bluntly, 'For all the poor devils who died today!'

Coutts flushed, but turned to Bolitho again.

'I have watched you. You are the right stuff, with the ability and the steel to lead men.'

Bolitho glanced at Pears' grim features and was shocked to see his expression. Like a man under sentence.

'Thank you, sir.'

'Therefore . . . ' the word hung in the damp air, 'I am offering you a new appointment as soon as you reach Antigua. With me.'

Bolitho stared, realizing what it would do to Pears. With Coutts back in Antigua, or probably in New York before *Trojan* reached harbour, Pears would have nobody to speak for him but Cairns. A scapegoat. Someone to use to cover Coutts' costly exercise.

He was surprised that he could answer without hesitation. It was all he wanted, the one opportunity to transfer to another ship, smaller, faster, like *Vanquisher* or one of the other frigates. With Coutts' patronage it would be the best chance he would ever get.

'I thank you, sir.' He looked at Pears. 'But my appointment is under Captain Pears. I would wish it to remain so.'

Coutts regarded him curiously. 'What an odd fellow you are, Bolitho. Your sentimentality will do for you one day.' He nodded, curt, final. 'Good evening.'

In a daze Bolitho went down a ladder and found himself in the wardroom, remarkably untouched by the battle.

Cairns followed him a few moments later and took his arm, beckoning to the wardroom servant as he did so.

'Mackenzie, you rogue! Some good brandy for this officer!'

D'Esterre appeared with his lieutenant and asked, 'What is happening?'

Cairns sat down opposite Bolitho and watched him intently.

'It *has* happened, gentlemen. I have just witnessed a misguided but *honest* man doing something which was right.'

Bolitho flushed. 'I—I didn't know . . .'

Cairns took a bottle from Mackenzie and smiled sadly.

'I was outside. Peering through a crack like a schoolboy.' He became suddenly serious. 'That was a fine thing you did just now. He'll never thank you for it, in as many words.' Cairns raised his glass. 'But I know him better than most. You gave him something to make up for what Coutts did to his ship!'

Bolitho thought of the schooner steering somewhere under *Trojan*'s lee. Tomorrow she would leave them and take with her his chance of promotion.

He got another surprise. He no longer cared.

# 15

## Another Chance

Bolitho stood in the shadow of the mainmast's massive trunk and watched the busy activity around the ship. It was October, and for two months *Trojan* had been here in English Harbour, Antigua, headquarters of the Caribbean squadrons. There were plenty of ships needing repairs and overhaul, but mostly because of the wear and tear of storms or old age. *Trojan*'s arrival had aroused plenty of excitement and curiosity as Captain Pears had brought her to rest, with the ensign at half-mast for her many dead.

Now, looking around the taut rigging and shrouds, the neatly furled sails and skillfully repaired decks, it was hard to picture the battle which had raged here.

He shaded his eyes to look at the shore. Scattered white buildings, the familiar landfall of Monk's Hill. A busy procession of boats, yard hoys, water lighters and the inevitible traders offering doubtful wares to the inexperienced and the foolish.

There had been a lot of changes, not only to the ship herself. New faces from other vessels from England, from ports up and down the Caribbean. All to be tested and worked into the rest of the company.

A Lieutenant John Pointer had arrived aboard, and because of his seniority had been made fourth lieutenant, as Bolitho had once been. A cheerful young man with a round Yorkshire dialect, he seemed competent and willing to learn.

Young Midshipman Libby, stripped of his acting rank, had gone to the flagship on one fine morning to face his examination for lieutenant. He had passed with honour, although he was the only one to show surprise at the verdict. Now he had gone, appointed to another two-decker without delay. But his parting had been a sad occasion, both for him and the other midshipmen. There were two more of those as well. Fresh from England, and in Bunce's view, 'Less than useless!'

Of Coutts they had heard nothing, other than he had returned to New York. Promotion or disgrace seemed unimportant in the face of the latest news which even now seemed impossible to grasp.

In America, General Burgoyne, who had been operating with some success from Canada in the earlier stages of the revolution, had been directed to take control of the Hudson River. He had advanced with his usual determination with some seven thousand troops, expecting to be reinforced by the New York regiments. Someone had decided that there were insufficient soldiers in New York and barely enough to defend the city.

General Burgoyne had waited in vain, and this month had surrendered with all his men at Saratoga.

There had been news of greater activity by French privateers, encouraged, and with good cause, by the military defeat.

*Trojan* would soon be ready to rejoin the fight, but Bolitho could see no way of retaining a grasp of a rebellious colony even if Britain commanded the sea-lanes. And with more French involvement, that was no certainty either.

Bolitho moved restlessly to the nettings to watch another trading boat passing *Trojan*'s glittering reflection. It was hot, but after the earlier months, and the torrential tropical downpours, it seemed almost cool.

He glanced aft, at the flag which hung so limp and still. It would be even hotter in the great cabin.

He tried to see Quinn as a stranger, someone he had just met. But he kept recalling him as the most junior lieutenant, when he had just come aboard. Eighteen years old and straight from the midshipman's berth, beginning as Libby was now for himself.

Then again, gasping in agony from the great slash across his chest. After all his quiet confidence, his determination to be a sea officer when his wealthy father wished otherwise.

These last weeks must have been hell for him. He had been released from his duties, and even if he retained his appointment would now be junior to the new officer, Pointer.

Because of the activity within the local squadrons, and the general air of expectancy of a French intervention in strength, Quinn's troubles had taken a low position in priorities.

Now, in this October of 1777, he was being examined by a board of inquiry in Pears' cabin. Just one short step from a court martial.

Bolitho looked at the other ships, so still in the sheltered harbour, each paired above her image in the water, awnings spread, ports open to catch the slightest breeze. Very soon these vessels and more beside would endure what *Trojan* had suffered under *Argonaute*'s guns. They would not be fighting brave but untrained rebels, but the flower of France. Discipline would be tightened, failure not tolerated. It made Quinn's chances seem very slim.

He turned as Lieutenant Arthur Frowd, officer of the watch, crossed the deck to join him. Like Libby, he had gained his coveted promotion, and now awaited an appointment to a more suitable ship. The most junior lieutenant, he was still the oldest in years. In his bright new uniform, with his hair neatly tied to the nape of his neck, he looked as good as any captain, Bolitho thought admiringly.

Frowd said uneasily, 'What d'you reckon about him?' He did not even mention Quinn by name. Like a lot of other people he was probably afraid of being connected with him in any way.

'I'm not certain.'

Bolitho fidgeted with his sword hilt, wondering why it was taking so long. Cairns had gone aft, as had D'Esterre and Bunce. It was a hateful business, like seeing the court martial Jack on a man-of-war, the ritualistic procession of boats for a flogging around the fleet, or a hanging.

He said, '*I* was afraid. So it must have been a lot worse for him. But—'

Frowd said vehemently, '*But*, aye, sir, that small word makes a world of difference. Any common seaman would have been run up to the mainyard by now!'

Bolitho said nothing and waited for Frowd to walk away to speak with the guard-boat alongside. Frowd did not understand. How could he? To reach a lieutenant's rank was hard enough for any youth. By way of the lower deck it was much, much harder. And Frowd had done it with his own sweat and little education. He would see Quinn's failure as a betrayal rather than a weakness.

Sergeant Shears marched across the quarterdeck and touched his hat smartly.

Bolitho looked at him. 'Me?'

'Yessir.' Shears glanced quickly at the men on watch, the sideboys and the sentry. 'Not doin' very well, sir.' He dropped his voice to a whisper. 'My captain give 'is evidence, and one of the board says, all 'aughty-like, "wot does a marine know about sea officers?"' Shears sounded outraged. 'Never 'eard the like, sir!'

Bolitho walked quickly aft, gripping his sword tightly to prepare himself.

Pears' day cabin had been cleared, the furniture replaced by a bare table, at which were seated three captains.

There were others present too, seated on chairs to either side, mostly strangers to Bolitho, but he saw the earlier witnesses, Cairns, D'Esterre, and alone, with his hands folded in his lap, Captain Pears.

The senior captain looked at him coolly. 'Mr Bolitho?'

Bolitho tucked his hat under his arm and said, 'Aye, sir. Second lieutenant.'

The captain to the right, a sharp-faced man with very thin lips, asked, 'Were you present on deck when the events which led to this investigation took place?'

Bolitho saw the clerk's pen poised above his pile of papers. Then for the first time he looked at Quinn.

He was standing very stiffly by the door of the dining cabin. He looked as if he was finding it hard to breathe.

'I was, sir.' How absurd, he thought. They all knew exactly where everyone was. Probably right down to the ship's cook. 'I was in charge of the upper gundeck when we engaged the enemy to starboard.'

The president of the court, a captain Bolitho remembered seeing in New York, said dryly, 'Forget the formality, if you can. You are not on trial here.' He glanced at the captain with the thin lips. 'It would do well to remember that.' His level gaze returned to Bolitho. 'What did you see?'

Bolitho could feel those behind him, watching and waiting. If only he knew what had been said already, especially by the captain.

He cleared his throat. 'We'd not been expecting to fight, sir. But the *Argonaute* had dismasted *Spite* without any challenge or warning. We had no option.'

'We?' The question was mild.

Bolitho flushed and felt clumsy under the three pairs of eyes. 'I heard the admiral express the view that we should fight if need be, sir.'

'Ah.' A small smile. 'Continue.'

'It was a bloody battle, sir, and we were sorely short of good hands before it began.' He sensed the scorn in the thin-lipped captain's eyes and added quietly, 'That was not meant as an excuse, sir. Had you seen the way our people fought and died that day, you would have known my meaning.'

He could sense the silence, like the terrible calm before a hurricane. But he could not stop now. What did they know about it? They had probably never had to fight with such inexperienced officers and so few seasoned hands. He thought of the man on the surgeon's table pleading for his leg, the marine who had been the first to die, falling from the top to drift in the sea alone. There were so many of them. Too many.

He said, 'The Frenchman came up to us and drove hard alongside. They boarded, or tried to . . .' He faltered, seeing the French lieutenant falling between the grinding hulls, his own sword red with blood. 'But we fought them off.' He turned and looked directly at Quinn's stricken face. 'Mr Quinn was assisting me up to that moment, and stood under the enemy's fire until action was broken off.'

The president added, 'Then *you* were taken below. Correct?'

He looked at Bolitho's tense features and asked, 'How old are you?'

'Twenty-one, sir. This month.' He thought he heard someone snigger behind him.

'And you entered the Navy at the age of twelve, I understand. As did most of us. In addition, you come from a distinguished seafaring family.' His voice hardened suddenly. 'In your *experi-*

*ence* as a King's officer, Mr Bolitho, did you at any time during this series of unfortunate events consider that Mr Quinn's behaviour was lacking in skill or courage?'

Bolitho replied quietly, 'In my opinion, sir—' He got no further.

The president persisted. 'In your *experience*.'

Bolitho felt desperate, trapped. 'I do not know how to answer, sir.'

He expected to be rebuked, even dismissed from the court, but the president merely asked, 'He was your friend, is that it?'

Bolitho looked across at Quinn, suddenly hating the three captains, the gaping spectators, everything.

He said firmly, 'He *is* my friend, sir.' He heard the murmur of surprise and expectancy but added, 'Maybe he was afraid, but so was I, as were many more. To deny it would be foolish.'

Before he turned back to the table he saw Quinn lift his chin with pathetic defiance.

Bolitho said, 'His record has been a good one. And I have had him with me on several difficult missions. He has been badly wounded and—'

The thin-lipped captain leaned over to look at his companions. 'I think we have heard enough. This witness has little to add.' He glanced at Bolitho. 'I understand that you declined a new appointment which Rear-Admiral Coutts was prepared to offer? Tell me, was that lack of ambition on your part?'

The president frowned, and then turned as feet moved heavily on the deck.

Without looking, Bolitho knew it was Pears.

The president asked, 'You wished to say something, Captain Pears?'

The familiar harsh voice was remarkably calm. 'The last question. I feel I should answer. It was not lack of ambition, sir. In my family we call it *loyalty*, dammit!'

The president held up his hand to still the sudden excitement. 'Quite so.' He looked sadly at Bolitho. 'However, I am afraid that in the case of Lieutenant Quinn loyalty is not enough.' He stood up, and throughout the cabin the spectators and witnesses lurched to their feet. 'The inquiry is adjourned.'

Outside, on the sunlit quarterdeck, Bolitho waited for the visitors to leave.

Dalyell and the new lieutenant, Pointer, were with him when Quinn appeared on deck.

He crossed over to him and murmured, 'Thank you for what you said, Dick.'

Bolitho shrugged. 'It didn't seem to help much.'

Dalyell said quietly, 'You have more courage than I, Dick. The cold-eyed captain scared hell out of me, just looking at him!'

Quinn said, 'Anyway, the president was right. I could not move. It was like being dead, unable to help.'

He saw Cairns approaching and added quickly, 'I shall go to my cabin.'

The first lieutenant leaned over the rail and watched the boats alongside.

Then he said, 'I hope we can get back to sea soon.'

The others moved away and Bolitho asked, 'Did the captain kill Quinn's chances, Neil?'

Cairns eyed him thoughtfully. 'No. I did. I witnessed it, but was less involved than you. Suppose you had been marked down by one of the Frenchman's sharpshooters, or broken by chain-shot. Do you think Quinn could have held the fo'c'sle and driven off the boarders?' He smiled gravely and gripped Bolitho's arm. 'I'll not ask you to betray a friendship. But you know, as well as I, that we would have been made to strike to the *Argonaute* if Quinn had been left in charge forrard.' He looked along the deck, probably remembering it, as Bolitho was. He said, 'There are more lives at stake than the honour of one man.'

Bolitho felt sick. Knowing Cairns was right, but feeling only pity for Quinn.

'What will they decide?'

Cairns replied, 'The admiral who commands here will be aware of this. It has taken long enough to come to light. He will also know of Quinn's father, his power in the City.'

Bolitho could feel the man's bitterness as he added, 'He'll not hang.'

After lunch the court was recalled, and Cairns was proved correct.

The court of inquiry had decided that Lieutenant James Quinn had been rendered unfit by cause of injury in the King's service to continue with active duty. Upon confirmation from the commander-in-chief, he would be sent ashore to await passage home to England. After that he would be discharged from the Navy.

Nobody outside would know of his disgrace. Except the one man who really cared, and Bolitho doubted very much if Quinn could carry that final burden for long.

Two days later, with Quinn's fate still unconfirmed, *Trojan* weighed and put to sea.

It would, it appeared, take a little longer.


Two and a half days after leaving English Harbour *Trojan* was steering due west, under reefed topsails and forecourse in a stiff following wind. It was a good opportunity to exercise the old and new hands together in sail drill, as with spray bursting over the poop and quarterdeck the two-decker pointed her jib at the misty horizon.

Apart from a few tiny islands far away on the starboard bow, the sea was empty. An endless deep blue desert, with long cruising rollers and white crests to display the power of the wind.

Bolitho waited on the larboard gangway, the taste of strong coffee warming his stomach, while he prepared to take over the afternoon watch in fifteen minutes' time. With so many new faces and names to grapple with, the constant efforts to discover the skilled hands from the clumsy ones, all of whom seemed to have five thumbs on each fist, Bolitho had been kept very busy. But he could sense the atmosphere in the ship all the same. Confused acceptance by the lower deck and an air of bitterness from aft.

*Trojan* was ordered to Jamaica, her lower decks crammed with a contingent of marines which the admiral was sending to enforce law and order at the governor's urgent request. Bad weather had wrecked many of Jamaica's local trading vessels, and to make matters worse there had been news of another slave uprising on two of the larger plantations. Rebellion seemed to be in the air everywhere. If Britain was to hold on to her Caribbean possessions she must act now and not wait for the French and possibly the Spanish to blockade and occupy some of the many islands there.

But Bolitho guessed that Pears saw his role through different eyes. While the fleet was preparing for the inevitable spread of war, when every ship of the line would be desperately needed, he was being ordered to Jamaica. His *Trojan* had taken on the task of transport and little more.

Even the admiral's explanation, that *Trojan* needed no escort, and was therefore releasing other vessels for work elsewhere, had had no effect. Daily Pears walked his quarterdeck, still watchful for his ship and the routine which ran her, but alone and quite removed from everyone else.

It could not be helping him now, Bolitho thought, to realize that hidden just below the horizon was the south-eastern shore of Puerto Rico, so near to where Coutts had committed all of them to a hopeless battle. In some ways it would have been better if the *Argonaute* had not broken off the fight. At least there would be a total victory to hold on to. Maybe the French had used their captain as a scapegoat, too?

But, as Cairns had said, it was better to be at sea and be kept busy than to swing at anchor, moping over what might have happened.

He looked down at the gundeck, at the milling scarlet uniforms and piled weapons as D'Esterre and the captain in charge of the marine contingent inspected and checked everything for the hundredth time.

'Deck there!'

Bolitho looked up, the sun searing his face like sand.

'Sail, sir! On the starboard bow!'

Dalyell had the watch, and it was at moments such as this that his inexperience showed through.

'*What? Where?*' He snatched a telescope from Midshipman Pullen and rushed to the starboard shrouds.

The look-out's voice was drifting with the wind. 'Small sail, sir! Fisherman, mebbee!'

Sambell, who was master's mate of the watch, remarked sourly, 'Lucky Admiral Coutts ain't here. He'd have us chasin' the bugger!'

Dalyell glared at him. 'Get aloft, Mr Sambell. Tell me what you see.' He saw Bolitho and smiled awkwardly. 'So long without sighting anything, I was off guard.'

'So it would appear, sir.' Pears strode on to the quarterdeck, his shoes squeaking on the seams. He glanced at the set of the sails and then moved to the compass. 'Hmm.'

Dalyell peered up at the master's mate, who seemed to be taking an age to make the long climb.

Pears walked to the rail and watched the marines. 'Fisherman. Maybe so. There are plenty of small islets there. Good places for water and firewood. Not too dangerous if you keep one eye open.'

He frowned as Sambell yelled, 'She's sheered off! Makin' for one of the islands!'

Dalyell licked his lips and watched the captain. 'Sighted us, d'you suppose, sir?'

Pears shrugged. 'Unlikely. Our masthead has a far greater vision than some low-lying hull.'

He rubbed his chin, and Bolitho thought he saw a sudden gleam in his eyes.

Then Pears said harshly, 'Hands to the braces, Mr Dalyell. We will alter course three points. Steer nor'-west by north.' He banged his big hands together. 'Well, *jump* to it, sir! 'Pon my soul, you'll have to do better than this!'

The shrill of calls and the immediate rush of seamen brought Cairns on deck, his eyes everywhere as he looked for a ship.

Pears said, 'Vessel on starboard bow, Mr Cairns. Could be a fisherman, but unlikely. They usually keep in company in these hard times.'

'Another privateer, sir?'

Cairns was speaking very carefully, and Bolitho guessed he had taken much from Pears' tongue in the past few weeks.

'Possibly.'

Pears beckoned to D'Esterre, who was being pushed and jostled by the extra marines as they sought to avoid the seamen at the braces and halliards.

'Captain D'Esterre!' Pears peered aloft as the yards squeaked round and the deck heeled over to the change of course. 'How d'you propose to land your men at Jamaica if there has been a further uprising?'

D'Esterre replied, 'In boats, sir. Land by sections above the port and take the high ground before seeking the local commander.'

Pears almost smiled. 'I agree.' He pointed at the boat tier. 'We will exercise landing the contingent at dusk.' He ignored D'Esterre's astonished stare. 'On one of those islands yonder.'

Bolitho heard him say to Cairns, 'If there is some damned pirate there, we will swamp him with marines. Anyway, it will be good practice for them. If *Trojan* is to act as a troop transport, then she will do it well. No, better than well.'

Cairns smiled, grateful to see a return of Pears' old enthusiasm. 'Aye, sir.'

The helmsman shouted, 'Nor'-west be north, zur!'

'Steady as you go, man.' Cairns waited impatiently for Bolitho's watch to relieve Dalyell and then said, 'I wish to God we could catch one of them again. Just to show Rear-Admiral bloody Coutts a thing or two!'

Pears heard him and murmured, 'Now, now, Mr Cairns. That will do.' But that was all he said.

Bolitho watched his men settling down to their duties while the rest went below to eat. He still believed that what Coutts had tried to do had been right. But his reasons were less certain.

Why was Pears taking the trouble to land marines for so trivial a sighting? Hurt pride, or did he expect to face an eventual court martial at Coutts' instigation over the *Argonaute* encounter?

He heard Pears say to Bunce, 'I intend to stand off as soon as we have landed the marines. I know these waters very well. I've an idea or two of my own.'

Bunce gave a rough chuckle. 'That you do know 'em, Cap'n. I think it may be God's will that we be here today.'

Pears grimaced. 'Most probably, Mr. Bunce. We shall have to see.' He turned away. 'And pray.'

Bolitho looked at Cairns. 'What does he mean?'

Cairns shrugged. 'He certainly knows this part of the world, as much as the Sage, I would think. I have studied the chart, but apart from reefs and currents, I see no cause for excitement.'

They both faced Pears as he strode across the quarterdeck.

He said, 'I am going aft to take lunch. This afternoon we will muster all hands and prepare the boats. Swivels in the bows of cutters and launches. Only hand-picked men will go.' He glanced at Bolitho. 'You can supervise the landing arrangements, and will take Mr Frowd as your second. Captain D'Esterre will command the land force.' He nodded and strode aft, hands behind his back.

Cairns said softly, 'I'm glad for him. But I'm not so sure he is acting wisely.'

Bunce muttered, 'My mother used to 'ave a saying, zur, about too wise 'eads on too young shoulders. Not good for 'em, she'd say.' He went to the chart room chuckling to himself.

Cairns shook his head. 'Didn't know the old bugger ever *had* a mother!'

• • •

*Trojan* closed to within a mile of the nearest island and then lay hove to while the business of lowering boats and filling them with marines was begun.

Most of the marines had been in Antigua for a long time and had only heard about the war in America from visiting ships. Although few of them knew why they were being sent across to the island, and those who did regarded it as something of a joke, they carried out their part willingly and in good humour.

The cheerful atmosphere made Sergeant Shears exclaim angrily, 'My Gawd, sir, you'd think it was a bloody 'oliday, an' no mistake!'

The sea was still very choppy and lively, and it took more time than calculated to get the boats fully loaded and headed for the shore. It was growing dark, and the sunset painted the wave crests amber and dull gold.

Bolitho stood in the sternsheets of the leading cutter, one hand on Stockdale's shoulder as he controlled the tiller-bar. It was difficult to see the cove where they were supposed to land, although it had looked clear enough on the chart. The grim truth was that nobody really knew the exact position of every reef and sand-bar. Already they had seen several jagged rocks, shining in the strange light and bringing a few anxious remarks from the crowded marines. In their heavy boots and hung about with weapons and pouches, they would go to the bottom before anything else if the boats were capsized.

D'Esterre was saying, 'Fact is, Dick, we may have been sighted already. They'll not stop to fight all these marines, but we'll not find them either!'

Another seething rock passed down the starboard oar blades, and Bolitho signalled with a white flag to the boat astern, and so on down the line. *Trojan* was only a blurred shadow now, and she had been making more sail even as the boats had pulled clear. She would use the prevailing wind to ride in the island's lee for some sign of results.

'Land ahead, sir!'

That was Buller in the bows. A good hand, as he had shown, his wood splinters apparently forgotten. He was lucky to be able to forget so easily, Bolitho thought.

Like darkly hooded monks some tall rocks rose on either side of the boat, while directly across the bows and the loaded swivel gun lay a bright strip of sand.

'Easy all! Boat yer oars!'

Seamen were already leaping and splashing into the surf on either beam to steady the boat as she drove ashore.

D'Esterre was out, waist-deep in water and calling his sergeant to lead the first pickets to the higher ground.

It was a tiny island, no more than a mile long. Most of the others were even smaller. But there were rock pools for gathering fresh water and shellfish, and wood to burn for any small and self-sufficient vessel.

Bolitho waded ashore, thinking suddenly of Quinn. He had heard him asking, pleading with Cairns to be allowed to come with the landing party.

Cairns had been coldly formal, almost brutal. 'We want experienced, picked men, Mr Quinn.' The last part had been like a slap in the face. 'Reliable, too.'

Midshipman Couzens was arriving with the next cutter, and the *Trojan*'s red-painted barge was following her. Bolitho smiled tightly. Frowd and the other marine captain were in her. Being held back in case the first boats had fallen under a deluge of shot and fire.

'Take your positions! Boat-handling parties stand fast!'

Stockdale strode from the shallows, his cutlass across one shoulder like a broadsword.

From tumbling confusion and whispered threats from the sergeants and corporals, the marines formed into neat little sections. At a further command they moved up the slope, boots squelching on sand and then on rough, sun-hardened earth.

An hour later it was dark and the air was heavy with damp smells, of rotten vegetation and seabird droppings.

While the marine skirmishers hurried away on either side, Bolitho and D'Esterre stood on a narrow ridge-backed hill, the sea ahead and behind them, invisible but for an occasional gleam of surf.

It seemed deserted. Dead. The unknown vessel had gone to another island, or had sailed north-west towards the Bahamas. If Sambell had not seen her for himself, Bolitho might have thought the look-out mistaken by a trick of light and haze.

'This is no Fort Exeter, Dick.' D'Esterre was leaning on his sword, his head cocked to listen to the hiss of wind through fronds and bushes.

'I wish we had those Canadian scouts with us.' Bolitho saw some seamen lying on their backs, staring at the sky. They were quite content to leave it to others. They merely had to obey. To die if need be.

They heard a nervous challenge and then Shears strode up the hill towards them. He carried a clump of grass or creeper to cover his uniform, which was why the sentry had been so startled. It reminded Bolitho of Major Paget's little cape.

'Well?' D'Esterre leaned forward.

Shears sucked in gulps of air. 'She's there, right enough, sir. Anchored close in. Small vessel, yawl by the looks of 'er.'

D'Esterre asked, 'Any signs of life?'

'There's a watch on deck, an' no lights, sir. Up to no good, if you ask me.' He saw D'Esterre's smile and added firmly, 'One of the marines from Antigua says they'd have lights lit and lines down right now, sir. There's a special sort of fish they goes after. No *real* fisherman would lie an' asleep!'

D'Esterre nodded. 'That was well said, Sergeant Shears. I'll see that the man has a guinea when we get back aboard. And you, too. You must have something about you to inspire an unknown marine to offer his confidences!' He became crisp and formal. 'Fetch Mr Frowd. We will decide what to do. Pass the word to watch out for anyone coming ashore from the yawl.'

Shears said cheerfully, 'They got no boats in the water, sir.'

'Well, watch anyway.'

As the sergeant hurried away D'Esterre said, 'Well, Dick, are you thinking as I am? A surprise attack on them?'

'Aye.' He tried to picture the anchored vessel. 'The sight of all your marines should do it. But two armed cutters would be safer. In case they are unimpressed by your little army.'

'I agree. You and Mr Frowd take the cutters. I'll keep the midshipman with me and send him with a message if things go wrong. So work your way round. No risks, mind. Not for a damned yawl!'

Bolitho waited for Frowd to join him, thinking back to Pears' casual reference to these small islands. It had all been clear to him. If the vessel was an enemy, or up to no good, she would run at the first hint of trouble. Towards the land and the marines, or more likely use the prevailing wind and put to sea again or hide amongst the islands. Either way she would find *Trojan* lying there, using the offshore current and wind. Waiting like a great beast to overwhelm her in a matter of minutes.

At sea, in open waters, there was hardly a vessel afloat which could not outsail the slow-moving *Trojan*. But in confined space, where one false turn of the helm could mean a grounding at best, *Trojan*'s massive artillery would make escape impossible.

Frowd remarked dourly, 'Boat action then.'

Bolitho watched him curiously. Frowd could probably think of nothing but his next appointment, getting away from the ship where so many had been his equals and were now expected to knuckle their foreheads to him.

'Yes. Pick your men, and let's be about it.'

He noticed the sharpness in his own voice, too. Why was that? Did he see Frowd's attitude as a challenge, as Rowhurst had once vied with Quinn?

With muffled oars the two cutters pulled away from the other moored boats and turned east towards the far end of the island, the wind making each stroke of the oars harder and more tiring.

But Bolitho knew his men by now. They would rally when the time came. They had done it before. It was strange to be pushing through the choppy water without doubts of these silent, straining men. He hoped they held some trust in him also.

It would be funny, if after all this stealth, they found only terrified traders or fishermen rising to the marines' rough awakening. It would not seem so amusing when they had to tell the captain about it.


'Somebody must be comin', sir!'

Bolitho scrambled through the cutter to join the look-out in the bows. He could see the two seamen he had put ashore, framed against the sky, one moving his arm above his head very slowly.

How loud everything sounded. The water sluicing around the two moored boats, the distant boom of surf and the hissing roar as it receded from some hidden beach.

They had reached this tiny inlet several hours ago and had made fast to get as much rest as possible. Most of the seamen appeared to have no trouble. They could sleep anywhere, indifferent to the rocking boats, the spray which occasionally spattered across their already damp clothing.

Frowd, in the boat alongside, said, 'It's gone wrong, I expect.'

Bolitho waited, realizing that the men on the shore were easier to see, more sharply defined against the dull sky. It would be dawn soon.

Stockdale said feelingly, 'It's Mr Couzens, not the enemy!'

Couzens came slithering down the slope and then waded and floundered towards the cutters.

He saw Bolitho and gasped, 'Captain D'Esterre says to start the attack in half an hour.'

He sounded so relieved that Bolitho guessed he had got lost on his way here.

'Very well.' *Attack.* That sounded definite enough. 'What is the signal?'

Stockdale hoisted the midshipman unceremoniously over the gunwale.

'One pistol shot, sir.' Couzens sank down on a thwart, his legs gripping on the bottom boards.

'Good. Recall those men.' Bolitho made his way aft again and held his watch against a shaded horn lantern. There was not much time. 'Rouse the hands. Make ready to cast off.'

Men stirred and coughed, groping around to get their bearings.

From the set of the current Bolitho could picture how the yawl would be swinging to her cable. He thought suddenly of Sparke, deciding on his attack. Pushing sentiment aside after the bloody fighting was over.

'Load your pistols. Take your time.'

If he hurried them, or shared his own anxiety over the brightening sky, somebody was bound to get muddled and loose off a ball. It only took one.

Stockdale swayed through the boat and then returned. 'All done, sir.'

'Mr Frowd?'

The lieutenant waved to him. 'Ready, sir!'

In spite of his tense nerves Bolitho felt he wanted to smile. *Sir.* Frowd would never call him by his first name in a hundred years.

'Out oars.' He raised his arm. '*Easy*, lads. Like field mice!'

Stockdale sounded approving. 'Shove off forrard! Give way larboard!'

Very slowly, with one set of oars pulling the boat round like a crab, they moved away from their tiny haven.

Frowd was following, and Bolitho saw the bowman training the swivel from side to side as if to sniff the way.

Couzens whispered, 'There's the corner, sir!'

Bolitho watched the jutting spur of rock, Couzens' 'Corner'. Once round it, they would be on exposed water and visible to any vigilant sentry.

It was brightening so rapidly that he could see a touch of green on the land, the glitter of spray over some fallen stones. Weapons too, and in the bows, leaning forward like a figure-head, the topman, Buller.

'Christ, there she be, sir!'

Bolitho saw the swaying mainmast and the smaller one right aft on the anchored yawl, stark against the sky, even though the hull was still in shadow.

A yawl, or dandy, as they were usually termed, would be just the thing for using amongst the islands.

He heard the gurgle of water around the stem, and from astern the regular, muffled beat of Frowd's oars.

Stockdale eased the tiller over, allowing the cutter to move away from the island to lay the yawl between him and D'Esterre's marines.

Soon now. It had to be. Bolitho held his breath, drawing his hanger carefully, although he knew from past experience that a tired look-out would hear little but his own shipboard noises. An anchored vessel was always alive with sound and movement.

But there was a long way to go yet. He said, 'Roundly, lads! Put your backs into it!'

The cutter was moving swiftly and firmly towards the yawl's larboard bow. Bolitho saw the anchor cable beneath the pole-like bowsprit, the casual way the sails were furled and brailed up.

The crack of a pistol shot was like a twelve-pounder on the morning air, and as somebody gave a startled cry aboard the yawl, an undulating line of heads, closely linked with muskets and fixed bayonets, appeared along the top of the island, then touches of scarlet as the marines continued to march in a long, single rank up and then down towards the water.

'*Pull!* All you've got!' Bolitho leaned forward as if to add weight to the fast-moving cutter.

Figures had appeared on the yawl's deck, and a solitary shot lit up the mainmast like a flare.

Across the water they all heard D'Esterre shouting for the yawl to surrender, and more confused cries, followed by the sound of cordage being hauled madly through blocks.

Bolitho momentarily forgot his own part in it, as with unhurried precision the line of shadowy marines halted and then fired a volley across the vessel's deck.

There was no movement aboard after that, and Bolitho shouted, 'Stand by to board! Grapnel ready there!' From a corner of his eye he saw Frowd's boat surging past, a grapnel already streaking towards the yawl's bulwark, while the selected men charged up with drawn cutlasses.

Yelling and cheering, the seamen clambered on either side of the bowsprit, seeing the crew crowding together near the mainmast, too shocked by what had happened to move, let alone resist. A few muskets had been thrown down on the deck, and Bolitho ran aft with Stockdale to ensure that no more men were hiding below and even now attempting to scuttle their vessel.

Not a man lost, and across the water he saw the marines waving their hats and cheering.

Frowd snapped, 'Privateers, right enough!' He dragged a man from the crowd. He had thrown his weapons away, but was so loaded with pouches of shot and cartridges that he looked like a pirate.

Bolitho sheathed his hanger. 'Well done, lads. I'll send word across to the marines and—'

It was Couzens who had shouted with alarm. He was pointing across the bows, his voice breaking, 'Ship, sir! Coming round the point!'

He heard D'Esterre calling through his speaking trumpet, his voice urgent and desperate. 'Abandon her! Man your boats!'

Frowd was still staring at the neat array of braced yards and sails as the approaching vessel tilted suddenly to a change of tack.

He asked, 'What the *hell* is she?'

Bolitho felt fingers tugging his sleeve, and he saw Buller, his eyes on the newcomer.

'It's 'er! Th' one I saw, zur! Th' brig which went about when *Spite* were dismasted!'

It was all tumbling through Bolitho's mind like a tide in a mill-race. The brig, the yawl waiting to load or unload more weapons and powder, D'Esterre's last order, his own decision which lay frozen in his reeling thoughts.

There was a flash, followed by a dull bang, and a ball whipped overhead and smashed down hard on the island. The marines were falling back in good order, and Bolitho could sense the change in the yawl's crew. Fear to hope, and then to jubilation at their unexpected rescue.

'What'll we do?' Frowd was standing by the capstan, his sword still in his hand. 'She'll rake her as she passes with every gun she's got!'

Bolitho thought of Pears, of Coutts' disappointment, of Quinn's face at the court of inquiry.

He yelled, 'Cut the cable! Stand by to break out the mains'l! Mr Frowd, take charge there! Stockdale, man the helm!'

Another ball came out of the misty light and smashed into one of the cutters which was bobbing beneath the stem. Before it heeled over and sank, its loaded swivel gun exploded, and a blast of canister cut down a seaman even as he ran to sever the cable.

With only one boat there was no chance to obey D'Esterre's order. Bolitho stared at the brig, his heart chilling with anger and unexpected hatred.

And he knew, deep down, that he had had no intention of obeying.

The great mainsail swung outboard on its boom, thundering wildly as the anchor cable was hacked away to allow the yawl to fall downwind, out of command.

'Put up your helm!'

Men were slipping and stumbling at the halliards, ignoring the dumbfounded crew as they fought to bring the yawl under control.

Bolitho heard a ragged crash of gun-fire, and turned in time to see the small after mast pitch over the rail, missing Stockdale by a few feet.

'Hack that adrift!'

Another crash shook the hull, and Bolitho heard the ball slamming through the deck below. She could not take much of this.

'Put those men on the pumps!' He thrust his pistol into Couzens' hand. 'Shoot if they try to rush you!'

'I've got 'er, sir!' Stockdale stood, legs wide apart, peering at the sails and the freshly set jib as the land swam round beneath the bowsprit. He looked like an oak.

But the brig was gaining, her deck tilting as she tacked round to hold the wind and overreach her adversary.

The yawl had two swivels, but they were useless. Like a pike against a charge of cavalry. And all the hands were better employed at sheets and braces than wasting their strength on empty gestures.

A bright ripple of flashes again, and this time the balls battered into the lower hull like a fall of rock.

Bolitho saw the flag at the brig's gaff, the one he had been hearing about. Red and white stripes, with a circle of stars on a blue ground. She looked very new, and was being handled by a real professional.

'We'm makin' water fast, sir!'

Bolitho wiped his face and listened to the creak of the pumps. It was no use. They could never outreach her.

Small, vicious sounds sang past the helm, and he knew they were in musket range.

Somebody screamed, and then he saw Frowd stagger and fall against the bulwark, both hands clutching a shattered knee.

Couzens appeared at the hatch, his back towards the deck as he trained the pistol down the companion ladder.

'We're sinking, sir! There's water bursting into the hold!'

A ball burst through the mainsail and parted shrouds and stays like an invisible sabre.

Frowd was gasping, 'Run her ashore! It's our only chance!'

Bolitho shook his head. Once on firm sand, the yawl's cargo, and he had no doubt now that she was loaded with arms for the brig, would still be intact.

With sudden fury he climbed on to the shrouds and shook his fist at the other vessel.

His voice was lost on the wind and the answering crash of cannon-fire, but he found some satisfaction as he yelled, 'I'll sink her first, *damn you*!'

Stockdale watched him, while beyond the bows and the sea which was being churned by falling shot he saw the headland sliding away.

Please God she'll be there, he thought despairingly. Too late for us, but they'll not live neither.

# 16

## Orders

As she floundered further from the island's shelter and into open water, the yawl rapidly became unmanageable. With so much damage below, and the dead-weight of weapons and iron shot, she was destroying herself on every wave.

The brig had changed tack again, sweeping away sharply to run almost parallel, while her gun crews settled down to pound the smaller craft into submission. There was no thought left of saving anything or anybody, and even the terrified prisoners were falling under the murderous cannon-fire.

Bolitho found time to notice that the brig, obviously new from some master-builder's yard, was not fully armed. Otherwise the fight would have been over long since. Only half her ports were firing, and he guessed the remainder were supposed to have been filled from the yawl's cargo. And this was her master's second attempt. The first had cost many lives, and the loss of the *Spite*. It seemed as if the brig had a charmed life and would escape yet again.

The deck gave a tremendous lurch and the topmast and upper yard fell in a mess of rigging and flapping canvas. Immediately the deck began to lean over, throwing men from their feet and bringing down more severed rigging.

From the open hatch Bolitho heard the violent inrush of water, the cries of the prisoners as the sea pushed through the frail timbers into the hold.

Bolitho clung to the bulwark and shouted, 'Release those men, Mr Couzens! The rest of you help the wounded!' He stared at Stockdale as he released the useless tiller. 'Lend a hand.' He winced as more shots whistled low overhead. 'We must abandon!'

Stockdale threw an unconscious seaman over his shoulder and strode to the side, peering down to make sure the remaining cutter was still afloat.

'Into the boat! Pass the wounded down.'

Bolitho felt the deck tilt and begin to settle more steeply. She was going by the stern, and the taffrail, with the stump of the after mast, was already awash.

If only the brig would cease firing. It needed just one ball to fall amongst the wounded and they would sink with the cutter. He looked at the swirling water and lively white crests. They would have a poor chance of survival in any case. On the island, which seemed to have moved a mile astern, he could see a few red coats, and guessed that the majority of the marines were running back to man the other boats. But marines were not seamen. By the time they managed to draw near, it would be over.

Couzens staggered towards him and gasped, 'The bows are out of the water, sir!' He ducked as another shot ripped through the mainsail and tore it away to rags.

Stockdale was trying to climb back on deck, but Bolitho shouted, 'Stand away! She's going down fast!'

With his face like a mask, Stockdale cast off the painter and allowed the current to carry him clear. Bolitho saw Frowd struggling aft to watch the sinking yawl, his fingers bloody as he waved his sword above his head.

The brig was shortening sail, the forecourse vanishing to reveal the rest of her neat hull.

Will they try to save us or kill us?

Bolitho said, 'We will swim for it, Mr Couzens.'

The boy nodded jerkily, unable to speak, as he kicked off his shoes and tore frantically at his shirt.

A shadow moved below the open hatch, and for a moment Bolitho imagined a wounded or trapped man was still down there. But it was a corpse, drifting forward as the water pounded between the decks. It was as high as that.

Couzens stared at the water and murmured. 'I'm not much of a swimmer, s-sir!' His teeth were chattering in spite of the sunlight.

Bolitho looked at him. 'Why in hell's name didn't you leave with the cutter then?' He realized the answer just as quickly and said quietly, 'We will keep together. I see a likely spar yonder . . .'

The brig fired again, the ball skipping over the wave crests, past the swaying cutter and between some floundering swimmers like an attacking swordfish.

So that was why they had shortened sail. To make sure the British force was totally destroyed. So that every officer would think again if in the future he saw a chance of seizing much-needed supplies.

The yawl lurched over, tipping loose gear and corpses into the scuppers.

Bolitho watched the brig. But for Couzens he would have stayed and died here, he knew it. If he had to die anyway, it were better to let them see his face. But Couzens did not deserve such a death. For him there must always seem a chance.

The brig was putting her helm over, her yards in confusion as she swung away from the drifting wreck. He could even see her name on the broad counter, *White Hills*, and a startled face peering at him from the stern windows.

'He's going about!' Bolitho spoke aloud without knowing it. 'What is he thinking of? He'll be in irons in a minute!'

The wind was too strong and the brig's sails too few. In no time she was rendered helpless, her sails all aback in flapping, disordered revolt.

There was a muffled bang, and for an instant Bolitho thought she had sprung a mast or large yard. With disbelief he saw a great gaping hole torn in the brig's main-topsail, the wind slashing it to ribbons against the mast even as he watched.

He felt Couzens clutching his arm and shouting, 'It's *Trojan*, sir! She *is* here!'

Bolitho turned and saw the two-decker, standing as if motionless in the haze, like an extension to the next pair of islets.

Pears must have judged it to the second, biding his time while the same wind which was hampering the brig carried him slowly across the one safe channel of escape.

Two bright tongues stabbed from the forecastle, and Bolitho could see the gun captains as if he were there with them. Probably Bill Chimmo, *Trojan*'s gunner, would personally be supervising each careful shot.

He heard the splintering crash as an eighteen-pound ball blasted its way into the brig.

Then, below his feet the deck started to slide away, and with Couzens clinging to him like a limpet he plunged over the bulwark. But not before he had heard a wild cheer, or before he had seen the bright new flag being hauled down from the brig's gaff.

Even at that range *Trojan*'s starboard broadside could have smashed the brig to pieces in minutes, and her master knew it. A bitter moment for him, but many would thank him all the same.

Gasping and spluttering they reached the drifting spar and clung on to it.

Bolitho managed to say, 'I think you saved *me*.' For, unlike Couzens, he had forgotten to remove his clothes or even his hanger, and he was grateful for the spar's support.

As he tried to hold his head above the choppy wave crests he saw the cutter turning towards him, the oarsmen leaning outboard to pull some of the swimmers to safety, or allow them to hang along either side of the hull. Further beyond them the other boats were coming too, the marines and the small party of seamen left to guard them doing better than Bolitho had expected.

He called, 'How is the brig?'

Couzens stared across the spar and answered, 'She's hove to, sir! They're not going to make a run for it!'

Bolitho nodded, unable to say anything more. The *White Hills* had no choice, especially as D'Esterre's boats were being careful not to lay themselves between him and *Trojan*'s formidable artillery.

The brig's capture might not make up for all those who had died, but it would show *Trojan*'s company what they could do, and give them back some pride.

*Trojan*'s remaining boats had been lowered and were coming to join in the rescue. Bolitho could see the two jolly boats and even the gig bouncing over the water. It took a full hour before he and Midshipman Couzens were hauled aboard the gig by a grinning Midshipman Pullen.

Bolitho could well imagine what the delay had done to
Stockdale. But Stockdale knew him well enough to stand off
with his overloaded boat of wounded and half-drowned men,
rather than to show preference for a lieutenant who was to all
intents safe and unhurt.

The eventual return aboard the *Trojan* was one of mixed
feelings. Sadness that some of the older and more experienced
hands had died or suffered wounds, but riding with it a kind of
wild jubilation that they had acted alone, and had won.

When the smartly painted brig was put under the command
of a boarding party, and the seamen lining the *Trojan*'s gangway
cheered the returning victors, it felt like the greatest triumph of
all time.

Small moments stood out, as they always did.

A seaman shaking his friend to tell him they were alongside
their ship again, the stunned disbelief when he discovered he had
died.

The cheers giving way to laughter as Couzens, as naked as the
day he was born, climbed through the entry port with all the
dignity he could manage, while two grinning marines presented
arms for his benefit.

And Stockdale striding to meet Bolitho, his slow, lopsided
smile of welcome better than any words.

Yet somehow it was Pears who held the day. Tall, massive
like his beloved *Trojan*, he stood watching in silence.

As Couzens tried to hide himself Pears called harshly, 'That
is no way for a King's officer to disport himself, sir! 'Pon my
soul, Mr Couzens, I don't know what you are thinking about,
and that's the truth!' Then as the boy ran, flushing, for the
nearest companionway, he added, 'Proud of you, all the same.'

Bolitho crossed the quarterdeck, his feet squelching noisily.

Pears eyed him grimly. 'Lost the yawl, I see? Loaded, was
she?'

'Aye, sir. I believe she was to arm the brig.' He saw his men
limping past, tarred hands reaching out to slap their shoulders.
He said softly, 'Our people did well, sir.'

He watched the brig spreading her sails again, the torn one
little more than rags. He guessed that Pears had sent a master's
mate across, while the marines searched and sorted out the
captured crew. Frowd might be made prize-master, it might
make up for his badly shattered knee. Whatever Thorndike did
for him now, or some hospital later on, he would have a bad limp

for the rest of his life. He had reached the rank of lieutenant. Frowd would know better than anyone that his wound would prevent his getting any further.

It was late afternoon by the time both vessels had cleared the islands and had sea-room again. It was no small relief to see the reefs and swirling currents left far astern.

When D'Esterre returned to the *Trojan* he had another interesting find to report.

The *White Hills'* captain was none other than Jonas Tracy, the brother of the man killed when they had seized the schooner *Faithful*. He had had every intention of fighting his way from under *Trojan*'s guns, hopeless or not. But the odds had been against him. His company were for the most part new to the trade of a fighting ship, which was the reason for a seasoned privateersman like Tracy being given command in the first place. His reputation, and list of successes against the British, made him an obvious choice. Tracy had ordered his men to put the *White Hills* about, to try and discover another, narrow passage through the islands. His men, already cowed by the *Trojan*'s unexpected challenge, were completely beaten when that second, carefully aimed ball had smashed into the brig's side. It had shattered to fragments on the breech of a gun on the opposite bulwark, and one splinter, the size of a block, had taken Tracy's arm off at the shoulder. The sight of their tough, head-swearing captain cut down before their eyes had been more than enough, and they had hauled down their flag.

Bolitho did not know if Tracy was still alive. It was an ironic twist that he had been firing on the man who was responsible for his brother's death without knowing it.

Bolitho was washing himself in his small cabin when he heard a commotion on deck, the distant cry that a sail was in sight.

The other vessel soon showed herself to be a frigate under full sail. She bore down on *Trojan* and with little fuss dropped a boat in the water to carry her captain across.

Bolitho threw on his shirt and breeches and ran on deck. The frigate was called *Kittiwake*, and Bolitho knew she was one of those he had seen at Antigua.

With as much ceremony as if they were safely anchored in Plymouth Sound, *Trojan* received her visitor. As the guard presented muskets, and calls shrilled, Pears stepped forward to greet him. Bolitho realized it was the post-captain who had been on Quinn's court of inquiry. Not the president, nor the one with the thin lips and vindictive manner, but the third officer who had, as far as Bolitho recalled, said nothing at all.

Sunset was closing in rapidly when the *Kittiwake*'s lord and master took his leave, his step less firm than when he had come aboard.

Bolitho watched the frigate make sail again, her canvas like gold silk in the dying sunlight. She would soon be out of sight, her captain free of admirals and ponderous authority. He sighed.

Cairns joined him, his eyes on the duty watch who were preparing to get the ship under way again.

He said quietly, 'She was from Antigua with despatches. She has been realeased from her squadron to go ahead of us to Jamaica. We are not outcasts after all.'

He sounded different. Remote.

'Is something wrong?'

Cairns looked at him, his face glowing in the sunset.

'Captain Pears thinks that the sea war will end in the Carribbean.'

'Not America?' Bolitho did not understand this mood.

'Like me, I think he believes that the war is already finished. Victories we will have, *must* have if we are to meet the French when they come out. But to win a war takes more than that, Dick.' He touched his shoulder and smiled sadly. 'I am detaining you. The captain wants you aft.' He walked away, calling sharply, 'Now then, Mr Dalyell, what is this shambles? Send the topmen aloft and pipe the hands to the braces! It is like a fish market here!'

Bolitho groped through the shadowed passageway to Pears' cabin.

Pears was sitting at his table, studying a bottle of wine with grim concentration.

He said, 'Sit down.'

Bolitho heard the pad of bare feet overhead, and wondered how they were managing with the captain away from his familiar place by the rail.

He sat.

The cabin looked comfortable and content. Bolitho felt suddenly tired, as if all the strength had drained out of him like sand from an hour-glass.

Pears announced slowly, 'We shall have some claret presently.'

Bolitho licked his lips. 'Thank you, sir.' He waited, completely lost. First Cairns, now Pears.

'Captain Viney of the *Kittiwake* brought orders from the flagship at Antigua. Mr Frowd is appointed into the *Maid of Norfolk*, armed transport. With all despatch.'

'But, sir, his leg?'

'I know. The surgeon has patched him as best he can.' His eyes came up and settled firmly on Bolitho's face. 'What does he want most in the world?'

'A ship, sir. Perhaps one day, a command of his own.'

He recalled Frowd's face aboard the yawl. Perhaps even then he had been thinking of it. A ship, any ship, like the armed transport written in his appointment, would have done.

'I agree. If he languishes here it will be too late. If he returns to Antigua,' he shrugged, 'his luck may have changed by then.'

Bolitho watched him, fascinated by Pears' authority. He had fought in battles, and was now taking his command to deal with God alone knew what in Jamaica, and yet he had time to think about Frowd.

'Then there is Mr Quinn.' Pears opened the bottle, his head to one side as the hull shivered and rolled before settling down on a new tack. 'He was not forgotten.'

Bolitho waited, trying to discover Pears' true feelings.

'He is to be returned to Antigua for passage to England. The rest we already know. I have written a letter for his father. It won't help much. But I want him to understand that his son only had so much courage. When it left him he was as helpless as Frowd with his leg.' Pears nudged a heavy envelope with the bottle. 'But he *tried*, and if more young men were doing that, instead of living in comfort at home, we might be better placed than we are.'

Bolitho looked at the bulky envelope. Quinn's life.

Pears became almost brisk. 'But enough of that. I have things to do, orders to dictate.'

He poured two large glasses of claret and held them on the table until Bolitho took one. The ship was leaning so steeply that both would have slithered to the deck otherwise.

It was strange that no one else was here. He had expected D'Esterre, or perhaps Cairns, once he had completed his duties with the watch on deck.

Pears raised his glass and said, 'I expect this will be a long night for you. But there will be longer ones, believe me.'

He raised his glass, like a thimble in his massive fist.

'I wish you luck, Mr Bolitho, and as our redoubtable sailing master would say, God's speed.'

Bolitho stared at him, the claret untouched.

'I am putting you in command of the *White Hills*. We will part company tomorrow when it is light enough to ferry the wounded over to her.'

Bolitho tried to think, to clear the astonishment from his mind.

Then he said, 'The first lieutenant, sir, with all respect...'

Pears held up his glass. It was empty. Like Probyn's had once been.

'I was going to send him. I *need* him here, now more than ever, but he deserves an appointment, even as a prize-master.' He eyed him steadily. 'As you did to Rear-Admiral Coutts, so did he refuse my suggestion.' He smiled gravely. 'So there we are.'

Bolitho saw his glass being refilled and said dazedly, 'Thank you very much, sir.'

Pears grimaced. 'So get the claret down you, and say your farewells. You can bother the life out of someone else after this!'

Bolitho found himself outside beside the motionless sentry again, as if it had all been a dream.

He found Cairns still on deck, leaning against the weather nettings and staring across at the brig's lights.

Before Bolitho could speak Cairns said firmly, 'You are going as prize-master tomorrow. It is settled, if I have to send you across in irons.'

Bolitho stood beside him, conscious of the movements behind him, the creak of the wheel, the slap of rigging against spars and canvas.

*I expect this will be a long night for you.*

'What has happened, Neil?'

He felt very close to this quiet, soft-spoken Scot.

'The captain also received a letter. I don't know who from. It is not his style to whimper. It was a *friendly* piece of information, if you can call it that. To tell Captain Pears he has been passed over for promotion to flag rank. A captain he will remain.' He looked up at the stars beyond the black rigging and yards. 'And when *Trojan* eventually pays-off, that will be the end for him.

Coutts has been ordered to England under a cloud.' He could not hide his anger, his hurt. 'But he has wealth, and position.' He turned and gestured towards the poop. '*He* only has his ship!'

'Thank you for telling me.'

Cairns' teeth were very white in the gloom. 'Away with you, man. Go and pack your chest.'

As Bolitho was about to leave him he added softly, 'But you do understand, my friend? I couldn't desert him now, could I?'

The next morning, bright and early, with both vessels hove to, *Trojan*'s boats started to ferry the wounded seamen across to the brig. On their return trips they carried *White Hills'* crew into captivity. It must have been one of the shortest commissions in sea history, Bolitho thought.

Nothing seemed exactly real to him, and he found himself forgetting certain tasks, and checking to discover if he had completed others more than once.

Each time he went on deck he had to look across at the brig, rolling uncomfortably in steep troughs. But once under sail again she could fly if need be. It was too close a memory to forget how she had been handled.

Cairns had already told him that Pears was allowing him to select his own prize-crew. Just enough to work the brig in safety, or run before a storm or powerful enemy.

He did not have to ask Stockdale. He was there, a small bag already packed. His worldly possessions. Pears had also instructed him to take the badly wounded Captain Jonas Tracy to Antigua. He was too severely injured to be moved with the other prisoners, and should be little trouble.

As the time drew near for him to leave, Bolitho was very aware of his own torn emotions. Small incidents from the past stood out to remind him of his two and a half years in the *Trojan*. It seemed quite unbelievable that he was leaving her, to place himself at the disposal of the admiral commanding in Antigua. It was like starting life all over again. New faces, fresh surroundings.

He had been surprised and not a little moved by some of the men who had actually volunteered to go with him.

Carlsson, the Swede who had been flogged. Dunwoody, the miller's son, Moffitt, the American, Rabbett, the ex-thief, and old Buller, the topman, the man who had recognized the brig from the start. He had been promoted to petty officer and had shaken his head in astonishment at the news.

There were others too, as much a part of the big two-decker as her figurehead or her captain.

He watched Frowd being swayed down to the cutter in a bosun's chair, his bandaged and splinted leg sticking out like a tusk, and hating it all, the indignity of leaving his ship in this fashion.

Quinn had already gone across. It would be difficult to stand between those two, Bolitho thought. Bolitho had already seen Frowd looking bitterly at Quinn. He was probably questioning the fairness of it. Why should Quinn, who was being rejected by the Navy, be spared, while he was a cripple?

Most of the goodbyes had been said already. Last night, and through the morning. Rough handshakes from gunner and boatswain, grins from others he had watched change from boys to men. Like himself.

D'Esterre had sent some of his own stock of wine across to the brig, and Sergeant Shears had given him a tiny cannon which he had fashioned from odd fragments of silver.

Cairns found him checking over his list of things which he was required to do and said, 'The Sage says that we're in for a blow, Dick. You'd better be going now.' He thrust out his hand. 'I'll say my farewells here.' He glanced around the deserted wardroom where they had shared so much. 'It will seem emptier with you gone.'

'I'll not forget you.' Bolitho gripped his hand hard. 'Ever!'

They walked forward to the companion ladder, and Cairns said suddenly, 'One thing. Captain Pears thinks you should take another officer to stand watches with you. We cannot spare a master's mate, and lieutenants are as rare as charity until our replacements arrive. So it will have to be a midshipman.'

Bolitho thought about it.

Cairns added, 'Weston will be acting-lieutenant as of now, and both Lunn and Burslem are better left here to finish their training. That leaves Forbes and Couzens who are young enough to begin again anywhere.'

Bolitho smiled. 'I will put it to them.'

Watched by the lieutenants and marine officers, Erasmus Bunce, the master, beckoned to the two thirteen-year-old midshipmen.

'A volunteer is needed, young gentlemen.' Bunce glared at

them disdainfully. 'Though what use either o' you will be to Mr Bolitho, I can't say.'

They both stepped forward, Couzens with such a look of pleading on his round face that Bunce asked, 'Is your gear packed?'

Couzens nodded excitedly, and Forbes looked near to tears as he shook his head.

Bunce said, 'Mr Couzens, off you go, and lively. It must be the Lord's blessing to clear the ship of your high spirits and skylarking!' He looked at Bolitho and dropped one eyelid like a gunport. 'Satisfied?'

'Aye.'

Bolitho shook their hands, trying to hold back his emotion.

D'Esterre was the last. 'Good luck, Dick. We'll meet again. I shall miss you.'

Bolitho looked across at the *White Hills*, seeing the wave crests rolling along her hull, making her sway more and more steeply.

His orders were in his pocket, in a heavily sealed envelope. He waited to go, but the ship held on to him.

He walked towards the entry port, seeing the gig rising and falling alongside. In for a blow, Bunce had said. Perhaps it was just as well. To hasten the break and keep him too busy for regrets.

Cairns said quietly, 'Here is the captain.'

Pears strolled across the quarterdeck, his coat-tails flapping out like studding sails, while he held on to his gold-laced hat with one hand.

'Prepare to get under way, Mr Cairns. I'll not lose this wind.' He seemed to see Bolitho for the first time. 'Still here, sir?' His eyebrows went up. ''Pon my soul . . .' For once he did not finish. Instead he walked across and held out his big hand.

'Be off with you now. My regards to your father when next you see him.' He turned away and moved aft towards the compass.

Bolitho touched his hat to the quarterdeck, and clutching his hanger to his hip hurried down into the boat.

The oars dipped into the water, and immediately *Trojan* fell away, the men on the gangways turning to continue with their work while others ran up the ratlines to loose the topsails again.

Couzens stared back at the ship, his eyes watering in the

wind. It looked as if he was crying. Unknown to Bolitho, it was the happiest day in the midshipman's short life.

Bolitho raised his hand, and saw Cairns doing the same. Of Pears there was no sign. Like the *Trojan*, he was letting go.

Bolitho turned his back and studied the *White Hills*. His for so short a time. But *his*.


As Bunce had predicted, the wind rose rapidly to gale force, and with it the sea changed its face from cruising white horses to long, violent troughs with ragged yellow crests.

The prize-crew got down to work in grim earnest, bringing the ship's head to the south as the wind backed and pushed them hard over, the yards braced round until they would not shift another inch.

Bolitho discarded his hat and coat and stood beside the unprotected wheel, his ears ringing to the roar of wind and sea, his whole body soaking with spray.

It was lucky the *White Hills* carried a spare main-topsail, he thought. The one which had been torn apart by *Trojan*'s first shot had been saved for patching but was useless for anything more.

Under reefed topsails and jib, the *White Hills* ran close-hauled to the south, away from the islands and danger.

Quinn, stiff-faced and barely speaking, worked with the hands on deck, and without him Bolitho wondered what he would have done. Couzens had the determination and loyalty of ten men, but experience in handling rigging and sails in a full gale he had not.

Stockdale came aft and joined the two hands at the wheel. Like Bolitho he was drenched to the skin, his clothing stained by tar and salt. He grinned through the drifting streamers of spindrift and bobbed his head at Bolitho.

'Real little lady, ain't she?'

For most of the day they ran with the wind, but towards sunset the strength fell away, and later still the bruised and breathless seamen managed to get aloft and set both mainsail and forecourse. The additional bulging area of canvas pushed the hull over further still, but held her steadier, and more firmly on course.

Bolitho shouted to Quinn, 'Take over! I'm going below!'

After the noise and confusion on deck it seemed almost quiet once he had lowered himself through the companionway.

How small she seemed after *Trojan*'s great girth. He groped his way aft to the cabin, a miniature of Pears' quarters. It was barely large enough to contain Pears' table, he thought. But it looked inviting, and too new to show signs of a previous owner.

He reeled as the sea boiled and thundered along the quarter, and then managed to reach the stern windows. There was no-where in the cabin, apart from a battened-down skylight, where he could stand upright. What it was like in the messes, he could well imagine. As a midshipman he had once served in a brig very similar to this one. Fast, lively, and never still.

He wondered what had happened to Tracy's other command, the captured brig which he had renamed *Revenge*. Still attacking British convoys and stalking rich cargoes for ready prize-money.

The cabin door banged open and Moffitt lurched through it carrying a jug of rum.

He said, 'Mr Frowd thought you might like a drop, sir.'

Bolitho disliked rum, but he needed something. He swallowed it in a gulp, almost choking.

'Mr Frowd, is he all right?' He must visit him soon, but now he was needed and would have to return to the deck.

Moffitt took the empty goblet and grinned at it admiringly. 'Aye, sir. I've got him propped in a cot in his cabin. He'll be safe enough.'

'Good. Get Buller for me.'

Bolitho lay back, feeling the stern rising and then sliding down beneath him, the sea shaking the rudder like a piece of driftwood.

Buller came into the cabin, his head lowered to avoid the beams.

'Zur?'

'You take charge of the victuals. Find someone who can cook. If the wind drops some more we'll get the galley fire re-lit and put something hot into our bellies.'

Buller showed his strong teeth. 'Right away, zur.' Then he too was gone.

Bolitho sighed, the aroma of rum around him like a drug. Chain of command. And he must begin it. No one else was here to goad or encourage his efforts.

His head lolled and he jerked it up with sudden disgust. Like George Probyn. That was a fine beginning. He jumped up and gasped as his head crashed against a beam. But it sobered him even more quickly.

He made his way forward, swaying and feeling his balance with each jubilant lunge of the brig's bowsprit.

Tiny cabins on either side of a small, square space. The wardroom. Stores, and shot garlands, swaying ranks of pod-like hammocks. The ship smelt new, right down to her mess tables, her great coils of stout cable in the tier forward.

He found the wounded Tracy in a cot, swinging in a tiny cabin which was still unfinished. A red-eyed seaman sat in one corner, a pistol between his feet.

Bolitho peered at the figure in the cot. About thirty, a powerful, hard-faced man, who despite his terrible wound and loss of blood still looked very much alive. But with his arm torn off at the point of the shoulder he would not be much trouble.

He glanced at the sentry and said, 'Watch him, all the same.'

The other wounded men were quiet enough, bandaged, and cushioned from the fierce motion by spare hammocks, blankets and clothing from the brig's store.

He paused by a wildly swinging lantern, feeling their pain, their lack of understanding. Again, he was ashamed for thinking of his own reward. They on the other hand knew only that they were being carried away from their ship, which good or bad, had been their home. And to where? Some home-bound vessel, and then what? Put ashore, just another cluster of crippled sailors. Heroes to some, figures of fun to others.

'There'll be some hot food along soon, lads.'

A few heads turned to look at him. One man he recognized as Gallimore, a seaman employed as a painter aboard the *Trojan*. He had been badly injured by canister during the attack on the yawl. He had lost most of his right hand, and had been hit in the face by wood splinters.

He managed to whisper, 'Where we goin', sir?'

Bolitho knelt down on the deck beside him. The man was dying. He did not know how he knew, or why. Others nearby were more badly hurt, yet bore their pain with defiant, even surly resignation. They would survive.

He said, 'English Harbour. The surgeons there will help you. You'll see.'

The man reached out, seeking Bolitho's hand. 'Oi don't want to die, sir. Oi got a wife an' children in Plymouth.' He tried to shake his head. 'Oi mustn't die, sir.'

Bolitho felt a catch in his throat. Plymouth. It might just as well be Russia.

'Rest easy, Gallimore.' He withdrew his hand carefully. 'You are with your friends.'

He walked aft again to the companionway, bent almost double in the space between decks.

The wind and spray were almost welcome. He found Couzens with Stockdale by the wheel, while Quinn was groping along the forecastle with two seamen.

Stockdale said gruffly, 'All 'oldin' firm, sir. Mr Quinn is lookin' at the weather braces.' He peered up at the dark sky. 'Wind's backed a piece more, Fallin' off, too.'

The bows lifted towards the sky, then came down in a trough with a shuddering lurch. It was enough to hurl a man from the yards, had there been one up there.

Stockdale muttered, 'Must be bad for the lads below, sir.'

Bolitho nodded. 'Gallimore's dying, I think.'

'I know, sir.'

Stockdale eased the spokes and studied the quivering maintopsail, the canvas ballooning out as if to tear itself from the yard.

Bolitho glanced at him. Of course, Stockdale would have known. He had lived with suffering for most of his life. Death would seem familiar, recognizable.

Quinn came aft along the pale deck, staggering to each swooping dip across the troughs.

He shouted, 'The larboard anchor was working free, but we've catted it home again!'

Bolitho replied, 'Get below. Work out two watches for me, and I'll discuss it with you later.'

Quinn shook his head. 'I don't want to be on my own. I must do something.'

Bolitho thought of the man from Plymouth. 'Go to the wounded, James. Take some rum, or anything you can find in the cabin, and issue it to those poor devils.'

There was no sense in telling him about Gallimore. Let the dying man join his companions in a last escape. The sailor's balm for everything.

A seaman, accompanied by Buller, ducked down the companion ladder, and Bolitho saw it was a swarthy Italian named Borga. It seemed as if Buller had already chosen a cook, and Bolitho hoped it was a wise decision. Hot food in a seaman's belly after fisting canvas and trying to stay inboard was one thing, but some foreign concoction might spark off a brawl. He glanced at Stockdale and smiled to himself. If so, it would soon be dealt with.

Another hour, and the stars appeared, the scudding clouds driven off like fleeing vagrants.

Bolitho felt the deck becoming steadier, and wondered what tomorrow would be like, how Bunce would have predicted it.

As promised, a hot meal was produced and issued first to the wounded, and then to the seamen as they were relieved from watch in small groups.

Bolitho ate his with relish, although what he was having he did not know. Boiled meat, oatmeal, ground biscuit, it was also laced with rum. It was like nothing he had ever had, but at that moment would have graced any admiral's table.

To Couzens he said, 'Are you sorry for your eagerness to join the *White Hills*?'

Couzens shook his head, his stomach creaking with Borga's first meal.

'Wait till I get home, sir. They'll never believe it.'

Bolitho pictured Quinn, sitting below with the wounded, and thought of Pears writing a letter to his father. *He tried*.

He thought too of the despatches he was carrying from Captain Pears to the admiral at Antigua. It was probably safer not to know what Pears had said about him, although it would certainly affect his immediate future. But he still did not really understand Pears, only that under his command he had learned more than he had first realized.

Bolitho stared up at the sky. 'I think we've seen the worst of it. Better fetch Mr Quinn on deck.'

Couzens watched him and blurted out, 'I can stand watch, sir.'

Stockdale grinned lazily. 'Aye, sir, he can at that. I'll be on deck, too.' He hid his grin from the midshipman. 'Though I'll not be needed, I'm thinkin'.'

'Very well.' Bolitho smiled. 'Call me if you're in any doubt.'

He lowered himself through the companionway, glad he had

given Couzens the opportunity to face responsibility, surprised too that he had been able to trust him without hesitation.

As he found his way to his small cabin, he heard Frowd snoring loudly and the clatter of a goblet rolling back and forth across the deck.

Tomorrow would be a lot of hard work. First to try to estimate their position and drift, then to set a new course which with luck would carry them to the Leeward Islands and Antigua.

On the chart it did not seem so far, but the prevailing winds would be against them for much of the passage, and it could take days to make good the loss of being driven south.

And once in Antigua, what then? Would the French lieutenant still be there, taking lonely walks in the sun, on his honour not to try and escape?

He laid down on the bench beneath the stern windows, ready to run on deck at the first unusual sound. But Bolitho was fast asleep in a matter of seconds.

It was noon, two days after leaving the *Trojan*, but a lifetime of new experiences and problems.

The weather was less demanding now, and the *White Hills* was leaning over on the larboard tack, with even her big spanker set and filled by the wind. The vessel felt clean and dry after the storm, and the makeshift routine which Bolitho had worked out with Quinn and Frowd was performing well.

Frowd was on deck, seated on a hatch cover, his leg propped before him as a constant reminder.

Couzens stood by the wheel, while Bolitho and Quinn checked their sextants and compared calculations.

He saw the seaman Dunwoody walk to the lee bulwark and hurl a bucket of slops over the side. He had just emerged from the forecastle, so had probably been with Gallimore. He had still not died, but had been moved to the cable tier, the only place where the stench of the great slimy rope was matched by his own. His wound had gone gangrenous, and it seemed impossible for any man to stand the misery of it.

Quinn said wearily, 'I think we are both right, sir. With the wind staying as it is, we should make a landfall the day after tomorrow.'

Bolitho handed his instrument to Couzens. So it was *sir* again. The last link broken.

He said, 'I agree. We may sight the island of Nevis tomorrow, and after that it will be a hard beat all the way across to Antigua.'

He felt a sharp sense of loss. The thought of losing the *White Hills* seemed unbearable. It was ridiculous of course. Just a few days, but what confidence she had given him, or had discovered in him.

Bolitho glanced along the sunlit deck. Even that no longer seemed so narrow and confined after *Trojan*'s spacious gundeck.

Some of the wounded were resting in the shade, chatting quietly, or watching the other hands at work with professional interest.

Bolitho asked quietly, 'What will you do, James?'

Quinn looked away. 'As my father pleases, I expect. I seem to have the knack of obeying orders.' He faced Bolitho suddenly. 'One day. If you want to, I—I mean, if you have nowhere to go, would you care to see me?'

Bolitho nodded, wanting to strip away his despair. It was killing him with no less mercy than Gallimore's wounds.

'I will be happy to, James.' He smiled. 'Although I've no doubt your father will think badly of a mere lieutenant in his house. I expect you'll be a rich merchant by the time I get to London.'

Quinn studied him anxiously. Something in Bolitho's tone seemed to comfort him and he said, 'I thank you for that. And much more.'

'Deck there! Sail on the weather bow!'

Bolitho stared up at the look-out. He tried to see the *White Hills* like a cross on a chart. There were so many islands, French, British, Dutch. This sail could be any kind of ship.

Since the *Kittiwake* had left Antigua anything might have happened. Peace with the American rebels, war with France.

With a start he realized they were all looking at him.

He said, 'Get aloft, Mr Quinn. Take a glass and tell me what you see.'

Frowd groaned as Quinn hurried past. 'God damn this leg! I should be up there, not, not . . .' By the time he had thought of a suitable insult Quinn was already hurrying up the shrouds.

Bolitho paced rapidly back and forth, trying to stay calm and unmoved. She was quite likely a Spaniard, southward bound for the Main and all its treasures. If so, she would soon haul off. She might think *White Hills* to be a pirate. In these waters you could choose from a dozen sorts of enemy.

'Deck, sir! She's a brig!'

One of the wounded men gave a thin cheer. 'She'll be one of ours, lads!'

But Frowd rasped painfully, 'You know what I'm thinking, don't you?'

Bolitho looked at him, his brain suddenly ice-cold.

Of course, it made sense. Cruel sense. And they had got so far. This time, he had believed, with success.

There was still a chance.

He held his voice steady as he called, 'Keep watching her!' To Couzens he added more quietly, 'We shall have a closer look at her soon enough, I imagine.' He saw the understanding clouding Couzens' eyes. 'Clear for action, if you please. Then load, but do not run out.'

He glanced along the deck, at the brig's small defences. Enough guns to rake the defenceless yawl, but if the oncoming vessel was Captain Tracy's previous command, they would be all but useless.

# 17

# *None So Gallant*

Bolitho waited for the deck to steady again and then trained his telescope across the larboard bow. He could see the other brig's topsails and topgallants sharply etched against the blue sky, but the rest of the vessel was lost in distance and haze.

If the vessel was the *Revenge*, her master would recognize the *White Hills* as soon as she was within reasonable distance. He might have done so already. To alter course away, to wear completely and fly with the wind would tell him what had happened quicker than any challenge.

Bolitho looked up at the masthead pendant. The wind had backed a point or so further. It was tempting to turn and run, but if the wind went against them again, and they were repeatedly made to change tack, the other brig would soon overhaul them. With only a small prize-crew to work the ship, Bolitho knew it would be asking too much for any man.

He said, 'Let her fall off a point, Stockdale.'

From the mainmast he heard Quinn call, 'I can see her better now! She's the old *Mischief*! I'm almost certain!'

Frowd swore. 'Bloody hell! We'd better show her a clean pair of heels!'

*In Gallant Company*

Stockdale said, 'Nor'-east by east, sir.'

Bolitho cupped his hands. 'Man the braces! You, Buller, put more men on the weather forebrace!'

He watched narrowly as the yards moved slightly to allow each sail to fill to capacity. But not enough to betray an attempt to escape.

Couzens came running aft, his hands filthy, his shirt torn in several places.

'Cleared for action, sir. All guns loaded.'

Bolitho smiled tightly. By *all guns*, Couzens meant the *White Hills'* eight six-pounders. She was designed to carry fourteen, and some swivels, but the sinking of the yawl had put paid to that. Eight guns, and only four on either beam. To try and shift a full battery to one side would certainly be seen by the other brig. She was growing in size at a surprising speed, and Bolitho could see the sun reflecting on metal, or perhaps the glass of several telescopes.

She was closing with the *White Hills* on a converging tack, bowsprit to bowsprit.

The *White Hills'* original crew had been new and raw, but the *Revenge*'s master would certainly know Tracy by sight. They must try and stand off. Keep up some sort of bluff until dusk.

'Land on the lee bow, sir!' The look-out had been keeping his eyes open too while Quinn watched the other brig.

Bolitho looked at Frowd, seeing his despair. The land was most likely to be one or more of the tiny islands which marked their course past Nevis and then fifty miles on to Antigua. It made it seem much worse. So near, yet so far.

'Brig's altered course, sir!' Then another cry, 'She's run up her flag!'

Bolitho nodded grimly. 'Hoist the same one, Mr Couzens.' He watched as the red and white striped flag ran up to the gaff and broke to the wind.

Frowd was straining up on the hatch cover. 'No use, blast his eyes! He's closing, and making sure he can keep the wind-gage!'

'He'll want to speak with us. To find out if we got the guns and powder. This brig was probably meant to join with him at some point.' Bolitho was thinking aloud and saw Frowd nod in agreement.

Stockdale pulled at Couzens' sleeve. 'Get the *real* flag ready, Mr Couzens. I can't see our lieutenant fighting under false colours. Not today.'

Frowd said despairingly, 'How can we fight, you fool! These privateers are always armed to the gills! They need to smash an enemy into submission as fast as they can, and before help can be sent to drive 'em off!' He groaned. 'Fight? You must be mad!'

Bolitho made up his mind. 'We will begin to shorten sail directly, as if we are about to speak with him. If we can get near enough without rousing suspicion, we'll rake his poop, do for as many of the after-guard as possible and then run for it.'

Stockdale nodded. 'Later we could shift two guns aft, sir. A stern chase is better'n nothin'.'

Bolitho made himself stand quite still, to give his mind time to work. He had no other choice, and this was not much of one. But it was either a sudden act of daring, or surrender.

'Take in the mains'l.'

Bolitho watched the few spare hands swarming up the ratlines. The other master would see the depleted crew, and might imagine they had been in a battle. The gash through the bulwark made by *Trojan*'s eighteen-pounder must be plain enough to see.

He levelled his glass on the other vessel, ignoring the shouts and curses as his men fought with the rebellious canvas. Frowd was right. She was heavily armed, and there were plenty of men about her deck, too.

He wondered what had happened to her original captain when she had been captured from under him. Fourteen guns and a determined company would make her a formidable enemy. Bolitho watched her tilting towards him, revealing her main-deck, the line of guns on the opposite side. None was manned, but on this side he could see a few heads peering over the sealed gunports, and guessed they were probably loaded and ready.

Moffitt crossed the deck and said dourly, 'You'll be needin' me, sir? I know how to speak to them bastards!'

'Be ready.'

He studied the set of each sail, the lively froth around the privateer's stem as she edged over even further, her yards moving as if controlled by one hand.

Half a mile. Not long now.

He shifted his glance inboard, seeing the quick, anxious gestures of his small company, even the wounded were craning their heads and trying to see above the weather bulwark.

'Come down, Mr Quinn!' Bolitho looked at Stockdale and Buller. 'See that our people keep their weapons out of sight.

When I give the word, I want those four guns run out as smartly as you like and fire at will. If we can mark down her officers we may use the surprise to fight clear.'

Quinn arrived beside him, breathing fast, his eyes towards the enemy.

'D'you think they are on to us?'

'No.' Bolitho folded his arms, hoping that across the glittering pattern of waves and spray he would appear more relaxed then he felt. 'They would have run down on us before now. They have all the advantage.'

If the wind chose this moment to change . . . He shut his mind to the possibility and concentrated on the sails and masthead pendant. The wind, which was fresh and steady, came from the north-west. The *White Hills* had her yards well braced, heeling on the larboard tack, the wind across her quarter. If they could just delay the other captain's suspicions, and then hold him off until dark, they might well lose him amongst the islands when daylight returned.

And even then, if the privateer's captain was so set on another victory and made further contact, they might be able to give him the slip further north, or in the narrows between Nevis and St Christopher. In those treacherous waters, off some deadly place like the Scotch Bonnet, they might even tempt their pursuer aground.

The only ally at this precarious stage was the wind. Both brigs were carrying the bulk of their sails, so either could tack or come about with agility if need be.

Stockdale observed, 'She must be steerin' almost sou'-east, sir. The wind right astern of 'er.'

Bolitho nodded, knowing Stockdale wanted to help, if only by making a professional comment.

The range had dropped to a mere quarter-mile, and it was possible to see the watching figures on the other vessel's poop and forecastle.

'When she tries to hail us, Moffitt, tell her captain that Tracy is sick, badly wounded after a brush with the British.' He saw the man tighten his lips. 'It's no lie, so keep it simple, eh?'

Moffitt said coldly, 'I'll see that he don't recover if them buggers board us, sir!'

Along the weather side the seamen were crawling on their hands and knees, like strange worshippers around the four small cannon. Ball and grape to each gun. It would not even be felt by a stately two-decker like *Trojan*. But one good blast across the enemy's quarterdeck might do the trick. Time, time, time. It was like a hammer on an anvil.

Two small shadows moved on the *Revenge*'s side, and Bolitho heard a murmur of anxiety from some of the wounded seamen. *Revenge* had raised two of her forward port lids, and as he watched he saw the sunlight touch a pair of black muzzles as she ran out the guns.

Frowd muttered uneasily, 'He *knows*, the bugger!'

Bolitho shook his head. 'I think not. He would run out a broadside if he was sure of an enemy, and maybe tack across our stern.' Again, it was like sharing his thoughts with those around him. 'He'll have been watching us all this time, as we have him. Tracy's absence from the deck will have been noted. If *Revenge*'s captain is newly appointed, he'll be wary of taking a chance, but unwilling to show fear or uncertainty to his men. Following a man like Tracy must be quite a task.'

He saw some of his seamen glance at each other, for support, to discover a new confidence. But he knew he was only guessing out of sheer hope.

*Revenge*'s captain might be even more experienced than Tracy. And at this very moment was using the *White Hills'* unchanged tack for one terrible bombardment, his guns already manned and ready to fire.

Moffitt took a speaking trumpet and climbed casually into the weather shrouds. It was far too early, but it might lull the enemy's caution.

If not, the fight would explode across this deck within fifteen minutes.

Bolitho said evenly, 'You men, carry Mr Frowd and the other wounded below. If we have to abandon, the quarter boat will be used for them only.'

Frowd swivelled round on his hatch cover like an enraged terrier.

'Damn your eyes, I'll not die like a sick woman!' He grimaced as the pain stabbed through him, and he continued in a more controlled tone, 'I meant no disrespect, sir, but try and see it my way.'

'And which way is that?'

Frowd swayed about like a bush in a wind as the hull lifted and sliced through the choppy water.

'If your plan works, sir, and I pray to God it does, it will be a chase which only luck and superior seamanship can win.'

Bolitho smiled. 'Perhaps.'

'But, as I suspect, we may have to fight, for God's sake let me play my part. I have been in the Navy all my remembered years. To end my time cowering below when the metal flies overhead would make my life as worthless as that of any gallows-bird.'

'Very well.' Bolitho looked at Couzens. 'Help the lieutenant aft and see that he is supplied with enough powder and shot to reload the pistols and muskets to give an impression of strength and greater numbers.'

Frowd exclaimed, 'That's it, sir. I ask for nothing more. Those devils will outnumber us four to one, maybe more. We can take a few with us if we can maintain rapid fire.'

It was incredible, Bolitho thought. The prospect of sudden death had been made suddenly stark and inevitable by Frowd's words, and yet the previous apprehension seemed to have gone. The waiting had been the worst part, the simple task of fighting and dying was something they all understood. It was like hearing Sparke all over again. Keep them busy. No time to moan and weaken.

He turned to watch as the *Revenge*'s jib and staysails quivered and flapped like tapered wings, and knew she was falling off a little more to run even closer to the *White Hills*. Nearer, she looked impressive and well armed.

Her hull was weatherbeaten and the sails stained and patched in several places. She must have been made to work and fight hard against her previous owners, Bolitho thought grimly.

'We will give her a few more minutes, Stockdale, and then you can bring her round to steer due east. It will be the obvious thing to do if we are to draw close enough to speak.'

He winced as a handspike clattered across the deck and a man retrieved it under a stream of threats and curses from Buller.

He saw the cutlasses and pistols by each man, the way they kept tensing their muscles as if carrying some great load while they waited and lived out each agonizing minute.

'Man the braces. Stand by!' Bolitho strode to the side and added sharply, 'Be easy, lads! Take your time.' He saw some of them pause to stare. After serving in a King's ship it was like a blasphemy to be told to take your time. He added, 'You are *landmen*, remember?' It was unbelievable that some of them could grin and chuckle at such a stupid joke. 'So forget you are prime seamen.'

Buller called, 'But not for long, eh, zur?' Even he was laughing.

'*Now*, Stockdale.'

With yards and rudder moving in clumsy unison, the little brig fell three points downwind, the *Revenge*'s masts appearing to slide astern until she was running on a parallel course, her bowsprit and jib boom just overlapping the *White Hills'* taffrail, and half a cable away.

Obediently, or so it appeared, the other vessel followed suit, dropping even further with the wind and leaning over on the larboard tack. Fifty yards separated the two brigs now, with the *Revenge* still slightly astern. Each alteration of tack had given *White Hills* a few more precious minutes and a tiny lead on her unwanted companion.

Frowd said between his clenched teeth, 'Thank the good Lord they have no prepared signals this time.'

'You sound like the Sage.'

But Frowd was right. The enemy could have examined them at leisure had they had the time to create an efficient form of signalling as in more professional navies.

Apart from the creaming water alongside, the resonant slap and boom of canvas, it was very quiet on deck.

Moffitt remarked, 'I can see one of 'em with a trumpet, sir.' He looked at Bolitho, his eyes calm. 'I know what to say. I'll not let you down.'

Rabbett said, 'You'd better not, matey. I've been in too many jails to rot in one o' theirs!'

Moffitt grinned and then waved his speaking trumpet towards the other vessel. Both brigs were moving swiftly on the same tack, and at any other time would have made a fine sight. Now, in their controlled advance, they each had had a quality of menace. Like two wary beasts, the one unwilling to fall into a trap, the other afraid of showing weakness to her enemy.

It was then, even as someone waved back from the *Revenge*'s quarterdeck, that the tension was shattered by a terrible scream. It was like something inhuman, a soul in hideous torment.

The seamen at the braces, or hiding beside their guns, peered round, horrified and then angry as the sound got louder and wilder.

Quinn gasped, 'What is it, in the name of God?'

Stockdale said, 'Gallimore, sir. His wound must 'ave burst.'

Bolitho nodded, tasting the bile in his throat, as he pictured the awful gangrenous, rotting flesh which had given off such a stench that he had had to move Gallimore to the cable tier.

'Tell Borga to silence him.'

He tried to shut out the screams, to exclude the picture of the tortured man below.

A voice came across the water, bringing Bolitho back to danger and reality.

'*White Hills* ahoy! What in hell's name was that?'

Bolitho swallowed hard. Poor Gallimore's last moments of terror had unnerved the enemy as much as his own prize-crew.

Moffitt yelled, 'Wounded man!' He staggered as the brig pitched through a steep-sided wave, but Bolitho knew it was an act. Moffitt was as nimble as a cat. But it gave more time. 'Had a brush with the English! Lost some good hands!'

The scream stopped with dramatic suddenness, as if the man had been beheaded.

Across the water the other voice asked, 'An' Captain Tracy? Is he safe? I've orders for him, y'see!'

'He's wounded right enough.' Moffitt gripped the shrouds with his free hand, then relaxed his fingers as he whispered over his shoulder, 'Them two guns, sir. Their crews have stood down.'

Bolitho wanted to lick his lips, to wipe the sweat from his eyes, anything to break the strain of waiting and watching the other vessel. Moffitt had seen what he had not even dared to hope for. Maybe it was Gallimore's screams which, added to Moffitt's outward confidence and the fact that the *White Hills* was the right vessel in almost the right place, had convinced *Revenge*'s captain that all was well.

But there was still the matter of Tracy's new orders. Probably details of the next rendezvous, or news of a supply convoy left open to attack.

In a few moments *Revenge*'s captain would have to face the fact he was now in the senior position. He was the one who would have to decide what to do.

Bolitho said quietly, 'He'll suggest we both heave to so that he can come over to us and speak with Tracy and see how he is.'

Quinn stared at him, his face like a mask. 'Will we go about then, sir?'

'Aye.' Bolitho stole a quick glance at the masthead pendant. 'The moment he decides to shorten sail and head into the wind, we'll use our chance.' He called to the nearest gun crew, 'Be ready, lads!' He saw an over-eager seaman struggling off his knees and reaching for a slow-match. 'Belay that! Wait for the word!'

The *Revenge*'s captain called, 'We'll heave to. I'll be over to you as soon as—'

He got no further. Like some terrifying creature emerging from a tomb, Captain Jonas Tracy lurched through the fore-hatch, his eyes bulging from his head with agony and fury.

He carried a pistol which he fired at a seaman who ran to restrain him, the ball smashing the man in the forehead and hurling him on his back in a welter of blood.

And all the time he was bellowing, his voice stronger than most of the men around him.

*'Rake the bastard! It's a trick, you damn fool!'*

From the other brig came a series of shouts and confused orders, and then like bewildered hogs the guns began to run out through the ports along her side.

Another seaman hurried towards the swaying figure by the hatch, only to be clubbed senseless by the pistol. That last effort was more than enough. Blood was spurting through the wad of bandages around his armpit, and his stubbled face seemed to be whitening even as he tried to drag himself to the nearest gun, as if the life was flooding out of him.

Bolitho saw it all as in a wild dream, with events and sequences overlapping, yet totally separate. Gallimore's sudden cries had lured Tracy's guard from his post. And who could blame him? Tracy's terrible wound should have been enough to kill almost anyone.

And *Revenge*'s captain's voice calling across to Moffitt must have somehow dragged Tracy from his unconscious state to sudden, violent action.

Whatever had begun it, Bolitho knew there was no chance at all of completing his flimsy plan.

He yelled, *'Run out!'*

He watched his men hurling themselves on their tackles, the four guns squeaking to the open ports with desperation matched only by despair.

*'Fire!'*

As the guns crashed out in a ragged salvo, Bolitho shouted, 'Stockdale! Put the helm down!'

As Stockdale and a helmsman spun the spokes, Bolitho dragged out his hanger, knowing that nothing, nothing on earth could change this moment.

He heard startled shouts from his own men and musket shots from the *Revenge* as like a wild animal the *White Hills* responded to the helm and swung up into the wind, sails shaking and convulsing, as the other vessel appeared to charge right across her bowsprit.

There were several isolated shots, his or theirs, Bolitho did not know. He was running forward, his feet slipping on blood as he tore past the dying Tracy towards the point of impact.

Like a great tusk the jib boom smashed through *Revenge*'s rigging and stays, the impact shaking the hull and deck with the force of going aground.

And still the wind, and the *White Hills*' impetus, drove them harder and faster together, until with a tremendous crash, followed by the sounds of spars splintering in half, the two brigs came together in a brutal embrace.

Bolitho's ears were ringing to the sounds of falling rigging and thrashing sails, of *Revenge*'s topmast, complete with topgallant and a mountain of uncontrollable canvas, plunging down through the drifting gunsmoke to add to the destruction.

But he was angry, wildly so, and could not control himself as he waved his hanger and shouted, 'Come on, lads! *At 'em!*'

He saw the dazed faces change to maddened excitement as they responded. In a small tide they charged towards the bows, while from aft Bolitho could hear Frowd and his collection of cripples firing across the arrowhead of water with every weapon they could lay hands on.

And here was the enemy's deck right beneath his legs. Staring eyes and wild shouts, while others struggled and kicked beneath the severed rigging and splintered woodwork.

A bayonet lunged out and sent a seaman screaming down into the smoke, but Bolitho let himself drop, felt his feet find their balance on the other deck, while on either side of him his boarding party surged forward to the attack. The man with the bayoneted musket swung wildly to face him, but Stockdale seized him and smashed the cutlass-guard in his mouth. As the man toppled away, Stockdale hacked him across the neck and finished it.

The first shocked surprise at seeing the *White Hills* turn towards them and deliberately force herself into a collision would soon give way to a rage and determination to overwhelm that of the boarders. This, Bolitho knew, but at a distance, as if it were already beyond his reach.

Once, as he ducked beneath a fallen yard to slash a man across the arm who was aiming a pistol at somebody, Bolitho caught a glimpse of his brief command. With her big mainyard sprung in two like a giant's longbow, and with the canvas and rigging piled over her forecastle like so much rubbish, she looked almost a wreck.

Beyond the debris, and licking above the thinning smoke, he saw a patch of scarlet, and realized that despite everything which had happened he had given the order to run up the colours, and yet could remember nothing about it.

'This way, lads!' It was Buller, brandishing a boarding axe and a pistol. 'Fight yer way aft!' Then he fell, his face set in an expression of complete surprise.

Bolitho gritted his teeth. Time, which they had won with such care, had run out.

From the *Revenge*'s quarterdeck came the crash of a swivel gun, and Bolitho realized that someone was still firing at the *White Hills*. Above the din of clashing steel, screams and curses, he heard answering shots, and could picture Frowd yelling defiance, and waiting to die.

Somehow they had fought their way to the midships part of the deck, where the piled debris of cordage and broken spars made every move doubly hard, but where, if you hesitated, it was asking to be killed.

He saw Dunwoody rolling over and over on the bloodied deck, struggling with one of the *Revenge*'s seamen, one hand cut to shreds as he tried to hold off the man's dirk while he groped for his fallen cutlass. Another man ran from the smoke, raised a boarding pike and drove it through Dunwoody's neck, pinioning his kicking body to the planking until the dirk stabbed him into stillness.

Bolitho saw it all, and as he struggled over an upended gig he found himself face to face with the *Revenge*'s captain. Beyond him he could see the abandoned wheel and the torn splinters standing up from the quarterdeck like quills, the sprawled bodies and crawling wounded who had fallen to the four doubly loaded six-pounders.

Bolitho ducked as the man's blade sliced above his head, caught his foot in a trailing rope and fell heavily on his side. He watched the blade rise and plunge towards him again, and held up his hanger to take the brunt of the blow. The numbing shock jarred his shoulder like a kick, and he saw the other officer turn and run aft, leaving Bolitho rather than face a sudden rally of the boarding party. Rabbett, his cutlass bloody to the hilt, Carlsson, the Swede, with a bayoneted musket he must have snatched from one of the brig's men, even Borga, the Roman cook, who held a dirk in either hand like one of his ancestors in the gladiators' arena, were still here and ready to fight.

On the far side of the deck he saw Quinn with the rest of the boarders, white-faced and with blood running from his forehead, locked in combat with twice his own number.

Bolitho saw Couzens and yelled hoarsely, 'Get back aboard! I told you to stay with Mr Frowd!'

He gasped and ducked as a shadow passed in front of him. Then with a sharp twist of his arm he brought the hanger round to lock with his attacker's cutlass.

The man was a petty officer of sorts and, he guessed, as English as himself.

'You've bitten off too much this time, *sir!*'

Bolitho felt the man's strength forcing him back, the blade inches from his chest. It was not that he was a better swordsman, but his voice, if not Cornish, was certainly from Bolitho's own West Country.

Moffitt rose shaking his head like a prize-fighter, the blood of another victim glittering on his cutlass.

'And *you!*'

Bolitho fell back with the petty officer on top of him. Moffitt's blade had been driven into his spine with such force it was a wonder it had not pinioned both of them.

Couzens was ducking and side-stepping wildly as figures staggered and kicked around him like madmen. Steel on steel, and from right aft a chorus of screams as a swivel exploded and burst apart amongst its own crew.

But he managed to shout, 'I came to help!'

Bolitho shook his arm, feeling him cringe, as he said, 'Take two men and get below! Tell them I want this brig set alight!' He knew the boy was terrified of him, his wildness, and his despair. *'Do it!'*

Shots were hitting the deck around him and making the

corpses jerk to their impact. The *Revenge*'s captain had sent marksmen aloft to mark down Frowd's puny challenge and to kill any of the boarders who looked like an officer or a leader.

Stockdale bellowed, 'Watch out, sir!' He lunged forward as a man rushed at Bolitho with a cutlass, but was not quick enough.

Bolitho saw the fury on the seaman's contorted features and wondered if he himself looked like that, if that was why Couzens had seemed so frightened of him.

The heavy cutlass grated across Bolitho's sword-belt, scoring the brass plate like a musket-ball.

Bolitho saw the man's expression change to fear, then to nothing as the hanger opened his face from eye to jaw and threw him screaming into the men behind him.

Bolitho felt sick, worn out and stunned by the savagery of battle. Couzens would not be able to fire the brig, and in any case they had started to cheer. The battle was nearly done. Like Quinn, he had tried.

There it was again, wild and uncontrolled. *'Huzza! Huzza!'*

Bolitho stared at Stockdale. 'That was no enemy!'

He swung round, dropping his guard for the first time, as through the fore-hatch came a sudden rush of dirty, unshaven figures.

Couzens was running with them, beside himself with ecstasy as he shouted, 'Prisoners, sir!'

He was pushed away by the released men as they snatched up fallen cutlasses, belaying pins, anything which could hit or maim their old captors.

Bolitho thought he must be going mad, and yet it was happening. They were obviously seamen captured in previous battles, maybe some from this very brig. But they charged through the dwindling boarding party like an avenging tidal wave, beating down the privateer's crew and hurling some of them over the side in their determination to seize the poop.

Bolitho shouted, 'Come on, lads! One last effort!'

Then, cheering and yelling meaningless words he ran with the rest, his arm like lead as he hacked and parried, cut and pushed his way aft.

A few shots were still hitting the deck nearby, and without warning a seaman slithered down a stay and snatched a pistol from his belt, his face frozen in concentration as he stared at the onrushing figures.

He must have known that nothing could save him, and yet

some last spark of anger or pride held him there.

Couzens found himself face to face with him. Bolitho saw what was happening, but was several paces away, and Stockdale further still.

Bolitho shouted hoarsely, 'You shoot and I will kill you!'

The man's eyes did not even flicker, and Bolitho knew he was going to fire, he could even see the trigger starting to give under his finger.

A figure bounded over a pile of tangled sails and threw himself between the pistol and the stricken Couzens, so that the shot was almost muffled.

Bolitho ran and caught Quinn as he fell. He did not see Stockdale's big cutlass swing, but heard just a sharp grunt as the other man died.

Bolitho held Quinn and lowered him to the deck. He knew he was dying and there was nothing he could do. The ball had entered his stomach and there was blood everywhere.

Quinn gasped, 'Sorry... to... leave... you... sir.'

Bolitho held him firmly, knowing Stockdale was guarding his back and that Couzens was kneeling on the deck beside him sobbing, uncontrollably.

'*Dick*,' he said. 'Remember, eh?'

He felt near to tears himself. What made it worse, if that were possible, was the cheering. Aft, in another world, his jubilant sailors and the released captives were hauling down the flag, watched by the *Revenge*'s captain who had been badly wounded in the last charge.

Bolitho said quietly, 'We won, James. It's done.'

Quinn smiled, his eyes looking up through the torn rigging and sails.

'*You* did.'

He was finding it difficult to speak and his skin looked like damp wax. Bolitho unbuttoned his shirt, seeing the great, cruel scar from Quinn's first battle.

With his free hand he loosened his cross-belt and said gently, 'And you were supposed to be a passenger. But for you, young Couzens would be dead. I'll see they know about it in England. About your courage.'

Quinn's eyes shifted to Bolitho's face. 'I'm not afraid any more,' he coughed and some blood ran down his chin, 'Dick.'

Bolitho was about to speak when he saw the light go from Quinn's eyes. Like a candle being snuffed out.

Very carefully he lowered Quinn's shoulders to the deck and then stood up.

Stockdale touched his elbow. 'Be easy, sir. The people are watchin'.'

Bolitho nodded, his eyes almost blind with strain and emotion. 'Thank you. Yes.'

He faced the weary but triumphant seamen. It had been a near thing. But these men had done as well as anyone could. They deserved every last effort, no matter how he was feeling.

He said quietly, 'That was well done. For a company so small, there could be none so gallant.'


Three days later the two prizes sailed into English Harbour under the eyes of the whole squadron.

It had been a hard three days. Repairing damage just enough to carry them to Antigua, selecting the released prisoners and sharing them between the two brigs.

It should have been a proud moment for Bolitho, but the sadness of Quinn's death was still with him when the look-out reported land in sight.

He had taken command of the *Revenge*, and one of the first jobs he had ordered after rigging the jury-mast, and burying the dead of both sides, had been the removal of her new name, beneath which Jonas Tracy had painted the favoured motto, DON'T TREAD ON ME, with the serpent insignia for good measure.

As the land had grown out of the sea haze, and the two brigs had tacked carefully towards the harbour, a patrolling frigate had run down on them to investigate.

Couzens had called, 'What shall I tell them, sir?'

Stockdale had looked at Bolitho's features and had thought he had understood.

He had said, 'I'll do it, Mr Couzens.'

Then he had cupped his big hands and had shouted across for all to hear.

'His Majesty's brig *Mischief* is rejoining the fleet!' It had been a very special moment for him as he had added, 'Lieutenant Richard Bolitho, *in command*!'

# ALEXANDER KENT